Twenty-Eight Years

Telma Rocha

WORD TREE PUBLISHING

WordTree Publishing

Twenty-Eight Years Copyright © 2022 by Telma Rocha.

First Edition

ISBN: 978-1-9990667-2-7 (paperback)

ISBN: 978-1-9990667-5-8 (ebook)

Cover design by: Terry Rocha

Interior Formatting by: Indie Publishing Group

To all my girlfriends. You are to me what Cassie is to Jenna.

BOOKS BY TELMA ROCHA

The Angolan Girl
From Far And Wide
Twenty-Eight Years

Twenty-Eight Years Ago

1989

PROLOGUE

Ripped from Her

EIGHTEEN-YEAR-OLD HOLLY MILLS paced in her spacious bedroom of her parents' four-thousand square foot, two-storey brick mansion, located in the prestigious Forest Hill neighbourhood of Toronto. She walked in circles for several hours before having had enough of her parents and calling the taxi. At half past ten, she grabbed her jacket and lipstick and slipped the items into her Gucci purse—a gift from her mother—and walked out into the chilly night to meet the taxi at the front iron gates of her family home's driveway. When she opened the door and stepped inside, the driver turned to peek into the back.

"It's just me," she said, suspecting he was looking for more passengers.

As the taxi pulled out of the long driveway, Holly's heart raced. No turning back now. She watched the taxi driver as she recalled her last conversation with her mother, then shoved it aside and leaned back into the seat. When the taxi pulled into the busy parking lot of the bar, her heart raced even more. She was doing this. Her shaky hand found the door handle, and she pulled and stepped out into the night. Against her better judgment, she handed the bouncer a fake ID she had paid for with birthday money. She had no business going into the bar. It was dangerous for a young, attractive girl her age with shiny red, waist-length hair and big blue eyes to walk into a bar alone, one full of guys looking at her like she was a prize. But she entered anyway to spite those who supposedly loved her, knowing they would be livid if they found out. They rarely asked where she was going. Her parents' absence from her life made it easy to get away with that, and so much more. Sometimes she wondered if she did these things to get her parents to notice. While Holly was a strong, independent young woman, she craved attention from them, but that wasn't something she often received—unlike elaborate gifts—so she had stopped expecting it. She reminded herself of that as she prepared to walk in through the crowd of men and women and have them stare, since she expected to look younger than most.

The place was bigger than it appeared from the outside. There were a few randomly placed tables around the perimeter of a dance floor facing a stage large enough to hold a full-size band. But tonight, the only ones on stage were people using the ledge as seats, as most other seats were full. Careless Whisper by George Michael blasted through the speakers and Holly couldn't help sway to the rhythm of the music. She loved that song.

Many occupied stools hugged the bar counter as two pretty female servers wearing cropped tops and teased bangs rushed to deliver orders to the impatient guys banging their fists. Holly's nostrils filled with the smell of stale smoke, and she made a funny face at the last wave. Older grey-haired men and middle-aged women, smoking and hitting on each other, equally occupied the bar. She stood, unsure of what to do. It didn't take long for someone to notice her. Holly had barely made it in five feet when a slightly older guy caught her eye. He was about her height. His face was perfect, symmetrical, with smooth skin. She guessed him to be in his early twenties. Likely only five years older than her. She was good at guessing people's ages. He stood at the edge of the dance floor holding a drink, smiling at her; she looked away, feeling flushed and hot. He continued to stare. She looked over both shoulders to see if his eyes were meeting someone else's, but no, there was no one behind her—nothing but an empty hallway with a sign that read 'Washrooms' and an arrow pointing away from her. He gestured with his hand for her to come to him and she took one shaky step to test the waters, then another, until they were only a few inches apart.

Careless Whisper ended and as The Reflex by Duran Duran began, the crowd grew rowdier and sang along. He told her his name; she barely registered it, then he asked her something else, but she couldn't hear because of the sound of the music. He leaned in and spoke directly into her ear as he pushed strands of hair away from her face, making her melt at his touch. They were still on the dance floor, and he took her hand and led her toward the bar. He ordered something for her, but she couldn't make out what it was. She accepted the first drink, something clear in a shot glass, then a second, and a third.

Crazy for You by Madonna began, and the crowd settled, allowing her to hear better. They spent the next couple of hours in conversation. Holly only telling him the bare minimum about herself and, sometimes, it wasn't even the truth that left her lips. He spoke more than her, and although he talked about himself a lot, she reminded herself she still didn't know him.

Then, suddenly, she jumped as his big hand touched her knee. With the other, he continued to caress her face.

"You're so beautiful. It should be illegal for you to be out by yourself," he said, just before the room spun out of control.

She grabbed the counter for support. "I think I should go home."

"You sure know how to drive a guy crazy."

She hadn't thought she'd done anything to make him crazy as she held her head, keeping it from spinning.

After slamming down another shot, he slapped some bills on the counter. She was feeling less than normal. Her head buzzed; the music was too loud, her thoughts all jumbled. She hadn't planned to leave the bar with him that night, not at all. That was not her intention. She was only looking for a little attention, to prove she could demand it. She had only planned to take the free drinks since she was short on money, underage, and carried a fake ID; she thought she'd never see him again after this night. Innocent enough. Nothing more. This night was not about getting with someone. She had never been with someone that way before, so she took that seriously—until now. This night was different. This night was about getting away from her parents, like a toddler having an outburst in the middle of the grocery store floor. But *was* she being rebellious when they didn't know where she was? She should have known she was hurting herself; she was smart enough to know this with the straight A's she received in high school, and being on the honour roll, and choice of any university. But she thought about it and decided she didn't care. She was simply having fun—she deserved that. A few more months, she'd be nineteen and wouldn't need the fake ID anymore. As her head spun, her stomach growled. She hadn't eaten since lunch, and even then all she'd had was bread dipped in hummus. That was hours ago and long gone from her system, allowing the alcohol to take control faster.

Holly knew she should call a taxi and leave, but somehow, she allowed him to take her hand and lead her outside. She considered asking if he was driving her home. With her hand locked in his, he led the way and passed many cars and she wondered which was his, but he continued to lead her away from the parking lot. They ended up in the back of the parking lot, far away from the building. She wasn't sure how they got there. He was so smooth, both with words and touch, caressing her cheeks, stroking her arms—charming, even. He once again pushed her hair away from her face—her melting point. She'd kissed boys before, but never with this much intensity. None had ever touched her with such eagerness as, oh, what was his name? touched her. When he touched her hair, she gave in and allowed him to take advantage of her youth and innocence on that breezy night of the Toronto streets.

In the back of the parking lot behind the bar, not feeling the cold because of the alcohol, Holly Mills smiled at the thought of what her parents would think if they found out. All she was thinking during the act was not of this young man she allowed to take advantage of her, but that her parents should have paid more attention, should have asked more questions, and maybe she wouldn't be in this place allowing this stranger to do this to her. If only they knew where she was at that moment—her mother would be livid! That made her smile.

∞

Once the alcohol was out of her system and she was thinking straight, Holly told herself that if she didn't think about that night anymore, it wouldn't exist—at least not in her mind. She filed it away and never gave it another thought. She'd lost her virginity to an almost stranger at eighteen; that wasn't the end of the world, surely. No. She knew it wasn't. She'd go on with life as if it never happened. She knew she'd never see the guy again, as she knew nothing about him. His name was as absent in her mind as her parents were in her life.

∞

Things, however, didn't go according to Holly's plans because a few weeks after that poor decision, her flat stomach bulged, and she knew in her empty heart that her life, as she once knew it, would be no more. Suddenly, the bad decision turned into a horrific nightmare. Her favourite blue jeans no longer hugged her nicely curved thighs but remained unzipped and unbuttoned to allow the bump to escape from within its tight space, covered by a large, oversized shirt to conceal her secret. Instead of booking an appointment with her doctor to get medical attention she did more sit-ups, crunches, leg lifts—anything to conceal her expanding belly and, undeniably, the child rapidly growing within her.

She hid the pregnancy well, too well, especially from her parents. She continued to attend school, determined to finish her last year before heading off to university; was that even still an option, considering her situation? As the school year came to an end, her classmates questioned her rapid weight gain, and with each accusation and assumption came quick excuses and denial, blaming the chips she said she snacked on most nights, which was true as chips and cereal made up her diet most days. But who was she kidding? By the time Holly was sixteen weeks, when most women began to show, she looked like she was much further along, and with missed menstrual cycles, there was no denying the fact that she was pregnant.

Day after day, week after week, month after month, she tried desperately to hide her midsection from everyone, including her parents. They were the most oblivious of all, too consumed in their own lives and success to notice her growing predicament.

She had no babysitting money left, so she took her mother's credit card one day to buy more oversized sweatshirts and jogging pants. It was all she could wear to keep her secret safe. The housemaid who came three times a week to clean, cook, and do laundry looked at her new choice of wardrobe one afternoon as she dropped off a freshly washed load into Holly's room, and while setting it down on the bed, tilted her head to the side and offered to help. Holly thought it was odd the housemaid noticed something was wrong when her parents thought she was simply gaining weight.

Despite all that, she went to school most days, but while there, distanced herself from all, eating lunch alone. She got a job, one that paid more than babysitting. Taking the bus to and from the café where she worked, avoiding everyone who talked to her or made eye contact, provided an opportunity for her to think about life and what she was going to do. She wanted to disappear forever and get that night and the guy that had sweet-talked her into having sex out of her mind once and for all.

During the bus rides, she sometimes wrote letters to the unborn baby—giving advice of sorts, as if she were in any position to give anyone advice. But she had nothing else she could do, and this gave her a sense of accomplishment.

~

By the time she was six months pregnant, she hadn't yet seen a doctor, still living in her world of shame. The oversized sweaters had to be stretched daily to keep up with the growth. Her parents were still unaware of her situation—as far as she knew. They'd not once said a word, but then they had rarely seen her as of late. One day Holly came home from work and found a pamphlet on her bed for a weight-loss program and attached to the pamphlet was a note in her mother's pristine handwriting:

> Holly,
>
> Call this number and sign up for the weight control program. They can help. I suppose I can go with you to your first appointment if you like. Please provide enough notice so I can clear my schedule if I must go with you
>
> Mom

Of course, the rapid weight gain concerned her mother. That was not ladylike, not sophisticated enough for their family. What would her mother's precious friends think? Certainly, that would be her biggest concern. Holly rolled up both the letter and pamphlet and, with one big swoop of her wrist, it flew across the room and landed in the expensive trash bin.

~

When Holly was almost seven months pregnant, she woke up extra tired and had a nagging pain in the middle of her navel, and when she used the washroom, there was a pinkish stain on her underwear. Unsure of what that meant, she ignored it. Her parents were already at work, as they usually were each morning—off building their empire, fighting others' fires, just not their own. But Holly knew the fires burning under their roof were much more damaging.

Holly was supposed to be starting university soon, having finished her last year of high school in June, but was working in the meantime.

She considered staying home that morning, but forced herself to shower, dress, and go to work, regardless of the consistently increasing pain. Going to work, even though she hated it there now, helped fill her days and keep her mind sharp and occupied. She usually rode the bus, but not wanting to sit for longer than necessary, she took the subway to get there faster. While she rode through the tunnels on that painful morning, as she made her way to work, there was a popping sensation in her groin; she felt wetness on her seat, and a warm liquid trickled down her legs. She looked at her seat, and there was a puddle of water. People stared, but no one offered help, and her skin prickled, evidence of what was happening. Not now. No. No. No! She took one last deep breath to calm her racing heart before the pain intensified. Seconds later, when the train arrived at her stop, she remained seated; the pain so strong it choked the life out of her. So, instead of getting off with most of the other passengers, she remained seated in the wet, and travelled three more subway stops to the one closest to Toronto General Hospital. When the train jolted to a stop, Holly grabbed her stomach to make it through the next blow, then forced herself to stand and walked out the door. She collapsed beside the track onto the dirty, disease-covered platform, alone; she screamed out in pain as she received the next punch to her belly. Instantly, a group of curious people gathered to look and stare, but no one offered help, again. She let out a deep, anguished cry with each blow, until a well-dressed woman approached, bent to Holly's level, and asked if she could walk. It took all of Holly's strength to move her head sideways, and then she blacked out as someone yelled something about blood.

❦

When Holly awakened, she was in the hospital with a team of medical professionals at her side, rushing as they checked her vitals and tried desperately to stop the bleeding. An older gentleman with a stethoscope yelled orders to others, and within minutes they transported Holly to the operating room for an emergency caesarean. She was in grave danger;

she'd heard them say. The medical team worked fast to stop the bleeding; so much blood poured over the crisp white sheets. Her eyes remained locked on the red stains as the anesthesiologist prepared her for surgery.

The moment filled her mind with thoughts of her life—of her destiny, a future she'd no longer have as it was being ripped from her, like her baby was about to be ripped from her womb. Her mind wandered to the letters she'd written. She only had five letters, and had hoped to write more, but those would have to do, she thought hazily. As she slipped into unconsciousness, Holly remembered the letters were in her bag. She always carried them with her, and knowing this was the end, hoped that someone would find them and, one day, deliver them to her baby.

Her baby, she thought. Then heard someone counting backwards.

"Five, four, three—"

Her mind went dark.

꩜

After they put Holly to sleep, she dreamt. She no longer thought about her predicament, or how she'd tell her parents what she'd been hiding for almost seven months. This was the end for her. In her hazy, fading, dream-like state, a doctor, who looked much like the one who was operating on her, said that there was not one, but *two* baby boys.

꩜

Dear Baby,

My worries about the future are growing as fast as you're growing inside me.

I still haven't told them about you. They must have noticed I've been spending a lot of time in my room but haven't asked why. They don't even know that I sleep most of the day, but that's okay. I got this. I can do this on my own. Eventually, they'll see me for me and realize the truth. Until then I just need to get through having you grow one day at a time.

It's best they don't know about you—easier that way, at least until I've figured out what to do when you get here. When they discover you, they will have a lot of questions and ones I can't answer, so for those reasons, I haven't told them or anyone else. You remain my biggest secret. I've already been thinking of names for you. If you're a girl, I'll call you Maddie, and if you're a boy, Joshua or Josh for short. Or maybe Liam. Yes, Liam seems more appropriate. I'm torn between the two boys' names. I'll wait until you're in my arms and then I'll know if you're a Josh or a Liam. One look will be all I need to decide, but until then, you'll remain my precious baby.

But don't worry, baby, you won't be alone in this world. I'll be there for you always and forever.

With Love, Mommy

PART ONE

Twenty-Eight Years Later

2017

CHAPTER 1

Vibrant Energy

JENNA TAYLOR WAS dressing for yoga class when her fiancé, Josh Harrison, entered the bedroom of their apartment with his demands.

"When?"

She stopped pulling up her pink and black Lululemon leggings and turned to him. "When what?"

He sat on the edge of the already made bed, arms crossed. "You know what. Why are you pretending?"

She blew out a breath. "Is this about the baby thing again? Josh, you know where I stand. I want children, but we're still young. We're not even thirty or married. We have our entire lives to start a family. What's the urgency?"

"There's no urgency."

Jenna licked her lips. "It looks that way."

"If we start a family sooner than later, it gives you more time to jump back into your career when the kids are older."

Jenna looked into the mirror and adjusted her matching pink and black Lululemon tank top. Her stomach was nice and flat. Having a baby would change that. She reached into her top dresser drawer for a matching scrunchie and pulled her over-grown, straight brown hair into a high ponytail with a few face-framing wisps left out. There, that would do.

"That's the thing. I don't want to jump back into my career *later*. I'm not ready to leave yet. My career is only getting started. A baby would derail my advancement," she said.

Josh squared his shoulders. "That's not true."

"Of course it is. It's easier for men. You know that. I'd have to deal with the pregnancy, parental leave, and all while being replaced by the next newest graduate. Not going to happen to me. Not before I've made it further as a journalist."

Josh stood, arms still crossed. Jenna glanced at her watch. It was almost time for her to pick up her bestie from university, Cassie. She waited to see if Josh had anything else to say.

"I'm not waiting any longer. I'm done. Either you're with me on this, or you're not. But I need to know." He walked out and slammed the bedroom door.

Jenna stood, wondering if she'd heard him correctly. Did he just give her an ultimatum? She left the bedroom to search for him. His briefcase was still on the kitchen chair, but she couldn't find him.

As she drove to Cassie's apartment, she ruminated over the horrible things he'd said. How could he make her choose? Was she not as important to him as he was to her? Josh knew Jenna's career was essential to her wellbeing and that having a family would alter the carefully crafted balance she'd created. Not finding an alternate reason for his outburst, she blamed it on stress over his father's health.

❦

The sour smell that emanated from people overextending themselves hung in the air of the downtown Toronto yoga studio as the instructor demonstrated the awkwardness of the next stretch. Josh's accusatory words from that morning rang in Jenna's ears, breaking her concentration while she held the chair pose less elegantly than the trainer.

The middle-aged yoga instructor, who was more flexible than Jenna at almost twenty-eight, brought the class down from a complex move to a safer stretch, then led them into the final meditation. The music changed as if it was in sync with her teaching techniques, and perhaps the instructor planned it like a choreographed dance. Jenna's mind wandered during the meditation; she didn't have the mental ability to sit and not think. That was a waste of time, but she loved the challenge of tangling up her body into odd, pretzel-like shapes. It felt good to stretch the stress away, especially after *that* particular morning and Josh's harsh words. Besides, she'd promised Cassie that she'd commit to the program Cassie signed them up for without even consulting her—the nerve!

Jenna sat cross-legged, back straight as a pin, arms hovered over her knees, thumb and index finger forming a circle but not touching. Her eyes should have been closed, but she peeked at Cassie. Cassie was chewing gum and glanced at a guy two rows ahead while she, too, sat in the same pose. At least Jenna wasn't the only one having a hard time concentrating. Jenna's gaze met Cassie's. They giggled, and the instructor let out a disgruntled moan and hard stare. Bringing her attention back to the meditation, Jenna tried to force her mind to think of nothing. How was it possible to think of nothing?

When the instructor relieved the class from the torture of silence, Jenna rolled up her pink yoga mat; her favourite, the one with an elephant. She grabbed her matching water bottle and caught up to Cassie. Cassie was already chatting up the cute guy who had joined two weeks late. They looked like they were in an intense conversation, eyes locked on each other, and Jenna smiled as she watched them interact. Jenna admired Cassie for her gift in getting others engaged in deep conversations; she drew people to her with her overt bubbliness and vibrant energy.

When Cassie glanced at her, Jenna pretended to chew gum to

remind Cassie to not chew while she talked. Cassie got the hint and stopped. Cassie was always chewing gum, and sometimes forgot and chewed aggressively—not her most flattering quality. But her long, blond, centre-parted hair, oval-shaped face, and high cheekbones were very flattering. Which was likely why the guy was hanging off Cassie's every word, gum-chewing and all.

The gum-chewing caused Jenna's insides to boil. It was a pet peeve of Jenna's, but her best friend's habit, so she put up with it. Cassie leaned into the new guy and the corners of his lips quirked further up. Jenna smiled and walked out of the studio to her car, the wind kissing her face.

While she waited, she applied hand sanitizer and watched as the hustle and bustle of a busy Toronto workday got underway. Men in suits walked while talking on their phones, and women with high heels made their way to Union Station, a few stopping to bend and adjust their shoes. The CN Tower stood tall, hovering over the city; its elevator making the fast ascent to the top. While Jenna watched the Toronto craziness around her, her mind wandered to Josh again. The words he had spoken earlier ached in her heart. She thought she was over it, but the tightening of her chest revealed she wasn't. He couldn't have meant what he said, she hoped. Could he? No. Certainly not. He'd had outbursts like that before.

"Hey, so sorry for keeping you waiting, girl. I couldn't resist an introduction to the cute guy." Cassie climbed into the passenger seat as Jenna started the ignition.

"I know. It's okay. I've only been waiting for twenty minutes. It's not like I have a life and job to get to."

"I wasn't that long," Cassie protested.

Jenna knew better and glanced at the dashboard; it was seven fifty, class ended at seven thirty. Jenna pointed to the time. "Buckle up. I have to be at the office by nine thirty. You've already made me late. I should make *you* call Rachel." Cold crept into Jenna's bones at the mention of *that* woman's name, and she shivered.

"It's freezing in here. Why didn't you turn the heat on?" asked Cassie.

"There's only a quarter of a tank of gas left. I didn't want to risk it."

"Since when do you drive with such little gas?"

"I didn't have time to stop this morning. But don't get me started on why."

"So?" Cassie flipped through the radio stations. "What happened? Did Josh bring up the 'issue' again?"

"He did. He gave me an ultimatum. I think."

"Hmmm..." Cassie stared straight ahead. "I have an idea. It's a big one, but it might help the situation."

"I'm listening."

"I know getting pregnant isn't something you want, but there are other options."

"I know," said Jenna.

"Adoption is one of them. There are many older children that need loving homes. If you considered adopting a child, it might be easier."

"I've thought about it."

"You never told me you and Josh were considering adoption."

"We haven't talked about it in great detail. But it was an option we discussed briefly for the future. He wants a family. I'm not ready for what comes with being pregnant, and the risk of jeopardizing my career. Plus, you're right. There are many older children that need homes, so we'd be giving one something they'd otherwise not have. I'd consider adoption one day, just not now."

"So, how did the ultimatum end?"

"I don't know, Cas, it just all seems so rushed. This sudden desire for Josh to have a family."

"Think about it some more. Adoption could be the answer."

Jenna shook her head. "The issue isn't that I don't want to get pregnant. I want a family; you know that. The problem is, I don't want a family *now*. Biological or not, that's irrelevant. That's the issue. He wants a child and I'm not ready. I've told him I want to wait a few years, but he doesn't see the point in waiting. I even told him we could explore adoption more when that time came." Jenna shook her head again. "I mean, why rush it? We're not even married yet. If my parents stopped talking to me for so long when I moved to France at eighteen, what do you think they'd do if I got pregnant out of wedlock?"

"It's different now, you're older, you're not a teenager."

"I know, but still. My parents aren't even the issue here, I'm not sure why I brought them up."

"I don't get Josh sometimes," said Cassie.

"Ha! Guess what? I don't get him either, and I live with him."

"What's his rush, anyway? You're both still so young. Most men his age aren't thinking about starting a family. Have you asked him why he's in a hurry to have a kid?"

"I have," said Jenna.

"And?"

"I think he's looking for someone to call his own."

"How so?"

"He has this urge lately to belong, if that makes sense?"

"Not really."

"His desire to be a father began when his dad got sick. I think it scared him. The thought of losing his father and not having any other close relatives alive must have pushed him over the edge. He's got cousins and an uncle, but no immediate relatives other than Billy. I think the thought of losing his dad scared him. He's told me this in so many words."

"What's wrong with Billy? I didn't realize he was sick."

"We don't know yet. Josh has another appointment tomorrow. It's probably a nasty cold or flu, but it's been three weeks and he's not feeling better. He's always tired, and he's had a fever on and off."

"Orange juice," Cassie said, unexpectedly.

"What? You want juice?"

"No, that's way too much sugar for me, you know that. It's for Billy. Tell him to drink one glass of orange juice a day. It will help. I watched a YouTube video on natural health remedies."

"Cas, I love you, but there isn't a simple solution to every problem. Those videos exaggerate and prey on vulnerable people, like you."

"Who are you calling vulnerable? Look, I know you don't believe in half that stuff, but if you look at problems from a unique perspective, like art, for example, you can analyze it and find specific things to target."

"I wish this problem were that easy, Cas."

"Perhaps it can be!"

Cassie lived in a tiny one-bedroom apartment about a five-minute drive from Union Station, but with the Toronto traffic, it always took longer. When they pulled into the parking lot, Jenna glanced at the time. "You know, we really should have found a closer yoga studio. It would save us time if we could walk."

"Yeah, well, this one offered a discount. Maybe next round."

Next round? She eyed her delusional friend. Cassie was planning on dragging her through this longer than the current commitment. Well, she'd think of a way out.

"I don't mean to be rude, but get out."

"I'm going." Cassie reached into the backseat to grab her stuff. "Be sure to tell Josh to give his dad a glass of orange juice a day."

Jenna rolled her eyes. "Okay, sure!"

"But it needs to be one hundred percent pure orange juice and not the crap stuff you buy for cheap."

"Got it. Now get going. I have to get to work. If I'm late, Rachel will have my head *again*. Sors d'ici!" *Get out.*

Cassie stepped out and blew Jenna a kiss. "Oh boy, you're speaking French, so you must mean business. No idea what you said, but okay. I'm going. Ciao, girl. Call me later tonight if you want to have coffee and talk about Josh. I'm free, unless that cute guy from yoga calls, then I'm busy." She winked and walked away with her yoga mat and water bottle. She stopped midstride and turned.

Jenna rolled down the passenger-side window to hear. "Quoi?" *What?* Sometimes when Jenna got frustrated she'd throw out French words. French came just as easily to her as English, as she was bilingual.

"I almost forgot. Call your mom today," yelled Cassie.

"My mom, why?"

"I saw her last night at the grocery store, and she went on about how you never answer when she calls."

"Seriously? You saw my mother and you only mention it now?"

"Sorry, it slipped my mind. And don't worry about Josh. I'm sure he didn't mean what he said," she yelled from the apartment building door.

Jenna shivered, rolled the window back up, and drove away. It wasn't like she was purposely ignoring her mother's calls. Her mother just had a way of calling when Jenna was smack in the middle of something important. And as for Josh, Cassie must be right; he didn't mean what he'd said. She'd go home, smooth things over, and tonight she'd order his favourite meal: chicken wings and fries from the pub down the street.

❧

Jenna lived less than five minutes away from Cassie in a condo just off of Lakeshore Boulevard, but, again, with traffic, sometimes it took longer.

Jenna parked in the underground parking and dashed through the hallways, making her way to her apartment. She eagerly pressed the elevator button and after a few seconds, took the stairs two at a time. It was faster than waiting for the elevator. When she approached the door, she stood and stared at the fifth-floor apartment she shared with Josh before walking inside.

While the building faced the waterfront with views of Lake Ontario, their balcony view offered nothing more glamourous than cars to stare at, although, out in the distance, skyscrapers surrounded them when they looked up. They sat out enjoying wine on the balcony from time to time, stretching their necks to see the tops of the buildings lit up at night.

She was envious of the lake-view apartments and hoped to have one someday. She had just started her new job at the magazine and was working her way up when she and Josh moved in together, so they had taken the less expensive apartment to save for a house. But lately, things had been shaky, and she couldn't imagine a house in their future after what he'd said that morning. As if their five years together meant nothing.

When she walked through the door, the apartment was dark and silent.

"Josh?" She waited for a reply, but the only sound was the annoying humming of the old refrigerator. He must have left for the office already. Josh was a criminal defence attorney and normally started his day working from home when not in court.

Jenna walked through the apartment looking for clues as to where he must be, thinking maybe he was out for a run. There was no paperwork scattered anywhere, his laptop was not where he normally kept it, and his briefcase was not in the front hall closet. The apartment was small, so there couldn't be many places for him to be. She went into their bedroom. Although it was tiny, there was a walk-in closet they shared, despite Jenna claiming she needed more space. Josh had a corner of the closet where he kept his few shoes, unlike the full shoe rack opposite Josh's corner where Jenna kept her different coloured pumps. When Josh asked why she had so many shoes, she explained about needing options, but he seemed to not understand her when she said that and rolled his eyes at her, which she ignored.

His brown leather belt and shoes were not in their usual spot. Jenna sighed. It was rare to not receive a call or text when he left for work. Had he decided that he didn't care anymore? With her mind racing, she jumped in the shower to get ready to face her day—to face Rachel. Convinced Josh just needed to blow off steam, she decided to deal with him later.

CHAPTER 2

Unsettled Thoughts

JOSH HARRISON ALWAYS began his workday at home, but that morning was different; he couldn't stop his mind from wandering. He'd been an early morning riser since he was little. His dad taught him that if he could wake up early and get important things done first, the rest of the day would be a breeze. That advice had stuck with Josh throughout his life and into his career as a junior attorney. He'd graduated with a law degree at twenty-five, passed his bar examination and completed the LPP program soon after. Josh attributed that success to being a morning person, like his father.

But that morning, there had been no working at home. The stillness in the apartment got under his skin, contributing to his confusion. After the argument, Josh had gone for a morning run along the waterfront paths, hoping to shift his thoughts away from Jenna. When he'd returned, he had showered, dressed, then prepared a black peppermint tea with no sugar to go, having decided to stop at his dad's before heading to the law firm.

Unsettled thoughts filled his mind as he drove, and that made it difficult to concentrate. He aimed to see his dad every day, but that didn't always happen; life got busy. But considering his dad's current health, he was making more of an attempt. The last time Josh saw him, his dad had said he was feeling tired, beaten up, and his legs hurt. That reminded Josh of a fever. He had taken his dad's temperature. The thermometer had read thirty-six point five Celsius, so he wasn't concerned and had called yesterday instead of stopping by.

When he arrived at the house, his dad didn't greet him at the door as usual. Butterflies fluttered in his stomach as he pulled into the driveway and saw the empty porch. The outside lights were still on, and that was odd because his dad didn't waste electricity. Josh used his key to let himself inside and couldn't remember the last time he had used it. The lights were off, the coffee pot empty, save for the dregs from yesterday's brew. Josh called out to his dad, but he didn't answer. A bead of sweat trickled down Josh's forehead. Josh searched and found him in bed—dressed in the same clothes that he had been wearing when Josh saw him two days ago. Josh looked at the time and gasped. His dad never slept in.

Josh squared his shoulders and stared at his dad before waking him. His dad was pale and thin, with sunken cheekbones.

"Dad, wake up."

His dad didn't stir, so Josh rubbed his shoulder. His skin was too warm. Another trickle of sweat ran down Josh's cheek. He left his dad to check the thermostat outside the bedroom door; he had set it at twenty-five degrees Celsius. Josh ran his fingers through his hair, wondering why his dad had set it so high, and turned it down to room temperature.

From inside the bedroom, his dad moaned and laid still. When he tried to move, he grunted as if his bones were about to break off his fragile body. Josh observed from the doorway. How had he gotten like that in such a short time? Two days ago, he'd looked healthier, had been walking about. But now, he appeared as if he was on his deathbed. Unable to bear the heat any longer, Josh took off his suit jacket and set it on the back of a chair next to the bed. He ran to the kitchen to get his cell phone from the briefcase Jenna gifted him last year on his birthday and called the doctor's office. It went to voicemail. He checked the time again and frowned; the office didn't open until nine. He left a message asking for a call back right away and explained Billy's situation, and with the phone still in hand, rummaged through his dad's bathroom drawers, searching for a thermometer. His dad was still asleep, so it was good that he'd purchased a newer, faster thermometer that scanned foreheads, unlike the antiquated one his dad had that went under the tongue or armpit. As Josh placed the thermometer before his dad's forehead, it beeped, showing it'd taken a reading. The temperature on the display read thirty-nine point one. The number jumped out from the small display and gave Josh a wave of panic. He ran his hands through his hair, deciding there must be a mistake, so he retook the temperature, same result. He breathed heavily and considered calling an ambulance but didn't want to overreact because of a fever.

His father was sixty-one and, before falling ill, was full of life. He walked five kilometres daily, drank plenty of water, and refrained from red meat. Not that there was anything wrong with red meat. Josh enjoyed a good steak now and again, but his dad often imparted his beliefs to Josh about how to keep a body in top-notch shape. It had worked for him. His father had worked out most of his adult life, so he looked good too, until then.

"Dad, come on, get up."

"Mmm."

"Dad. Can you hear me?"

"Son, is that you?"

"Come on Dad, get up, I'm taking you to the hospital. You're burning up."

It took some effort, but before long his dad awakened, and Josh helped him dress into fresh clothes. Josh had to put socks and shoes on for him because he was too weak to bend over.

"Dad, do you have everything you need? Health card?" His dad pointed to his wallet on the kitchen table.

Josh slipped his muscular arm under his dad's boney one, trying to take most of the weight as they walked to the car. His dad could barely stand by himself. Josh considered calling emergency services again.

"I'm not sure why the rush, son. It's most likely just a cold, and you dragging me out is only going to make me more tired."

"I'm not arguing, Dad. Let's go."

"Can't an old man just sleep in for once?"

"You're not old. But sure, after you've seen the doctor. I'll bring you back and you can nap. Let's go."

Leaving his suit jacket and briefcase behind, Josh placed Billy in his prized black BMW sedan, a car he'd always wanted and had purchased with his last work bonus, then buckled up his dad's seatbelt. "You'll be fine, Dad. I'm sure of it. I don't want you worrying about anything."

"I know, son. You're the one making all the fuss."

Josh chuckled, knowing his father was right.

When they arrived, Josh pulled the BMW into the emergency parking lot, ran to grab a wheelchair, and helped his father into it. As they went through the automatic double doors and headed to the triage station, a pretty young nurse greeted his father by name.

"Mr. Harrison, hello sir, what are you doing here again so soon?"

Josh spun his head. "What do you mean?" Josh asked the nurse, out of confusion. "My father hasn't been here for almost two years; you must be mistaken." But as Josh said that, he realized she couldn't be mistaken—she'd addressed his father by their surname.

The nurse glanced from Josh to his dad, and her smile faded as she turned to speak to his dad, leaving Josh's question unanswered. "Can you walk, sir? If so, come around to the desk so we can assess you. If not, I'll wheel you in."

"I don't think I can walk."

"I'll come to get you. You stay put."

"Can someone please tell me what's going on?" demanded Josh.

"Son, go sit down. I'll explain everything. I promise," said his dad.

"We'll call you as soon as we assess your father."

The nurse took his dad into the triage room, and Josh stared into the glass as nurses and doctors shuffled their way in and out, giving orders, punching keys on the computer's keyboard. When the nurse wheeled his dad around the corner, Josh observed as nurses greeted his father by his first name. Some said they were seeing too much of him lately, and that he'd better not be making that a habit. Others said he'd looked better and asked him what happened since the last time he was there. Confused and unsure of the nurses' reactions toward his dad, Josh shook his head, grabbed an older issue of the magazine Jenna worked for, and took a seat in the waiting room—there was nothing else he could do.

While he sat with his leg shaking, a mom with two young children sat across from him. Josh watched as she tried to console the child on her lap, patting the baby's bum. The other child coloured in a book on the seat next to her. As Josh stared at the mom, their eyes locked. Josh understood her sorrow. He saw her pull her eyes away from his and went back to her crying baby—trying to soothe him. Josh's gaze lingered on the baby. His thoughts went to Jenna and the fact that she wouldn't give him a child. He hadn't thought of Jenna since seeing his dad. His thoughts were spiralling out of control. Did he mean what he'd said to her earlier that morning? He'd forgotten he'd given her an ultimatum and didn't know if he would follow through with it. Was he just needing to blow off steam, as Jenna often said? Questions brewed. Answers lacked. He felt sick to his stomach, dizzy, and unfocused as he waited with the magazine on his lap, unopened, listening to the screaming baby.

CHAPTER 3

Much Opportunity

AFTER A QUICK, hot shower, Jenna stood in the small walk-in closet searching for an outfit for her afternoon of meetings. She combed her wardrobe for something comfortable but classy. The magazine she worked for, Brandy Thyme, had a business casual policy, including no ripped jeans. She'd risked wearing them once on a Friday when she had no meetings—thinking she'd be safe in her office as Rachel had meetings all day. But Jenna's rebellious move didn't go unnoticed. By the end of the workday, she'd received an email from Human Resources. Rachel had complained. Her jeans weren't even that ripped, but whatever! From that day on, Jenna had adhered to the policy like one watched a carefully planned diet. That was how she handled all aspects of Rachel.

While dressing, she glanced at her phone for messages from Josh, but there were none. That was odd. The argument must still have him upset. While trying to put him out of her mind, after a quick makeup routine and pulling her hair into a ponytail to save time, she got dressed in skinny jeans, an off the shoulder loose blouse, and a pair of red heels. It was late March, so the weather was cool, and the mornings in Toronto were sometimes even chillier because of the lake-effect. So, she layered a neutral blazer over the outfit before grabbing her black trench coat. Satisfied, she picked up her red bag and headed out the door, ready to face the day.

Her days depended on what happened in the world, what decisions others made. It could go from interviewing a new chef to attending an art gallery opening. The only constant in her job was, unfortunately, Rachel. Her thoughts often travelled to Rachel when she was in a sour mood; Rachel had that affect. Rachel made her work life more complicated by failing to tell her things and changing deadlines at the last minute. Jenna learnt to work with her, to say things she knew she wanted to hear. Usually, it was enough to keep Rachel off her back. Her main issue with Rachel was that she couldn't trust her. Rachel had already screwed Jenna over more than once. She took credit for things undeserved and didn't give Jenna important details that left her chasing minor facts like a cat chasing its tail.

Glancing at her phone, Jenna's blood boiled because Josh hadn't yet sent a text telling her he'd gone into the office early. He knew she'd worry when she got home from yoga, and he wasn't there. He was always there, and the days he wasn't, he'd let Jenna know. But she knew why today was different. They had fought. The ultimatum hung in the air, stale, unmoving. How dare he make her choose? What *would* she choose if he was serious? Breathing heavily, she typed out a text from within the elevator of her office building.

Jenna: Nice of you to let me know you wouldn't be home when I got back. You don't have to be a jerk about the baby situation. It's not as if I said I NEVER wanted kids, just not now!

After she pressed the Send button, she regretted it immediately. It was too harsh. She quickly typed another text.

Jenna: Can you call me, please? We need to talk about this morning. I don't like how you left things!

She stared at the second text before pressing the Send button, wondering if she should change 'you' to 'we'. She didn't want Josh to think she was blaming him. Although he started it. On reflex, she pressed Send. She regretted it again and wished she could recall not only the last message, but both. Doing that through text was not right. Even she knew that, but her pride was at stake and had gotten the best of her. She slipped her phone back into her bag and ran her hands down the front of her blouse, smoothing out a few small wrinkles when the elevator door opened.

∽

The magazine was near the core of Queen Street West, Toronto, the famous, former home of the popular MuchMusic channel from back in the eighties and nineties. Jenna never watched MuchMusic but remembered her parents blasting rock music as the videos played on the bulky television when she was little. The building the magazine was in was a block away from where the entertainment had taken place.

The magazine specialized in all forms of the arts: music, visual arts, dance, and culinary. It featured Canadian artists; some were famous, others not so well known.

Rachel's contorted face, along with her tightly pulled-back hair and arms crossed over her chest, was the first thing Jenna saw when the elevator doors opened.

"You're late, again." Rachel clicked her tongue, waiting for a response.

"No, I'm not."

Rachel's tongue clicked again. "I need the story typed up and on my desk in an hour. No excuses."

"Yes, I know you need the story—"

Rachel interrupted Jenna mid-sentence. "You were to have it to me first thing this morning. Where have you been?"

Jenna glanced at her watch, wondering if she was late or if Rachel was making stuff up, an attempt to discredit her again. She hadn't checked the time since she pulled into the parking lot, and she had five minutes to spare then. It couldn't have taken longer to park and ride the elevator. When she saw the time, she let out a sigh of relief. "I'm not late. I'm early. One minute, to be exact." Jenna extended her arm to show Rachel her wristwatch.

Rachel waved Jenna's arm away. "That means nothing. If the report is not on my desk when I return from the kitchen, that makes you late, despite the time on that cheap watch. I can't sit around waiting for you to decide you're ready to put your career first."

Jenna sighed; her watch was not cheap. It had been an engagement gift from Josh. Jenna reminded herself to breathe, like in yoga.

"Rachel, I have the piece. I wrote it first thing this morning when I got up. I thought I'd emailed it. I'm positive I did. Are you sure you checked your inbox?"

Rachel raised her eyebrows questioningly.

"I mean, you could have missed it," said Jenna, taking a risk, being bold and brave.

"I don't have time to sift through hundreds of emails looking to see if you've followed through with your duties and print it myself. Who do you think I am, *your* secretary? I want it on my desk by the time I'm back with coffee."

"Of course she does," muttered Jenna under her breath. Jenna had already expected this, so she had printed a copy of the paper at home after she'd emailed Rachel. She suspected Rachel would be too lazy to check her email and print the piece. Because of Rachel, Jenna never missed a beat, and for that she was grateful. She knew Rachel didn't even realize that in her rude, controlling, and snarky ways, she was helping Jenna. She let Rachel think she was beating her down with the way she treated her, but Rachel's aggressiveness and unfairness were only teaching her how to do her job better: to be faster, more efficient, and always be one step ahead. She reached into her briefcase, pulled out the piece, and waved it in front of Rachel. Rachel walked away, ignoring her, so Jenna called after her.

"I wouldn't want you to have to carry this to the kitchen. I'll drop it off on your desk as requested. Pronto!" said Jenna.

Jenna turned on her heel, suppressing a smile. She wouldn't give Rachel a chance to find another fault with something she forgot to do. It tempted her to turn around and see the look on Rachel's face, but she forced her feet to move forward and not give Rachel the satisfaction of the last word.

Jenna's office was next to Rachel's, and Jenna knew that was deliberate. When Jenna walked into Rachel's large, pristine office, the familiar scent of lavender hung in the air; Rachel always had a scented diffuser plugged in. Jenna giggled as she thought that the inviting scent was necessary, since the person who occupied the space was uninviting. It tempted her to pull the diffuser out, but she decided not to stoop to Rachel's level.

She dropped the folder on Rachel's desk and picked up a pen. Resisting the urge to leave a nasty note, she put the pen down. Good lord, it was still early morning and already the encounters with *that* woman were challenging. She left Rachel's office with the scented diffuser still plugged in and no nasty note and headed into her office. She needed a coffee, but after dropping her bag, she saw a note on her desk in Rachel's handwriting reminding her that Rachel needed the piece, the same one she just dropped off. Jenna grunted, tore the note, and tossed it into the trash. The trashcan was too far, so the note landed inside one of her spare shoes she kept there for emergency outfit-matching. Deciding those looked better than the red heels she wore, she swapped footwear and headed to the kitchen.

The kitchen had streamers hanging from the ceiling, and balloons plastered to the walls. Jenna wondered whose birthday it was. Aleshia from accounting entered, wearing a birthday hat and a Hawaiian lei around her neck. A swarm of people followed, singing happy birthday. Jenna wished Aleshia well, poured enough cream into her mug to resemble a light mocha colour, and headed back to her office, leaving the celebratory gang to their happiness.

Jenna was lucky to have an office. Rachel wasn't pleased about that, as the executives had made the decision against her advice. But because Rachel couldn't do anything to reverse the choice, she had insisted on the office next to hers. The darn woman! Jenna stretched her neck and took a sip of the steaming coffee and instantly relaxed. That was her first cup of the day. She always waited until she got to the office to have that first cup. It was easier to keep the total cups consumed to three if she didn't start too early. Anything over three cups, and Jenna got the jitters and had difficulty sleeping.

Placing the mug down next to her laptop, she booted it up and opened her email. To her surprise, there was an urgent email from Rachel marked 'JENNALYN READ ASAP' in the subject line: Rachel always used Jenna's full name in email correspondences, and Jenna swore she only did that to make herself look smart. Everyone else addressed Jenna by her nickname, but that wasn't good enough for Rachel; she couldn't be like everyone else. The email read:

Jennalyn,

When you read this, come see me right away. It's extremely important.

Rachel

Sent from my iPhone.

"Hmmm," said Jenna, aloud. It surprised her to receive that, since she already got scolded earlier. The timestamp showed Rachel sent it minutes ago. Why had Rachel not talked to her at the elevator? Jenna grunted, frustrated that Rachel had found yet one more thing to harp about.

Taking her coffee, notepad, and pen, she walked to Rachel's office. The door was closed, so she knocked lightly, trying to exude a calmness that she hoped would rub off on Rachel.

"Come in." Rachel's voice was sharp and loud.

Still protected from the closed door, Jenna took a deep breath to ready herself before turning the knob and pushed the door open just enough to slip in.

"Rachel," Jenna tried to sound composed and collected. "I read the email. I assume this is about the piece. As you can see, it's on your desk." Jenna pointed to the folder on the corner of Rachel's desk in case she'd missed it.

"Sit."

Jenna remained standing.

Rachel cleared her throat. "This is not about the report."

"If it's not about the report, then what?"

"I thought I told you to sit." She pointed to the chair in front of her desk as if there was another option. Rachel picked up a piece of paper and studied it for a few seconds before continuing. "I'm sure you've heard of the small office we're opening in Quebec City?"

Jenna sat. "Oh, that," Jenna said in a relieved voice. "Yes, of course. Everyone's heard of the new office. There were several memos sent."

The magazine was expanding into Quebec City, and that was precisely why now was not a good time for Jenna to think about a family. There was much opportunity for her with all the recent development and staff growth. Jenna knew Rachel wouldn't be able to oversee all the journalists on her own, and if the board hired another senior editor, Jenna wanted her name at the top. She didn't want old-fashioned prejudices about her being a mother to sacrifice career advancement. She knew it was wrong, and that legally no employer could ever hold that against any woman. But in working at *Brandy Thyme,* and with her experience overseas, she knew that the prejudices still existed. Jenna wanted to be the powerful female that didn't give her male co-workers something to hold over or against her.

"Well," continued Rachel, looking directly into Jenna's eyes, "there's a temporary position opening in that location. It's going to be six months to a year's contract. The candidate will oversee coverage of the arts festival and a few other art shows that are scheduled to happen in the next year. If that goes well, we'll hire junior French-speaking journalists to work under the candidate." Rachel's eyes shifted from Jenna's back to the paper she held. "Despite my input, your name came up as *the* candidate, considering you are bilingual and suitable for the position."

Jenna grabbed the arms of the chair to steady herself, afraid that she'd topple over. She tried to speak but couldn't find words.

Rachel clicked her tongue. "Jenna, did you hear me?"

Jenna forced herself to find her voice. This was the moment she'd waited for, that enormous opportunity that would allow her to break out from the others and finally let her move up. "Yes. I heard you." She was trying to sound composed, in charge.

"I expected more enthusiasm from you. You should know, this was not my idea. I told the executives you were not ready, but they insisted on you. They charged me with convincing you, so you must go or it will make me look bad."

Jenna's mind wandered to the reality of the situation. Yes, this was the big break she'd wanted and been waiting for, but that monstrosity of an opportunity also came with a magnitude of complications. She wanted to yell 'Yes!' from the top of her lungs. To run straight out of the office and go home to pack. She was ready for that, wanted it fiercely. But there was Josh.

"I am excited and honoured, but..."

Rachel ignored her and continued as if there was no possibility that Jenna would decline.

"We'll set you up with an apartment paid for by the magazine. And the company will cover all travel expenses. I need you to leave by next week."

Jenna sat up straighter. "Next week?"

"Yes. I know it's soon, and it doesn't leave much room for planning. But we must get you there right away. We've already missed out on too many stories."

Jenna, unsure if she'd even heard Rachel correctly, asked, "I'm sorry, what are you saying exactly?"

"You need to take the position, Jenna. It's already yours. There's no

other option. Trust me when I say that I wish circumstances were different, but the executive team wanted you, and frankly, I think it will be
best for you and me if you go."

"How so?"

"Even though you're not the most suited for the job, the distance
might do us good."

"If I'm not the most suited, then why was I chosen?"

Rachel clicked her tongue. "Your guess is as good as mine. You are
fluent in French, both written and verbal, but that's about it."

Was Rachel trying to get rid of her? Either way, it was an opportunity of a lifetime. Jenna wanted to yell 'Yes!', but said, "Rachel, I
appreciate this opportunity, but I can't accept it."

Rachel scrunched up her nose. "What. Why?"

"I have a fiancé, a life here, you know this. I can't just up and leave."

"That's a lame reason to turn down this opportunity, and you know
it. It's only temporary. Six months to a year and then you can return to
your little life here."

"I still can't move, even if it's only for six months."

"Well, if this is really about the fiancé, then take him with you. The
apartment will be big enough for two, I'm sure."

"It's not that easy."

Rachel clasped her hands together over the desk. "All right. I'm losing patience. What is the actual issue? For someone who's just received
an opportunity of a lifetime, you are being ungrateful. Perhaps I should
convince the executive team to consider Greg. He's also bilingual and
qualified."

"Greg? Seriously, you're going to compare me to Greg? You know
I'm more qualified than he is. Besides, my French is way better than his."

"Well, that remains to be heard," said Rachel with a smirk.

What a bitch, thought Jenna. She hesitated, then forced herself to
speak the truth that was trapped; the truth she was avoiding.

"Josh, that's my fiancé. He'll never move to Quebec City, not even for six months. You know he's an attorney? I'm sure I've mentioned it before."

"Enough is enough. I don't care if he's the president of the United States. You need to get your priorities straight and your ass to Quebec City."

Jenna sat back in her seat. "My priorities?"

"Yes, your priorities. You know what those are, don't you?"

Jenna considered the question. What *were* her priorities? She thought back to the argument that morning; Josh telling her they must have a baby or she'd lose him.

"Listen, I'm busy and don't have the time to sort out your personal life. I'm not your therapist. Figure it out, Jenna. Make it work. Make it happen, fast. You want the promotion, don't you?"

"Yes, of course I do. It's an opportunity of a lifetime, but..."

Rachel ignored the 'but' again. "Yes, it is. And this is *your* opportunity. It's being handed to you on a silver platter. You'll be the lead reporter there with editor potential. Isn't that what you're after, and wanted for so long?"

"Yes, but not in Quebec City!"

Rachel looked out the window and leaned back. She crossed her arms in front of her. "I need a formal answer, in writing, in forty-eight hours. The next executive meeting is in two days, at ten in the morning. I need your definitive answer by then."

Jenna looked at her hands, fingers intertwined on her lap. "I don't need forty-eight hours. I'm giving you my answer." She took a deep breath.

"Choose your next words wisely," said Rachel.

"I can't go."

"You'll be jeopardizing your career if you don't take this opportunity. There will never be another chance like this."

"I know. I realize that."

"You're positive?"

"Unfortunately, yes," said Jenna.

"Okay. Well, that's that then." Rachel looked at her watch. "I have another meeting, so you need to leave."

Jenna knew she should get up and leave fast since she'd annoyed Rachel, but when she tried to stand, her legs were shaky, and she wasn't sure she could carry her coffee mug without spilling it. She tested her legs and stood, holding onto the back of the chair until she felt confident in her stance.

"Oh, and Jenna."

"Yes?" She looked back at Rachel from over her shoulder.

"The piece was not in the format I wanted. Fix it. You have thirty minutes."

Jenna walked back to her office and called up the second copy of the piece she had ready and attached it to an email with the subject line 'THE FORMAT YOU DIDN'T WANT'. She pressed 'send' without a moment's hesitation on having used all capitals.

❧

Rachel was right, it was a tremendous opportunity and if Jenna were single, she'd jump at the chance to move to a new city, a new apartment, and be the top reporter. But her life had been so complicated lately: focusing on her career, not wanting to set a wedding date yet, and holding off on having kids. Yet that seemed to be all that Josh was interested in. They got engaged a year ago, and knew they'd have a long engagement, but lately Josh was getting antsy, impatient, and even talked about flying to Jamaica to elope.

He'd always wanted a large family but had a small one. His mother died of cancer when he was young, and he had no siblings. He'd often told Jenna that he felt there should be more, and Jenna always told him it was his mother's death at a young age that left him feeling lonely.

Jenna knew in her heart there was no way Josh would move. He wouldn't leave the law firm, or his dad. It wouldn't even be fair of Jenna to ask, and she couldn't go without him. She didn't want to live for six months to a year in a different city. As much as she loved her career, she loved Josh more. He was her rock and security in all the uncertainty in the world. She'd had to turn down the opportunity, even though secretly she'd admitted it would be nice to be working far away from Rachel for a few months—a quiet reprieve. Rachel's words rang in Jenna's ear: 'Well, that's that then.' Jenna decided on the same, she'd not give it another thought. She wouldn't even tell Josh about it; there was no point.

Thinking of Josh, she realized he still hadn't responded to her last text. She suspected he must be in court and forgot to tell her—that must be the reason for his silence. Jenna brought her mug to her lips then recoiled; the coffee had gotten cold, and she despised cold coffee, so she headed back to the coffee station, drained the cold liquid, and poured herself a new one. With the mug in hand, she stood at the coffee station, staring into nothing as her co-workers discussed her mental state from the kitchen door, not daring to approach her. She must have given off a terrible vibe. And then she remembered the yoga instructor saying she could set the mood for the day, so she forced herself to walk, head held high, into her office. She was constantly scanning her phone for text messages from Josh, but the only one she received was from Cassie.

Cassie: He texted me. Yippy!

Jenna: Who texted you?

Cassie: Who do you think, girl? The hot yoga guy. We're having coffee later!

Jenna: Yay. I'm happy for you, Cas. Does the hot yoga guy have a name?

Cassie: Don't laugh, okay?

Jenna: I've never laughed at anyone's name before!

Cassie: Well, this might be the million-dollar moment! And you might think he's meant for you, not me.

Jenna: Stop the suspense, please?

Cassie: Bernardo!

Jenna loved the name Bernardo! She used to have a family dog named Bernardo when she was young, and she always said that if she ever got another dog, she'd name him Bernardo again. They joked about how obsessed Jenna was with that name. Despite her day, Jenna laughed out loud.

Jenna: LOL ☺ HAHAHA! He looks like a Bernardo!

Cassie: Yeah, he really does, doesn't he?

Jenna could always rely on Cassie to make her laugh. After reading the last text, she set the phone down and went through the rest of her work emails, and by noon she still hadn't heard from Josh. But the courts would break for lunch soon, so she called to check in. She wasn't sure where they stood after that fight. The phone rang four times before it went to voicemail. She hung up without leaving a message and wanted to wait fifteen minutes in case he was still in court. But after eight minutes, she called again; the second call went to voicemail as well. She typed out a quick text.

Jenna: Hey, call me when you get a chance. Are you in court today?

Jenna: Are we okay?

Jenna gazed at the phone for a few seconds, waiting for a reply, and just as she was about to set it down and go get a sandwich from the food truck before her meetings began, her phone buzzed.

Josh: Not in court today. Can't talk though. I'll call you later, okay?

Jenna: Why weren't you home this morning when I returned? Is everything okay?

Josh: No!

Her instincts had been right. He was still upset.

Jenna: I'm sorry about this morning. I didn't mean to upset you. When can we talk?

Josh: Not everything is about you. I'm at the hospital with Dad. Waiting to see the doctor, not sure what's going on, but he seems to know a lot more than I do.

Hospital? Since when? She had many questions, but texting was not the right way to ask them.

Jenna: I'll leave now. Be there soon!

Josh: No!

Jenna: ???

Josh: Don't come!

Jenna: Why?

Josh: I need to deal with this and having you here will make it worse.

That made no sense and caused her to do exactly the opposite. She packed up her laptop and tossed it into her briefcase as she sprinted to the elevator. On her way, her mother called, but she let it go to voicemail. She wasn't in the mood to deal with her. Jenna texted Rachel, telling her there'd been a family emergency and that she'd be out of the office for a couple of hours. She didn't elaborate or apologize for her absence. Before putting her phone back in her bag, she typed an email:

Rachel,

Please accept this email as my definitive answer to the job offer. I'm sorry, but I must decline the opportunity. I can't, under any circumstance, take the position in Quebec City. It won't happen and if that means I'm jeopardizing my career or any future promotions, then so be it. Please pass along my appreciation for the consideration to the board.

Thank you,
Jenna

Looking over the email for typos as she rode the elevator to the parking garage, she was satisfied she'd said all that needed to be said and, without further hesitation, pressed Send and braced herself to face Josh. He hadn't said what hospital they were at, but Jenna took a chance and headed for the nearest one.

CHAPTER 4

Time Crawled When Chaos Sped Through Air

IN THE HOSPITAL room, Josh paced, not sure what else to do as he waited for the doctor—the anticipation made breathing difficult. He knew he'd upset Jenna with his last text, but he was being honest. His phone was in his back pocket when it buzzed. He braced himself to read her reply.

Jenna: My job is to be there for you. I'm on my way.

She'd taken it better than he'd thought.

Josh: I said, don't come.

Jenna: I know what you said, but I'm still coming. Besides, when do I ever listen?

She was right, she never listened before, so why start? He didn't want to see her but couldn't stop her from coming. Having her there would make it harder to push her away. He had what he thought was a solid and smart strategy. He'd give her space and when she got lonely, she'd realize how much she needed him, wanted him, and only then would she want what he wanted. It's not like he had asked if he could knock her up today. He just wanted a plan, some idea when they'd start their family. He wanted a child to hold and cherish, and lately that need had intensified deep within. He couldn't explain the sudden desire, the strong want for marriage and a baby. But it was there, constantly lingering and burning a hole in his heart.

From across the room on the bed, his dad shifted from his side to his back, breaking Josh's concentration. "Dad, you doing all right?"

"Mmm."

"I don't know what that means. Do you need something?"

His dad's eyes were closed, but he nodded to let Josh know he was okay. They were in a private emergency room, and his father still hadn't told him anything, but something big was indeed happening, and he wondered how he could not know. Josh knew everything about his dad, or so he'd thought. The hospital staff knew him, and they'd treated that visit as if it were a routine trip—perhaps it was. Perhaps there *were* things his dad hadn't told him.

"You promised to tell me what's going on. I'm still waiting," said Josh.

Billy's eyes were still closed when he spoke. "Son, I already told you I want to wait for the doctor."

Josh blew out a breath. "And you say I'm the stubborn one."

Unable to do nothing, he gave up trying to get his dad to talk and took out his phone again. He pulled the thin white sheet over his dad's shoulder and sat on the chair next to the bed and read work emails. He read three emails but didn't know what they were about. His eyes had read the words, but his mind focused on his dad. He reread the first, gave up, and slipped the phone into his pocket and resumed pacing.

After a few minutes of pacing, Josh checked the time. Ten minutes had passed. Time crawled when chaos sped through air. Jenna's office wasn't far, so if she was on her way, then she would be there momentarily. Josh was not sure what he'd say. He was not sure he could even look at her without feeling a stab of pain. She had hurt him with silence earlier that morning more than she could have damaged his heart with words. Josh wanted her to know that, and to feel the emptiness and pain that she had inflicted on him by not agreeing to have a baby.

Her voice pulled him out of his reverie. It was distinctive, loud, and carried down the hallway. She was asking for his dad. A woman's voice said she couldn't go beyond the locked doors. They restricted it to family.

Josh walked to the door to hear better.

"Billy is my father-in-law; my husband is with him. Please let me be with them."

What a good liar she was. The door to the emergency area buzzed, and Josh listened for the familiar click of her heels as she made her way. The clicking grew louder the closer she got. Suddenly, the clicking stopped and the door swung open. Josh backed up from the door to avoid it hitting him.

"There you are! It's like fighting a pack of wolves to get to you two." She looked at Josh's dad and went to him. She placed her hand over his forehead. "How are you feeling, Billy?"

"Jenna, dear, you didn't have to come here for me."

"Of course, I did. You're my family." She glanced at Josh as she said that, but Josh looked away.

"I've seen better days, my dear."

"Has the doctor been here?"

"No, we're still waiting," answered Josh. "Jenna, can I have a word outside, please?"

She hesitated for a few seconds. "Billy, I'll be back, okay? I'm not leaving, so don't worry."

"Sure, dear." Billy patted her hand.

She patted his shoulder, then followed Josh out. Josh shut the door behind him so that Billy didn't hear the conversation. He had enough to worry about. Josh leaned up against the wall, trying to put distance between them. Jenna moved a foot closer and tried to embrace him, but he pushed her hands away.

"Josh..."

A man dressed in a white overcoat holding a clipboard approached just in time to save Josh from having to answer her questions.

"Are you Mr. Harrison's son?"

"I am." Josh held out his hand and said his name.

"I'm Dr. Danes. Can we have a word inside with your dad?"

"Of course." Josh turned to Jenna. "Wait here, okay?"

"No way. I want to be in there too."

Josh's back was to Jenna, so he looked into the doctor's eyes, enlarging his own, pleading.

"I need to discuss things with father and son only. You can wait there." Dr. Danes pointed to a single chair at the end of the hallway.

Josh mouthed the words 'thank you' to the doctor and entered the room, not allowing Jenna to argue. Josh couldn't help noticing Dr. Danes already knew his dad.

"Are you the emergency room doctor?" asked Josh.

"No, I'm an oncologist."

Oncologist. The word rang in his ears. Josh considered he'd heard wrong. He must have misunderstood.

Dr. Danes sat on the chair next to the bed, chart in hand. "Billy, I'd say it's nice to see you again, but we both know what me seeing you again means."

"Nice to see you..." Billy stopped to cough, then continued, "too, doc, even under..." more coughing, "these circumstances."

Josh rushed to the sink to get his dad a cup of water.

"Here, drink." After his dad had a sip and the coughing subsided, he added, "I think I've been patient enough. When is someone going to tell me what is going on?" He turned to Dr. Danes. "Why are you here? We don't need an oncologist. And how do you know my father?"

Dr. Danes put down the clipboard. "Billy, you know it's time? You can't keep going through this alone."

"What's going on?" Josh asked again, but Dr. Danes held up a hand to silence him.

"Billy, do you want me to do it, or do you?"

His dad sat up straighter, let out a cough, and took another sip. His gaze lingered on Josh. "Son, sit." Billy motioned to the edge of the bed. And Josh did as he was told. He sat close to his dad and noticed how dry his lips were as he licked them. "It's cancer, son. I didn't want to tell you until there was a need to worry. I've managed this far. But seems I can't hide it anymore, as you can see." He brought his arms up as high as he could, which wasn't high at all, and shrugged—defeat showing.

The room spun. Josh gripped the bed for support. His father was his life; the anchor that kept him safely docked while the world created ripples from the waves. Cancer. Of course it was cancer. Josh twisted his hands together; his fingers formed a pretzel-like shape. He didn't look at his father when he spoke. "How..." The words choked him; he cleared his throat and tried again. "How long have you known, Dad?"

His dad hesitated, as if he were afraid to tell Josh the truth. Josh thought he probably was.

"How long?" Josh repeated. "I can deal with it, but I need to know everything."

"Four months."

Josh squared his shoulders. "Four months? You've gone through this alone for that long?"

"I'm so sorry I didn't tell you from the beginning, son."

Josh stood, walked to the sink, and looked at his dad from a distance. He shook his head, then returned to the bedside and placed his arms around his father, unable to be upset with him. "How... bad is it?" he asked, hesitation seeping from his voice. He was afraid to know the answer.

"If I may. It's metastasized," cut in Dr. Danes. "We need to begin treatment immediately. Your father has avoided it. But it's time."

"How bad?" asked Josh.

"The cancer is spreading fast. It started in his prostate but has dispersed into other organs." He looked at his clipboard for a moment before continuing. "I'm sorry."

"So, it's bad?"

"Yes, it is."

Josh stretched, lifted his shoulders, and leaned his head back into the crevice. "What sort of treatment are we talking about?"

"Your father and I have discussed the options at great lengths. But I'll give you the summarized version. Radiation and chemo are the recommended treatment plan, but it comes with great consequences, as you probably know."

"It'll make him sick," confirmed Josh.

"Unfortunately, yes. Your father will lose energy, lose weight, vomit, but it's the best treatment plan that offers him the greatest chance at survival. We'd need to start aggressively, so if your father agrees, I'm recommending an admittance to get started right away. After a week, we'll reassess and possibly, he could go home and continue outpatient treatments."

Josh processed the information, shaking his head vigorously. "What's the prognosis? Will he be fine after all this?"

"Mr. Harrison, as you must know..."

"Please, call me Josh."

"All right then, Josh. There are no guarantees in life, especially in medicine. Your father has stage four cancer, so he will need to be emotionally strong for the next few months and stick with this treatment, and even then..." Josh noticed him hesitate, likely contemplating his next words. "He might end up in hospital longer, or dare I say, worse."

"So, there's a *good* chance we *can* beat this?"

Dr. Danes pushed his glasses up his nose. "Yes, there's a chance."

Josh noticed Dr. Danes omitted the word *good*. He turned to his father and scratched his head. "Dad, why wouldn't you have told me when you found out? Why wouldn't you have come to me? I can't believe you've been going through this alone for so many months. I don't understand. Did you think I couldn't handle it? Didn't you trust me?"

"Son, can we not do this now, please?"

"Do what Dad, talk about the truth?"

"Son, please."

"Please what, Dad?" Josh scratched his head again. "You didn't trust me. You didn't have faith in me."

Dr. Danes cleared his throat. "Mr.... My apologies, Josh. You said I could call you Josh?"

Josh nodded in reply.

"Josh, you must understand. Your father was only looking out for you. He didn't want to worry you. At first it was only a small spot on his prostate and as soon as we discovered that, we removed it."

"My father had surgery, and I didn't know?"

"You knew, son."

"I'm pretty sure I'd recall you having surgery."

"Remember the hernia?" asked his dad.

"I do. It was a few months ago, while I was away on business. I was so upset that you had booked a procedure while I was out of the country, but you said it was a minor hernia. You lied about that?"

"It wasn't a hernia," said Dr. Danes. "That was the story your father told you. He didn't want to pursue treatments, because he knew it would make him sick. It was his choice, and I had to respect his wishes. All I could do was counsel him. He was in the hospital for a couple days and we sent him home with a nurse to check up on him daily for a while. I tried to get him to agree to the radiation then, but you know your father better than I do, so you know how stubborn he is."

"Stubborn is an understatement. Seems you know my father rather well."

"A relationship between a doctor and patient is important—and confidential," he said in an apologetic tone. "I'm sorry we kept you in the dark, but Billy is my patient and I need to respect that."

That was too much for Josh. He needed to clear his head. "I can't... I need air. I'm going to get a tea." Josh's hand was already on the doorknob, but he turned to ask one more question. "What's going to happen next? Today, I mean?"

"I've recommended an admittance." Dr. Danes looked at Josh's dad for approval, and he nodded in agreement. "All right. I'm glad that's settled. We're waiting for his room to be ready upstairs. In the meantime, a nurse will be in to set the intravenous. Now's a good time for you to get some air."

"Go on, son. I'll be fine. Clear your head. I know this is a lot to take in."

Josh didn't want to leave his dad, but his throat was closing fast. The room was suffocating him, and he needed to get out before he stopped breathing. He'd forgotten about Jenna, their fight, that she didn't want kids, and that she was in the hallway waiting. He remembered her as he walked out of the room and saw her sitting at the end of the hallway, face in her hands. As if she sensed him, she looked up, stood rapidly, and ran toward him. Her heels clicking uncontrollably: tap, tap, tap.

She rubbed his arms when she approached. "How is he?"

Josh recoiled from her touch and walked away, but she called after him. He stopped in between two occupied stretchers, avoiding her eyes. He couldn't make sense of his jumbled thoughts. Without realizing he'd even spoken, he said, "We need time apart. I can't do this anymore, not like this."

Jenna stood behind him, her hand hovered just above his arm. "What do you mean? What's going on?"

Josh squared his shoulders, grabbed her arm, and led her outside so they could have space and privacy. They were getting in the way in the emergency hallway. Once outside, he ran his hands through his hair. "I'm moving out."

"No, you're not. Don't be ridiculous. Is this about this morning?"

"I'm staying with my dad for a while. I need time to think about what I want, and this will give you time to think about what you want from me."

"You need time to think so you're moving out? Just like that?"

"That's what I said. It's not negotiable."

"Not negotiable? What the hell, Josh? I'm not a client. I'm your fiancée. You can't throw out words like 'not negotiable' right after telling me you're moving out."

"Don't make this harder."

"What's going on?" she asked in a soft tone.

"I'm moving out, that's what's going on."

Likely due to shock, Jenna took a step back to grab onto the 'No Parking' sign for support. "Just like that? You decided on a whim that you're moving out?"

"Yes. Just as easily as you said you didn't want to have kids with me. I understand how easy it is to make a life-changing decision on a whim," he said, not meeting her eyes.

"Is that what this is about? Josh? Because if you recall, I never said I didn't want kids. I only meant now. You know that, and you're blowing this way out of context."

She ran her fingers through her hair, and Josh heard her breathing quicken.

"It's decided. I'm moving out." Josh stood frozen, looking away, hands in his pockets.

"For how long? Are we talking a day or two? Or..."

"Months, maybe longer. Who knows?"

Maybe longer. Who knows? Her face was red, and she balled her fists at her sides while tears formed. "You know what? Don't bother. You're a jerk! If it's me you need to get away from, then you can have the damn apartment."

"Jenna..."

What the hell had he just said? Josh shut his eyes for a second and opened his mouth to tell her the truth: he didn't mean to be so abrupt with her. He was in shock and needed to be near his dad. He was going to ask her to be patient as he realized he was being unfair, but she stopped him when he spoke her name.

She raised her hand, her palm facing him. "Stop. I don't want to hear anymore. I have something to tell you, too." She continued without giving him a chance to get a word in. "They have offered me a new position with the magazine for six months. *Maybe* longer. Who knows!"

Josh stood, hands in his pockets still, listening.

"In Quebec City." She continued, "I've accepted the offer and leave next week, but I'll stay with Cas until then. So, you're getting what you want. You're getting rid of me. It's over."

She walked away and out of his life before he could even explain the cancer, the treatments, that Billy will need him. He opened his mouth to call for her, but stopped. He didn't have to explain anything because she'd already decided to leave him. She was going to leave all along. Is that why she was being so supportive earlier, wanting to come to the hospital? Was she trying to soften the blow? What a selfish, heartless bitch. You think you know someone until your world blows up and you find out you never knew them at all. How could she have done that to him, to them? She didn't even consider asking him to go with her. Not that he could have, because of Billy and his career, but that was beyond the point. He would have liked if she had considered him. But she didn't, and that proved his suspicions; she cared more about her career than him. Josh watched her walk away and disappear behind cars, hoping she'd look back and change her mind. But she never did. She'd only thought of herself, and Josh was glad that he'd found out how selfish she was. With his head hung, he went back inside and made his way to his father. At least he was free to care for Billy—no more distractions.

CHAPTER 5

A Sudden Realization

JENNA STOOD IN the hospital parking lot, shaking and worrying her legs would betray her. She looked around, unsure how she got there. The parking lot was full, and her car was nowhere. The last thing she remembered was Josh's squared shoulders and echoing voice piercing her ears, saying he was moving out. She couldn't believe after getting engaged and five years of being together that he'd cast her out like a worn glove—one that no longer fit. She repeated his words, hoping they'd take on a new meaning. He was moving out. That was what he said—wasn't it? Did he even love her? He'd repeated the words, but she doubted their meaning. Wasn't their love supposed to be unconditional? She'd thought it was.

Too consumed in misery, she'd forgotten about Billy. She knew she was being selfish and considered going back to find out if he was okay; he was almost her father-in-law. But the thought of seeing Josh made her stomach hurt. Instead, she sent a text.

Jenna: I should have asked about Billy. I hope he's okay?

Josh: He'll be fine.

Jenna: Give him my best, will you please?

Josh: Will do.

Will do? That was all he had to say? Jenna's world spiralled out of control as she tried to find her car but couldn't remember where she'd parked. She thought she had parked beside the exit, but obviously did not know. Panicky and unsure of what to do, she pressed the alarm button on the key fob. The alarm blasted in front of her. Good lord, it was there the entire time. How had she not noticed? She shook her head in frustration. Now that she'd located the car, she was in a hurry to get inside. Not paying attention, she stumbled over the parking block and placed her arms on a car next to her to break the embarrassing fall. Jenna righted herself and tested the unsteady ground while she tried, desperately, to get inside. Fumbling with the key fob, unable to unlock the door, she grunted in frustration. The unlock button wasn't working, so she kicked the tire to relieve stress. It didn't relax her. She pressed the unlock button repeatedly in a rapid motion with no success. The more she struggled with the lock, the more cars spun around her. Jenna threw herself down and sat on the cold parking block to avoid another fall. She rested her arms on her knees and formed the familiar circle you often see during meditation by bringing her thumb and index finger almost to a touch. Visualizing the yoga instructor, she tried to calm her inner thoughts but didn't have the concentration for it. She reached for her phone, but the display was blurry, and she returned to the meditation pose and tried to focus on breathing, and after a few minutes, her heartbeat slowed. Rechecking the phone, she breathed a sigh of relief that her vision was back to normal. With the display on her phone legible again, she dialled Cassie. Cassie picked up on the first ring; it was as if she had been expecting her call.

"Oh good, just the person I need. You must have read my mind. I'm getting dressed for my lunch date with that hot yoga guy, a.k.a. Bernardo, and can't decide on black or blue jeans. I'll snap a pic wearing each and send them to you. Okay?"

There was a lot of background noise: shuffling and hangers clanking together. "Cas, I need your help." The background noise stopped.

"What's wrong, girl? Is it Rachel? Because if she's got you this upset again, I'm going over there and—"

Jenna interrupted. "No, it's not Rachel," she said in between sobs.

"Well, what then? Wait. I hear beeping. Where are you? I thought you'd be at the office today?"

"I'm at the hospital..."

"What!"

"But I'm fine. Well, physically anyway. I think... other than the dizziness."

"I'm getting in my car. I'm on my way. What happened?"

Jenna wasn't sure she could speak coherently. Her breathing was out of hand again, so she constantly reminded herself to relax, take deep, slow, and controlled breaths.

"It's over, Cas."

"What's over?"

"He's moving out."

"Girl, you're not making sense."

"Josh ended it. He told me he was moving out."

"Oh girl, Josh is an idiot, and he isn't going anywhere. Don't worry about that. He's probably had a bad day. I know his type."

"What's his type?"

"The kind that will try to control you into doing what he wants."

"I don't think that's what this is about, Cas. It's really over."

"But why? Over the baby thing? And why are you at the hospital? You still haven't explained that?"

She poured her heart out as Cassie drove to the hospital, refusing to let her go.

"Okay, girl, I'm pulling in. Wave so I can find you. Oh, never mind, I see you sitting on the curb. I'm coming," she said and hung up.

Jenna sat motionless as Cassie found a nearby parking spot and sat next to her. Cassie leaned in close and wrapped her arms around her.

"Oh girl, you're freezing."

Jenna shivered. "I'm not that cold, but I should have worn better shoes. I can't feel my toes."

"I'm so sorry this is happening to you." Cassie looked around the full parking lot. "We need to get out of here. Can you drive to the coffee shop on the corner? We can sit, have a coffee, and chat? You can tell me all about your idiot fiancé."

"Idiot ex-fiancé," corrected Jenna. "And my car door won't unlock. I think I broke it." Jenna waved the key in annoyance.

"Let me see that?" Cassie grabbed it, and with one swift click of the unlock button, the door unlocked. Cassie looked at her with raised eyebrows and tilted her head to the side. "Did you do the breathing thing like the instructor taught us?"

Jenna rolled her eyes. "I tried."

"Come on, let's go. I'll drive. You leave your car here, and we'll come for it later."

Jenna got into Cassie's car and applied hand sanitizer. Cassie got into the driver's side, reached in her bag, pulled out a pack of gum, and offered one to Jenna.

"No thanks. Wait, what about your date with Bernardo?"

"Hot yoga guy doesn't have priority over my best friend."

"I'm sorry I ruined your lunch date."

"Ahh, it's no biggie. If a guy can't understand the importance of a bestie needing help, then he's not the guy for me. Doesn't matter how hot he is." Cassie winked, and Jenna smiled for the first time since she'd left the office.

∾

"I still can't believe he just announced he was moving out. That must have felt like he slapped you in the face. I mean, it's unlike Josh. I know I've had my issues with him in the past, and I used to say he didn't deserve you, but still. There's got to be more to the story than what you're telling me."

The 'issues' that Cassie referred to were mostly jealousy on Cassie's part when Jenna and Josh got together. Cassie often told Jenna that Josh was too controlling, demanding and took up too much of Jenna's time.

"There isn't more to tell you. That's it."

"Really?"

"You don't believe me?"

"Of course, I do. You're my best friend, you know that. I'm here for you and will always have your back, but this is out of character, even for Josh."

"Cas, I wish there was more to it, but that's not the case. He said he was moving out and wasn't sure for how long."

"And you're really leaving next week?"

"Yes."

"Don't you think you should stick around in case...?"

"Cas, I won't chase him. He left me, remember? I'm not that girl that will chase a guy that doesn't want me."

"I know. I'll support you no matter what, but are you sure this is what you want?"

"Cas, I've never been surer of anything in my life. This move will be good for me."

Cassie offered Jenna her apartment and, since Jenna had already told Josh she'd be out of their apartment, she accepted. She planned to return one last time to pack while Josh was out.

A sudden realization hit her. "Shit."

"What now?" asked Cassie.

"I need to get a hold of Rachel right away. This is terrible."

"You're not making sense again, girl."

"This is bad, Cas." Jenna stood and hastily gathered her belongings.

"I know, girl, but we'll get through this together."

"I turned down the job offer earlier. It completely slipped my mind until now."

"You didn't!"

"I need to get back to the office to discuss this with Rachel."

"I'm sure that can wait. Take some time to process the breakup first. You might even decide that moving isn't what you want."

"It is. Josh ended things; I can't stay. This promotion is what I need. I must get to the office and explain before they offer Greg the job."

"Greg, the dude that hits on you at every Christmas party? They'd never consider him! But no worries. I'll take you back to your car. We'll meet at the apartment later and I can help you pack."

"That sounds great. I'll call you in a couple of hours. You're off work right?" Cassie was a receptionist at an insurance broker.

"I'm off the rest of the week. Call whenever you're ready."

Back at the hospital parking lot, they hugged, and Jenna squeezed for an extra few seconds to show how much she appreciated Cassie. When she was back inside her car, she grabbed her phone from her bag and dialed Rachel. The phone rang once, twice, three times. "Please pick up, please pick up..." said Jenna before voicemail kicked in. "Shit," she said aloud. She hung up without leaving a message and tried again. It went to voicemail a second time, but she left a desperate message and wasn't sure Rachel would understand her babbling. While at a red light, she emailed her. Jenna needed Rachel to get these messages before they offered the job to Greg. That cannot happen. No way. Impossible. Jenna increased her speed, looking for police cars.

She arrived at the building minutes later with a lineup in the parking garage elevator. There's never a lineup! She contemplated taking the stairs, but her shoes weren't the most comfortable, so she took her chance and waited for the elevator, tapping her foot on the polished garage floor while she waited. When the elevator door opened, she pushed past a group standing in her way, discussing financial projections. Jeez, doesn't anyone use boardrooms anymore? When the elevator stopped on her floor, she ran straight to Rachel's office, but found it empty. Shit.

"Hey Vanessa," said Jenna to the receptionist, "where's Rachel?"

The pretty co-op student looked bored filing her nails and glanced at Jenna. "How am I supposed to know? I'm not her assistant."

"Do you know if she's left the building? Can you tell me that?"

Still filing her nails without looking at her hands, she answered, "I saw her walking with her mug about five minutes ago. Did you check the kitchen?"

Seriously. If she knew, why didn't she say so? Jenna resisted the urge to reach over the desk and strangle the girl.

When Jenna entered the kitchen, Rachel was standing at the sink, stirring her coffee. Jenna was grateful to have found her, but prayed it wasn't too late.

"Rachel, I need to talk to you."

Rachel turned with a frown. "Oh, goody, look who's decided to work today."

"Rachel, did you get the voicemail or email message I sent a few minutes ago?"

"Your messages are not my priority. I've been in meetings, the ones you should have attended as well. Do you think I have nothing better to do than to sit around checking messages?"

"Can we talk, please?"

"I'm busy."

"Rachel, please, it's about the job. Something changed. I want it. I want to explain why I turned it down earlier."

"How do you know I haven't offered it to Greg?"

"I don't, but sure hope you haven't."

With her coffee in hand, Rachel walked toward the door, then turned. "Well, are you coming or what? I don't have all day."

❧

She got the job and let out the breath she didn't realize she'd been holding. At the end of their meeting, she'd asked for the next two days off to prepare for the move, but Rachel declined, giving her only the rest of the afternoon. Jenna knew better than to push her luck. She was fortunate that Rachel had not yet informed the board about her earlier decision.

Later, while still at the office, she worked on her to-do list. When

her list was complete and she was sure she had missed nothing crucial, she searched for apartments in Quebec City. With the help of a
French-speaking real estate agent, she had virtual tours and then went
to her apartment to pack. She wanted to get there and be out before
Josh got home. That afternoon, she and Cassie packed Jenna's belongings and moved them to Cassie's apartment. As she'd shut the door
behind her and locked it, her fingers had lingered on the doorknob,
aware that it was the last time she'd be there. With her car jam-packed,
she'd started the ignition, and Jenna's eyes had lingered on the building,
remembering the day they had moved in. Time for a change. She'd put
the car into drive and as the building faded in her rear-view, she didn't
look back.

❧

They tried to find room in Cassie's apartment for her stuff, even though
they only packed personal items and some kitchenware, leaving furniture
behind. Cassie's apartment wasn't big, but would do. The apartment she'd
be leasing would come furnished.

In the evening, before the second live virtual tour with the same real
estate agent for one contender, Cassie made them drinks: Kahlua and
vodka. Jenna wanted the drink to relax. Cassie sat in on the virtual tour
with Jenna and agreed it was the one; although the tour was in French
and she complained she understood little, so Jenna had to interrupt the
agent often to translate. That night, she signed the electronic lease for
six months, starting March thirty-first, the day before her twenty-eighth
birthday. She'd celebrate alone in a foreign city. Perfect. This would be
her year of transformation.

CHAPTER 6

Bienvenue à Québec

THE NEXT WEEK, Jenna hadn't heard from Josh. He hadn't called or even texted when he got home to discover her stuff gone. She had expected him to call and felt a pang of hurt when he didn't. It was like Jenna never existed. So be it; that part of her life was over, and she knew she must move on.

❧

It was finally moving day, and that morning Jenna visited her parents to let them know what she'd been doing and what was happening in her life. Until then, she hadn't told them about the breakup and that she was moving. It was easier to wait until the day of, tell them, then leave. She would avoid desperate calls from her mother trying to convince her to stay. She was about to repeat history and hadn't realized it until she drove to her parents' house.

❧

When Jenna had moved out of the family home ten years ago, her parents, less than pleased about the arrangement, had said she was too young to be on her own. That statement had gotten to her because her brother, Kris, had moved out at the same age to travel with his boyfriend, Xavier. That hadn't been an issue, but Kris went with Xavier, and she was going alone. She'd wanted to show them she was in charge of her life, even if she was female. Her entire existence she had lived in her brother's shadow. Her parents had encouraged Kris to do what he wanted, find true love with whomever he chose, live his life the way he'd dreamt, but with Jenna, they had pushed her to find a good man who could provide for her, so she could give him many children, and learn to cook for the family. Her parents were old-fashioned, but that was not her; it had never been. Jenna had often argued with them about who should do the cooking. Her parents still lived like they had when they were young. Her mother did everything for her father, and that had driven Jenna crazy over the years—the way he took advantage of her mother. Jenna had reflected on her upbringing and realized that her mother was only following in the footsteps that Jenna's grandmother had paved. Jenna had decided to be the female in her family to break the chauvinistic mentality. Eventually, Jenna became fed up, and when she turned eighteen she wanted out—to explore the world. She had convinced herself she needed no man to take care of her. She'd yearned for independence. Two weeks before her eighteenth birthday, she had gathered all her saved money and booked a flight to France, leaving on her eighteenth birthday.

"Happy Birthday to me," she had said the day she'd purchased the ticket. She had told her parents on the day she'd left.

Her mother had clasped her hand over her mouth: "How long will you be away?"

"I don't know, Mom, a few months maybe."

Her mother hadn't pretended to hide the tears. When her father had heard her mother's sobs, he'd come behind her mom and wrapped his arms around her, asking what was wrong. "It's your daughter, Brian," her mother had said. "She's lost her mind. She's throwing her life away." Her mother had stormed out, her father followed.

"Young lady, go to your room. We'll discuss this later," said her father. But by the time they had returned, she was no longer there.

It was a coincidence how both major events played out at the same time of year. Fate?

⚮

Jenna's parents, Brian and Kate, lived in Toronto, along with her brother, Kris. He lived with Xavier since he'd moved out. Her brother and his boyfriend lived in a tiny apartment and claimed they needed little because they travelled often. They had created an internet business selling merchandise, and it had done well. That business venture afforded them the luxury to take off for a few weeks, several times a year. Although both her parents and brother lived close, the family only saw each other a few times a year on birthdays, Christmas, and Thanksgiving. Their relationship hadn't recovered from the blow that Jenna threw at them all those years ago, and here she was, giving them yet another.

Her parents were up early and already having coffee when she arrived unannounced. She had called Kris to ask if he could meet her there, but Xavier informed her he was out. She had hoped to only have to do this once.

She took a deep breath and rang the doorbell.

"Jenna, what a surprise," said her father, holding the door open. "Your mother just made coffee. Would you like a cup?"

Jenna accepted.

"Great, she'll get you one." Then he turned to her mother, "Kate, get coffee."

Of course, it was her mother who prepared the coffee. It was always her mother; some things never changed.

Over two cups of coffee, Jenna updated her parents on the breakup, her new job, and apartment. Her parents took the news well, considering what she'd dropped on them. Her escapade years ago must have toughened them up. And as Cassie had mentioned, she was older and not eighteen, like she was the last time she'd left abruptly.

They stood at the door together and her mother's eyes pleaded as she said she wanted a call from her the moment she arrived in Quebec City, and at minimum, once a week; Jenna nodded in agreement. Her mother still called her every few weeks, but Jenna seldom picked up and only returned the call after her mother begged to know she was all right.

"Do you promise?" asked her mother.

"Mom, I'll call you more often." She hesitated, then added, "I promise."

"And call your brother, too. I don't want him finding out from me."

"Mom, we both know you'll be on the phone with Kris tonight."

"Yes, and that's because he calls to check in."

Why had she said that? She immediately regretted going there. "Fine. I'll call him."

They said goodbye, and while walking to her car, she looked over her shoulder. Her father had left, but her mother remained glued to the front porch. Jenna waved and got in her car, but she hadn't even put the car into reverse when her phone rang.

"Hey Jeni, I missed you earlier. So sorry, but I had to run out. Xavier said you rang?"

"Hi Kris, I'm leaving Mom and Dad's. I had hoped you could have stopped by while I was here."

"Oh boy, did I miss some fun?"

"I had news to share."

"Oh, dang it! I missed the family fun!"

"Family fun?"

"I assume your news is exciting and why it required a visit. Mom and Dad would surely have been in a huff over seeing you when it's not your birthday. Wait! What day is it? I didn't miss your twenty-eighth birthday, did I?"

"Not yet."

"Phew. So, what's going on? Don't keep your big brother waiting any longer. I can't take the suspense."

"Where are you?"

"I'm back at home."

"Can I stop by?" she asked.

"Like, you mean right now?" She heard the anxiety in his voice.

"Yeah, but I won't be long, I promise."

"Well, if you must. I suppose I can take Effie for a walk later."

"Thanks for putting me before your dog."

"You sure you can't just tell me over the phone?"

"Kris!"

"I'm kidding. Come on over."

"Thanks, Kris. I won't stay long and promise not to mess up your routine. I know how much you dislike unexpected company."

"Anything for you, Jeni."

"I'll be there in ten minutes."

Her brother was something else. He came across as selfish, but he was the opposite: sweet and kind, just didn't always show it. After stopping at her brother's, she drove to Cassie's one last time before heading out of town. They had already loaded up her car before she left to see her parents. But she was running late, so promised to stop on her way out of town for a proper goodbye.

"Cas, thanks so much for being there for me this past week. I don't know what I'd do without you."

"I do! You'd be a basket case, but that's what best friends are for."

Cassie wrapped her arms around her, and Jenna promised to call when she arrived.

"I want a call tonight, and I don't care what time you get there."

"I'll miss you, Cas."

"And I'm coming to see you next weekend, so don't forget."

"You don't have to come so soon; I know you have a lot going on and you took time off recently already."

"Are you kidding me? I need to see my bestie's new pad. Besides, it's only an eight-hour drive."

"Only if you plan on not stopping to pee or eat."

"Okay, so ten, tops. If I take Friday off, and leave by three a.m., I can meet you for lunch."

"You're crazy, and that's what I love about you."

"So, it's a date?"

Jenna chuckled. "Yes, it's a date!"

After one last hug, Jenna climbed into her car, and the feelings that enveloped her were bittersweet. As she turned on the ignition, she looked around. Time to move on. Time to get a new life, and so after holding onto the memory of her best friend waving at her, and yelling Happy Birthday, she put the car into drive and left the life she had, alone. Her twenty-eighth birthday was going to be a year of transformation and new beginnings. She just had a feeling.

As the Toronto skyline diminished in her rear view, a wave of panic hit her stomach. She pushed the fear back down. She'd never let a man steer her life before, and she wouldn't start now.

Approximately six-and-a-half hours later, she left the familiarity of Ontario behind as the big, blue 'Bienvenue à Québec' sign greeted her from the side of the road, and all the bulletins, streets, and storefront names were in French. A couple more hours into the commute, she passed a house with a sign at the end of the driveway: 'Chatons Gratuits' *Free Kittens*. On a whim, she stopped. There was an enormous wicker basket lined with a blue and white blanket spilling over the sides. She peeked inside and her heart skipped as kittens tried to climb out but were too little and fell onto each other. Jenna wondered if it was too cold for them out there and wanted to take them all. Then her eyes landed on a white, extra furry kitten with one black spot on the back of the neck sitting alone in the corner, too frightened to attempt the climb. The kitten's eyes met Jenna's, and they locked as the homeowner approached.

"Interested in one?" asked the woman in French.

"I'll take that one," said Jenna without hesitation, flipping to French naturally.

She accepted an empty pop can box and placed the kitten inside on the passenger seat, hoping the kitten would be okay for the rest of the car ride. Jenna named her new companion Seul, which meant 'alone'—a representation of the next chapter. Before climbing into the driver's seat, she pulled out her hand sanitizer and doused it over her hands and forearms. With a shaky foot on the gas pedal, she and Seul made their way to a new city, and new life.

Jenna switched the radio stations until she found one in French, getting ready to embrace the new culture she'd be living amongst, and in French, sang along as Seul slept peacefully beside her.

CHAPTER 7

Meet Cute

JOSH HADN'T HEARD from Jenna since that day in the hospital—the day *she* left. He thought about her often, despite his busy days working and visiting his sick dad. That morning marked one week they'd been apart, so it was especially hard, and he couldn't help reminiscing about the day they met. Swallowed by feelings he couldn't sort through, he allowed himself to think about their meet cute.

❧

He knew right away she was The One. It only took one glance to be sure. Josh heard her voice in a café near the University of Toronto. She sat alone and aggressively punched the keys on her laptop at full speed, as if she were writing a typing exam. The foul word that had escaped from her red-polished lips was not one Josh would have expected, but when she spoke the foul language with so much passion, emphasizing the U in the f-bomb, his head had whipped around. His eyes met hers briefly before she looked away and muttered another foul word, but in

French this time. Josh wasn't bilingual but knew that word. Right after cursing, she frowned. She chewed her bottom lip and stared at the screen with enlarged eyes. Her expression made Josh smile, and the hunger pains in his stomach shifted and he couldn't put his finger on the unfamiliar sensation flowing through him.

When they first met, Josh had just graduated from York with his undergrad and had started law school. Part of him had known he couldn't afford the distraction of a beautiful woman at a time so focused on self-control and hard work, but the other part hadn't been able to resist. She had pulled him to her like a magnet and he realized that, even though he'd only heard her speak two words, she was special.

There was something about her. He needed to talk to her, to get to know her; of that he was surer than he'd been about anything. He bumped into a stranger carrying two coffees and, without taking his eyes off her, apologized for the lack of attention to his surroundings. Josh stretched his neck to get a look at her screen. He was desperate to read her words. Her shorter and lighter hair hung over her turtleneck. The sweater hugged her body, and Josh imagined pulling it off her. Strands of hair stuck under the folded neck made her look even cuter than she would have if placed perfectly.

For the first time since he saw her, her fingers stopped moving. She lifted her hand to her neck and placed her fingers under her hairline and pulled upward, allowing the stuck strands to join the others. Her silky, straight hair fell over her folded neckline now, instead of being jammed in a mess. Josh held his breath. Then her hands moved again. This time, she brought them up to her face and her small, delicate fingers adjusted the reading glasses—thick with bright red rims.

She went back to typing as fast as she had been before, and Josh remained frozen, breathless. Her head remained down, lifting it only to take a sip of coffee. She hadn't looked at Josh again, and his breathing intensified as he pondered how to get her to notice him. Josh found an empty seat and sat for several minutes before he realized others blocked him from her view, so after a deep breath and self-talk, he picked up his peppermint tea and moved tables. If only she'd look up. He tapped his foot, drummed on the table with his fingers and coughed, hoping she'd look his way, but she stayed focused.

After five more minutes of staring and hoping, Josh's heart skipped a beat as her head bobbed up for air—another coffee break. She shook the cup back and forth and frowned. It must be empty. She groaned, set it down, and continued typing. This was his opportunity. He sprinted to the counter and asked the barista if she remembered what the lovely girl with the red-rimmed glasses had ordered. The barista told him she was a regular and was drinking a dark roast drip coffee with extra cream, no sugar. Josh ordered an extra-large for her, and a new black peppermint tea with no sugar for himself. His palms were sweaty, and he had a hard time holding the cups. He didn't want to leave sweat marks on her cup, and that made him walk faster. When he approached, she still didn't look up—oblivious to the world. Josh considered his next move and cleared his throat to alert her to his presence. After waiting a long time, she lifted her chin to him with squinted, narrowed eyes.

"I don't remember ordering another?" she pointed to the cups in his hands.

"Ahh..." Josh couldn't find words. She was speaking to him, finally, and he was mumbling. He could be such a nob sometimes.

"Well, I could use it, so if it is a regular coffee with lots of cream, I'll take it."

She blinked her long eyelashes and Josh almost dropped the cups.

"You can set it down."

"Ahh," repeated Josh.

"Go on, I don't bite."

He cleared his throat to ready his voice, but before he spoke, she asked, "Do you not speak English? Je suis francophone." *I am French.*

"English. I speak English. And you... you didn't order another. I just thought..."

She tilted her head to the side and rubbed her neck. The fabric shifted slightly as she rubbed. Josh's insides turned upside down, watching that unintentionally sexy gesture. The bare section of her neck was so smooth. Her skin was so silky. He forced himself to tear his eyes away from her neck and looked into her eyes—safer to look there. She looked into his eyes and they both smiled. Josh let out a little giggle as he noticed her glasses had slid down again, and she adjusted them back up closer to the bridge of her nose, as she had before.

"I guess I got a little too excited thinking that was for me. Sorry."

She waved her empty cup at him and then sat it back down gently that time.

"It is."

Her eyebrows raised from above the lenses of her glasses. "Really? For me?"

"Yes. A dark roast coffee with extra cream, no sugar. It's how you like it?" Still standing, with his shoulders squared, Josh sat the cup down next to the empty one and put his hand in his pocket, not knowing what else to do.

Her eyebrows scrunched up again, and there was a tiny wrinkle between her eyes. Josh wanted to touch it, smooth it out, so he forced himself to keep his hand in his pocket.

She looked at the steaming coffee, then back at him. "Are you a stalker? Do I need to worry? Because, if you are, I need to know right away. Tell me fast."

Stalker? She wasn't wrong.

He decided on honesty, smiled, and said, "I'm no stalker, just an admirer."

"Well, you answered one question, but what about the other?"

"There were more?"

"If you'd paid as much attention to what I said instead of my face, you'd know I also asked if I should be worried?"

Right. She asked that.

"I don't think so," he said.

She smiled again after repositioning her glasses once more. "You don't think so? Interesting. You sure know how to sell yourself. Now you've confused me. Is that part of the plan?" She glanced at her watch, then continued. "Okay, if you're not a threat, then sit, but you'll have to be quiet for a few minutes. I need to finish this report for my boss, otherwise, I'll make you deal with Rachel; because I'm certainly not."

Josh did not know who Rachel was, or what report she was writing, but there he sat, watching her work for the next few minutes.

"There," she said and slammed her laptop shut. "Thanks for the coffee, by the way."

"You're welcome. So..."

"So... what?" she prompted.

He combed his brain for something intelligent to say; he was in law school after all, so why was it difficult? All he came up with was, "So, Rachel is your boss, I presume?"

"Yeah, I'm an intern at *Brandy Thyme Press* magazine. I work part-time while attending school."

"You want to be an editor or something like that?"

She smiled weakly. "Something like that. I'm taking journalism at Ryerson. Third-year. I need to get back to work, so be quiet or find a new table."

"You shut your laptop. I thought you finished."

"I took a slight break. I didn't want to be rude."

"That was a break?"

"Yes, now be quiet, please."

She flipped the laptop open, and Josh sat with one hand clenched around the hot tea, and watched her fingers aggressively press the keyboard once again. Her focus was enchanting. He knew she'd won him over and was head over heels for the mystery girl whose name he didn't even know.

That afternoon was their first date. After Jenna finished with the report, she announced she was hungry, and they'd left the café and shared a pepperoni, sausage, and bacon pizza in the park. The rest, as the famous saying goes, was history.

＠◯

He forced himself out of the memory. It would only increase the pain to think of the good times. Instead, he focused on her faults. He knew they were over, but it wasn't like her to not call or text. She hadn't even asked about his dad. But he'd said Billy would be fine; maybe she believed that.

＠◯

His dad became weaker after they admitted him, and Josh stayed at the hospital every chance he could. He even slept the night there a few times, despite his dad complaining that he was fine. Life was out of control as Josh tried to keep up with his caseload and care for his sick father. And, of course, Jenna's absence left a hole. But the other attorneys at the firm had picked up his slack and that helped. He didn't know if he'd be able to juggle it all without his co-workers jumping in to help.

It was a tough week, but if Josh was truthful, even though he missed Jenna, it was easier not to worry about her, too. He convinced himself it was normal to miss her, and it didn't mean letting her go was a mistake. Sadness was normal in a breakup, but after the meet cute memory, he pushed further thoughts of them away; there was no room or time for sorrow.

After a few more days, his dad's condition improved, and they were discharging him with homecare. Things would fall back into a routine soon.

＠◯

On his lunch break, instead of relaxing and reading as his colleagues suggested, he went to the pharmacy to pick up his dad's prescription. Josh was picking up his dad after work and didn't want to stop on the way.

As he waited in the prescription drop-off line, a hand tapped him on the shoulder. He turned and found Cassie standing a little too close to his face for his liking.

"Well, well, well. Look at you," she said with a frown. "Aren't you looking all smug standing here as if nothing happened?" She crossed her arms over her chest.

"I don't know why you're upset with me, again, Cassie, but now is not a good time." Josh turned to face the pharmacy assistant as he was next.

Cassie reached out to stop him. "Oh, no you don't. Not so fast, mister."

"What the hell is your problem?"

"You. Who else do you think is my problem?" Her lips gathered into a pout.

"Hold on a second," said Josh, holding up a finger to Cassie.

Josh handed the prescription to the assistant and waited for her to confirm the name, address, and insurance policy number for his dad.

The pharmacy assistant looked at the prescription for a few seconds and then named two different drugs and asked which the doctor had ordered. "I don't know. I'm sorry, but isn't it written there on the paper?" asked Josh.

"Yes, but it's not legible. I want to be sure; one is for treating cancer, and the other is for less severe ailments. Is this for cancer?"

"Yeah, it's the one for cancer," Josh confirmed, as he lowered his eyes.

"It should be ready in fifteen minutes. Are you waiting or coming back later?"

"I'll wait," said Josh to the pharmacy assistant.

He turned to face Cassie. "Now, what is *your* problem?"

"Cancer?" she asked.

"You heard that?"

"Is it Billy? Does he have cancer?"

"Yeah, he does. I found out last week. But why are you angry with me? Jenna's the one who left. How does that make me the bad guy?" Josh couldn't help noticing her twitch when he said that.

"Does Jenna know?"

"Know what?"

"About Billy?"

"No. I don't see how she would. I haven't heard from her since she left. Unless she's called him, but he would have told me, I think." His dad hadn't told him about the cancer, though. What else could he be hiding? Maybe he had talked to Jenna.

They moved away from the line as others complained they were in the way.

"How is she? Is she settled in her new place?" He didn't want to ask, didn't want to know, but asked anyway.

"She's fine, and she's getting settled, slowly. I'm actually on my way to see her first thing in the morning. Just picking up some protein drinks for the trip." She paused, and Josh felt she wanted to say more. "She said *you* were moving out."

There it was. He scratched his head. "Yeah, it's true. I said that. Things were... complicated. I've got my hands full with my dad and work. Speaking of that, I have to get back to the office and still have shopping to do."

"Don't let me keep you then."

Josh turned and walked away as Cassie called out his name. "What's Billy's prognosis?"

"He had a few bad days, but he's much better now. A little more radiation and it should kill the cancer, we're hoping anyway."

"It looks good, then? His survival rate, I mean?"

"Yeah, it does." Josh nodded, then added, "Tell Jenna..."

She prompted him to continue. "Tell her what?"

He cleared his throat. "We still need to divvy the furniture." Josh turned and walked out, doing no further shopping and without picking up the prescription.

CHAPTER 8

Life Lessons

AFTER WORK, JOSH stopped at the pharmacy since he'd left in haste because of the encounter with Cassie, then headed to the hospital. His face brightened when he saw his father; he was laughing at nurses' jokes, smile expanded ear to ear. They loved him there. The staff told Josh he brought sunshine to a grey day. That was his dad all right, even after receiving a cancer diagnosis.

Josh wanted to bring him to his apartment so he wouldn't be alone, but his dad wouldn't hear of it. Josh then suggested he'd stay at his house, but he wouldn't have that either. Stubborn man that he was.

He still hadn't told his dad about Jenna leaving. A part of him hoped he could keep it secret, but knew it was inevitable Billy would find out. He'd already asked about her many times because she hadn't been back to see him since that day in the emergency room. Josh said she was busy, but suspected his dad knew there was more to the story. His dad was an intelligent man, and Josh knew his father had a magical quality that enabled him to see right through people. Josh couldn't hide from him—emotionally—no matter how hard he tried.

Josh observed his dad from the doorway; he had a spring to his steps he didn't have before being admitted. Josh thought the time there had served him well. After the nurses completed the discharge papers and said goodbye, he escorted him out and put his father in the front seat of his BMW, and buckled him up.

Billy knocked his hands away. "I've got cancer, not two broken arms. Will you stop fussing over me like this, son?"

"Dad, I—"

Billy raised his hand to stop him. "I can still do some things. You must let me try."

"Sorry, Dad. I can't help it." Josh threw his arms up in the air, accepting defeat.

"Help it, or you'll drive me batty. You ever see an old man batty before?"

Josh thought about that. "No, at least not you, Dad. And stop calling yourself old."

"Well, you will if you don't stop fussing."

Josh walked around the BMW to the driver's side and minded his own business during the drive. He'd hired a personal support worker to prepare for his dad's return. The personal support worker had assured him there was enough of everything he'd need to be comfortable, including food, and she'd even dropped off a wheelchair in case fatigue set in again. Billy would continue his treatment as an outpatient for six weeks. After that, they would know if they were successful in killing the cancer cells. If not, they would discuss next steps, but Josh was confident, judging by the last few days, that Billy would be fine. He was one of the strongest people he knew.

"All right Dad, here we are. Do you need a hand getting out?" Josh asked first this time, respecting his dad's space and wishes.

"I think I'm good, son."

Josh threw up his arms again. "I'll lay off, then."

"Son, if I ever need help, you'll be the first I ask, okay?"

Josh attempted a smile, but his lips barely moved. "Deal."

The house smelled like Pine-Sol cleaner, the lavender scent from Josh's childhood, thanks to the cleaners Josh had hired.

"Would you like a tea, Dad? I can put the kettle on."

"Sure, that would be great, but only if you have a few minutes to stay and have one with me."

"Of course, Dad, I'm not going anywhere."

His dad raised his eyebrows, so not missing a beat Josh added, "That is, until you want to be alone, and then I'll leave." Raising his arms, he added, "Promise."

"Son, you know you're welcome here. That's not what I meant earlier."

"I know, Dad. I'm just teasing."

It was April and chillier than normal. Josh noticed his father shiver, so he turned on the gas fireplace long enough to take the chill out of the air. They sat on the bulging recliners next to the fireplace, blowing on their teas to cool them enough to drink without burning their tongues. Josh focused on the flames, changing and glowing.

His dad was the first to break the trance. "I'm listening, son."

"I said nothing."

"Exactly, and I think it's about time you do."

"What do you want me to say?"

"Start by telling me where Jenna's been this week?"

Josh lowered his head.

"I know something is up. She's never this absent, and I could tell something was wrong last time I saw her."

Josh kept his head hung, watching the liquid in his cup swirl rather than watching the fire. He didn't want to have this conversation with his father. He had known it was coming but hoped to avoid it longer and wanted to put more distance between the time since the breakup. It was too soon for him to talk about her without breaking.

"If you're not ready to talk, I understand. I'm here whenever you are ready."

Josh met his father's eyes. "She's gone."

"I gathered that much. Where to?"

Josh filled his dad in on the past week.

"So, it's over?"

"It's over."

"I'm sorry things ended this way." Billy shook his head repeatedly. "So, that was it? She just up and left with no explanation? Doesn't sound like our Jenna."

Josh knew exactly what Billy was implying. "You think I had something to do with her leaving, don't you?"

"I never said that."

"You didn't have to. I can tell it's what you're thinking. You believe I pushed her away. Pushed her too hard, put too much pressure on her about getting married and having a baby, and scared her? Isn't that the truth, Dad?"

"I don't know, son. Is it the truth?"

His father had a way of twisting things around and making him see more clearly. Josh thought back to how that day had played out. Was it his fault? He was the one who had announced first that he was moving out. He shook the thought away. It didn't matter; she had already accepted the job offer, and *she'd* already planned to leave *him*. That was not only the truth, but the reality. Josh must have made her feel better about her decision, because she could say she left because of him. She could shift the blame.

"Listen, son; I'm a wise, old man, and I know a thing or two about life and being committed to a woman."

"For crying out loud, Dad. You're not that old."

"Older than you, so by default, much wiser, too."

"You realize you're talking to a lawyer? We're pretty sharp."

"Yes, and by the time you're my age, you'll be unstoppable. Now listen up as your old man has some advice."

Josh prepared himself for another life lesson. His dad had been giving him insights, that he referred to as valuable lessons learnt from life experiences to him since he could remember. As far as Josh knew, Billy had started while Josh had been in his mother's womb. His dad would have wanted to maximize the lesson's impact.

Josh imagined his mother's swollen belly and his dad on his knees, head pressed up against the bump, giving him advice. The lessons may have happened even before Josh's mother died, but they had become more frequent after her death—more to learn after a loss.

His dad had a way with words. He always did. He used to take the most obscure situation and turn it into an example for Josh. Josh remembered being a young boy, barely able to comprehend what his dad was saying. It all sounded complicated and grown-up to him. But when his dad spoke the magical words, his ears perked up, and he listened intently, nodding to show his dad he was listening, even though most of the time he didn't understand the wisdom his dad was imparting. The life lessons happened mostly during drives to and from little Josh's soccer practises and games, on the way to birthday parties, or the grocery store to pick up much-needed items while his mother was at home preparing supper.

Josh smiled at the memory of these lessons and readied himself for another one.

"Son, do you remember when you were little, and you really wanted a pet, but you weren't sure which? Your mother had said you could have any pet, except for a cat because of her allergies. Do you remember?"

Josh laughed. "I remember."

"Yes, well, do you also remember that you came home repeatedly with someone else's pet?"

Embarrassed by the memory, Josh's face turned red. "Yeah, I do."

"Once, you brought home a small dog, he had a collar, and you just picked him up from his front yard and carried him home, remember that?"

"Wow, yes, I remember."

"Another time you brought home the neighbour's ferret. You said you found him in the driveway. You didn't realize that you couldn't just take what wasn't yours. Then the next week, you came home with a birdcage and inside was a budgie."

"Oh wow, now you're digging deep into the memories, Dad."

"You set your mind on something and went out to get it, even if it was not rightfully yours. You didn't care about that since you were young and selfish. Your mother and I had to teach you about belongings and to not take what wasn't yours—a normal lesson for a kid."

Josh listened intently. "What does any of this have to do with Jenna and me?"

"Have you not learnt anything from me?"

"Of course, I have."

"Well, son, then you should know that this has everything to do with you and Jenna. *You* want to get married, *you* want to have a family, not later but now. *You're* trying to take that decision away from Jenna— but it's not *yours* to make. That alone is a decision for her to make, and not because you want her to. That's not a good enough reason for her to agree to what you want."

Josh took a sip of his tea and listened.

"She's young, and a strong, independent woman. She's found this job she adores, and you're her first serious love. Bottom line: she wasn't ready. I know you've pressured her; you told me. You probably pushed her away more than you've admitted to yourself."

He was right, again. Josh had pushed her more than he should have. The fight that started them down that path was because he had given her an ultimatum. She didn't like to be backed into a corner and forced to do something she wasn't ready to do. Who would?

"It's important to know what you want, son, then go after it full force and with all your being, but never take what's not rightfully yours."

"So, what you're saying is that I need to let her go?"

"She's in Quebec City, isn't she?"

"Yes, she is. She left last week."

"Then you've already let her go. There's nothing more you can do, son. The decision is not yours to make—remember that, if nothing else. You can only control yourself. *Your* decisions, *your* choices, and *your* emotions. Everyone else's are off limits. You should know this better than anyone, being a lawyer."

Josh pondered his words. "You're right, Dad, so right."

"Now it's time to move on, son. And get your old man another cup of tea while you're at it. All this talking has kept me from drinking mine and now it is cold. You know how I don't like cold tea."

Josh chuckled and got up right away, happy that his dad needed him for a change.

"I'm on it, Dad."

After Josh had placed the new steaming cup on the side table next to his dad, Billy said: "There's one more thing we need to talk about, son. Something I need to explain to you. I should have had this conversation with you a long time ago. But like you, I worried too much about what your reaction would be, so I held off much longer than I should have. But now I'm at crossroads. I need to say this."

"More wisdom, another life lesson?"

"Not really. Not this time. But more important."

"Gee, now you've got me curious, Dad. What could be more important than life lessons?"

"What I'm about to tell you is more important than anything else. I just hope you understand and listen before you react. Okay?"

Josh's phone rang. It was one of his clients, and he ignored it and let it go to voicemail.

"Sounds intense, Dad. Is this about the cancer?"

"No. You'll understand, hopefully, when I tell you. Do you have time tonight? This might take a while."

His phone rang a second time, the same number. "One second Dad. Let me just get this, it might be important."

Josh took the call out onto the front porch. On the other end of the phone was an irate client. Something had gone down, and they expected him in court tomorrow for a last-minute bail hearing. Frustrated, he promised to be ready to defend the client. He needed to get back to the office to pick up the file and prepare for tomorrow's hearing. He dreaded leaving his dad, especially when he was getting serious, and had something so important to tell Josh, but he had no choice.

"Dad, I'm so sorry, but I have to go. I wasn't expecting this."

"It's fine, son. You go."

"What was it you wanted to talk about?" Josh checked the time. "We can finish our conversation first. I don't have to rush out just yet. I have a few minutes."

"It can wait."

"But you said it was important."

"It is, but we need time to have that conversation. I'm afraid a few minutes won't be enough. We've got time, still. I'm not going anywhere soon. Now go, deal with your client. I'll be fine here."

"And you promise this has nothing to do with you being sick?"

"I promise."

Josh walked out into the chilly April night, heading for his office, already switched into work mode, not giving a second thought to what his father wanted to discuss.

CHAPTER 9

Were They Comparable?

QUEBEC CITY REMINDED Jenna of many European cities with its old churches and grand architecture, many museums, cobblestone streets, and outdoor French-style cafés. Quebec City sat on the St. Lawrence River, which connected the Great Lakes to the Atlantic Ocean.

She'd visited Quebec City many times before, so the culture was not new to her, but now it was different; it would be her home, at least for the next several months, so she tried hard to fit in and spoke French when she visited a store or restaurant. French came as naturally to her as English, so she was right at home.

The weather was cooler than in Toronto. The average daytime high in April in Quebec City was only nine degrees Celsius, with low temperatures sometimes still below zero. Unlike Toronto, where she hadn't seen negative temperatures for the past couple of weeks and the daytime highs were already hitting the teens.

❧

Jenna stomped through her new apartment, picking up items, moving them, and then putting them back. Frustrated, she stood at the front door to examine what she'd done with the place and decided that once Cassie arrived, they'd go shopping to make it hers. She'd thought the apartment was perfect when she'd seen it on the internet and took the virtual tours, but now that she was there, she realized it was missing… something, but she couldn't pinpoint what. Her thoughts were all scattered. Today had not been a good day; she'd had much anxiety since she'd gotten up—thinking about her parents, Josh, her life, where she'd been and would end up.

Could she do this? Could she adjust? She'd tried to get as comfortable as possible, but since she had arrived, she'd had butterflies in her stomach—especially when she thought of Josh. Another ruined relationship.

While she waited for Cassie, she remembered her solo trip to Paris, France at eighteen and reminded herself that if she could do that, she could do anything. The France trip had been her biggest feat until recently, and she'd managed it with ease.

Of course, it had petrified her to take that enormous leap into the unknown. Who wouldn't be at that age? But her parents had pushed her over the edge, like Josh pushed her. She was so unhappy before that trip and leaving had changed that. She compared the two major events in her life, but were they comparable? She'd needed to see the world, explore. With focus, she'd stayed strong, wrote her parents a note, and left it on the kitchen table for them to find in their own time. She'd taken a taxi to the airport and called her brother on the way. Jenna had hesitated, then blurted the news.

"You're what!" her brother had said.

"Calm down. I know what I'm doing. Besides, I know the language."

"You do not know what you're doing and you're also hurting Mom and Dad. You know they mean well and are only looking out for your best interest," he'd said.

"I know. And say what you must say. I'm still going."

And she had.

As she'd walked towards the security gates at Pearson International Airport, she knew she'd damage her relationship with her parents. She knew things would never be the same, but without looking back, she'd kept her head held high and walked straight toward the gates. In time, she'd adjusted well there, so she'd adjust to Quebec City too. It was yet another move to another city at a different point in life.

By the time she had been in France for a few weeks, Jenna no longer had a bitter feeling deep within, no longer cried herself to sleep. She was the happiest she'd been in a long time. She was in control. It might take a few weeks now, too, but like in France, she'd make it through.

Jenna had lived in France for two years with a work visa, and during that time learnt all she could about journalism; it was there she fell in love with it. When her temporary placement ended, she'd called her parents to tell them she was coming home. She hadn't talked to them since she had left, save for one postcard she mailed once a month. After Jenna's inevitable return, she'd made a plan. Earning good grades in high school had given her a competitive advantage when she applied for the journalism program at Ryerson University. They accepted a limited number each year, and that year, Jenna was one of the lucky ones and started the following fall. It was the same school that Cassie was attending. That was where they met. It had all worked out then; it would work out again. She'd form a fresh plan. Only now, instead of France, it was Quebec City.

❧

"Hey girl, I've missed you tons," said Cassie, carrying her bags from the car into Jenna's new apartment. "Wow, girl, this is spiffy," she said while chewing gum.

Jenna chuckled at her choice of words. She hadn't thought of her new place as spiffy. Small, convenient in the downtown core, but not spiffy. Leave it to Cassie to use that word.

"Thanks. I'm still trying to figure out what's missing. Still doesn't feel like it's mine."

"Give it time. Ooh, is this the second bedroom?"

"Yes, it's small but perfect for a home office."

"And the apartment came with all this furniture, from what I remember, right?"

"Yep!"

"Hmmm, lucky you. I guess I can tell Josh that you don't need to divvy up the furniture, at least not immediately. You've got no more space for anything else."

On hearing Josh's name, Jenna stopped mid-stride. "You've talked to Josh?"

"Oops. I promised myself I wouldn't bring it up, but yes. I ran into him downtown, at the pharmacy." Cassie paused and looked at Jenna pointedly. "Well?"

"What?"

"Do you want to know what he said?"

"Nope."

"You're not curious if he asked about you?"

"Nope."

Cassie raised her eyebrows. "That's hard to believe."

"Okay. Maybe a little. I don't know." Jenna pondered whether she wanted to know and continued. "Fine. Tell me what he said. How was he? How did he look? Did he ask about me? What was he doing at the pharmacy? Is he sick? Is Billy still sick?"

"Wow. Slow down, girl. That's a lot of questions for someone who doesn't want to know anything!"

"Curiosity got the best of me, I guess. I was trying not to think of him, but now that you've brought him up, I can't stop."

"So sorry, girl. I didn't mean to dig up old wounds."

"It's fine. So, tell me."

"Patience, girl. We didn't talk long. He was picking up medication for Billy."

"I guess he's still sick?"

"He has cancer. Did you know that?"

Jenna couldn't find her words for a few seconds.

"Jenna, did you hear me?"

"What? Cancer? I didn't know. Since when? I can't believe Josh didn't tell me."

"I'm not sure, but it sounded like it was a recent thing, judging by his look. I can't remember if he said when. He didn't appear like someone who has had time to process it."

"What do you mean, Cas?"

"He said the words like they were eating him alive and like he's not had to say them many times before. I remember when my uncle died of cancer, my mother said the words differently after her grieving process. The way Josh said them reminded me of when my mom first found out about her brother. She pronounced the words slower and with pain."

"It makes sense now," said Jenna. "It explains a lot."

"What does?"

"That must be why he was so sick and why he went to emergency the day we broke up, when Josh announced he was moving out. But this makes little sense."

"You're confusing me. I thought you just said it made sense?"

"Billy being sick does, but Josh never told me he had cancer. That part makes no sense. All this time, he's never said a word about his dad having cancer. How could he keep this from me? We lived together; we were engaged! How could he not tell me something so serious?"

"Did you ever ask him?"

"If Billy had cancer? Of course not! I didn't know to ask!" Jenna had raised her voice to Cassie, something she'd never done before. "I'm sorry, Cas. I didn't mean to snap; I'm just frustrated. I would've helped him more, been there more, had I known."

"Don't sweat it. I get why you're upset. But maybe he had his reasons for not telling you."

"Like what?"

"I don't know. I'm just trying to make you feel better!"

"Did he say anything else?"

"Nope."

"How did the subject of furniture come up, anyway? That seems like an odd conversation, especially after discussing cancer."

"We'd finished talking. He walked away and then turned around and told me to mention you still needed to sort out the furniture."

"And that was it?"

"I'm afraid that's it."

"He can have it, for all I care. If you see him again, please tell him that."

"Hey, hold on a minute, girl. I'm not getting between the two of you. Besides, I only ran into him by chance, and I don't know when I'll see him again. Toronto is a big city; the chances of that happening again soon are slim-to-none."

"Whatever, let's get you settled in." Jenna grabbed one of Cassie's bags and slung it over her shoulder.

They walked arm-in-arm into Jenna's room.

Jenna told Cassie to put her bag in her closet. It was a two-bedroom apartment, but only one was setup as a bedroom, so Cassie would have to sleep on the couch.

Seul was curled up like a ball on Jenna's bed, sleeping comfortably. One paw covered her eye, and she didn't even raise her head when Cassie walked in.

Cassie stopped mid-stride. "What in the lord's name is that thing?" she asked, pointing to the little kitten sleeping peacefully.

Jenna peeked over her shoulder. "What does it look like?"

"Since when do you have a cat?"

"Since last week. Cas, meet Seul." Jenna approached the bed and reached her hand out to pet Seul on the neck. The kitten squirmed and then tucked her little head under her paws.

"What kind of name is that?"

"It's French for alone."

"Girl, are you going through a midlife crisis or something?"

"Something like that."

"A cat? I didn't even know you liked cats. I always thought you were more of a dog person."

"Sometimes people change. I've changed, or at least I'm trying."

"Well, I have just the thing to cure you of that so-called midlife crisis."

"I'm afraid to ask what."

"Me! You have me and for the entire weekend. You're so lucky. So, are you taking me out on the town or what? I'm starving!"

Jenna chuckled. "Yeah, let's go. I know this great place downtown that serves the best poutine."

"I'm ready," said Cassie, her bag hanging off her elbow. "Can we walk? I'd like to walk to see more of the city."

"Of course. I told you the apartment was conveniently located, remember? I wasn't kidding."

Jenna grabbed her bag, and they linked arms and walked out into the sunny but cool afternoon, her mind still preoccupied with the news about Billy. She contemplated calling Josh or Billy. She wondered if Billy even knew that they'd broken up. He probably did, and most likely wouldn't want to hear from her. Josh would have painted an ugly picture about the breakup—shifted the blame to her.

As they walked through the streets of Quebec City, exploring both upper and lower town, Jenna pointed out all the little hidden cobblestone pathways that led to even more to see. Cassie was in awe, as that was her first time there.

As they passed a horse pulling a carriage, Cassie squealed. "Can we ride one of those through the streets while I'm here?"

"Sure, Cas."

"I feel I won't have time to see it all," said Cassie, constantly scanning her head from side to side.

"You won't; because there's too much to see, but that just means you'll have to come back again sooner than later."

"Deal. But can we at least also fit in a walking tour or a hop-on hop-off bus tour?"

Jenna giggled, as she had known Cassie would want to do a lot of sightseeing. "Sure, we can do that too."

Jenna tried to put Josh and Billy out of her mind, so she pointed out some cute shops she thought Cassie would like. Cassie couldn't keep her eyes still for one second, constantly scanning the storefronts. It was a sunny spring afternoon, and although a cool chill in the air, perfect to spend with a best friend shopping, eating pastries, and drinking coffee. So why did Jenna feel so desolate inside? She pondered over her mood as Cassie continued to take in the city views, but she had no answers that made sense. They shopped until the hunger began and Jenna became embarrassed by the sound her stomach made.

❧

At the restaurant, they found a table near a window and Jenna quickly pulled out her phone to check her work email for messages from Rachel. It was nice for Jenna to not have to see that woman every day, although she found with the distance, Rachel hid behind emails and texts and was even crueller. There were no new emails in her inbox in the last twenty minutes—fantastic! No major emergency on the Rachel front was one less worry. She might relax and enjoy lunch with her best friend, after all.

She'd missed Cassie a lot that past week: missed meeting up for coffee and lunch. They used to do that often as they worked close by. After the weekend, she didn't know when they'd see each other again, so she wanted to cherish their time together.

The restaurant wasn't fancy; it was more like a café. All the outdoor sidewalk seating was full, so they had to sit inside. Jenna put away her phone, and after dropping their jackets on chairs to save seats, they went to order at the counter. Jenna scanned the menu she'd already come to memorize in the short week she'd been there, even though she already knew she'd order the poutine. Poutine was her favourite, despite her not doing well with cheese. She often ordered it but picked off most of the cheese curds that laid over top of the French fries and brown gravy; it made her mouth water thinking of the food.

Cassie stared at the menu, then reminded Jenna she didn't know how to read French. Jenna made a few suggestions when a silhouette appeared in her peripheral vision; her head jerked to look at him. He stood a few feet from her, but his posture, his side profile, bone structure, was too familiar. He turned his head. Her eyes locked on his face—a face she knew but was still different. She blinked a few times to clear her vision, not trusting what she saw. It had been that kind of day. When she re-opened her eyes, nothing changed. The new yet familiar eyes stared back. She searched his face for clues—for something—anything that would make sense. He smiled at her weakly, and his cheeks turned a fiery red. She looked away, flushed at him having caught her staring, but despite her embarrassment, she couldn't keep her eyes peeled from his face for long. When she glanced back at him, he was still looking at her. His weak smile expanded and lit his face—Josh's face.

Almost.

CHAPTER 10

The Look-a-Like-Game

CASSIE AND JENNA constantly saw look-a-like people on the many trips they'd taken together over the years. In Cuba, they had seen Jenna's older neighbour. In New York City, they'd seen Cassie's cousin, and in Jamaica they saw Rachel. Jenna ran in wet flip-flops toward the opposite direction when Cassie pointed out the Rachel look-a-like. They had played the look-a-like game for so long they expected it on trips, so when Jenna first set eyes on the Josh look-a-like, she couldn't help thinking that was it—what else could it be?

She considered the possibilities; he could be a relative, although she didn't recall Josh mentioning any relatives in Quebec City. Jenna knew about two cousins in Nova Scotia, but not here.

She nudged Cassie's arm, and when Cassie looked up, she stared too, then raised her eyebrows.

He stood in the lineup's front, next to order. Jenna was a few feet away when he ordered in French; he must be a local.

"Thé à la menthe, poivrée, sans sucre." *A black peppermint tea with no sugar.*

She gasped and almost fell. As he waited for his tea, he glanced at Jenna, then squared his shoulders and, with his firm jawline visible to Jenna, turned toward the barista.

"Merci!" *Thanks!*

Jenna's heart skipped a few beats as she steadied herself.

The stranger's phone chimed, and before he reached into his pocket, he pushed his shoulders back the way Josh often did. The main physical difference was the hair; this guy's was a reddish tone. Frozen, she shook her head to clear the Twilight-Zone feeling she had. Before he walked away, he glanced at her again with that same big smile that reached his eyes.

"Jenna, they're waiting for our order."

She heard Cassie's voice, but the words didn't register.

"What's wrong?"

"I..." Jenna lost her voice.

"Can you give us a minute, please? We're not ready yet," said Cassie to the cashier.

"Bien. Qui est le prochain?" *Fine. Who is next?* asked the cashier with annoyance in her voice.

Cassie grabbed Jenna's arm and led her back to the table they'd reserved.

"Jenna, you're scaring me. What's going on?"

Jenna remembered to focus on breathing, to regain control. "I'm fine. I'm sorry. It's just... did you see that guy?"

"The Josh look-a-like? Yeah, I did! Pretty striking resemblance."

"I'd say."

"Probably the best one yet! Hopefully, he doesn't live close, so you don't see him often. What would the odds be if he's a neighbour?"

"Oh my gosh," said Jenna.

"Imagine that. You leave to get away from Josh and find a Josh look-a-like. Only you, girl, only you!" Cassie shook her head.

"Cas, it's not funny."

"Sorry, I didn't mean to upset you."

"Cas, it's more than just looks. The way he moves. When he pushed his shoulders back the way he just did, I swear I was looking at Josh."

"I hadn't noticed that. But then I don't pay that much attention to Josh, obviously." Cassie rolled her eyes.

"I'm telling you, Cas, it's more than just looks."

"Maybe they're related, a cousin probably. That's possible."

"His only cousins live out east."

"Maybe they are on vacation. You've never met them?"

"Never."

"There. I'm sure he's a cousin. Or perhaps we've just met our match to the look-a-like game."

Leave it to Cassie to always joke. Jenna smiled for the first time since controlling her breathing. The techniques they taught in yoga were effective if you applied them. Jenna knew she must remember to use them more often, especially during stressful times.

"Okay, girl, don't look, but he's coming up behind you."

"What?" Jenna turned as soon as Cassie told her not to.

"I said don't look."

"Bonjour, mesdames!" *Hello, ladies.*

He stood closer than before; his almond-shaped eyes, the contoured lines on his face—too close.

"Puis-je vous rejoindre?" *Can I join you?* He pointed to an empty chair.

Cassie couldn't have understood what he said but understood the gesture and jumped in before Jenna spoke. "All yours." She pushed the chair out with her foot.

"Merci. Je m'appelle Liam." *Thanks. I'm Liam.*

Jenna quickly interjected in French to let him know Cassie didn't speak French. She didn't want her friend feeling awkward or left out.

He cleared his throat as if he needed to ready his voice and then switched to English. Liam looked to Cassie, then back to Jenna. "My apologies to your friend," he said in French.

His strong French-accented English sounded different from how

Josh spoke. "Lucky for me, I speak English. And for the record, I rarely do this."

"Rarely do what, exactly? Drink black peppermint tea with no sugar? That's a pretty specific drink to order." Jenna said.

Cassie kicked her from under the table. Jenna glared at her; Cassie scowled back, rolled her eyes, and Liam raised his eyebrows at the exchange.

"Don't mind my friend here. She's had an off day," said Cassie.

Liam began answering in French and then quickly stopped himself and answered in English. "You noticed my drink of choice."

"It was a pretty specific order," said Jenna.

"Not really, just a plain peppermint tea. I always drink that. But that is not what I meant when I said I rarely do this."

"What did you mean?" asked Jenna.

"I meant I rarely approach pretty ladies in coffee shops."

"Oh, sorry," said Jenna in a soft tone.

Liam sat across from them. Cassie pretended to be busy reading on her phone, and Jenna knew she was pretending because Cassie rarely read. She was more of the texting type.

"Are you ladies ordering anything?"

"Right, our orders! I'll go," said Cassie.

After Cassie left, there was an uncomfortable silence. Each waiting for the other to speak first. Jenna twirled her fingers on the table, wondering how Cassie would order anything with her lack of French.

Liam cleared his throat and broke the silence in English. "I hope I am not intruding and if I am, just say the word and I will leave."

"No," said Jenna too quickly. She forced herself to slow down. "You're not intruding. My friend and I are just having lunch. But I see she's only brought back drinks."

"I have told you my name, so what are yours?"

After Jenna told him, he said, "I like those names."

"They're short for Jennalyn and Cassidy, but no one ever calls us that," said Cassie, setting two coffees on the table. "*Café* was the only thing they understood. Sorry."

"I like those names even better," said Liam as he sipped on his peppermint tea, blowing on it first before taking each sip, just like Josh.

"So, are you two visiting?"

"I'm a recent local. I've only been here..." Jenna stopped to think about how long. "Six days."

Liam raised his arms in a welcoming gesture. "Bienvenue!" *Welcome!* "Where are you from?"

"I'm from Toronto. Cassie is visiting for the weekend."

"If you need someone to show you around, let me know."

"How about you? Any family in Toronto? A cousin your age? And how is it you speak English so well?" Jenna blurted without intending to.

Sometimes her mouth ran wild, and she couldn't control it. It had gotten her into trouble at work with Rachel, not being able to hold her tongue. At that same instant, her phone chimed, and she looked down on her lap where she'd left it. It surprised her to see a text from Cassie since she sat across from her. Before she swiped the screen to unlock and read it, she caught the message as it flashed on the screen before disappearing.

Cassie: Damn, girl. Too many questions! Pull it back a notch!

She left the phone on her lap and glanced at Cassie. Her fingernails clicked hard and fast against the screen. That was more like her.

"I have been to Toronto recently for art shows, but I do not know anyone there well, definitely no family... that I know of." Jenna noticed the way he lowered his eyes when he added the last part. "I do not recall where I stayed, but it was near a park and a university," he added.

"That doesn't help much. There's a few universities in Toronto," said Jenna.

"Interesting city, though," he continued. "Always busy with hustle and bustle, no matter what day it is. But I am sure you know."

"Are you an artist?" asked Jenna.

He wore casual clothing, like most artists she interviewed. That was another difference Jenna noted between Liam and Josh.

"I paint. I have a studio and storefront down in the lower city. I mostly paint local scenery to sell to tourists. Occasionally, I will take on custom orders and the odd portrait, but scenery is my primary focus."

Jenna's phone chimed again.

Cassie: Okay, so now we know they aren't relatives. He's an artist, so unlike Josh. COMPLETE OPPOSITES!

The phone chimed again.

Cassie: And look at his ripped jeans. I've never seen Josh wear ripped Jeans. He's more of a formal suit kind of guy. Definitely just a look-a-like!

Growing annoyed at Cassie texting from across the table, Jenna typed a quick reply:

Jenna: Josh is an attorney, so he has to wear a suit most days.

Cassie: Hello... red hair?

Jenna: Stop texting. This is beyond rude!

Peeking from the top of her eyes, Jenna saw Liam's eyes go from her and Cassie and then back to her again. Good lord, did he know they were texting each other?

"You two appear busy, so I will just go." Liam stood, hands in his pockets.

"No, don't leave. I'm sorry, that was rude. It was a friend; she can be a bit much and annoying. But I've dealt with her now," said Jenna, dropping her phone onto her lap a little too hard. It hit her knee and she winced.

Another ding.

Cassie: Annoying??? I'll argue that I'm not annoying!

Jenna saw the text flash on the screen but ignored it.

Seconds later, one last text she read fast before it disappeared from the screen:

Cassie: He's cute. He's into you. I'm leaving to go buy that cute top that's hanging in the window across the street. Meet up later. Have fun! YOU NEED A DISTRACTION 😊

Jenna lifted her head casually, not wanting to show her phone had her attention. She couldn't tell Cassie not to leave, not in front of Liam, and she didn't want to be alone with him. Great!

Cassie excused herself moments later, taking her coffee with her, and Jenna placed her hands under her legs to prevent them from fidgeting.

"Your friend is something else. Is she always this... chipper? Did I use the right word?"

"Chipper is a grand word to describe Cas."

"You said you were new in town. So, what brings you here from Toronto? A boyfriend perhaps?" He raised an eyebrow as he said 'boyfriend'.

"Oh no, no boyfriend... not anymore. He stayed behind." Her voice grew softer as she spoke about Josh.

"I'm not sorry to hear, but feel I should say I am."

"Don't. It's for the best. It's a long and complicated story."

"So, if you did not follow the man of your dreams here, then what brought you to Quebec City?"

"Work. Just work."

She grew more comfortable the longer they sat alone, so Jenna tested her hands by allowing them to escape from under her legs.

She searched his features now that they were alone, and Cassie wouldn't judge her for staring. Her heart skipped a beat when he squared his shoulders again. She imagined what he'd look like with darker and shorter hair instead of his red shaggy cut and imagined him speaking without the accent. Josh, not Liam, stared back. She shook her head to clear the image of Josh and forced her mind to not go there. If he was a relative, she'd find out, but for the afternoon, Cassie was right. She needed a distraction, so she allowed herself to ease into superficial conversation with the familiar stranger.

Continuing to speak in English even though they were alone, they discussed her life, and she told her more about her job and the move, but she left out personal details about her relationship with Josh. Curious to know more about him, she shifted the conversation and asked about his past relationships. He told her it had been a couple of years since he'd dated anyone seriously and that he was still waiting for the girl of his dreams. He looked at her hard when he said that, and so Jenna moved to a safer topic and asked about his artwork. The more she learnt, the more she realized there was a piece she could write on him. Jenna mentioned that to him.

"Wow, I cannot tell you how excited I am about having a feature written on me. I hope I am interesting enough for such an honour."

"Are you kidding me? You're exactly why I'm here. There's so much talent, and it's my job to find it and tell the world about it."

His smile reached his eyes again as he turned his face so that she had a direct view of his side profile. Again, it was almost Josh's profile she saw. Not exactly but similar. He then turned his head to the other side.

"I get it now. I finally understand why you have been staring at me."

"What?" She hadn't expected him to call her out on it. The nerve of him!

"You are wondering which side of my face will photograph better for the article. Am I right?" He turned to show the other side of his face again. "Well, which wins? Right or left? I favour the right, but what do I know?"

Jenna let a breath of air escape heavily. "Yes, that's exactly it!"

They chatted for the next hour, and Jenna found the conversation flowed easily. But when her stomach growled loudly, she remembered she hadn't eaten yet, and knew Cassie must be hungry too.

"I really should be going. I don't want to leave my friend alone much longer. She came here to see me after all."

"I understand. I am sorry if I have kept you longer than I should," he said.

"I enjoyed the chat."

"Me too." He studied her, then added, "A lot. Here," he reached out his hand, "give me your phone."

"Why?"

"So I can put my contact information into it."

Jenna handed the phone to him and couldn't help noticing how he looked at her as he punched his name and phone number into her phone. She didn't want to send the wrong message by staring so much, but the resemblance to Josh made it difficult to peel her eyes away. The uncanny resemblance could only mean one thing; they must be relatives. She reviewed his contact, curious to learn his last name: Garnier. There were no Garnier relations to Josh that she knew about, but she would find out who Liam Garnier was.

"Can I have yours?"

"My what?" His name had distracted her.

"Your number?"

Of course he'd want her number, too. She considered that. If she gave him her number, he might take it the wrong way, and she couldn't blame him for her reactions toward him, but she couldn't tell him the real reason she couldn't peel her eyes off him. She wanted to keep things professional, so she said, "I've got yours. I'll call you in a couple of days to set up a meeting to see your studio and to interview you."

He raised his eyebrows as she said that, and it didn't go unnoticed.

"Looking forward to it," he said, not taking his eyes off her.

She was halfway to the door when he called her name. She turned and almost bumped into him as he'd followed closely behind. He surprised her with his next question.

"Can I take you to dinner, maybe tomorrow night?"

The dinner invite took her aback. Not wanting to hurt his feelings, she smiled and said, "I appreciate the offer. But I can't. I have Cassie with me for the weekend." She knew using Cassie as an excuse was not right, but she liked Liam enough to not want to hurt his feelings. Besides, if she were being honest, she was pleased he'd found her attractive. It had been years since a cute guy had asked her out and she could say yes if she so desired, and despite everything, a part of her wanted to say yes.

"Right, your friend! Of course. Okay, some other time? We can figure it out when you call me?"

"Maybe some other time."

He frowned when she said 'Maybe.' "You will call for the interview?"

"That I can promise," she said, and walked out of the restaurant and across the street, unable to believe what had just happened and how bizarre the resemblance was between Liam and Josh.

∽

Jenna could see Cassie from the large storefront window. Cassie stood, a bunch of clothes draped over her arms, talking to a saleslady. She had a frown and Jenna figured she was having a hard time communicating.

When Jenna entered, Cassie's eyebrows knit together. "That was fast. I had expected to shop more. I haven't even tried half of the stuff on yet. But thank goodness you're here. I keep asking questions in English and everyone answers me in French!"

"You know some basic words, Cas. If you attempt to communicate in French, it will be easier for you. Besides, I was with him for almost an hour."

"So? Give me the juice."

Jenna shrugged. "I'm doing a piece on him for the magazine. We're setting up a time next week."

"*And?*" Cassie asked, exaggerating the word.

"*And* nothing." Jenna moved some tops around on a rack, trying to distract herself from the questions.

"That's it?" Cassie dropped the bundle of clothes on a table and crossed her arms over her chest. "You found a professional contact, but nothing more? Seriously?"

"What else did you expect?"

"Well, let's see; dinner plans or at least another coffee date, for starters."

"This wasn't a coffee date; this was a business meeting." Jenna didn't dream of telling her about the dinner invite. It would send Cassie over the edge if she knew Jenna had declined.

"Right. Maybe to you it was."

"What's that supposed to mean?"

"Come on, girl. Didn't you notice the way he looked at you? It won't be long before it's more than business."

"Cas, be serious."

"I am being serious."

"Josh and I only broke up two weeks ago. It's too soon to be dating."

"You don't have to sleep with him right away!"

"Cas!"

"I'm only saying that it could be good for you to at least go to dinner, enjoy yourself, make some friends here. It will help to get over the breakup. I have more experience in this than you, so trust me. Besides, if you're going to be here for six months or more, you need a replacement for me, so why can't it be a cute guy with a nice bum?" She winked at Jenna.

"You looked at his butt, Cas?"

"Did you just meet me today?"

"Sometimes I think I have the craziest best friend."

"I try, but holding that title doesn't come easy."

"Come on, let's shop. I see a pair of jeans I want to try on," said Jenna, excited to be shopping—that was her distraction. She didn't need to have dinner with a cute guy with a nice bum who was interested in her. She just needed to buy some cute clothes and maybe a new purse and matching shoes. Retail therapy—that would do the trick.

They spent the rest of the afternoon shopping and munching on takeout poutine. Their growling bellies were finally silenced. By the time they'd visited most shops in the area, they each had more bags than they could manage.

Struggling as they walked, fumbling with the bags, they passed a unique little shop with local paintings in the display window. Jenna recognized one of the Montmorency Falls, (*Parc De La Chute-Montmorency*) between Beauport and Boischatel, and twelve kilometres from the centre of Quebec City. Jenna hadn't yet visited the falls, but she'd researched it and seen many photos and was planning on taking Cassie there tomorrow. She had the entire day planned; visit the falls, then hike the trails and attend a guided tour. She'd also booked a reservation for her and Cassie at a sugar shack (*cabane a sucre*), where she looked forward to introducing Cas to an authentic sugar shack meal consisting of: pea soup, baked beans, cretons, ham, sausages, and of course, heaps of maple syrup poured over the top. Jenna loved her dessert and couldn't wait to try the maple sugar pie. She had a fun-filled day planned for them tomorrow and they were lucky to be in town before the season ended.

The painting of the falls in the storefront window was the best replica she'd seen of the falls yet. Curious, she peeked inside. To her surprise, Liam stood at the counter helping a customer. She backed up from the window, but not before he looked up, saw Jenna, and waved. He returned to help his customer wearing that same big smile that reached his eyes. Jenna hadn't realized they'd wandered down to lower Quebec City as they were busy chatting. Great—now he'd think she'd followed him. She was definitely sending a message she wished she could retrieve.

"What is so interesting in there?" asked Cassie, peeking over Jenna's shoulder.

"Nothing, let's go." Jenna grabbed Cassie's arms and dropped a bag, but Cassie stayed put.

"Well, well."

"Stop it. Can we go?" asked Jenna.

"What do you know!" said Cassie.

"Oh, be quiet and get your head out of the gutter. I didn't know his store was here. Well, I knew it was in the lower part of town. He'd mentioned it, but not here specifically."

"Right!" Cassie said with a grin.

"Cas, I'm serious."

Cassie dropped all the bags. "Well, aren't you going inside? Now that you've 'accidentally' bumped into him again."

"Of course not. And why are you using air quotes around 'acciden-tally'? I didn't know this was his store."

"Girl, you sure have a way of attracting what you're trying to run away from."

Jenna dropped her bags too and crossed her arms. "Why do you mock me so?"

"Because I love you. Don't be so touchy. Come on. I need another coffee." Cassie placed her arm through Jenna's, and they walked away.

"Cas! Our bags."

"Oh, geez. Did we have to buy so much stuff?"

They giggled as they once again tried to figure out how to carry it all. Just as they'd strategically placed all the bags over their arms, the door to the store opened.

"Hey, you *are* here! Wait. Why are you girls leaving so soon?" asked Liam. The same big smile that reached his ears touched Jenna's heart, and she gasped and smiled back, walking toward him while her heart did a funny little skip.

༄

The three of them spent the evening together, had a late dinner, and Jenna had to admit she'd forgotten about Josh for the first time since the breakup.

CHAPTER 11

The Girl of His Dreams

C'ÉTAIT MAGNIFIQUE. *THAT was magnificent.*

That was what Liam thought when he walked out of his store and saw Jenna standing there. He had not expected to see her so soon after their coffee date. After they had parted earlier, he couldn't help but feel disappointment that she had not given him her number. He had wanted it so bad, but didn't want to push her. He'd sensed she was holding back and assumed it was because of her recent breakup with the nob who had let her go. She had his number, and so left the rest to fate. And there she was again. It was fate after all.

When she walked toward him, he had held his breath, unable to believe she was approaching. He had dinner plans with his mom and dad that night, but when the girls suggested dinner, he did not hesitate and called his mom and dad to explain that he had just met the girl of his dreams and needed a rain check.

"Elle doit être une fille spéciale?" *She must be a special girl?* asked Pat, his mom.

"Vous n'avez aucune idée à quel point." *You have no idea how much.*

His mom had giggled and told him she loved him and that he could have dinner with her and his dad any other time.

When their night ended after dinner, he'd walked the girls back to Jenna's apartment and, after she closed the door after him, he'd stood with his back pressed against the door, unable to believe his good fortune.

Il avait rencontré la fille de ses rêves. *He had met the girl of his dreams!*

He'd never been surer of anything in his twenty-eight years.

CHAPTER 12

Another Moment of Silence

ON MONDAY MORNING before Cassie left, they squeezed in one last tourist stop that they hadn't gotten to over the weekend; Fairmont Le Château Frontenac, which was on the top of Cassie's list. Its stunning views of the sparkling St. Lawrence, intriguing massive structure comprised of over six hundred rooms, and the many European touches made that hotel a UNESCO World Heritage Site. The girls had breakfast sitting outside in the crisp breeze while admiring the scenery.

Soon after, Cassie left, and Jenna had her apartment back. She did a workout video in her living room because she still hadn't joined a gym. Once finished, and before heading into the shower, she picked up her phone to check the time. Eight, not too early, so he should be up. She would make the call—needed to make it. Not calling had eaten at her over the weekend, although she'd hidden her sorrow from Cassie, not wanting to dampen the mood.

There was a landline at Billy's and the only form of communication, as Billy didn't own a cell phone. Technically he did, but the Christmas gift from her and Josh from two years ago was still in its original package. Billy had refused to succumb to the times, clinging to his landline.

Jenna knew the landline was in the kitchen, and she tried hard to remember Billy's morning routine to figure out where he'd be. Because he was sick, she didn't want him to rush to get to the phone. Her goal was to make the call before Josh arrived. She was positive that he wouldn't miss his morning visit with cancer hanging over their heads. She wondered what Billy would think about hearing the landline ring on Monday morning. The only person who often called was Josh. She knew that because Billy had commented that it only got used by her or Josh, and occasionally Billy's brother.

Jenna didn't recall the number by heart, so she scrolled through the contacts on her phone. When it rang, she got butterflies in her stomach. Suddenly she remembered that Josh might be there because he'd said he was moving in with Billy. She'd forgotten that and considered hanging up, but pushed through and let it ring, and after the third ring she rehearsed her message in case voicemail kicked in.

Billy answered on the fourth ring.

As she readied her voice, she wondered if he'd recognize her, not expecting her to call.

"Billy, hi. I hope this isn't a bad time, but if it is, I can call back. It's... it's Jenna."

"Jenna, my dear, I know it's you. What a surprise. How are you?"

"I'm fine, thank you, Billy. Can you talk for a few minutes?"

"Certainly, my dear, what's on your mind? Josh isn't here, though, if you're looking for him. Thought I'd throw that out in case it was him and not my charm you were looking for bright and early on a Monday morning."

"It's you I want to speak to."

"All right, dear, I'm all ears then. What's on your mind?"

Jenna walked into the bedroom and put the phone on speaker to free her hands. She remembered a morning video check-in with Rachel; she was running late.

"Billy... I... heard about the cancer. I'm so sorry."

"Don't be sorry. You didn't make me sick, so why are you apologizing?"

"It just seems like something people say. How are you holding up?"

"You know me, hard as stone, and stubborn as a bulldog."

"Billy, you can let down your guard and talk to me. How are you really?"

"I've seen better days, my dear, but I'm hanging in there. I'm surprised that you know. I didn't think you and Josh had been in contact since...."

Jenna suspected he wanted to say, 'Since you left,' but hoped, despite what Josh might have said, that he held back because he knew his son, and he most likely also knew that if she left, it was because Josh pushed her. She and Billy had had that conversation often about her relationship with Josh. Billy was someone Jenna could talk to easily about anything. He listened well, and always gave good, constructive advice while being sensitive.

"You're right, we haven't spoken."

"How did the news travel to you so fast?"

"I found out from Cassie, my best friend. Do you remember her, 'the pretty bubbly blond' as you called her at my birthday party last year?"

"Ahh, yes, the pretty bubbly blond. Of course, I remember her."

"Cassie and Josh ran into each other, and Josh mentioned it. That's how she found out. I wish you would have called. You know you can call me anytime you need anything? It doesn't matter that Josh and I are no longer together. I'm still here for you. I love you, Billy."

"I love you too, dear. That's sweet of you, and thank you. I appreciate your concern, but you've got enough on your plate. How's Quebec City?"

"Quebec City is as impressive as I remembered, and I'm adjusting okay. It's a little lonely without... Cassie here, but I'm doing all right considering." She'd almost said *without Josh* but changed her mind last second.

"I'm sure you'll meet people to keep you company."

"Work has me pretty busy, so not much time to meet new people.

But enough about me. I didn't call to discuss my move. How are you really? You feeling okay, Billy? I realize it's an odd question with you having cancer, but I guess I just wondered how you're handling it?"

"Chemo is a bitch, that's for sure."

Jenna didn't think she'd ever heard Billy swear before. "Are you... I mean, does it...?"

"Spit it out dear, what is it? Just ask what's on your mind."

"How bad is it?"

"I have my days, some better than others."

"I'm praying that you have better days." Jenna held back a sob. She didn't want Billy to hear her crying. "I wish I was there to help you."

"There's not much you could do if you were here. Josh has it covered. He's even hired a personal support worker to look after me every day."

"That's good. I'm glad he got help, but please remember to call me if there's anything I can do. I know I'm far, but if there's anything you need that I can do from here, paperwork for insurance forms or anything like that, I'll do it. We don't even have to tell Josh if it would be uncomfortable for you."

"Why would that be uncomfortable for me?"

"I'm not sure," Jenna considered his question, then added, "I suppose there's no reason it would be."

"I appreciate the offer. Thank you, my dear. You've always been like my daughter-in-law, and I spoke to others as if you already were. I was certain you would be one day. I'm sorry things didn't work out between you and my son. You holding up okay?"

Jenna lowered her eyes and stopped rummaging through her closet. "I'm sorry things didn't work out, too, and I'm doing okay, really I am. Funny, the other day, Cassie and I met someone who looked so much like Josh. He shocked me when I first saw him, and I had to look twice. He even works close to my apartment. So, I'll see him often. That's painful, but I'm sure I'll manage. What are the chances of that? A Josh look-a-like only a few blocks from me."

There was a thick silence on the other end. Dead, complete silence.

Jenna checked the phone display to see if the line was still active—perhaps the call dropped.

"Billy? You still there?"

No answer. She checked the phone a second time—the call was still active.

"Hello, did I lose you?"

"No, I'm here," said Billy's shaky voice a moment later.

"It went silent there for a minute. I thought I lost you."

"Must be a poor connection."

"I guess. Did you hear what I last said about the Josh look-a-like?"

"I did."

"What do you think about that?"

"I'm not sure I understand the question, dear?"

"I guess I'm just looking to get your thoughts. It's ironic, isn't it? We break up and I move away and now have to see his features on someone else."

Another moment of silence. "I guess Josh has a common face. I'm sure you'll see it through many strangers for a while since he'll be on your mind while you grieve the loss of the relationship."

Jenna hadn't planned to bring that up, but since they were discussing it, she asked about what had bothered her all weekend.

"Billy, it's more than just a resemblance. Even the way he moves reminds me of Josh. It's a little too eerie."

Billy was silent again, so she continued. "Do you have relatives in Quebec City? Any nephews the same age? His name is Liam Garnier. Does the name ring a bell?"

"No. I've never heard the name," Billy said without hesitation. "Jenna, I have to go. I have a doctor's appointment and still have to get ready."

"Okay. I'm sorry for babbling away. I won't keep you anymore. I just wanted you to know I'm thinking of you."

"Thank you, dear. Don't be a stranger. Call anytime you feel like talking to an old man."

"I promise I will call again soon," she said, then stopped for a second, wondering if she should add what was on her mind. "Billy? One more thing."

"Yes, my dear?"

"Can you not mention to Josh that I called?"

"Why is that, dear?"

Jenna wondered why she'd asked. "Truthfully, I don't know why. I suppose it makes no difference if he knows. Never mind that I asked."

"If you want me to not say anything, then I won't."

"Thanks, Billy."

They hung up, and seconds later she jumped into the shower then dressed in the outfit she had picked out while they chatted, and pulled her hair into a messy bun piled at the top of her head with a few wisps hanging to the side. Jenna hoped to beat Rachel to the call as she was almost always late, grabbing a last-minute coffee. So Jenna thought she had time to be online and ready on the screen when Rachel entered the Toronto boardroom. But her plans failed. When she pressed the 'join meeting' icon on her laptop, the boardroom was already full, and Rachel's face filled the screen.

"You're late," Rachel's sharp voice blared through the speakers.

Jenna looked at the time on the bottom of the screen and smiled when she realized she wasn't late. She had five minutes before the meeting began, but she bit her tongue, smiled, and said, "Good morning, everyone."

PART TWO

Three Months Later

CHAPTER 13

No Distractions

JENNA LEFT THREE months ago, and Josh hadn't heard from her since—not a text, phone call—not even a postcard, and he knew how much she loved to mail postcards everywhere she went. She'd forgotten about him as fast as she'd packed her bags. That was fine; he'd kept busy taking care of Billy and working at the firm, so that prevented thoughts from travelling to her too often. Today he'd be in court and next week they had the dreaded but expected medical appointment to find out if the radiation and chemo treatments were successful. He'd booked that day off to take his dad. Normally he'd just take a couple of personal hours, but for that appointment, he wanted no distractions.

He expected good news and planned to take Billy out to lunch to celebrate, so didn't want to have to rush back to the office. Because of his upcoming day off, he had a lot he needed to get done; therefore, he focused on the many tasks at hand, juggling three at a time. By the end of the workday, he was hungry, having only had a quick sandwich at the courtroom, but with case notes to prepare for a meeting with a client the next morning, he had no time to cook. A food delivery service Josh had hired delivered his dad's meals, so his dad didn't need him. He wanted nothing more than to sit at a bar, order a beer and chicken wings and fries, and review his notes; he decided he'd do just that.

His paralegal, Lainey, stood at the doorway of his office. She placed papers on his desk, and when she bent forward, remained leaning over the desk a little too long, with her chin resting on her hands. Josh looked away, avoiding her tanned, toned arms. Lainey had been overly friendly toward Josh since the breakup, but he was not going there—especially not with her. She was cute with a slim figure, high cheek bones, big brown eyes, and to be honest, it would be nice to have female company; he hadn't been with anyone since Jenna, but she wasn't the right one because he wouldn't mix work and pleasure. That always ended badly. But today, he was optimistic about the appointment, and he could use her help with the case review. Using that as an excuse, he allowed himself the freedom to invite her to dinner; she agreed with zero hesitation, making Josh question if he'd done the right thing.

⁂

They went to a downtown pub Josh often frequented near the CN Tower. Josh made a mental note to go up the tower again soon; he loved going up the CN Tower. It was one of his favourite things to do in Toronto. He'd stand for hours at one of the lookouts, contemplating cases.

The CN Tower's construction finished in 1976 and they named it after the railway company that built it. It stood 1,818 feet tall, welcoming close to two million visitors each year. The high views provided him with most of his inspiration for tough cases.

After ordering drinks, he opened his laptop bag, pulled out the laptop and turned it on.

Lainey looked at him with a hopeful stare and asked, "Why the hurry?"

"We have a lot to go through."

"Let's take a minute to enjoy the drinks. We have all night."

Josh peeked at her from above the laptop and caught her winking. Confident his dad was okay for the evening, as he had spoken to him on the way to the bar, Josh said, "You're right. There's no hurry. We do have all night, don't we?"

"I'm game if you are." Another wink from Lainey.

"I don't have any place to be, so we can relax and chat for a minute, enjoy a drink before we start on the case review."

"Sounds perfect." She reached out her hand, inches from his.

"Why not?" said Josh, permitting himself to be with her.

After the server brought the drinks, Lainey inched out her arm across the table further and placed her hand on his.

"You work too hard as it is. You need to relax more, it's good for you."

Her touch caused Josh to become jittery, and he tried to avoid her eyes peering into his, so he looked at the bar. To his surprise, Cassie stared at him; her mouth hung open. She sat next to a fit-looking guy with straight-cut hair and pearly-white running shoes. Cassie raised her eyebrows at Josh, and their locked eyes remained glued. Josh wanted desperately to look away, but he couldn't pull his gaze off her because seeing her brought back a flood of memories about Jenna. He'd done well keeping his thoughts from going to Jenna. And in one instant, that disappeared.

Josh glanced at Lainey. She followed his gaze and her eyes landed on Cassie, too. She reached out her other hand and took both of Josh's in hers. Cassie frowned and refocused on her date, leaving Josh staring at the back of her ponytail.

Josh pulled his hands out from under Lainey's. "I think it's time we review that case."

Lainey glanced to Cassie once more, than asked, "Do you want to move to a different table? Perhaps one a little more private?"

"Why would we need a more private table?"

Lainey shifted her gaze to Cassie again for a quick second. "I just thought perhaps it might be uncomfortable with her so close." She pointed in Cassie's direction and tried to hide her finger behind her glass, but it was so obvious. Josh noticed Cassie had her head turned toward them again and rolled her eyes at the gesture.

"Nope, I'm fine here."

"You sure you're fine? Who is she anyway?"

"She means nothing to me."

"The way you two locked eyes suggested otherwise." She tilted her head to the side.

"It's not what you think."

"Okay, then I have nothing to worry about."

"Why would you worry otherwise?"

"I just meant... it doesn't matter. As long as you're comfortable here, I'm good too."

"I'm good." He raised his drink to his lips.

For the rest of the evening, he noticed Cassie turn to look at them often. It appeared she was trying to be discreet, but Josh knew better. She never waved or even approached their table, not even after paying the bill and leaving—neither did he. Both pretended the other wasn't only a few feet away. Better that way. Their relationship had always been odd. As close as she and Jenna were, Cassie always put up a wall with him and he never understood why.

Three months. Three long, but busy months. He had been doing so well, but suddenly thoughts about Jenna became accompanied by a stabbing pain again. He thought he was over Jenna, but it only took seeing Cassie to remind him of what he had and lost—or threw away.

"Cheers!" said Lainey, raising her glass.

"What are we cheers-ing to?"

"Anything we want. How about... us?"

He hesitated, then clanked his glass with her glass as he and Cassie locked eyes one last time just before she walked out of the bar, a scowl on her long face.

CHAPTER 14

Leap of Faith

FOR THE PAST three months, Jenna had seen Liam at least once a week, but as friends only and not allowing him into her heart. She'd placed a barrier between them, welcoming only friendship, feeling it was too soon for more. But his closeness had become one that she couldn't be without. He was her first and only friend in Quebec City, and he helped fill the lonely days with laughter, dinners, and movies.

Jenna had spent the day at the Quebec City office in meetings and yearned to get outside to enjoy the last part of the warm evening.

As she packed up her laptop and shoved her notebook and pens into her briefcase, her phone chimed. Trying to multitask, with one hand she picked up the phone and swiped to unlock the screen.

Cassie: Josh has a girlfriend! You, girl, need to make a move, NOW!

Cassie: It's time. Stop sitting around and doing nothing but working or I'm coming up to sort out your romantic life for you ☺

She read the text as she zipped up her bag, and after a long and exhausting day, that was not what she wanted to learn. While alone in the elevator, she reread the first text to be certain. She frowned, learning her eyes had not betrayed her as she had hoped; a pang of jealousy ran through her. She threw the phone a little too hard into her bag and it clanked into something, probably keys, but she didn't care. If she broke it, it would ease her from further depressing news. She couldn't deal with it, not that soon, so she shifted her focus to Liam instead.

∞

The piece she did on Liam had turned out to be fantastic, and they'd celebrated a few times over champagne, never crossing the friendship line. Liam had quickly become her confidante when Cassie was not around. She'd even told Liam all about Josh, the breakup, about Billy, and even touched on her relationship with her parents. He'd said he understood her needing time and space and had been a gentleman, not making a move or making Jenna feel uncomfortable.

She'd also researched his past, trying to form a connection to Josh, but hadn't gotten far due to work demands. She hadn't, however, told Liam that.

Over the last few weeks, Cassie had bugged her often, saying that if Jenna didn't take things seriously, Liam would get bored with the friendship and Jenna would miss her chance. Jenna had tried to convince Cassie that wasn't what she wanted, but Cassie always dismissed her when she went there. Not that she didn't find him attractive—the opposite. Jenna hesitated to take things to the next level because she was unsure of what that meant, and if her attraction was because of the resemblance between him and Josh. That part constantly nagged at her and kept her up at night. She reminded herself daily that it wasn't a good idea to date someone who resembled her ex so much. That would make it more complicated. She knew therapists agreed; she'd consulted one via the confidential therapy session offered from work. So, rather than fighting her instincts, she pretended she didn't find him attractive and avoided settings that were too romantic, such as late-night strolls by the waterfront. That had happened only once, and she feared she'd accidentally invited the intimacy. Since then, Jenna had strengthened the barrier when they were together.

＠

As she walked through the parking garage to her car, she pulled her phone out and texted Cassie back:

Jenna: Josh is free to date whomever he wants!

Cassie: You aren't even the least bit curious to know who he was with? Come on, I know you are.

Jenna feared that her silence would answer the question. She was right.

Cassie: Okay, since you're not asking, I'll tell you. Drumroll....

Jenna: Will you just say it already!

Cassie: Pretty sure it was the bitch from his work, Lainey! I only met her that once at the magazine open house, but I remember her eyes on Josh, even then.

Lainey? She *was* a bitch. Jenna had suspected for a long time that Lainey had a thing for Josh. She had seen the way Lainey looked at him at Christmas parties—eyeing him as if Jenna were invisible. Jenna had said nothing, because Josh never gave her a reason to believe that he reciprocated. Instead, she had batted her eyes back to Lainey and pulled Josh closer. That was usually enough to have Lainey refocus her attention on someone else's significant other.

Watching the numbers appear on the elevator, she counted back from five, then forced herself to get it together. It was none of her business anymore, so Josh could date, and if Lainey was his choice, then so be it. But if Josh could date, then Jenna could too—couldn't she? She wasn't ready to admit that aloud, so to keep Cassie from thinking she cared, Jenna asked about her dating life instead.

Jenna: I knew she had a thing for Josh.

Jenna: So, tell me about you. How's the dating thing with Bernardo going?

Cassie: Bernardo-who?

Jenna: We've moved on from Bernardo, got it!

Jenna: Yea, he turned out to be a bit much of a mama's boy for me. But there's a new guy I met at the gym. He's more my type. ☒

Jenna: We're moving on from yoga guy to gym guy. Cas, I can't keep up with you!

Cassie: Stop changing the subject. How about Lainey and Josh?

Jenna: I don't care. Really. I'm fine, Cas, and over him already!

Cassie: Right!

Cassie: Call me if you need to chat. I'm here for you, girl. XOXO!

Jenna stared at her phone, but instead of calling Cassie, she pressed the call button next to Liam's name. She held the phone glued to her ear as she walked to her car; he answered on the first ring.

"I was just thinking about you. You must have read my mind."

"Hey, I'm leaving the office, and wondered if you had dinner plans tonight? Or maybe you've already eaten. I know it's late."

"I have not, and I am starving. I am also dressed up from an earlier meeting with no one to take out, so, if you are asking me out, I accept."

Jenna chuckled, picturing him dressed up and wondering what that meant. She'd never seen him in anything but torn jeans and a T-shirt and jacket.

"What do you have in mind?" she asked.

"I will come to your place and we can walk downtown. We will find a spot, I am sure."

Jenna thought about it and almost said she'd changed her mind and was going to stay in, but Cassie's text flashed before her mind and pushed her to take a leap of faith.

"I'll be home in less than ten minutes."

"I cannot wait to see you," said Liam.

CHAPTER 15

Considerate Of Her Feelings

LIAM HAD BEEN thinking about Jenna and wishing he could take her out to dinner when his phone rang. It was her. He'd answered right away, but then regretted it, hoping he had not sounded too eager. He was afraid to scare her off. He had not stopped thinking about her since the day they met, three months prior, and although she kept him at a distance, he never gave up hope but promised himself he would give her space. He knew she was getting over a long-term relationship, and the last thing he wanted was to be her rebound. He would wait for her forever. He had enjoyed their time together the last three months, even if it was only as friends, and even if he was usually the one to suggest they get together. But tonight, she'd called him and suggested supper. Good fortune had found him again, and he could not be happier.

He'd scrambled to find a last-minute reservation somewhere nice and quiet. He did not want distractions and did not want to risk not getting a table. He wanted the luxury of having her all to himself, even if only for one supper. He reminded himself not to read too much into the evening to avoid disappointment. Every time they were together, he hoped she would lean in for a kiss, and once she almost had, but backed away, so he did not push her. That was him—considerate of her feelings. He respected her and cared too much to force her to do something she was not yet ready to do.

After double checking how he looked in the mirror and fixing his jacket, he grabbed his wallet and headed to the closest flower shop on the way to Jenna's. He skipped along with a renewed hope in his step, stopping to place a ten-dollar bill in a homeless man's dirty and tattered box held together with duct tape. His smile was so wide that even the homeless man stared and smiled back.

When he arrived at Jenna's apartment, he was eager to knock but forced himself to wait and counted to ten to not appear hurried. When Jenna opened her door, Liam's smile widened even more and he handed her the flowers.

CHAPTER 16

The Spinning Inside Her Head

JENNA AND LIAM walked to a quiet restaurant in the upper part of town, away from the hustle and bustle. Liam asked in French for a table in the back. The soft, dim lighting, classical music in the background, and candlelit tables created the romantic atmosphere Jenna had previously avoided. Pushing the reluctance away, she smiled and followed the host to their table. Liam was a gentleman and pulled her chair out for her; he'd not done that before, and she wondered why he bothered with the extra gesture that night.

"You look nice, by the way. The sports jacket over the T-shirt sets you apart from your regular attire," she said.

Liam grabbed the lapels. "I am so glad you think so. You look extra dressed up as well," he said.

"Oh, this is nothing. I just threw on some jewellery and heels since I was at the office today."

"That is not the only thing that has changed."

"What do you mean?" she asked.

"You seem more... eager, willing today."

"Eager and willing? To do what exactly?"

"Maybe those weren't the right choice of words. Sometimes I get mixed up when speaking English. But I prefer to speak English with you. It helps me to practice the language."

"Your English is great, Liam. So, what did you mean, then?"

"You just seem different. That is all. So, tell me, what brought about the change?"

Liam stared at Jenna; it made her heart race. Unsure of what to say about his comment, or what to do, she asked: "Shall we order drinks?"

Liam smiled and said, "Sure, let us do that."

After a while, the server came around to offer more wine. "Oui s'il vous plaît!" *Yes please.* "Et les faire venir." *And keep them coming,* she added, almost slurring her words. Jenna was soon on her third glass.

"You sure you want another glass?" Liam asked with concern in his voice and a raised eyebrow.

"You don't know how bad I need another drink right now."

Jenna took a big sip of the wine, and her head was foggier than ever. She knew she was going to be in trouble tomorrow, but all she could think about was the gorgeous, kind gentleman in front of her and the fact that Josh had moved on with Lainey. The wine consumption was the least of her worries. The food had arrived, but Jenna was yet to touch it.

"Here," said Liam, pushing the plate of food closer to her, "eat something before you get sick."

Jenna barely managed a few tiny bites of the appetizer, and when the main course arrived, she didn't touch it either.

When the server cleared their plates, Liam asked if she wanted to go back to his place to have coffee and sober up.

"Only because my place is closer, so makes more sense," he quickly added.

"I'm not sure that's a good idea. Maybe I should go home. I need to go to bed."

"Fine. But I am walking you home. You are not walking alone."

"I'm fine," she argued, as she stumbled trying to get up from the chair.

"No, you are not. You can sleep on my couch. I do not think we will make it to your place anyway, not in your condition."

"Fine, but I'm paying for supper. I invited you out."

"I already paid the bill."

"What? When? I didn't even notice."

"My point exactly. Come on. My couch is very comfortable."

Liam's apartment was only a few minutes from the restaurant, and as he took Jenna's hand and led her down the street, her thoughts spun out of control. She was questioning everything suddenly. Why was she pushing a perfect gentleman away? Why did she care so much that Josh was out with Lainey? Her thoughts became a jumbled mess. The alcohol clouded her memory of the events from before dinner and its details.

Because of the dizziness, she tripped over a rock and Liam's muscular arms caught her around her waist before she fell. It felt so comforting to be held again. It was a warmer evening than most, so he'd taken off his sport jacket. She looked at his bare arms; his bulging biceps peeked out from under the T-shirt. She ran her hand in slow motion down the length of his arms and moved in closer—his face inches from hers. She remembered one night a few weeks ago when they'd gone out for coffee and tea and he'd leaned in so close to her, but she'd pulled away last minute. Tonight, she was the one leaning in closer.

"Jenna, Qu'est-ce que vous faites?" *What are you doing?*

"Shush, say nothing and kiss me."

"I am not sure that is a good idea."

She didn't take her eyes off him. "Why?" she whispered. "I got the feeling these last few weeks you've wanted to kiss me."

"I have. Since that first day at the coffee shop when you were checking me out."

She chuckled. "I wasn't checking you out." She slapped his shoulder lightly. His face was an inch closer.

"I think you were. You could not take your eyes off me then, and you are having a hard time now."

She swallowed the saliva that had accumulated in her mouth.

"Umm..." she muttered.

"Did you think I did not notice?"

She found her voice. "It was only because you reminded me of someone I know."

"Oh yeah? I bet I am better looking than he is," he said, giggling.

She grunted, "You don't know how odd it is that you say that. But if you've wanted to kiss me for so long, why are you telling me to stop now?"

"Because you had too much to drink."

"So?" she countered.

He closed the gap by one more inch; their noses touched.

"Why are you staring at me so hard?" he asked.

"*Intently* is the word I'd use. But I already told you."

He raised his eyebrow. "Tell me again?"

"I want you to kiss me."

He smiled, and it reached his eyes. "We are back to that kissing game again, are we?"

"I'm willing to play if you are," she said.

"I'll play on one condition."

"What's that?" she asked.

"You must answer this next question correctly. How many fingers am I holding up?"

Seriously? Was he using the old medical test on her? How cute. She looked at his hand and counted aloud. "Five." Then she closed her eyes and leaned into him as his lips brushed against her lips and a tingling sensation swept through her entire body as the heat of his lips penetrated onto hers. This was the first guy she'd kissed since Josh, and she wasn't sure if the sensation represented excitement, fear, or both.

He pulled away for a second. "You okay?" he asked her.

"I'm better than okay," she assured him, and pulled him in for another kiss.

Her heart was beating fast, and she wasn't sure if it was the alcohol, the news about Josh and Lainey, the breakup, or the kiss, but suddenly she had an urge to be with Liam. She held him close, their lips glued together as they kissed deeply. He ran his fingers through her hair and then wrapped his hand around the back of her neck. Jenna didn't know what to do with her hands, so she wrapped them around his neck and let them slide down his back to his waist. They stayed that way for a long time, embraced in each other's arms, kissing passionately on the sidewalk of a busy Quebec City street and only breaking for air every so often.

"Come on." He grabbed her hand, ran, and pulled her along with him down the street.

"Slow down, I'm in heels."

When they got to his apartment, he picked her up effortlessly and carried her up the stairs, still kissing her.

He put her down long enough to search his jacket pocket for his keys. She stumbled, and he grabbed her waist to keep her from falling again, then unlocked the door, picked her back up and carried her inside. They stumbled the rest of the way until they got to his bedroom door, tripping on running shoes in the hallway. Opening the door with his foot as she was still in his arms, he carried her inside and laid her on his unmade, messy bed full of clothes. Jenna moved up, as she was hanging off the edge, and with her eyes called him to her—pleading. He leaned in and positioned his warm, muscular body over her as she desperately reached for his zipper. She ran her hands down his arms, down his flat stomach, and then reached behind to touch the cute bum that Cassie had mentioned, and she let the moment take her to where it would naturally go.

For the next couple of hours, Jenna thought of nothing but Liam: not Josh, not Billy, not work. Nothing. That night was about Liam, his warmth, his touch, his gentleness, as he caressed her and swept her away into the bliss that she didn't realize she'd missed. She let herself go and gave herself to him fully.

❦

After they made love—twice—they laid in bed on their backs staring at the ceiling, neither speaking for a long time. Liam broke the silence first.

"Avez-vous soif?" *Are you thirsty?* he asked.

"I'm not sure what I am."

He turned to his side and scooped her into his arms. His heart beat against her bare chest. "I think we both need water, especially you."

"Why me?"

"To dilute the alcohol."

"Oh, right." Jenna licked her lips, and they were dry. She swirled her tongue around the inside of her mouth; it was raw and scraped the inside of her cheeks. "Yeah, I think I do need water, and lots of it." Her stomach growled. "And maybe a snack, if you have food. I don't think I ate much at supper."

"Stay here. I will see what I can find." Liam slipped out from under the covers, broad chest and backside exposed, and grabbed a pair of abandoned shorts that were on the floor from earlier and slipped them on. As Jenna watched him pull on his shorts, she laughed because he tripped over some clothes and almost fell.

After he left, she looked around: a pile of clothes on the floor in the corner, the closet door open revealing its many contents messily thrown in. No organization. Clothes piled high on his large dresser, the cabinet barely visible underneath. Books scattered in another corner. Different from how she and Josh lived. No. Different from how she lived. There was no longer *them*, just her. Liam returned minutes later with two tall glasses of water and a tray of cheese, crackers, and assorted deli meat. She took the glass and drank most of its contents in one gulp.

"That feels better," she said, as she set the glass down on the nightstand, took a piece of meat and a cracker and snuggled back in under the covers. She wasn't sure what to make of the situation, of Liam, of them together. She was still trying to process her feelings about what she'd done, what she'd let happen, when he asked her how she was feeling and what was going on inside her head.

She turned to him. Not wanting to talk about herself, but eager to learn more about him. "Liam, you know so much about me, but I hardly know anything about your past. Let's talk about you for a change."

"That is not so. You know a lot about me. Besides, I enjoy talking about you." He stroked her hair, then continued, "But what else do you want to know about me?"

"You told me you grew up here, but you never told me where you were born?" she asked, to distract Liam from his intense stare.

"That's right. Been here almost my whole life."

"You said 'almost' so where were you before?"

"I was born in your city."

Jenna had taken the last sip of water and choked, then coughed to cover it up.

"Toronto?" she asked for confirmation.

"The one and only."

Another coincidence? How had she not known? Why hadn't she asked before?

It took her a minute to regain her voice. "Toronto, wow. I didn't know. You said you'd been there for art shows but didn't mention being born there."

"You never asked where I was born. Besides, it means nothing to me. This is home."

"How did you end up here?"

"I'm adopted. My real mother, originally from Toronto, died at birth. Sad story, I know. I never knew my biological father, either. My adopted family are from Quebec. I was a baby when they chose me, only months old. They are my genuine family, even though we do not share blood. We could not be any closer, really."

Jenna froze, empty water glass still in hand, unable to control the spinning inside her head. Her hand shook, so she set the glass down. She cleared her throat to ready her voice for the next question.

"Were you an only child? Did your biological mother have any other children?"

"I am not sure. I suppose it was possible. I asked no one or looked into it. I do not even know if Mom and Dad know."

"Really? Weren't you curious? I mean, to find out if you had siblings?"

"I have siblings. A sister and a brother from my adopted family. I do not consider them any different from any other family. Blood relation or not, that does not matter. I do not think we could have been closer had we been born from the same parents."

"That's interesting. I'd have been curious. Do you know your biological mother's name?"

"I do. The adoption agency told Mom and Dad her first name. It was Holly."

"Holly," repeated Jenna, as the name rolled off her tongue.

"That is all the information I have, though. Maybe if I had grown up in an unfair situation, a less loving family, I would have wanted to know more about my past, but I have always felt loved—wanted. Mom and Dad have never treated me any differently than their biological kids. There was never a hole to fill, so I suppose that was why I never wanted to find out more. That is simply a part of my past that, I suppose, will stay buried and I am okay with that."

Jenna shifted under the covers. "How old were you when you found out your parents adopted you? And how did you find out?"

"Interesting you ask because I feel like I have always known. I do not remember a time that I did not know. They told me the truth when I was young. I do not remember exactly when, but it was even before I started school. I remember going school shopping for the first time with Mom and asking her in the lineup at the checkout if I was really her son, even though I did not come out of her belly. She looked at me with such warmth and love in her eyes. She took my little hand in hers and squeezed it, then kissed the top of my head and said, 'Absolument'."

Absolutely. "I knew immediately that I was the chosen one, as they called me from that day forward. Mom and Dad constantly reminded me that while they did not create me, they *chose* me, and that meant just as much, if not more. Mom and Dad always said it was important for me to know the truth and they worried that if they did not tell me as soon as I was old enough to understand, that one day would turn to weeks, then months, then years, and then I would be a teenager and it would be too late to break the news to me without breaking my heart. Mom and Dad said that the longer you wait to reveal the truth, the harder it is to confess. They did not want to face that. They did not want me growing up in a lie. That was why they told me when I was little that I did not come out of Mom's belly. They told me before I could barely understand what they were saying."

"Do you remember the day they told you?"

"Not too well, but I remember playing with my Tonka trucks just before going school shopping and Mom and Dad asking me to sit with them. That memory stands out, and so I think that was the day they told me, but I do not really remember the conversation."

"I just realized I've known you over three months, and I don't even know your birthday."

"It is on September one. I will be twenty-eight," he said.

Jenna was sitting close to the edge and nearly rolled off the bed, grabbing the side for support—September first rang in her ears.

September first... it couldn't be.

September first... he'd be twenty-eight.

September first—Josh's year and day of birth.

"You okay Jenna?"

"Fine. I'm fine. I'll be fine."

September first.

September first.

September first.

Going through it again and again in her head, she convinced herself she must have dreamt that he said September and had actually said *October* first, not September. Or maybe November? She couldn't remember and didn't trust herself after all that wine she'd consumed earlier. She decided she'd eat more of the sausage and crackers. It would make her think straighter. She was sure the wine had affected her ability to understand what he was saying. Things would be clearer in the morning—or so she convinced herself.

Munching on another piece of meat, she suddenly stopped chewing and swallowed hard. Her stomach filled with butterflies. "Liam?"

He was busy chewing, so nodded to acknowledge her.

"Did you use a condom? I thought you did, but... some of it was... foggy."

Liam swallowed, picked up another cracker, and shoved it into his mouth. "You really do not remember?"

"I remember you pulling one out of your drawer, but then the next thing I remember is you inside me, and I just don't remember you putting it on."

"We never made it that far. Jenna, you kept telling me to hurry, and said it was okay. You said repeatedly you had us covered."

"I did?"

"You really were tipsy, weren't you?"

Jenna had been laying with her eyes closed but when she heard that, her eyes shot open. "I don't even remember saying that."

"You did, a few times. You grabbed the condom from my hand and threw it across the room. Look." He pointed to where it was on the floor, package ripped open but its contents still inside.

"Oh," she said.

"You are on birth control?"

"Yes, I'm on the pill. No worries. It's all good. Everything is fine."

Forgetting everything she'd learned tonight about Liam, and convincing herself she'd misheard it all, she snuggled back into Liam's chest and closed her eyes while her head pounded out of control. It was late, well after midnight, and the events of the evening caught up to her and before she knew it, she drifted off to sleep, wrapped up by Liam's warmth.

She hadn't expected to stay the night. She hadn't expected that night to happen at all. As sleep took her and dreams began, she dreamed of a woman named Lainey, and of calendars. The only month inside the calendar was September, and the calendar kept flipping pages, each with September written across the top.

The next morning, when she awakened, she thought she had the most bizarre dream. Why had September and the name Lainey plagued her through the night? Then muscular arms pulled her into them, and her memory cleared.

"Bonjour ma belle!" *Good morning beautiful,* he said.

She remembered where she was and what had led her to dinner and, inevitably, to Liam's bed. She remembered the wine, and that she'd learnt the truth about Liam after they'd slept together. Oh gosh, how would she ever get past that? She needed one person, her person. She needed Cassie.

CHAPTER 17

Hands Full

"WHAT THE HELL do you mean, he didn't use a condom? Jenna, that's not like you," said Cassie on the phone later that morning. Jenna had already filled Cassie in on the discoveries from last night about the two men sharing the same birth date, and Liam being adopted and born in Toronto. But since Jenna sprang on her the news that she'd slept with Liam, Cassie parked the earlier information and moved onto Jenna's carelessness. Jenna hadn't wanted to tell her as much, but she'd never kept something that big from her before.

"Trust me, Cas, I know how careless it was. I haven't been able to stop thinking about it since."

"At least you're on the pill and won't get pregnant."

Jenna didn't answer right away.

"Jenna, you *are* on the pill?"

Jenna remained silent.

"J e n n a... why aren't you answering me?" Cassie asked, accentuating Jenna's name.

"I am, but I might have missed a pill or two this month."

"Exactly how many pills did you miss? One or two?"

Jenna stared at her birth control package. She was afraid to admit that she'd messed up badly.

"A few."

Cassie let out a breath. "You're screwed, girl."

"Thanks for the support, Cas."

"You're so screwed."

Jenna knew being on the pill was supposedly over ninety-nine percent effective in protecting against pregnancy, but she didn't know what the statistics were when you missed several in a cycle, so she quickly called up Google to find out. "According to Google—" she began.

Cassie breathed heavily into the phone, then interrupted her. "This is a lot of information for you to spring on me in one phone call. I haven't even had my morning coffee yet."

"You! How do you think I feel?" Jenna placed the package of pills back in the cupboard and shut down Google. She didn't want to think about the statistics, not yet. She didn't even know if she'd come across a reputable site. She had placed little importance on taking the pills because she hadn't planned on having sex.

"I suppose there's nothing you can do now but hope."

"The only thing I can do is worry for the next several weeks."

"I'll worry right alongside you, girl. So what are you going to do about Josh and Liam?"

"What I do best; research their history. I'll get the actual story, gather proof, and then I'll approach Josh with it."

"Aren't you going to say anything to him until then? This is his life we're talking about."

Jenna considered that. "Exactly, so I need to be one-hundred-and-ten percent sure about this before I flip his world upside down, so no, not yet. I might consider calling Billy though, probe a little, and see what I can learn from him without giving much away. I can't believe that if I'm right it means Billy has kept this huge secret all these years."

"What about Liam?"

"What about him?"

"You're not telling him either?"

"No, not yet."

"Why? He already knows he's adopted, so the shock won't be as big," said Cassie.

"You're right, but my first obligation is to Josh. He's got more to lose. I need to focus on this. I should have focused on it sooner."

"I think perhaps you mixed up your priorities. I agree Josh has more to lose, but why do his feelings need more protecting over Liam's? Josh isn't even in your life anymore, but Liam is. Besides, how could you have focused on this sooner? You didn't know until last night."

"Part of me has always known something was off about them. They are just too similar for it to be a coincidence."

"Still. Don't beat yourself up over it."

"Eventually, if what I think is the truth ends up being accurate, I will tell Liam. Of course I will. I care about his feelings, too. But for now, nobody other than you will know until Josh knows the truth. Despite our history, I owe him that."

"I don't think you owe Josh anything, but you've got my word."

"Thanks, Cas."

"You've got your hands full, girl, but if anyone can pull this off, it's you. Keep me posted, okay?"

As Jenna hung up the call, she was already on Google searching through adoptions, deaths, and any other related information from twenty-eight years ago; she was eager to find the truth. She had her hands full, all right. Cassie had been right.

CHAPTER 18

One More Day

*L*IAM COULD NOT believe the night he'd had. It was the best night of his life. He could have stayed in bed with Jenna wrapped up in his arms all day. But when she had awakened and found him staring at her, she had a long and forlorn look on her face and was in a hurry to leave. He'd wanted to make her breakfast and bring it to her on a tray with a flower in a vase like in the movies—such a romantic as he was. But she left before he could even offer to make her coffee, much less food.

He laid in bed for a long time, contemplating their night together. It had been sweet, intimate, but he hoped to God he had not pushed her away by sleeping with her. He knew she had baggage, and the last thing he wanted was to add to her burdens. He hoped last night had not happened too fast for her.

He sent a text message, rather than calling, so she would know he was thinking about her. A text message was less invasive. He didn't want to appear pushy. A text allowed her to respond on her time, without feeling pressured. He stared at his phone, hoping for a reply. None came. While he missed her already and wanted to see her again, he decided he'd give her a day before reaching out again. He had waited three months, he could wait one more day, but it would be a long twenty-four hours.

CHAPTER 19

Excuses

A WEEK HAD PASSED since the night Liam and Jenna slept together. One full week, and a day hadn't passed that Jenna hadn't heard from him at least once. He texted or called every day to make sure she was okay, and to check she didn't regret their night together. She wasn't sure if she regretted it, so when he asked, she changed the subject and blamed her busy schedule on work. She had been busy, but it wasn't work that consumed her time.

Every day when he checked in, he asked her to meet for breakfast, but she made excuses and said she had early morning meetings. When he suggested lunch, she said she'd be in an interview. When he offered to cook her supper, she said she was meeting clients in the evening. She hated lying to him, but it was awkward for her to be around him, knowing what she knew about him—about his life. Liam wanted to spend every day with her, and all she wanted was to figure out what was important to her and what she was going to do, so the excuses poured out.

But then his latest text sounded pleading, and Jenna didn't want to hurt him anymore, and she needed to talk to him, so agreed to breakfast in the morning.

∽

That week she'd been so immersed in research on Josh and Liam's history that she'd completely forgotten about the possibility that she could be pregnant. She googled how long before she could get tested, and also googled, again, the statistics of missed pills. She stared at the laptop screen, reading the information. The words blasting from the article had her stomach in a tightly formed knot. It was fine. She'd be fine. Things would work out. She'd get her period next week as expected. Missing a few pills one month when she'd been on the pill for so many years wouldn't be an issue, she convinced herself.

Having had enough of reading about how likely it is for a woman to get pregnant after missing pills, she began a new search about adoptions, deaths, and hospital records from September 1, 1989. Using her notebook as a tool, she reflected on what she'd already learned over the last week. She had to pull some tricky strings to get the information, but Jenna was persistent and had gotten the help of the adoption agency. Adoptions were open in Canada, but that one, all those years ago, had been different. Without the adoption agency's help, she likely wouldn't have found out anything, but being a reporter made that easier. She didn't tell the adoption agency who she really was, instead she posed as the long-lost sister. At first, they were hesitant to speak with her, but with some convincing, she got them to open up. In one week, she'd located the hospital records of the births, discovered that Holly Mills, a young girl of eighteen years, died that day giving birth to fraternal twins—boys. She'd also found the adoption papers and knew that Billy Harrison was not Josh's biological father. Billy and his wife, Maria, adopted Josh when he was two. He'd lived with Billy and Maria since he was born, originally placed in their home as a foster child, but that case headed toward adoption relatively quickly.

After Holly died, Brenda and Bob Mills, Holly's parents, named the babies and gave them up for adoption. Josh and Liam were the original names listed on the official papers as well. It was all there, in black and white, in Jenna's possession to do something with, but she didn't know what. It didn't surprise Jenna that Billy had kept the baby's given name. She'd considered he'd wanted Josh to have something that linked him to his past. But what did surprise her was that Billy hadn't told Josh.

Holly's parents were still alive and in their early sixties. Jenna hadn't contacted them yet, but she considered it only to get more answers as to why, when their daughter died, did they not keep the twins? From the research she'd done on the couple, money wasn't an issue, not even then. They could have hired help if that was the problem, but they'd chosen to give up their dead daughter's babies. The form they'd signed to relinquish parental rights was dated September first, so they'd decided on the same night and hadn't even given it time to consider other options. Jenna found that troubling and wanted—needed—to understand.

From the research she'd done, Holly's parents had had zero contact with their biological grandchildren, or at least no documented contact. A few quick internet searches revealed that Holly's parents were still wealthy. They owned multiple apartment buildings, and the rental income alone from the rental properties generated enough cash flow for them to live off. They'd retired and moved to Quebec City almost ten years ago. Interesting. Jenna wondered if that was a coincidence. Holly's father had owned a medium-sized tooling business outside Toronto, and it did well. He'd sold the business for millions about ten years ago, just before the economic downfall, and was listed a shareholder for many public companies. He was also the chair of many high-up, well-known boards. As a couple, they were classy and influential in society, and even before Holly died, they'd held a high level of social standing. So, why would two wealthy grandparents of an only child not want to maintain contact with their grandchildren? That was the question Jenna knew only they could answer.

Liam might have run into them over the years, with them living in Quebec City, but Liam had told Jenna he didn't know his biological family, so if their paths had crossed, he'd have been oblivious. During her research on Holly's parents, Jenna reached out to a personal contact and discovered the Mills were regular contributors to one of the largest art and gallery museums, and had been for years, and were also donators to the local arts scene. That was odd; because from what she'd learnt, neither of them were artists.

It wasn't difficult for Jenna to find the information. By then she'd made several contacts in the QC arts scene and chatted them up often over coffee, claiming to be interested in doing a profile on the couple for the magazine. Jenna wondered what Brenda and Bob Mills would say if they knew a local journalist was looking into their past. She imagined they'd considered no one would discover their secret since it was so carefully orchestrated and tightly wrapped years ago.

The cause of Holly's death on the coroner's report was postpartum hemorrhage, however, Jenna found the obituary in an old newspaper clipping and the cause of death listed was different. The obituary stated Holly had died suddenly from a medical condition. Why the discrepancy? Why had the Mills covered up the pregnancy?

The information consumed her all week. She couldn't eat, sleep, and she couldn't concentrate on work. She knew Rachel had noticed her absence, even from afar, and threatened to have her called back to Toronto so that she could keep a closer eye, insisting that Jenna needed babysitting.

Jenna knew she hadn't performed well at work compared to her usual standards, but this was important, and she couldn't let it go. She was in too deep to not give it her full attention. How had her life become such a web of a mess in the last few days? How would she break the news to Josh, to Liam? That, she couldn't fathom. Her mind wandered to Billy and how he'd kept it secret all these years. Should she tell him she knows? What would his reaction be? Would it make his health worse? She determined it would, and so put off making that call. Jenna had called Billy a few times to check in on him, but she hadn't drummed up the courage to call that past week. How could she go on about life when she knew that big of a secret? It would be impossible. Jenna was unsure of what to do, and for someone always in control, that lost feeling was foreign. She missed her best friend being nearby.

∾

As she sat staring at her notebook, her phone rang—Rachel. "Shit," she muttered, as she wasn't in the mood for her demands, but knew she couldn't avoid her any longer.

"Hey Rachel," said Jenna, trying to sound nonchalant.

"Don't you dare, 'Hey Rachel' me. What the hell is going on there?"

"Rachel, I can explain—"

"You've been avoiding my calls. Haven't replied to my emails, and your last submission was not up to our standards."

"If you just give me a moment to—"

"This piece doesn't have enough depth to make the local paper, much less a feature in one of the most respected publications in the country. Are you suddenly unaware that social media killed the magazine star? If we lose a single subscriber this month, that's on you. I will send you to personally grovel if any of our advertisers read that fluff and back out. Everyone is watching you, Jenna."

"I know, but—"

"If this is what it's going to be like, I'm recommending to the executive board that you return at once. We'll get someone else with more spunk and vigour out there to cover the local arts scene. Someone interested in doing a good job."

"Rachel, stop. Please."

Rachel clicked her tongue. "What's your excuse? I can't wait to hear what you've come up with."

"I've been working on a story," she blurted unintentionally, to save herself from getting fired. "It's a big one, and a good one, but I'm still researching and collecting data."

"I'm listening."

"I found some trails of anonymous donations to various arts organizations that seem to come from the same source, and wouldn't it be great for Brandy Thyme to find out who they are and run an exclusive feature on one of the most financially dedicated arts supporters in the country?"

"Interesting."

"Okay, you agree, good. Will you let me continue on this path?"

"I want an update on it every few days."

"That's fair. Look, I know you don't like me, but you need to trust me, okay? This story will be better than great. I promise."

"Don't pretend to know what I like or dislike. Besides, this has nothing to do with my relationship or personal feelings toward you; this is business. Straight up business, that's it. I'm your boss, although you're eight hundred kilometres away. You still report to me. Do you understand?"

"Yes."

"When I call, you pick up. When I email, you respond promptly. Those are the terms of the contract."

Jenna took a deep breath. "I understand."

"You have until the deadline for the next issue to bring me the story, or your career with this magazine will be over."

Jenna hung up the call and threw her phone across the room and, thankfully, it landed on the chair. Rachel had put so much pressure on her, she'd buckled and blurted what Rachel wanted to hear. Why had she said she had a story? What the hell had she committed to? She wouldn't pretend that she hadn't thought about the feature, the exposure of the wealthy, high-society couple, the local famous artist, there was a story there, but that was also Josh and Liam's life she was messing with and although Josh was a jerk and left her, he was still Josh. She couldn't hurt him, wouldn't hurt him or Liam.

Still threatened by Rachel's words, Jenna dialled her again and said in haste: "Rachel, there was an up-and-coming local band gig a few nights ago, and I covered it with the intention of it being the next feature. There's a story there with an interesting angle. I have the draft, but just didn't have time to polish it. If I get it to you for copy editing by eight tomorrow morning, we can still beat the deadline for the next issue."

"You have until seven. If the story is not in my inbox by then, don't bother submitting it. I'll use someone else's work as a feature for the next issue instead."

Feeling a pang of jealousy, Jenna asked, "Whose? And please don't say, Greg."

"At least Greg's story has life, unlike the crap you submitted."

"You'll have the new story by seven. I promise."

Jenna knew Rachel didn't even get out of bed until seven. She was also positive she wouldn't look at her email until she was at the office well after nine, but Jenna was in no position to argue. She was doing damage control.

"Seven," repeated Rachel. "Not a second later, or Greg's piece gets the spotlight. And don't make promises you can't keep," she added, and hung up.

Jenna rubbed the back of her stiff, strained neck. After putting away the research on the twins, she focused on the story from the other night. She hadn't lied about attending the gig, but what she lied about was having the draft. She had written nothing—not one word. All she had were the handwritten notes and a bunch of recorded French interviews on her cell phone. Jenna blew out a breath and got to work. She stayed up the entire night writing, revising, editing, proofreading, and at five in the morning, when the sun peeked over the horizon and her eyelids grew heavy, she pressed the Send button. When the sun made its way fully over the Earth, she sunk into her covers, eyes already closed.

CHAPTER 20

Sometimes the Craziest Things That Happen Are Things We Rarely Plan

HEN JENNA AWAKENED a few hours later to her phone ringing, the sunshine through the window was so blinding she had to use the sound of the ringtone to find the phone. When she found it, and her eyes came to focus, she saw Liam's name on the display and remembered their plan to have breakfast. "Shit," she yelled into the room before answering. She swiped the call in a panic and apologized profusely, telling Liam that something came up and she wouldn't make it. That time, it wasn't a lie.

"Everything okay?" he asked with concern in his voice.

"Yeah, it's fine. It's just a piece I was late in submitting to my editor. I pulled an all-nighter to get it done."

"You have worked so hard this week. How is it you were late?"

It impressed her he'd noticed the little slip-up. "I have put in a lot of hours, but I haven't worked on this story."

"What other story are you working on?"

"Funny you should ask."

"Funny? You are writing comedy now?"

"Ha! You're the funny one here. But seriously, it's one I'm ready to tell you about."

"I am listening."

"Not now. It needs to be in person. Can we meet for supper?"

"I cannot today because it is my night to run the storefront. My part-time girl has tonight off and why I suggested breakfast. Unless you are up for a later supper? The store closes at eight. Is that too late?"

Desperate to talk to Liam, she said, "That works."

When she hung up, her palms were sweaty, and her heart was beating fast. She remembered the yoga breathing techniques, but they didn't help. She'd decided that morning to tell Liam what she knew. Jenna had awakened remembering her dream. In it, she'd told Liam about her discoveries, and after waking up to him calling, took it as a sign. He needed to know—everything.

⌒∾

On the way to the restaurant, she applied hand sanitizer and called Cassie for reassurance. Cassie agreed he should know and reminded her it would be less of a shock than telling Josh, since Liam already knew his parents had adopted him.

"You can also use this as a practice run," said Cassie.

"Practice run for what?"

"For when you tell Josh."

"Right, that."

Butterflies fluttered in her stomach again.

"You're going to have to face that, eventually."

"I know. I just can't think of it right now. Listen, I'm here and have to go."

"Call me afterwards. I'm here for you. Love you, girl."

"Love you too, Cas. Thanks for being there, but it might be late so don't wait up for a call."

"I don't care what time it is, I'm here, so call whenever."

She hung up, satisfied she was making the right decision. When she opened the door to the restaurant, Liam was already there, squared shoulders, smiling, and waiting.

"So sorry I'm late."

"Ce n'est pas un problème." *It's not a problem.* "I just got here, too." He stood to pull out her seat for her.

Jenna took a seat across from Liam and hid her shaky hands under her legs.

"I have missed you this week. I was getting worried you were avoiding me. You okay?" he asked.

"I'm fine," she lied.

She took her phone from her pocket and hid it on her lap and sent a quick text to Cassie.

Jenna: So nervous!

Cassie: You've got this, girl XOXO

Realizing Liam saw her texting, she said, "Sorry, that was just Cassie. I'll put the phone away."

"It is okay if you need to call her. I can wait."

"No, that's not important," she said, and slipped the phone into her bag.

After they exchanged pleasantries and ordered, Liam finally asked: "So, what is this story you want to tell me about? You had me wondering all day."

"I think we should wait for our drinks."

"Ahh, it is *that* kind of story, is it?" he said then added: "It is a good thing we ordered wine."

"Wow, you sounded like Cassie there for a minute."

After the server poured her glass, Jenna took a long sip, applied hand sanitizer, and placed her hands under her legs again. She didn't know where to start, so jumped right in.

"Liam, there's a reason I've been avoiding you this week. I ended up going down a rabbit hole with research for a story."

Liam scrunched up his nose. "A rabbit hole?"

"Yes, you've heard the saying I'm sure? It's from the nineteenth century novel by Lewis Carroll, *Alice's Adventures in Wonderland*?"

The blank look on Liam's face revealed to her that he'd never heard the term.

"Forget it. The research wrapped me up pretty tightly and, until I had all my ducks in a row, I couldn't see you. I needed to make sure I had all my T's crossed and I's dotted."

"Were the ducks inside the rabbit hole? Jenna, I'm confused."

"Oh, Liam, forget about that. I have information about your biological family." She waited for him to react, but he remained stoic. "I know who your biological mother was, and I found your grandparents. They live here. Can you believe that?" She waited again for him to say something—he said nothing. "You have a twin brother. Liam, it's..." She cleared her throat and continued. "It's Josh, my ex."

She looked at him, curious why he hadn't yet said anything. She waited and silently counted to ten to give him a chance to take it in before she spoke again. When she got to seven, her palms grew even more sweaty. At eight, she picked up her wine and gulped the rest down. When she got to nine, she gripped the underside of the table, then applied more sanitizer, got to ten, and continued with a shaky voice.

"When I first met you, you shocked me because of the resemblance. I considered maybe you were cousins, but never imagined you'd be immediate family. The night we slept together, when we laid in bed afterwards, was the night I figured it out. You telling me your birth date did it."

She searched his eyes for signs of something: anger, regret, relief, but his expression remained stone cold.

"Here." She handed him an envelope. "It's all in there. The proof you need that I'm not a lunatic."

Her legs shook, so she used her hands to settle them as she waited for him to speak. The server arrived to fill their glasses. Neither of them acknowledged or thanked the server.

She assumed Liam was in shock, so gave him time to process what she'd told him. She pulled out her phone and sent Cassie a text.

Jenna: Oh my gosh. I've told him. He hasn't said a word!

Cassie: He must have said something! What's he doing?

Jenna: Nothing, no words. Zero. He's just staring at me like he wants to kill me!

Cassie: Oh boy, not good.

Jenna: What do I do?

Cassie: Okay, let me think. I got it... he's in shock. Give him a few minutes.

Jenna: How many?

Cassie: I don't know! How much time would you need if it were you?

Jenna: This is bad. Okay, I'll give him space. Thanks!

She put the phone back in her bag and crossed her arms over the table, waiting.

After a long silence, he cleared his throat and spoke in French. "So, I mean nothing?"

His question caught her off guard. "Quoi?" *What?*

He continued in French. "Is that why you agreed to go out with me? Because I reminded you of your ex? Were you ever attracted to me for *me*, or was it just the resemblance that drew you in?"

"Liam, I—"

"Did you come here to find me?"

"No, of course not. Meeting you was a coincidence."

"And how dare you go digging into my past! You knew I was not interested in knowing. I was pretty clear about that! I told you I was happy. I have a family; how do you think this will make them feel? This will crush Mom and Dad. Did you think of them? I bet you didn't. I bet all you thought about was your precious story. You journalists are all alike."

She didn't want him to read the truth splattered over her face, so she looked away, afraid the look would betray her.

"Damn it, Jenna, look at me. I deserve that much."

He hadn't spoken to her in so much French since the first day they met. It was natural, though, for people to revert to their native tongue when angry. She continued to respond in French as well.

"I'm so sorry, Liam. I never planned for this and especially not to upset you."

"You've done a good job of that."

"We were at the same place at the same time and…."

She stopped when he picked up his napkin, wiped his mouth, and slapped three twenty-dollar bills on the table. "This should cover the supper we ordered," he said, stood, and walked away.

"You're leaving?"

"Yeah, I am leaving."

"Liam, please, don't do this. I told you because I wanted to be honest with you. I didn't want our…" she hesitated for a moment, unsure what to call this thing between them, then pressed on. "I didn't want our relationship to start with lies."

"It started with a lie the day we met."

"That's not fair. I didn't know when we first met."

"You should have told me I reminded you of your ex."

"I know, but I didn't think it was important then."

"Not important?" He studied her face. "Sometimes the craziest things that happen are things we rarely plan." He tilted his head to the side, then continued. "I never planned on falling as hard in love with you as I have."

He walked toward the front entrance and was out the door before his words registered in Jenna's ears.

Her phone chimed.

Cassie: So… how did it go? Has he said anything yet?

Jenna sobbed into the phone as the server asked if she needed a refill.

CHAPTER 21

Time

JOSH HELD ONTO his dad's arm tight as he helped him into the car, wondering what was going through his mind. "Are you nervous, Dad?"

"Son, I have advanced cancer. What else can they possibly tell me that will make my day worse?" he asked.

Josh thought of a few things the doctor could say that would be worse: the cancer had spread, the treatment was not working, he was dying, but Josh didn't say any of that. Instead, he forced a fake smile and drove, not looking at his father. Neither said a word during the drive.

After they checked in at reception, they sat in the office, waiting patiently for Dr. Danes to tell them if the treatment was successful. His dad had been acting strange since Josh picked him up; he was quieter than usual and wouldn't look Josh in the eye. Josh speculated that, despite his bravery, he worried about the news. Hopefully, he didn't know something that Josh didn't—that wouldn't be a first.

The door opened and Dr. Danes walked in wearing a serious look. But when his eyes met Billy's, his face softened.

"I'm sorry to keep you waiting," said Dr. Danes as he held a file and walked across the room and sat behind his desk opposite them. He opened the file, glanced at it, and shut it swiftly, setting it aside. He folded both arms over the table and cleared his throat. "Billy, I'm sure it won't be a shock to learn your body is rejecting the treatment."

Josh's hand moved to take hold of Billy's while his eyes remained locked on the doctor.

"I understand," said his dad.

Josh turned. "Wait. What? You do? Because I don't." He turned his head to face Dr. Danes, eyes pleading. "Can you repeat what you said? I must have misunderstood...."

Dr. Danes shook his head. "You didn't. It's not looking good. We've done all we can. I'm sorry."

The doctor's words rang in Josh's ears. He refused to accept that—refused to believe. "Pardon me? What exactly are you saying?"

"I'm saying that it's best from this point forward for you to spend every moment with your dad as possible. He doesn't have much time left."

Josh couldn't believe what he heard; their time together, limited. There'd be a mere moment soon when his dad would suddenly not be there. Josh couldn't fathom going through life without him. He turned to his father. "Dad, how can this be? I thought things were going well. You told me you were feeling okay."

His dad's face revealed his secret. "I have been feeling okay, son, but not the way you think."

"What other way is there? Either you're doing well on the treatment and it's working, or you're not. You told me you were well."

"Son, it's not that black and white."

"Sure it is. What else is there?"

"I can be okay while the treatment fails. I'm not referring to my body's reaction when I say I'm okay."

"Then what, Dad?"

"I'm okay, mentally, with all of this. I've made my peace with it."

Josh ran his hands through his hair and squared his shoulders. "You're sicker than you've been letting on, aren't you, Dad? You knew you weren't getting better, didn't you?"

"Yes, son, I knew my time was up, even before today."

Josh shifted his attention back to the doctor. "No. I'm not accepting this."

"I'm afraid you must come to terms with the reality," said Dr. Danes.

"No, I don't. There's got to be something we can do. Something we haven't tried? A trial?"

His dad interjected, "Son, please."

"Billy, if I may?" asked Dr. Danes, then faced Josh. "There is something more you can do."

Josh leaned forward in his seat. "I'm listening."

"Be there for your father. Do things he wants to do while he still has energy. Enjoy each other's company. He doesn't have much time, so make the time he has meaningful."

Josh brought his hands up to his head. "How long are we talking about?"

"It's always hard to guess how long someone has...."

"How long?" Josh repeated louder.

The doctor considered his question. "In my professional opinion, a few months, maybe a year. The cancer is spreading fast."

Three words rang in Josh's ears: A few months.

Josh hoped that if he repeated the words, perhaps they would change—take on a new form, a new meaning, but they choked him instead. His father had a life sentence, but Josh was the one dying. Before they left, they reviewed everything that must happen from then on: what to expect, what to do in such situations, and continued medication use. Dr. Danes spoke slowly and clearly to ensure Josh understood as he prepared him, not his father, for the worst-case scenario.

As they walked through the halls to make their way out, several nurses stopped to say hello to his dad. A reminder of how loved he was.

Once outside, the walk back to the car was a quiet one, and it was Billy who broke the silence first.

"Son, are you all right?"

Josh stopped mid-stride. "Dad, how is it you're asking me if I'm all right. Shouldn't it be the other way around?"

Tears welled, and he looked away to hide them from his dad. His dad put his limp arms around him, and Josh let the tears fall free while his dad held him.

"It'll be fine, son. I'm okay with this. I've lived a good life. I'm ready to be reunited with your mother."

"You're ready to give up, to leave me?" His voice was louder than he intended it to be. "How can you say that? I'm not letting you give up. *I'm* not giving up. There's got to be more we can do."

While still holding him, his dad patted his back. "You heard the doctor, there's nothing more to do."

"There's always something."

"What am I supposed to do, son? Keep fighting a losing battle? Live the rest of my days in misery? I won't do that. If God has called me, I'll go peacefully, and you need to let me go when the time comes."

Josh refused to let go of his father and clung tight. "You're all I have. You're it, Dad. There's no one else." He pulled away slightly, enough to look him in the eye, and his dad put his arms around his shoulders, comforting him as if Josh were the one who only had months to live.

"I think it's time you and I had a long-overdue talk, son."

"About what Dad, what else is important now?"

"There is something important that I should have brought up years ago. I tried to tell you the other day, but it didn't work out."

"I forgot about that," said Josh.

Suddenly, his dad's complexion turned white; he stumbled and luckily his arm was still around Josh's shoulders, so he grabbed on for support.

"Dad, what is it? What's wrong?" Josh held up his father, keeping him from falling.

"Feeling dizzy. Can you just take me home, son? I'm not feeling the greatest."

"I'm taking you back inside."

"No. Take me home. I mean it; take me home now. I'll have a nap then we can have the talk."

When they arrived, Billy was fast asleep, curled up in the passenger seat. Josh woke him and helped him into the house and into his bed, taking off his shoes and tucking him under the covers. His dad remained awake long enough to whisper good night.

Josh went to the kitchen to make himself a cup of peppermint tea, grabbed a blanket and tossed it over his shoulders, and sat next to his father the entire night, watching him sleep as his chest rose and fell with each breath. Josh counted the number of times he breathed, holding his own breath, hoping each of his dad's breaths wasn't the last.

CHAPTER 22

The Situation Called for Improvisions at Its Best

IT WAS NEARING the end of August, eight weeks since Jenna had slept with Liam. Seven since the night at the restaurant when she'd told him the truth, after which he'd announced he'd fallen in love with her and stormed out. She'd tried to reach him several times since, but he never returned her calls. Once, he sent a text, and all it said was:

Liam: I need time.

So she gave him time.

The temperatures broke record highs. The tiny air conditioner in Jenna's apartment worked constantly, and even stopped, unable to keep up. Summers in Quebec City weren't as hot as in Toronto, but still hot enough.

Jenna was up before the six thirty morning alarm, hair already drenched in sweat, stomach in tightly formed knots. Today was a big day—the day she'd visit Holly's parents. It was time. Meeting and interviewing them was the last missing piece of the deep rabbit hole she'd climbed into. She'd received an extension from Rachel on the story because she'd gotten lucky with another for a significant feature that issue, so Rachel hadn't pressed her too much about the big one she had promised. It relieved her because she wasn't planning on submitting anything about the twins. She'd only been stringing Rachel along to avoid getting fired. She knew she'd have to face her eventually but put that aside and continued—already in so deep. She couldn't stop and needed to interview the grandparents to get the last bit of information to complete her story—one she most likely would never share with the world.

Jenna had reached out to the grandparents as a reporter writing a piece about their generous contributions to the local arts fund, and the publicity thrilled them. That was what they were about and what brought the couple joy, Jenna learnt. She considered she could write an interesting enough piece on them alone that she could submit—a limited, one-sided story, not mentioning Holly or the twins. She wasn't sure what angle she would take with them, or if she'd even tell them all she knew. She would play it by ear and see where the interview went naturally, focussing on their arts involvement and generosity over the years. If an opportunity presented itself to dig deeper, she'd jump on it. If not, she'd figure it out. It wasn't like her to not have a plan, but the situation called for improvisions at its best. What she didn't want was to leave having gained nothing and losing half a day of work—that couldn't happen. She was already in too deep with Rachel as it was.

Jenna selected her outfit carefully: a slim black pantsuit that hugged her thighs and waist just a tad more than she last remembered, a cream collared button-down blouse that peeked through the jacket's lapels, and black pumps. For a splash of colour, her red bag. She surveyed herself in the full-length mirror that leaned up against the wall in her room and pressed down the jacket, then walked out the door—jittery nerves and nausea running through her.

From her research, she knew the couple lived in a wealthy part of the city. It was the same size home they'd had in Toronto, where Holly grew up. Jenna's stomach was queasy—obviously more nervous than she'd allowed herself to believe. Even coffee hadn't sat well. When she pulled up to the estate, the property, gated by an electronic fence with a keypad, took her breath away. Jenna didn't know the code, so pressed the white button on the brick pillar to announce her arrival, and within a second the gate opened, revealing a grey stone driveway lined with a darker stone leading to the gigantic, two-storey, all stone Victorian-style house she'd seen in photos she'd found online. As Jenna put her car into park, a sudden wave of nausea washed over her and she looked around for something to use, just in case she got sick, but there was nothing but stone and gardens. She pushed the nausea down, willing it away, but it did the opposite and reared its ugly head. She sprinted to the nearest garden, bent over the base of a magnolia tree, and vomited at its roots. Thank goodness the tree hid her from the front window views of the house. She grabbed onto the tree for support because her legs were wobbly and betrayed her. She was dizzy, and not confident that the wave of nausea was over, so she stood, hunched over for another few minutes—waiting for another blow. When the nausea passed, she collected herself, wiped her mouth and searched through her purse for gum or mints; she wished Cassie was there, as she'd have gum for sure. Jenna found an old candy from a restaurant she'd been to with Josh. It had been a Japanese restaurant, and she recognized the wrapper. That was when her life was simpler, when she and Josh were together. She shut the thought down as fast as it came and, although the candy was over six months old and the wrapper stuck when she tried to unwrap it, she popped it into her mouth. The stale sweetness felt like a soft blanket as it touched her dry lips. She swirled it around her tongue, trying to mask the bitter taste from the vomit. She patted down her blouse beneath the blazer and held her breath as she applied sanitizer, gagged, and walked toward the front door.

A well-dressed woman with no wrinkles or grey hair opened the door, but Jenna knew she was older than she appeared. The woman opened the door wider, revealing the inside of the house from behind. Wow. These people were wealthier than she'd thought, which raised more questions about why they'd given up the babies when they had so much money to care for them. They could have afforded to hire full-time help by the look of their front foyer alone, so money wasn't the issue—clearly.

Jenna wasn't sure if she should speak English or French. They were originally from Toronto and had lived there their entire lives, except for the last ten years. She started with French, considering they'd become accustomed to it over the years.

"Bonjour!" *Hello*, said the woman. "You must be Miss Taylor?" she continued in French.

"Yes, but please call me Jenna. And you must be Mrs. Mills."

"Oui," *yes*, she said, then continued, "the one and only. But please, call me Brenda."

"You have a beautiful home, Brenda."

"Yes, we are aware of its grandness and beauty. Thank you. Please follow me, we can sit in the living room." She led the way and Jenna followed, admiring the house as she crossed the entryway into the enormous living room with high, coffered ceilings, thick trim, and grand wood pocket doors.

She stopped in front of a large entrance leading to a sitting room. One without a television. "Will this suffice?" asked Brenda, pointing to the Victorian-style couch in the room's centre. "Or will you be needing a table to write? If so, we can move to the dining hall."

"This is great, thank you. I'll be taking some notes, but I'd also like to tape the interview, if that's okay?"

"That's fine by me. We are familiar with how you reporters work. My husband should be along momentarily, but we can get started." Brenda looked at her wristwatch. "It's early. Would you like a coffee and a biscuit? They baked them this morning."

"They?"

"The kitchen staff, of course. Would you like one?"

Of course they had kitchen staff.

At the thought of putting anything in her mouth, other than the candy she already chewed and swallowed, her stomach flipped, and she feared she'd be sick again.

"No, thank you. That's kind of you, but I've already had breakfast," she lied.

At the same moment, a housemaid entered and set a tray of coffee and biscuits on the coffee table. Jenna tried to breathe from her mouth, to avoid the smell making her already upset stomach even more unhappy. When she was sure she could speak without vomiting, she pulled out her phone. She started by asking Brenda about their connection to the arts when neither she nor her husband were artists.

Brenda had the straightest posture Jenna had ever seen. Not only was her back straight while she sat, but her legs also formed a ninety-degree edge as they hung off the couch, and her hands crossed over her knees. Her feet wrapped around each other in pristine heels that looked like she'd never worn them outdoors. Jenna felt self-conscious about her own shoes not being so well kept and tried to tuck them up behind the couch leg.

"Everyone asks that, and the answer is simple. We merely love art. Always have. It goes no further, I'm afraid. So the answer to this common question isn't as romantic and glorious as most people hope."

Jenna considered her answer and nodded. They continued with a few more rudimentary questions; Brenda's easy answers, rehearsed. Mr. Mills had yet to make an appearance.

"Shall we wait for your husband before proceeding?"

"No need. He'll be along shortly. He most likely got stuck on a business call. He's in his study, but knows you're here."

Feeling another wave of nausea hit, Jenna asked what she went there to ask, before she felt too sick and had to leave. She worked best under pressure, and her upset stomach causing her so much stress lit a fire under her.

"Tell me about your daughter. Holly was her name?"

Brenda stiffened even more. Jenna studied her face for clues about what she must be thinking. But the woman's face remained stoic, revealing nothing. She reached out and picked up a glass of water.

Jenna pressed on, still speaking in French. "I understand Holly passed away at eighteen, and the obituary said she died of an undisclosed medical condition, but from my research, I discovered she died giving birth to twins." Jenna waited for a moment before adding more. "Do you have any comment?"

Brenda dropped the glass, and it shattered when it hit the large-plank wood floors just as a hefty man entered the room. She recognized him from photos. Josh and Liam's grandfather. Jenna saw the resemblance amongst the men. He had red hair, just like Liam.

"I'm sorry to keep you two ladies waiting. I hope you at least got started without me." He looked from his wife to the glass shattered on the floor. "Darling, is something wrong?" he asked.

"Bob, get the cheque book," said Brenda to her husband, then clasped her hands together. "Who are you? And how much do you want to keep quiet?"

"I'm not here for your money." At that moment, Jenna felt the need to throw up again. "I'm sorry. I'm not well and need a washroom," she said, placing her hand over her mouth with urgency.

"Oh dear," said Mr. Mills, "right through there." Still standing at the room's entrance, he pointed down the hall, and Jenna ran into the guest bathroom, not even closing the door behind her. She cut it close as it was, nearly missing the toilet.

After she'd gathered herself and rinsed out her mouth, she washed her hands but still checked the medicine cabinet for hand sanitizer as she left her purse in the sitting room, but found none. She returned to the sitting room and before she spoke again, applied the sanitizer. Bob and Brenda Mills were sitting side by side on the couch, their lips in a tight line—no evidence of shattered glass.

"So, if you're not here for money, then why are you here?" asked Brenda.

"To talk. I want answers."

"How far along are you?" asked Brenda, her hands crossed over her lap.

"Oh no, you're mistaken. I'm not pregnant, just a little off today, is all," said Jenna as she swallowed back another urge to vomit. She must remember to lay off the sanitizer until she felt better.

They were fidgety compared to before Jenna had dropped the bomb. Mr. Mills was breathing heavily while Brenda stared into Jenna's eyes. "I have to hand it to you. Of all the reporters and interviews we've done over the years, you're the first to state that fact about Holly."

Jenna leaned into the phone to ensure the recorder was picking the voices up clearly. "Are you admitting to your daughter's cause of death?"

"How did you find out?" asked Mr. Mills.

"Dear, that's a silly question. She's a reporter. She's just smarter than the others. It was only a matter of time before it came out. I just never thought it would take twenty-eight years."

Bob Mills reached out to take his wife's hand, and she patted his in return. "If we tell you the truth, will you promise to write from our perspective and only include the details that we approve of?" asked Brenda, tilting her head to the side.

"The truth is always what I write." Jenna checked again to make sure the phone was still recording. "Ready when you are," she said, placing the phone closer to the couple so that it picked up each spoken word.

Brenda took a deep, long breath before speaking. "I don't know how you found out, but yes, Holly was pregnant at eighteen; although, we didn't know."

"You didn't know your daughter was pregnant? How can that be?"

"Well. I should have said that we refused to believe the truth. We were in denial. It's a long story. I don't even know where to start."

"Why don't you start at the beginning?" suggested Jenna.

And so, Brenda did.

PART THREE

Twenty-Eight Years Ago

CHAPTER 23

She's... In Trouble

Twenty-Eight Years Ago - 1989

BRENDA MILLS KNEW what was happening with *everything*. She knew what was coming next and what to do about every situation—or so she thought. She sat in her Toronto board meeting, deciding, throwing out suggestions, and being in control. She exuded confidence whenever she walked into a room, forcing people to stare and hear what she had to say because she always had the solution to problems. There wasn't any business-related matter that she couldn't face with ease. Her husband, Bob, also sat on many boards and chaired a few. Together, the Millses built their empire with a grace and elegance that everyone who knew them admired. The Millses owned many businesses and were silent investors in others. When Brenda and Bob had met at university, they had known they were perfect for each other and made plans to build their empire almost right away—the plans came to fruition as they became a prominent family in society, and one of the wealthiest in their neighbourhood. Brenda was proud of what she and her husband had accomplished in their eighteen years of marriage.

When Brenda became pregnant with Holly, the news devastated her because she didn't think it was the right time in her career. She worried it would cause a derailment, but one of the first investments they had made in a public company had done well and the dividends were handsome enough that they could hire a full-time nanny to help take care of the baby. With the help of the nanny, Brenda didn't miss one beat in her career. She was fortunate to be in a position where she could hire help; she knew that, but she didn't consider herself lucky, not by any means. That was not luck. It resulted from hard work, late nights, and much dedication, and not because she carried a rabbit's foot on her key chain—that would be superstition and not luck.

⁂

Brenda hoped to have socialized her daughter by then. At eighteen, they should have introduced her to society, but Holly was too stubborn, not placing enough importance on things, not even her health. When Holly turned sixteen, Brenda had tried to convince her to attend a 'coming of age' sorority. But Holly laughed, so that conversation ended. Despite her wishes, Brenda put the idea of having a debutante daughter aside, telling herself that, eventually, her daughter would see the importance of presenting herself to others. But now at eighteen, she'd regressed rather than progressed. Holly was cranky towards Brenda, distant, hardly around, and when she was near, she kept to herself and ate in her room.

How she looked toward the end of her life was a disgrace. She'd gained so much weight. How Holly could have let herself go that way, and so quickly, was what consumed Brenda's every waking thought, outside of business of course. Once, Brenda considered the possibility that Holly was with child, but then shoved the thought aside, never going there again.

Brenda hated to admit Holly was an embarrassment. Brenda had to make excuses whenever someone asked how Holly was after they'd comment that she looked different. Brenda had assumed they were referring to the weight gain and would say she hadn't been feeling well and blamed her expanding body on health issues. She refused to believe the weight gain was due to any other reason.

She pushed thoughts of her daughter out of her mind and refocused on the faces staring at her around the conference room table—that was what she did best, and so it was where she channelled her energy.

Her assistant walked into the room; her head hung with an apologetic tone. "Mrs. Mills, I'm so sorry to interrupt but there's a phone call for you on line one."

"Gina, please take a message. We're in the middle of something important," said Brenda, waving her arms.

Her assistant cleared her throat. "Yes, I know, but this is... more important."

"Good lord, what can be more important than this." She waved her arms around again.

"It's...."

Her assistant stopped and looked around the room. Brenda noticed bold and serious eyes were on her, waiting for her assistant to leave so they could continue. The assistant hesitated, but Brenda pressed her.

"Well?" said Brenda, raising her eyebrows. "We haven't got all day. Either say what you must or get out."

The assistant took a loud breath. "It's your daughter. She's in the hospital, she's..."

Confused at what the assistant spoke, Brenda asked, "She's what?"

"She's... in trouble."

CHAPTER 24

Dear Baby

Twenty-Eight Years Ago - 1989

BRENDA MILLS STARED at her assistant, waiting for more information, but when she didn't offer any, Brenda searched her face for clues as to what she knew, and the sombre look revealed pity.

"Please excuse me," Brenda said to everyone sitting around the board-room table. "I won't be a minute. I need a moment to sort this out."

Outside in the hall, her assistant picked up the phone and pressed line one and handed the receiver to Brenda. Brenda listened and heard the words 'pregnant' and 'in labour', then slowly allowed the phone to slip from her hand. It fell, and the base dangled in mid-air; Brenda collapsed. The office staff rushed to her side.

Once Brenda came to, her assistant called for her husband who was in another meeting and drove them to the hospital. Brenda and Bob, hurried through the emergency room doors and asked where they could find their daughter. The nurse requested the spelling of the name, looked it up on her list, and her face changed from a smile to sadness.

"I'm sorry. Can you have a seat there? I'll have the doctor come speak to you at once. He'll be here momentarily and can explain everything," said the nurse.

Brenda clutched her husband's arm; her long fingernails dug deep into his skin. Bob led them to the waiting room as the two took a seat, eager to sort out the nonsense about their daughter being in labour. Two minutes later, the doctor stood before them, a poignant look on his face.

"Are you Mr. and Mrs. Mills? Holly Mills' parents?"

"Yes, can you clear up this misunderstanding? They told me on the phone my daughter was in labour. How absurd. I don't know what nonsense my daughter is up to, but I assure you—"

The doctor interrupted her and urged them to move to a private room and closed the door behind him. He cleared his throat before he spoke. "I'm sorry. Your daughter died while giving birth to twins. We did all we could to save her."

Brenda stood, took a step closer to the doctor. "That's not possible. Our daughter was not pregnant. You have the wrong person. Let me see the girl so I can put a stop to this rubbish and get back to work."

"I'm afraid we have made no mistakes. She had identification in her purse."

"Well then, whomever you think is my daughter, has stolen the identification." Brenda looked at her husband for support, but he remained still and said nothing.

The doctor stared at them with an expressionless look. "Will you both come with me, please?"

❧

Moments later, the doctor escorted Brenda and Bob into a lifeless room. When a nurse pulled back the blanket from Holly's head, Brenda screamed, then stared at her daughter's pale face, searching for clues that it might not be her, but when her husband gasped behind her, there was no pretending anymore. Bob threw himself on top of Holly's body while Brenda walked out, wanting to be alone.

She wandered the halls for two hours before she looked through the glass window at her two new grandbabies in the incubators, but she wasn't seeing the babies. Instead, she stared into nothing. She hadn't shed a tear for her daughter; her mind was too busy racing with thoughts on how to fix the situation. Determined she had the answers, she left the babies and went to the nurses' station to make a call, one so critical it would change lives, including hers and her husband's. When she finished with the call, she returned to the nursery to watch the babies once again—convinced she had done the right thing. Brenda watched them, wrapped up, sleeping, and oblivious to her deciding their fate. Bob soon joined her and wrapped his arms around her shoulders. They remained silent for a long time standing side by side, but alone.

Bob was the first to break the silence. "I thought I might find you here. You left so suddenly."

"There was nothing left to see once they showed her to us."

"Have you been here the entire time?"

"I walked around for a bit. Did some thinking."

"I thought perhaps you'd want to spend a few minutes alone with her to say goodbye."

"What is the point? She won't know I'm there. It's not like she can hear me."

"No, but still. It's unbelievable, isn't it? How is it that we didn't know?" He then turned to his wife. "Did you know?"

Brenda nodded. Bob squeezed her tighter, and she laid her head on his shoulder. He wept, she didn't.

"Who were you on the phone with?" Brenda remained silent and he pressed on. "I saw you at the nurses' desk on the phone."

Brenda cleared her throat to prepare for what she needed to say. "Bob, I know what we need to do."

"There's a lot we need to do, but we'll get through it one item at a time. We'll get help for the babies. But first thing is to arrange the funeral..."

"I know that, and it's already set in motion. I mean; I know what to do about them." She pointed to the babies on the other side of the glass.

"What's that?" he asked, not taking his eyes off the babies.

"I thought long and hard about this. We can't keep them. We need to give the babies up for adoption. It's the only way to save our reputation."

Bob let his arms drop from her shoulders. "Adoption? Brenda, have you lost your mind?"

"I have not and that is precisely why I know this is the right thing."

"We don't have to decide so soon. We should take a day or two to think about this first. This isn't something we should decide lightly. They are our grandchildren."

"I don't need to think about this. This is all I have been thinking about for the last two hours." She lifted her head from his shoulder and faced him. "I've done it already. I have made the call to the Children's Aid Society; they are on their way."

"What have you done?"

"I've done what needs to be done. After today, we won't discuss this anymore. This is the only way, Bob; we've worked too hard to get to where we are to have this ruin our social standing. Can you imagine what the press would say if they got wind of this? A pregnant teenaged daughter, what a scandal this would create. We cannot have that."

"Brenda, we lost Holly. Are you even thinking of that?"

"Of course, I *am* thinking about her. That is why this has to be the only way."

"And what will we say was her cause of death?"

"It's already taken care of. She died from hemorrhaging from a fall to the head. Our lawyer is on his way to make sure none of this," she gestured towards the two babies, "gets out to the public." Brenda walked away from her husband, clenching her Louis Vuitton bag tight to her side, head held high.

"Where are you going? Don't walk away from me."

Brenda turned around. "What else is there to say?"

"Don't I have a right to voice my opinion? What if I want to be a part of my grandchildren's lives? You're taking that choice away from me, from us. It's not fair."

"Bob, you're reacting emotionally. It is what you do. I'm thinking this through logically. It is what I do. In time, you'll understand why I did this." She walked away again, and then turned around one more time and added, "I am doing this for us."

As she was on her way to the front lobby to meet with the lawyer and the Children's Aid Society representative, the nurse that was with Holly during the delivery saw her and stopped her just before she entered the elevator.

"Mrs. Mills, I've been looking for you. I wanted to give you these." She handed a stack of papers to Brenda, who took them reluctantly.

"What is this?"

"They look like letters. They were in the inside pocket of your daughter's purse. I didn't want them to get lost or tossed, so I took them to give to you personally. I thought you might like to have them."

Brenda took the letters just as the elevator door opened, inviting her in. She walked through and tucked the letters into her bag. She didn't want to read her daughter's last words for fear that it could persuade her to change her mind, but she was curious and searched deep within herself to find the confidence she had earlier when she'd decided on the babies' futures. When she found that confidence again, she took a deep breath, and sat at one of the uncomfortable couches in the lobby and, while waiting for the meeting she'd set in motion, she pulled the letters out of her bag and read them while she allowed her guard to fall and wept for the first time in years.

❧

Dear Baby,

I felt you kick today, and it sure felt like there was more than just one of you, but I'm sure that's just my imagination. I don't think twins run in my family; besides, if there were two of you, I'd know. I think I'd be bigger, although as I look down at the space you occupy, you sure take up a lot for a little thing.

I caught them talking about me today, and it wasn't pleasant. They were complaining about how I'm amounting to nothing, spending my days locked in my room not accomplishing anything. Little do they know I'm doing the most important job of all—growing you.

Let them complain, let them talk all they want because in the end, when they see you, they'll understand. People will always judge, it's human nature, but what we must remember is to not let those judgements affect who we are or our decisions about ourselves and others. When you're judged someday, my baby, let those judgemental thoughts float right over you. You must be stronger in life than them; show confidence in all you do, and you'll surely do great things if not extraordinary. I can't wait to hold you in my arms.

Love Mom

Brenda looked up from the letter, astonished by what she'd read. Those were her daughter's words of encouragement and survival. Brenda would never have guessed.

The lawyer and Children's Aid representative hadn't yet arrived, so she quickly opened another and continued to read.

Dear Baby,

I'm not sure how much longer I can conceal you. It's getting harder each day. Some days I think I should tell them. Once, I made it down the staircase and stopped mid-stride and ran back to my room. They were busy looking through papers and didn't see me.

From my calculations, you're due in November and it's now mid-July; we're almost there, little one.

I'm looking forward to cooler weather again, so I don't look odd wearing large sweaters in the heat of summer. I know I keep telling you to not worry about what others think of you, and it must seem that I'm doing the opposite. But, baby, I have a reason and that reason is one I'm not yet ready to deal with, but I promise you, I will soon.

Love Mom

As Brenda folded the second letter and put them all back inside her purse, a man and woman she didn't recognize asked if she was Brenda Mills. She wiped the tears she had let escape and stood with an air of confidence.

"Yes, I'm she. Now let us get this done and over with, shall we?"

PART FOUR

Twenty-Eight Years Later

CHAPTER 25

Much Communication
Without Speaking

Twenty-Eight Years Later - 2017

ENNA SHUT THE recorder off once Brenda finished her story. "I'm sorry. I realize that must have been difficult to relive. And thank you for being so honest about your past."

"You wanted the truth, so that's what I gave you. We didn't know our daughter—didn't know… didn't want to believe she was pregnant. I asked myself repeatedly; how could that be? I should have known. Perhaps deep down I did. We should have picked up on the sudden laziness, sleeping all day, the baggy clothes—but we ignored it. I focused too heavily on attending charities and social gatherings to have been there for our daughter when she needed us most. We paid off the funeral home to keep the cause of death private. Despite our attempts to keep the pregnancy secret, many people in town discovered the truth, but kept it discrete." She looked at Jenna. "Until you came along."

Brenda glanced at her husband. He looked at her and nodded, so she continued. "We named the boys Joshua and Liam, knowing those were boys' names Holly liked, and we never once looked back. Although both adoptions were closed, our lawyer discovered a couple adopted the first twin, Joshua, in Toronto. I couldn't go to the grocery store and not scan the face of every little boy, wondering if he was the boy. We weren't expecting to be so close to the other boy either, but having Liam right here made us curious about him. Odd how we ended up living in both cities where each grew up. We didn't know Liam was in Quebec City when we first moved here. That was a coincidence, believe it or not. We found out who adopted him, and what school he attended, and without meaning to, we kept tabs on him throughout the years, from a distance, of course, never wanting to interrupt his life. Over the years, we discovered his love of art, and it wasn't until he graduated high school that we donated regularly to the arts foundations. It was our way of helping, of saying we're sorry."

"Why didn't you ever search for Josh when you were in Toronto like you did Liam?"

"I don't think we..." she looked at her husband, then said, "I don't think I was ready then."

"Have you ever met Liam?" asked Jenna.

"Yes, once, about three years ago. I was shopping when I realized I was standing in front of his store. I froze, contemplating what to do. Then, against my better judgement, I walked in and browsed through the artwork. He saw me walk in, and I was the only customer, so he offered help. We chatted for a bit; such a lovely young man he's grown to be. I bought one of his most expensive pieces that day."

She pointed to the cream-coloured wall above the couch where an enormous portrait of Quebec City's downtown hung, covering most of the wall. The liveliness of the painting transformed the room. Jenna stood to inspect it and, on the bottom right of the portrait, was Liam's name.

"This is Liam's painting," said Jenna.

"Yes. It's the one I bought that afternoon." Brenda tilted her head. "Do you know Liam well? Is that why you're here?"

"I do. I know them both well, especially Josh. I've known Josh the longest."

Brenda looked at her husband for a bit too long. He stared back, both their hands shaking in their laps. Bob nodded and gestured with his eyes towards the cabinet that sat tall at the front of the room. There was much communication without speaking. Jenna wondered if that's what happened when a couple stayed together as long as they had.

Bob stood and walked to the cabinet and pulled out a medium-sized box. He handed it to his wife with another gentle nod; she acknowledged it by placing her hand over his.

"Jenna, these are the letters Holly wrote to the baby while she was pregnant."

"I imagine they're deeply personal and painful to read again," said Jenna.

"Yes, they were the first few times, and it's still hard, but at least now I can read them without locking myself in my bedroom for the next three days. Twenty-eight years ago, when I read them for the first time the night she died, they almost broke me; I almost called off the entire thing. Then I reread them all when the boys found homes, and I spent the next few years working on putting myself back together—mentally. I couldn't undo what I had done."

"Would you have wanted to if you could?"

"I'm not sure. I have mixed emotions. I'd like to think so."

"I'm sorry."

"Don't be sorry. This isn't your fault. You're only here for the truth, so, here," she handed Jenna the stack of letters. "Of course, I need them back, but you're welcome to make copies and share them with the boys if you so wish, whenever you feel the time is right."

Jenna took the stack from her. "Are you sure you want to share these?"

Brenda looked at her husband again, probably for more confirmation that they were doing the right thing. "Yes, I'm sure."

"How many are there?"

"There's five in total."

"Thank you for trusting me with them." Jenna couldn't believe she had a stack of letters in her possession written by Josh and Liam's birth mom. She took a few deep breaths to control her emotions.

"I'm sure one day I will share these with them, but I don't know when. They don't know about you. At least Josh doesn't. He doesn't even know he's adopted."

"I wondered about that."

"But thank you. I'll get these copied and returned by next week, if that's okay?"

Both Brenda and Bob nodded when Jenna's phone rang while it sat on the coffee table. On the display, clear as day, was Josh's name. Jenna didn't know why he was calling but knew it must be important. She hadn't heard from him in months. What could he want? Jenna looked at the phone, then at Brenda and Bob, who both stared at the name on the display.

"I'm sorry, I have to answer this, please excuse me." She picked up the phone on the third ring, anxious she'd miss it.

"Josh?" she said into the phone softly so that her voice didn't carry.

"Jenna, I need you. Can you come to Toronto?"

"What's wrong?"

"It's my dad, he's gone. He died moments ago."

"Oh Josh, I'm so sorry. Were you with him?"

"Yes, I was. I called an ambulance; he was feverish and unresponsive. He passed away shortly after we got here. I'm still looking down at his still body, waiting for him to take another breath, but he's gone, so he'll never breathe again."

"I wish I was there to comfort you."

"How soon can you get here?"

"You want me there? Really?"

"Yes, I need you."

"Are you sure? I mean, after everything that's happened?"

"Jenna, I really need you. I don't know what to do. I'm falling apart. Please come help me. I have no one else."

"Okay. Of course, I'll come. I'll book an early flight."

∽

Later at night, while laying in bed not able to sleep, Jenna unfolded the stack of letters and read each one carefully—several times over.

∽

Dear Baby,

Today was the day it hit me; I was going to be a mother. I'd known I was pregnant for a while, but today it all became real. Today you moved inside me—an extraordinary and exhilarating feeling.

You came into my life unexpectedly, but that doesn't mean that you're not welcome. In fact, I'm thrilled to have you—something of my own—something real. I have a lot of things, but it's all superficial and meaningless. With you, things are going to be different. I already know you will be my world. You will change me and hopefully others around you, too.

Please believe me when I say it's not their fault that they are the way they are. They're just too consumed by what's happening around them to see what's right before them.

But that's okay, baby, because when you come along, you'll change everything, including them. I have this feeling you will change their world and mine—we will change them together because one look at you, and their hearts will surely melt.

Baby, I already love you to the moon and back.

Love, Mom

CHAPTER 26

Lifeline

JOSH LET HIS phone slip from his hands, staring at his lifeless father. When he'd taken his last breath, Josh had immediately called Jenna like a reflex. She'd promised to book a flight first thing in the morning, so he only had today to get through without her. He wasn't sure why he had called her—that was an impulse. He considered calling back to tell her he didn't know what got into him and didn't need her, but who was he kidding—he needed her, more than he cared to admit.

There was a gentle knock. "Josh, is there anyone you want me to call?" asked Dr. Danes, standing in the doorway.

"No. I'll take care of it."

"You need to let him go. That's what he asked of you, remember?"

"Yeah, I remember," said Josh, as he walked out of the hospital room, head hung, contemplating if he had done the right thing by calling Jenna and begging her to come. He didn't want to come across as weak, but that was what he was, without his lifeline—without his father.

The hours after his father passed melted into one uncomfortable moment as he paced the hospital hallways looking for answers, but found he had only more questions.

CHAPTER 27

You Can't Control the Situation But You Can Control Your Reaction

FOR TWO DAYS, Jenna awakened before the alarm, despite having tossed, turned, and worried most of the night thinking about Billy being gone. She wiped her sleep-filled eyes with the back of her sleeve, rushing to the washroom, heading straight for the toilet. Last night's cereal she'd had for supper felt like a volcanic eruption as it made its way back up. She was sitting on the cool ceramic floor next to the big white bowl, thinking about Billy and welcoming the crispness of the tile on her bare legs, trying to comprehend how this was happening. It *couldn't* be happening.

Using her fingers, she counted back the number of weeks since she and Liam had sex; eight weeks ago—NO! The reality struck her hard, preventing her from breathing, so she grabbed a towel that hung over the tub and bit on it. When she could breathe in from her nose and out her mouth again, she crawled back to her room, sat on her bed and checked the calendar on her phone to be sure—eight weeks.

"Shit, shit, shit," she muttered out loud.

She needed to catch a flight to Toronto in a couple of hours. She had yet to shower, pack, and prepare mentally to see Josh again.

Josh

Pregnant

Eight weeks

Billy's death

Those six words echoed repeatedly in her head. How could she face Josh while she was pregnant? It was the one thing he'd wanted her to give him, and now... how was she going to look him in the eye knowing that what he'd always wanted, she had without him?

She sat a while longer, contemplating life. After another bout with the toilet and, convinced the cereal was all gone, she forced her legs to hold her up, used the counter for support and splashed cold water over her face.

Jenna hadn't talked to Liam since the night he told her he'd fallen in love with her. He didn't know she was pregnant, and for the time being, she intended to keep it that way. She hadn't even told Cassie about the pregnancy last night when they spoke, because Jenna hadn't been sure then. She let out another yawn; there was nothing she wouldn't give to crawl back into bed for another hour, or even just a few minutes, shut her eyes, and pretend today was a normal day. The thought of a few more minutes in bed was heavenly. But she didn't have that luxury. She needed to get to the airport. It was a short flight, but she convinced herself she could nap on the plane. Looking forward to napping gave her the motivation to pull herself together and get on the flight to see Josh and deal with Billy's death. She couldn't believe cancer took him from them so soon. She should have called him more. She should have booked the first flight out to visit him when she found out. Now it was too late. She'd never hear his words of wisdom, or his calming voice again.

Josh

Pregnant

Eight Weeks

Billy's death

No matter how hard she tried, she couldn't get those words off her mind.

⁘

After walking off the plane, she sanitized her hands as she saw Cassie waiting, chewing gum and holding two large Starbucks cups, one in each hand. The scent of the sanitizer upset her stomach again. Cassie's Louis Vuitton knockoff bag dangled off her elbow. When Jenna approached, Cassie handed her a cup. Jenna took it hesitantly. She loved Starbucks coffee; it was a favourite, but when the sweet vanilla scent of the tall latte reached her nose, she gagged and handed it back before running down the airport hallway to find the nearest washroom.

Cassie followed closely behind. "Girl, wait up. Where are you going?"

"Washroom."

"Slow down. I'm in heels. Is something wrong with the coffee?" Jenna looked over her shoulder and saw Cassie sniff her cup, then take a sip. "Tastes fine to me."

"No, it's not the coffee, it's me. Having an off day today."

"Off day?" Cassie repeated, "Then all the more reason you need Starbucks in your life."

Thinking her nausea passed, Jenna stopped in front of a magazine stand. To appease her friend, she took the cup, raised the rim to her lips, and let the hot liquid touch her tongue. She gagged and ran inside the washroom. Cassie followed.

"Hey Jenna, you okay in there?" Cassie stood outside the stall, knocking.

"Just give me a minute, Cas."

"Unlock the door, Jenna. Let me in."

Jenna reached up from behind to unlock the door; her face still turned towards the toilet, just in case.

"Oh, girl, what's wrong?" Cassie hunched down to be at the same level as her.

Jenna looked up; she no longer saw the two Starbucks coffees. She wondered if Cassie discarded them, knowing the smell was upsetting her stomach, and she was thankful she couldn't smell the sweet vanilla scent any longer. Cassie reached out her hand and pulled Jenna's hair back from her face.

"Cas, I'm pretty sure I'm pregnant."

"What? Wait... back up a minute...." She raised an eyebrow. "Liam's?"

"Yes. There has been no one else since Josh, you know that."

"Just making sure!"

Cassie placed her purse on the hook that hung on the back of the door and held back Jenna's hair as she got sick again. "I remember now. You missed those pills. Have you had a pregnancy test?"

Jenna wiped her mouth with her sleeve. "Does it look like I need one?"

Cassie brought both her hands to her head. "No, but it's still the next step."

"I know, I'm sorry for snapping at you, Cas. I'm just frustrated and disappointed in myself."

"I don't understand how you let this happen! You're always in control of everything."

"Look, I know, okay? I messed up and have no one to blame but myself. Please don't get on my case and remind me of what could be one of the most irresponsible decisions I've made. Please?" she begged.

"I'm sorry. How can I help? What do you need me to say?"

"I need you to be my supportive best friend, not my mother. I've already got one of those who's sure to have a word or two about this."

"I'm here for you, Jenna. You know that. I'm just worried, that's all."

"I'm worried too."

"Have you told Liam? What did he say?"

"No, I haven't told him yet."

"I need to stand for a bit. My leg is cramping," Cassie said, stretching as best she could in the confined space. "Do you have more that needs to come out, or are you good for now? How did you manage on the plane?"

"I slept, thankfully."

Jenna tested herself by turning around and looking away from the toilet. "I think I'm okay. As long as I don't eat, drink, or smell anything, I should be good."

"Let's go. We need to get you booked in with the doctor while you're here. Unless you've already found a new one in Quebec City?"

"I haven't, so that's a great idea."

"You should listen to me more often, I'm full of them." Cassie teased as she took Jenna's arm and her suitcase in the other hand. Her phone rang from within her bag. "Oh, hold on! Give me a second to get this." She fumbled, and by the time she pulled the phone out, it had stopped ringing. "Darn it."

"Was it important? Do you need to call them back?" asked Jenna.

Cassie looked at the display. "No, not important. Just this new guy I'm seeing. But I'm not too sure about him. He's too corky for me, so he can wait."

"Okay, then." Despite her complicated life, Jenna smiled because of Cassie's eventful one.

❦

Before calling Josh, Jenna had a two-hour nap. When she awakened, she called Josh to check in and tell him she'd arrived. She failed to mention she got there in the morning; he'd ask why she hadn't called earlier.

He answered on the first ring. "Jenna, finally! Are you here?"

"Hey, Josh, yes. I'm at Cassie's. She picked me up from the airport."

"I could have picked you up, but you didn't tell me what time your flight landed. I texted and called several times, but you didn't respond. I was getting worried."

"My phone was on airplane mode, sorry." Why he worried when they hadn't spoken since the breakup was a mystery.

"I'm at the funeral home. There's so much to figure out, so many decisions needed, and I can't seem to make any. Can you meet me now? I really need you."

"Of course, that's why I came. I'll have Cassie drive me. Text me the funeral home name and address."

"Will do, and Jenna..." he began, then stopped.

"Yes?" she prompted.

"Thanks for coming. I know it's not your problem anymore since we broke up months ago. You didn't have to come running to my rescue, but I'm glad you did. I can't get through this without you. I'm falling apart. I really need you, more than I've ever needed anyone."

His words hurt, but she forced herself to be strong for his sake, and Billy's memory. "Josh, no matter what happened between you and me, Billy was family. I loved him, too. Of course, I'd be here. It would have upset me if you hadn't called."

After they hung up, Jenna checked her phone for missed messages. If she missed texts and calls from Josh, what else has she missed? There was a text from Rachel asking her to check in that afternoon at one. That was two hours ago.

Jenna sent her a quick reply:

Jenna: So sorry, but there's been a family emergency. A death. I'm in TO. Landed today. I'm going to need a few personal days to deal with this.

She waited for a reply, but when one didn't come, she checked the phone to make sure it sent the message. It was odd Rachel hadn't replied right away.

⁂

Jenna and Cassie walked through the funeral home's enormous doors and at the water dispenser, cup in hand, was Josh staring at the carpet. He turned when the door chimed and went to them. Seeing Josh after many months of not even talking to him pulled Jenna back to their old life. She took a step closer and wrapped her arms around him. He squeezed her back, holding on tight and for a lot longer than she thought necessary.

After a long silence, he said: "Thanks so much for coming. It means a lot to have you here." He released her, letting each finger linger. Cassie gave him her condolences and asked Jenna if she wanted her to wait in the car.

Josh jumped in right away. "That won't be necessary. I'll drive her back. We might be here a while." He looked at Jenna, then added, "If that's okay with you?"

"Yes, that's fine." She turned to Cassie next, "Cas, I'll see you later at your place, okay?"

Cassie gave her friend a quick hug and left, saying nothing further to Josh.

Josh took her hand and led her inside the meeting room where the funeral director waited. Josh introduced Jenna by her name—the title of ex-fiancée omitted. The funeral director asked who she was concerning Billy, and Josh let out a forced cough.

"Billy was family," Jenna said, and the funeral director seemed satisfied with her reply and continued to ask the gruelling questions that Josh couldn't answer. Jenna could see it was too much for him, as a bead of sweat accumulated on his forehead and his leg shook under the table.

"I need more water," he said and walked out, leaving Jenna alone with the man.

"This is the fourth time in the last hour he's gone for water, and we haven't gotten past the initial questions yet. He still needs to answer them before we can move forward. I know this is a troublesome time, but we need to get the arrangements completed today. Do you think you can talk to him?"

Jenna's stomach was in knots, but she pushed back the desire to run to the ladies' room.

"I'll try. Perhaps if he can go through the questions in a more relaxed atmosphere, it'll be easier."

"I'm up for trying anything at this point. What do you have in mind?"

The funeral director gave Jenna a list of items that Josh needed to decide on. Jenna promised they'd be back in a couple of hours with decisions.

"Okay, good luck," he said as he walked Jenna out. Josh was back standing at the water dispenser, his face long and sad.

"Come on, let's go." She grabbed his arm and led him outside.

"I can't leave. That guy needs me to decide on stuff, and I can't seem to even think straight."

"That's why we're leaving. We're going to figure this out together."

"Together? You promise?"

"Yes."

"Where?"

"Someplace away from here. Come on. I have an idea." Jenna took him by the hand, and they walked to the nearest coffee shop. She held her breath when they walked in and slowly let out some air. Confident she wouldn't get sick, she told him to find seats and she'd order. When she returned, Josh had his face in his hands and his elbows were up on the table, hair dishevelled.

"Here's your peppermint tea," she said, placing it down in front of him. "I know it's hard. I've lost people close to me before, my grandparents, my cousin who was more like a sister. I'm not saying that you'll never forget, but what you can do is learn to cope and remember Billy the way he would have wanted to be remembered. You can't control the situation, but you can control your reaction. Those were your dad's famous words, remember?"

"I know what I need to do, it's just so damn hard."

"Yes, it is, and you need to be strong so you can take care of things. It won't end with the funeral arrangements either."

"What do you mean?"

"You know what I mean. You're going to have to sort out his finances, decide what to do with the house. Those are decisions that will fall on you, Josh."

"You'll be here, to help me through it all?" His eyes were pleading, begging for something that he was afraid to ask for.

His question caught Jenna off guard. When he said, 'through it all,' she wondered what he meant. The funeral arrangements, or *all* meaning afterwards. She took a moment to consider her response and answered on the assumption that he referred to the funeral arrangements only.

"Of course. I'll be here for the funeral. I wouldn't be anyplace else. I'll help you with ALL the funeral arrangements as best I can."

Josh's eyes flickered. "Just the funeral arrangements? What about the rest? You said it doesn't end after the funeral."

She needed to say something before he expected the impossible.

"Josh," she whispered his name. "The rest is up to you. I live eight hundred kilometres away. I'm not sure how long I can even stay. I've asked Rachel for a few days off, so I'll stay until the funeral, but then most likely will leave right after."

His eyes pleaded with her. "But I can't do this without you," he said again.

He'd pushed her away, and now he needed her to fix his life. How was that fair? It overwhelmed her. She shook her head; now wasn't the time or place for that. He needed her because his dad's death broke him. His hands were on the table, crossed, rolling his thumbs; that meant he was in deep pain. In all the years they'd known each other, Jenna had never seen Josh this broken.

"I can still be there for support, just not here physically. You can call me anytime."

He looked at her empty hands. "Are you not drinking anything?" he asked.

"No, I'm good. I've had enough coffee today," she lied.

He reached out, then took her hand in his. "I'm sorry about—"

"Josh, don't. I don't need an apology from you. This is not about us. This is about your dad."

She pulled her hand out from under his and she reached into her bag and pulled out the information sheet the funeral director had given her. "This is what I need from you."

An hour later they'd gone through the list, and Jenna had made notes on the wishes for the funeral. Exhaustion crept in, and Jenna yawned several times. She tried to cover it up, but failed. Josh asked why she was so tired so early in the day and she lied and said it was because she was up late working.

When they got back to the funeral home, Jenna told Josh to wait while she dealt with the funeral home director. When she returned, he stood beside the car, hands in his pockets.

"Jenna, I can't thank you enough for doing that. This place makes me not able to think straight. Every time that guy asked a question, I heard nothing but chatter. I couldn't even make out what he was saying."

"It's done now. All taken care of."

"Are you hungry? You must be. It's past suppertime."

Jenna was starving and her stomach growled as he mentioned food, but she couldn't eat, or it would end badly.

"Not really," she said, hoping Josh couldn't hear the noise coming from inside her stomach. "Cassie and I ate before she dropped me off."

There was noticeable disappointment in his eyes.

"Jenna," he said her name softly, then kicked a nearby rock, "do you want to come back to our apartment and stay there? It's totally fine with me."

"*Our* apartment?" she repeated. "It hasn't been *our* apartment for months," she reminded him.

"Technically, it is. Your name is still on the lease," he said. Then added, "Of course, I'll sleep on the couch... if that's what you prefer."

"I'm staying with Cassie."

There was that same disappointed look on his face.

"Jenna," he said, and reached out his arm to stroke her hair.

She took a step back. "Josh, don't. Please take me to Cassie's."

He lowered his arm. "Okay, no problem." With his head hung, he swung around to the driver's side and got in the car without saying another word. Jenna remained frozen, unable to move, but eventually got in the car and neither spoke all the way to Cassie's.

CHAPTER 28

Long-Winded Love Confession

*J*ENNA'S PHONE HAD been on silent since she first got to the funeral home, and so she hadn't heard the many message notifications, but when she checked she saw Liam had called twice and left a voicemail. It was the first time he'd called in weeks. Pressing play on the voicemail, Jenna braced herself to hear his voice. He'd left the message in English, his normal way of communicating with her. That bout in French at the restaurant had only been because he was angry.

"Hey Jenna, I am sorry I have not been in touch since I walked out on you that night. Believe me when I say I have wanted to call, but I needed time to process what you told me. I needed space to think about the news, and you, and the time away did me a world of good. But just because I have not called does not mean that I have not thought of you. You are all I think about. Every time a woman with your hair colour and length walks by, I hold my breath and hope she is you. When my phone rings, I wish for it to be your contact on the screen, even though when you have called, I didn't answer. When someone walks into the store, I long for you to appear at the door. Right after the night we spent together, I realized I was in love with you. I want to make things right between us. I enjoy having you in my life and now that you have been in it, I want it to stay that way. I understand why you did not tell me sooner, and I am okay with it. Truly, I am. Just call me back Jenna, so we can talk, please. I am sorry it took me this long to call. I won't make that mistake again."

Jenna had put the phone on speaker, so Cassie was standing beside her and heard Liam's long-winded love confession. Cassie raised her eyebrows, waiting for Jenna to say something.

"Don't look at me like that," said Jenna.

"Like what, exactly?"

"You know what I'm talking about."

Cassie shook her head. "He loves you!"

"Yeah, so he said."

Cassie stood with her arms crossed. "Well? I need details. You can't just let me hear that voicemail and then not tell me more."

"First, I didn't let you hear the voicemail. You were snooping. Second, I have no further details."

"Argg, you're so cryptic, girl."

"I'm not being cryptic. I just need time to process this."

"Did you make a doctor's appointment?"

"Yes, tomorrow morning at ten."

"Okay. I won't be able to get off work, but if you drive me, you're welcome to keep the car."

"Thanks, Cas. That'll be great."

"Maybe by then, you'll be able to tell me more about Liam."

"You never give up."

"Nope!"

❦

Later at night, Jenna stopped at her parents' house for a quick visit since she was in the city, and they tried to force her to eat, but she couldn't. She didn't want to stay long and, when she announced after a brief visit she was heading out, they stood before her, arms crossed. They said Kris and Xavier were on their way to see her and that it would be rude of her to leave so, out of guilt, she stayed. They must have called Kris the minute she had arrived.

Her brother and Xavier arrived fifteen minutes later, and they all sat and had tea, except Jenna didn't touch hers. She pretended to sip on it and dumped the liquid down the sink when no one was looking. They already knew about Billy's passing, having read Jenna's texts earlier, so when they said their goodbyes, her parents told her they'd see her at the funeral.

When Jenna got back to Cassie's, she tried to eat plain toast and tea. It was the first thing she'd eaten all day. She kept one piece of toast and half a cup of green tea down and felt a sense of relief, thinking maybe the worst was over.

"So, what's new with you these days, Cas?" Jenna asked, as they sat on the couch together. "You haven't mentioned the corky guy anymore. Is there a different guy I don't know about? Someone you're keeping from me? Is that why you hardly call anymore?"

"I call you all the time."

"Not as much as I call you, but nobody's counting."

"Remember that guy who called when we were at the airport?"

"Yes, I remember. You missed his call then and said you weren't too sure about him because he was corky. Is he The One?"

"Nope, but turns out he has a cute cousin."

Jenna chuckled. "Of course he does."

They spent the rest of the night watching romantic comedies on Netflix. Cassie with her big bowl of Smartfood popcorn and Diet Coke and Jenna with her plain, unsalted soda crackers and ginger-lemon water. When Jenna called it a night, Cassie got up and turned off the lights and retired to her room, so Jenna checked her phone again. Still no message from Rachel. Forcing the thought of Rachel out of her mind, Jenna placed the phone under her ear and laid on the couch, pressed play on the voicemail Liam left earlier, and by the time the message was over, her eyelids grew heavy, and she fell asleep. She awakened partway through the night, covered in a blanket and with a pillow under her head. Cassie always looked out for her. The phone she had fallen asleep with was on the coffee table and no longer glued to her ear. Jenna reached for it and pressed play on the same voicemail one more time before dozing off again for the rest of the night.

∽

At the doctor's office the next morning, she sat in the waiting room, munching on soda crackers again. They seemed to help a little, and she was glad Cassie packed them. Jenna hadn't thrown up since yesterday, so that was a good sign. When it was her turn to see the doctor, he took her blood pressure, and asked her many questions. She answered as honestly as she could remember. He handed her a slip of paper and told her to go next door for bloodwork.

"How long before the results come in?"

"We should know by tomorrow. My secretary will call you."

Before Jenna left, she told him that if the test was positive, she'd need an obstetrician in Quebec City.

"You can discuss that with my secretary once we know."

Jenna thanked him and left. As soon as she was outside, she called Josh to check on him. She'd expected he'd have called her by then. While she was on the phone with Josh, Liam called on the other line; she stared at his name for a moment while Josh spoke and she considered putting him on hold to answer it, but at the last minute, let Liam's call go to voicemail. When she finished with Josh, she checked her voicemail—there were no messages and she tried to hide the disappointment. She didn't want to call Liam back when there was so much going on. She wanted to wait so she could give him her full attention.

She drove to Billy's house to meet Josh and finish the last-minute preparations, and to pick out an outfit for Billy to wear for the viewing. Josh said he couldn't do it alone and needed her. By the time they finished, she rushed to pick up Cassie from work and when they got back to her apartment, all Jenna could do was take off her shoes before she fell onto the couch and dozed off thinking about tomorrow; it would be a hard day to get through having to say a final goodbye to Billy.

CHAPTER 29

The Surrounding Trees Spun Out of Control

THE FUNERAL HOME visitation would begin at nine a.m., followed by the burial service. Not wanting to be sick during the ceremony, Jenna skipped her morning coffee and only had dry crackers and lemon water. Cassie drove Jenna, despite her parents' offer to pick her up. She wanted to get there early enough to calm Josh should he need it, and so when she saw his name on her phone, it surprised her to hear from him an hour before she was due to be there.

"Are you on your way?" asked Josh.

"Yes, just leaving the apartment. Where are you?"

"I'm here. Just arrived. Can you hurry? I hate being here without you. I need you, Jenna."

"I'll be there by eight-twenty, the latest."

"Who was that?" asked Cassie, as they made their way to Cassie's car.

"It was Josh. He's already there and wondered where I was."

"Geez, he's sure clingy these days!"

"Cas, don't be like that."

"Like what?"

"He just lost his father, so cut him some slack. I'm a comfort for him, and that's why he's leaning on me. He's got no one else."

"What about his uncle, Billy's brother?"

"They're not that close."

"Hmmm. Convenient."

"What's that supposed to mean?" asked Jenna.

"Nothing, let's go."

Josh held up rather well during the visitation, considering. From the moment Jenna arrived, he clung to her hand and never let go, dragging her with him into the limousine that followed the hearse. On the way to the cemetery, Jenna took a moment to check her phone; a missed call from her doctor's office—her stomach fluttered. She didn't have time to call back until after the burial, but once it was over, she excused herself to get some privacy and called back.

"Ms. Taylor, I was about to call you again," said the receptionist, after Jenna announced herself.

"I saw you called earlier, but I was at a funeral."

"I'm sorry to hear that."

"Thank you. Do you have good news?"

"Yes. It's splendid news. Congratulations! Ms. Taylor, you're going to be a mother."

The surrounding trees spun out of control, and Jenna feared they would break free from their roots. The people gathered around the burial site spun with the trees in one big, jumbled mess, like the tornado in the scene in The Wizard of Oz. She reached for something to grab, but there was nothing. She looked toward the crowd for Cassie, but she was nowhere in sight. Jenna bent over, thinking she'd be sick, and held on to a tombstone to steady herself.

"Ms. Taylor, are you still there?"

"Yes, I'm here."

"The doctor instructed me to call in a prescription for you. It's Diclectin. Did the doctor talk to you about this?"

Jenna wasn't sure, but answered anyway, "I think so."

"It will help with morning sickness. He mentioned you'd been having a hard time keeping food down."

She was going to be a mother.

"Is the pharmacy you use still the same? The doctor mentioned you've moved out of the province."

She was going to be a mother.

"Here's the address I have on file." She read it as Jenna's mind continued to repeat the same words over and over and over.

She was going to be a mother.

Jenna didn't correct her about the pharmacy. She couldn't think straight enough to do so.

She was going to be a mother.

"All right. I'll call over that prescription for you pronto. I'm still looking into obstetricians in your city, so I'll call you with an update once I've found someone."

Jenna hung up without saying goodbye.

"Jenna, what's wrong?" said a familiar voice from behind her. Josh placed his hands on her shoulders, trying to comfort her, as if he wasn't the one who had buried his father.

"Just feeling a little lightheaded. I'll be fine."

"Have you eaten?"

"Not much."

"Come by the house for the reception for Dad. He'd want you there."

Knowing that Josh needed her, she said, "Okay, I'll ask Cassie to take me."

"I can take you."

"You have enough to worry about today."

"Jenna, seriously? Come with me, please?" He reached out his hand. She took it. "I'll bring you back to Cassie's place whenever you want to leave. No expectations. I promise."

Together, they walked hand in hand back to the crowd that was still gathered around the burial site. Off to the far side was Lainey, and Jenna felt a pang and then wondered why it bothered her to see that woman there. Cassie suddenly appeared from behind the crowd, and when Jenna's eyes locked with hers, she couldn't help but tell her everything with the look in her eyes.

⟢

The reception was bittersweet with many friends and extended family members of Josh's that Jenna hadn't seen in years. The house was full, so she didn't see Josh for a long time and assumed he was keeping busy with guests paying their respects. Jenna was still trying to process that she would be a mother. That hadn't sunk in yet, no matter how many times she said the words. She was standing alone at the kitchen sink, rinsing a glass as she contemplated her life when he found her.

"Hey, there you are," said Josh, turning up at the doorway. "Do you want to take a walk with me? I need to get out of here for a bit. I could use some company."

She set the glass down. "Sure."

They walked for a few minutes before Josh spoke. "I can't thank you enough for being here these last two days. It means a lot, and I know Dad would have appreciated it, too. He loved you like a daughter."

Jenna wasn't sure what came over her. Was it the baby, Liam's voice-mail, or the funeral? But she blurted out the question that she expected wouldn't leave her lips for a long time.

"Josh, I need to ask you something important."

"Sure, what is it?"

"Did Billy ever talk to you about your past, possibly another family?"

Josh stopped walking and looked at her straight on. "What other family? Like whom, exactly? You know my entire family. And what part of my past are you asking about? You know everything I do."

And much more, she thought. "Your birth?"

He chuckled, then said, "Well, I'm not sure he ever talked about it. I mean, what's there to say, unless something unordinary happened when I was born, I don't think he'd ever have a reason to bring it up. Why? And what do these questions have to do with my father's funeral?"

"It doesn't. Not with the funeral anyway."

"Jenna, you're acting strange. What do you want to ask me? Whatever it is, just ask."

"I've already asked it."

"But your question made no sense. There's more to it. What is it?"

"It's not a question really, it's more of..."

"What? Why are you being evasive?"

They'd reached a bench in a small park. "Josh sit. I have something I need to tell you."

Jenna didn't want to bring it up. She had planned to wait but couldn't keep it in any longer; it was killing her to keep that tremendous secret about his life.

"Jenna, you're scaring me."

"Josh, I discovered something. Something big. I found out by accident, of course. I didn't go poking around for no reason. It sort of found me, in a way. And once I became suspicious, I had to find out the truth, and I did."

"Truth about what? Please just say it."

"Josh, I found out the night you were born that your mother also gave birth to another child. You have a twin brother. His name is Liam."

Josh let out a chuckle. "Jenna, have you been drinking? I'm the one who should get drunk today, not you."

"NO! I have had nothing to drink in days except for lemon water and green tea. I'm serious."

He shook his head. "Why?"

"*Why* what?"

"Why are you trying to hurt me? I don't get you, Jenna. I've just buried my father, and you spring on me this nonsense about my parents having had another child? That... I have a brother, a twin? Did they decide two babies were too much, and they'd just keep one, and what? They flipped a coin, and I was the lucky one they kept?" He shook his head more. "Do you realize how absurd you sound?"

"No, that's not what happened, not exactly."

"Would you stop speaking in riddles? What, then? What's with the nonsense about a twin brother?"

That was her chance to say she was sorry, didn't know what got into her, or that she'd had too much to drink, but she said: "You were both given up for adoption."

The world went still when the words left her lips. She wished she could take them back as she bent forward and vomited.

CHAPTER 30

It Had to Be a Lie

SHE'D LOST HER mind. There was no other explanation. Josh concluded she'd gone crazy, and it was stress causing her to say such ridiculous things and vomit. He watched Jenna hunched over, getting sick, and as much as he wanted to help, he didn't want to be around her at the moment. How dare she ruin his beloved father's legacy by speaking about something that was so untrue—preposterous!

"How dare you say such words? How dare you shatter the image that I have of him this way? I never thought you had it in you to be so cruel. My father loved you like a daughter, and you repay him on his funeral day by saying something so outrageously untrue."

He walked away, leaving Jenna bent over, still vomiting. Where in the world had she gotten the idea, and why? He didn't understand. He walked briskly, hands in his pockets, trying to rationalize... what, exactly? The lie she'd told? Because it had to be a lie. His father would never lie to him about that. Somehow, deep down, Josh convinced himself of that and kept walking back to the house. If his parents had adopted him, his dad would have told him when he was little. There would have been conversation after conversation to ensure Josh was okay and understood. His dad would have explained it all to him years ago—included that in the life lessons. His dad would never have kept that from him; he was too honest, too kind, and would have wanted Josh to know the truth. So why was Jenna trying to hurt him?

CHAPTER 31

Curveballs

HUNCHED OVER, JENNA watched Josh walk away and tried to call out to him. But every time she took a breath, another wave of nausea hit. If only Cassie were there. She wanted to reach out to her and even pulled out her phone, but didn't call. She couldn't leave things with Josh that way. No. He needed to understand the truth—how that came to be. The information she'd collected would surely allow him to believe her. But she had brought none of it to show him; she hadn't expected to tell him. It must be the pregnancy that had gotten to her.

She tried to compose herself and walked back to the house. Some guests had left, and the only ones that remained were family: Billy's brother, his brother's wife, their grown children from out east, and of course Lainey was still there. What the hell was she doing there amongst family? Lainey adjusted her dress and walked up to Jenna, but Jenna pretended she didn't notice her and picked at a serving dish layered with cheese and crackers.

"Jenna?" said Lainey, holding out her hand.

"I know who you are," said Jenna, ignoring Lainey's hand.

"Oh, is that so? I don't think we've ever met before."

"Yes, we have. At the Christmas parties for the past five years. You were always the one with your eyes and hands all over my fiancé."

"Ex-fiancé," Lainey corrected, a little too quickly.

Jenna's eyes flickered at how fast Lainey had added that jab. "He is my ex now, yes, but I was referring to past tense. He was my fiancé when you tried to hit on him."

"No need to bring up the past. Let's just leave that where it belongs, okay? Besides, I wasn't hitting on him."

"Do you want something?" asked Jenna, with irritation in her voice.

"I have a message from your ex. He's out clearing his head and doesn't want to see you anymore today, so you better leave." She stood in front of Jenna, arms crossed, her weight shifted onto one hip. At that same moment, Josh walked through the front door and headed down the hall, his head hung and hands still in his pockets.

Jenna said, "Excuse me," and pushed past Lainey.

"Where do you think you're going?" Lainey yelled from behind Jenna.

"That's none of your business."

Jenna ran, eager to get away from Lainey and desperate to find Josh. He was in Billy's room, sitting on the bed with his face in his hands. Watching him from the open door for a few minutes, Jenna realized what she'd done—what she'd ripped from him. She shouldn't have blurted it out the way she did, and she wished she could take it back, but she couldn't. She needed to learn how to control her big mouth.

She knocked once. He didn't stir or even look up. She knocked again—nothing. She knocked a third time and said, "Hey, it's me. Can I come in?" She waited for an invitation, but when one didn't come, she begged, "Please, Josh, we need to talk."

"No offence, Jenna, but you're the last person I want to see. I have nothing to say to you and you have nothing I want to hear."

"I got the message from Lainey. I get you don't want to see me, but..."

"What does Lainey have to do with this?"

"You called her with a message for me, well she told me."

"Get your facts straight again. She called *me,* asked where I was, and I told her I needed time away from you. Because it was the truth."

Jenna took a few steps into the room. "Josh, I think you want to hear what I have to say, but you're in denial, and I get that. What I threw at you is a lot to take in. It's huge, but it's the truth. I didn't mean for you to find out like this. I was being overly emotional with the... because of the day." Jenna had almost said 'with the pregnancy,' but stopped herself in time. "I'm sorry about how and when I told you, but I'm not sorry that I did; because you deserve to know the truth."

He pulled his hands away from his face. "Do you even realize what you're saying? You're telling me the man I just lost, the man who's been my anchor, my life, my mentor, the man I've called Dad since I can remember, is not my biological father?"

"I know, Josh."

He stood and took a few steps from the bed. "No, you don't. Did you ever think for a minute that perhaps I wouldn't want to know? Did you think of me at all?"

"What kind of question is that? Of course, I thought about you. You're the one I thought about throughout all this."

"Doesn't seem that way to me. I bet you've discovered some big story that you'll print in your precious magazine soon—that's it right, a major story? Is my biological mother some famous actress worth writing about? Is she? Is that why you're doing this? Do you need me to know the truth before the article gets printed, so I'm not blindsided? Is that it? Answer me, damn it!"

Tears welled in Jenna's eyes. She never expected him to be so cruel. She never expected that reaction; sadness, confusion, loss, were what she'd planned for, but not anger.

Josh placed his hands over his face again. "Can you leave? I can't do this. Maybe someday I'll be ready to discuss it, to learn the truth, but not now. I need you to leave. Go back to your life in Quebec City. Go back to your new friends, your stories, and whatever else you've been doing. Just leave me alone."

"Josh, please," she begged.

He lifted his hand to silence her. "If I'm ever ready to talk about this, I'll contact you. But, if this will hit the news or magazine, please give me a heads up before it goes public. That's all I ask. Now leave, please."

"It's never going to print; it was never about a story. It was about discovering the truth for you."

"That changes nothing. Leave."

As she walked out of Billy's bedroom, determined to leave as fast as she could, she remembered she had no car. While she waited outside for the Uber, from the large front window she saw Lainey walking into Billy's bedroom, surely going to comfort Josh.

While Jenna waited, she pushed back tears and googled pharmacies near her in Quebec City, then placed a call to the doctor's office and requested they send further prescriptions to her new pharmacy. She didn't plan on staying in Toronto long enough to need the one here anymore. It was time she got her life together, and changing pharmacies and being seen for an examination was the first step. It was time to move forward and figure out what she was going to do. Life had a way of throwing curveballs, and unless you caught them, you'd get hit hard. That couldn't be her—she wouldn't allow it.

When she got off the phone with the doctor's office, she booked her flight. She'd leave the next day. Satisfied with the decisions she made; she checked her work emails. There was finally a response from Rachel.

Jennalyn,

Effective immediately, you are under suspension without pay for failing to do your job. This is a written notice that is officially being put in your file. Human Resources will contact you with the details of the suspension.

Rachel.

Suspension? For how long? How could Rachel suspend her for

taking a few days to attend a funeral? Great. That was the last thing she needed.

Later that evening, Jenna leaned on Cassie and sobbed over all that had happened until her phone rang.

Startled to see the magazine's number on her phone, she picked up right away. "I'm going to take this outside," she said to Cassie and waved as she walked out into the hallway.

Moments later, Jenna was back in the apartment.

"Is everything okay?" asked Cassie when Jenna returned, surely even more bright-nosed, with blotchy eyes.

"No, it's not. Rachel fired me."

Cassie's eyes enlarged. "Oh, shit. I'll get the vodka," she said. Then added, "Oh wait, that won't help you, but it'll help me help you. So, it's still needed. Wait here." She ran off.

When she returned from the kitchen, she was holding a bottle of vodka and a glass of lemon water and handed the water to Jenna.

"Girl, you've gotten yourself into quite a pickle these days." She took a long swig of the vodka straight from the bottle. Jenna stared, wishing she could be more carefree like Cassie.

CHAPTER 32

Never Let Fear Stand in the Way of What You Need or Want to Do

JOSH WOKE UP in a sweat. He had dreamt of one of his dad's life lessons.

❧

They were driving to Josh's soccer practice and while stuck in traffic, they watched on the side of the road as a fairly large bird picked away at its prey. The prey looked like a fish from Lake Ontario. It was a rather large fish, and the bird ate from its centre. Then a bald eagle swooped in and brought the smaller, lone bird, competition by flying in from behind. But before the eagle landed, the smaller bird grabbed half the fish and flew away, leaving the other half of the carcass.

Little Josh, perplexed by this, asked his father: "Daddy, why did he only take half?" Little Josh hadn't realized that the fish wasn't whole the entire time he watched the bird pick at it.

His dad smiled, welcoming the question as he prepared his answer. "Well, son, that's a good question. The smaller bird knew that while he was bigger than the fish, the fish was still large, and he wouldn't be able to carry it whole, so the entire time we've been sitting in traffic, the bird formed a plan."

It hadn't looked that way for little Josh at all. It had only appeared to be a bird picking at a fish, but he asked more questions anyway, curious.

"What kind of plan, Daddy?"

"Well, son, the bird split the fish in two."

"Why, Daddy?"

"Because he knew he couldn't easily carry the whole fish. So, if another predator came along—which inevitably one did as we just witnessed—he'd be prepared to take half and flee rather than stay and fight."

Still confused, little Josh asked, "Instead of splitting it in two, why didn't he just eat until he was full? He'd surely have been able to fill his belly in the time we'd watched him. That way he wouldn't have had to carry anything." Little Josh thought he was being smart.

"Yes, that would have been one way, but think about it logically, son. He'd have to forage for his food again later. This way he can take it back with him and eat a little at a time. Make it last. With this plan, the bird has secured himself not only supper, but also tomorrow's breakfast and lunch. Son, in life we must plan for all possibilities, and this means not just right now, but also the future. We must think ahead. If you always have a plan, then life will seldom surprise you. If the bird had no plan, the eagle that swooped in would have likely caused the smaller bird to lose it all."

Little Josh didn't understand, so he changed the subject. "Daddy, how much longer until we get to soccer? I have to pee."

His dad smirked. "That's because you didn't plan and go before we left the house as I told you to, son."

❧

The next few days passed like a blur, despite Josh not working, yet he remained busy. He had taken a few days off from the firm to deal with life. The other lawyers offered to cover his workload to allow him time to cope and heal. But it wasn't working, as he did little healing, although his father's affairs kept him busy enough, and he also knew the time off would do him good. He struggled with basic things, and that was unlike him. There was so much to do; decisions to make, plans to put together, and he couldn't do any of them right. Every choice he made left him feeling as if it was wrong only minutes after having made it. Each plan he formed revealed a big flaw. He was much better at being productive at work than getting his life in order.

As hard as he tried, he couldn't get Jenna off his mind. What she'd said rang in his ears, day and night, plaguing him like a terrible storm. What upset him most was that Jenna was great at her job and never got things wrong. She was the reporter that, when set out to search for a story's details, went all out and stopped at nothing. She was accurate, thorough, and because she broke the news to him already, must be one-hundred-and-ten percent, without-a-doubt, sure about what she'd discovered. Jenna never got facts mixed up, so what she said must be true.

Josh hadn't yet allowed himself to think about the deeper questions circling in his mind: Who were his biological parents? Why did they give him up? Who was his twin brother? And the most painful: why didn't his dad tell him?

The phone rang, interrupting his thoughts. It was the name of a law firm, one Josh recognized. Upon answering, he learned his father had hired a lawyer to contact him after he passed. It stunned Josh that his dad would hire a lawyer, since he was one. That couldn't be good. The lawyer advised Josh that his dad had left him something that he needed to pick up personally. Josh checked the time and learned they were still open, so he headed out to get the mystery package.

At the lawyer's office, Josh sat waiting to be called in, his mind preoccupied.

"Mr. Harrison, please sit. I know this must be difficult. My condolences to you," said the lawyer after introducing himself.

"Thank you, but can you tell me what this is about? You know I'm a lawyer?" asked Josh. "Why would my dad hire you when he had me?"

"Yes, your father told me. I met him only recently. However, he didn't want you to know about me until after he died. He left this letter with specific instructions for you to pick it up personally. I just need you to sign here to acknowledge that you have picked it up and you can be on your way."

"A letter? Why wouldn't he have left it with my Uncle Mike?"

"I can only assume that he didn't want the letter getting lost or opened by someone other than you."

Reluctantly, Josh took the letter, gripped it tight, and walked out. He took a deep breath before he read it.

Dear Josh,

By the time you read this, I'll have passed, but will still be with you in spirit. I'll always look out for you, always love you. You were my pride and joy for all my life. You brought me more happiness than anything else in this entire world. I'm so proud of the man you have become and of what you've been able to accomplish in only twenty-eight years. I can't imagine what you'll do in the next twenty—surely many more great things and I'll still be your biggest cheerleader.

You're probably wondering why I hired another lawyer to give you this letter and you're most likely confused about why I'm even writing. I didn't want to leave this world not telling you the truth. I considered leaving this letter with your Uncle Mike, but I worried he'd forget. He doesn't have the best track record, as you know. He didn't take after me that way. A lawyer was the most reliable way. I needed to know that once you lost me, you'd learn what you should have learned when you were little, but I was too cowardly to tell you—too scared. I'm so sorry, my son, but know that I tried many times over the years, especially as of late. The longer I waited, the harder it was to bring up. Then when I got sick, there were a few times I tried Remember that day at my house when you got that call from your office and had to leave? I was going to tell you that day. Had you not rushed out, I would have. A cancer diagnosis gave me the determination to tell you, but I got so sick and so quickly, that I didn't have the energy or strength left to do it in person; hence, this letter. Son, please sit before you read further. The next few words will hurt like crazy.

My dearest son, your mother and I adopted you as a baby.

When you were born, your biological mother died giving birth to you and your twin brother. Another family adopted your twin, and your mother and I took you in as a foster child when you were only weeks old. You were premature and had to be incubated for a few weeks, and that's the only reason why it took weeks and not days. One look at you and we longed to bring you home. After holding you in my arms for the first time, I knew I could never let you go again, and we applied for adoption right away. It took two years, but you were eventually legally ours, forever. Your mother and I loved you so deeply and so strongly that we couldn't have had a bigger heart towards you had you been born from your mother's womb.

God meant for us to be a family from day one. I'm sure it was always His plan. When I lost your mother even though you were little, you were the one that gave me life. You were the one that gave me the strength to live. Losing your mother ripped me apart, but you mended me back together. If you had not been in my life, my son, I don't know what would have happened to me after I lost her. I did not give you your life, but you sure gave life to me. You were my gift, my guardian angel, and now I'll be yours.

I don't, unfortunately, know any details that I can share about your birth parents or even your twin brother. But I have enclosed the adoption records, and it contains the name of the adoption agency. Perhaps, if you are curious, you can contact them and it will aid as a start in your search. I'm sorry that I have no more information to offer.

As I write this letter, I can feel myself weakening and so I must end it now. It's taken all I have to get this written. But it was important to me to leave this world knowing you'd have the truth.

You must believe me when I tell you this, my son. And you are my son. I've loved you and always will love you more than life itself. The only thing I ask of you is forgiveness for not telling you sooner. I hope you can understand how fear kept me from telling you. Please remember all the life lessons from over the years and have this be the biggest one.

<u>Never let fear stand in the way of what you need or want to do.</u>

I leave you now with much regret and one last request for forgiveness.

Love always and forever, Dad

Josh wiped a tear, and then carefully folded the letter and put it in his pocket.

PART FIVE

Three Months Later

CHAPTER 33

The Knowledge Freed Him

THREE MONTHS WAS long for Josh, but when it measured the time since burying his father, it didn't feel like much at all. In some aspects of his life, Josh had done well in the past three months: He'd won every case, dealt with his dad's finances, and donated most of the furniture to the cancer association, but he had done nothing with the information that Jenna had sprung on him. That morning, however, there was a nagging feeling inside him and so he called his Uncle Mike. Uncle Mike agreed to meet Josh for lunch, and so they met at a restaurant down the street from the firm. He didn't tell his uncle over the phone why he'd asked to meet, and Josh assumed Uncle Mike thought he'd want to discuss his dad. Which, in part, was true, but Josh also had another agenda. He wanted answers, and not from Jenna. It had been too long since he and Jenna had spoken, and he wasn't comfortable talking to her yet, especially after how he'd left things.

He left his car at the firm and walked down the street to meet his uncle, phone glued to his ear as he talked to a client about an upcoming hearing. As he walked through the busy streets, he passed many homeless people laying helpless on the sides of the road, tucked tight up against buildings, but he never stopped or even looked at them—too preoccupied with his own devastation to notice the homeless people's turmoil.

Josh and his uncle spent the next hour together. Josh sipped on peppermint tea and Uncle Mike went through coffee like it was water. After Uncle Mike's third cup and Josh's first, Josh finally found the courage to bring up what was on his mind.

"Uncle Mike," he began, and then clenched his hand around the empty mug for something to do. "Do you know who my biological parents were?"

Uncle Mike had taken a sip of coffee and choked on the hot liquid. He took a moment to regain his composure and cleared his throat a few times to find his voice.

"Josh, I didn't know your dad told you. He didn't tell me you knew."

"He didn't tell me personally. He left me a letter. But I already knew."

At Josh's response, Uncle Mike's eyebrows knit together. "From whom? Who told you? Few people knew, and your parents swore them to secrecy twenty-eight years ago." Uncle Mike looked directly into Josh's eyes. "Who on this Earth told you?"

"Jenna."

"Jenna? How did she know? Your dad wouldn't have told her before telling you, unless he was afraid to confront you himself and asked Jenna to…"

"No, that's not it. He didn't tell anyone. Jenna discovered it by accident, somehow, although I'm not sure how."

"What do you mean?"

"I didn't let her explain. I told her to leave the day of the funeral and I haven't talked to her since."

"You've known the truth for three months and have kept it to yourself? Aren't you curious to know more?"

"Yeah, I am. That's why we're sitting here."

Uncle Mike blew out a breath. "Tell me about the letter?"

"Here, you can read it."

After his uncle read the letter, he folded it back up. "That was so long ago. I never thought I'd have to think through the fine details so many years later. I know nothing. Your parents discussed little with me. I don't know who your biological parents were. I believed Billy when he said they didn't know, either. They mentioned the adoption was to be a secret and that your new life would be the only life you knew," said Uncle Mike.

"Why did they even consider adoption in the first place? Why didn't they have a child of their own? Weren't they able?"

"Your parents had so much love and wanted to share it with a child who needed it. They'd often said they wanted to adopt a baby, and possibly have one of their own later."

"Jenna had mentioned the twin, somehow even she knew about that."

"Well then, it sounds like you know what you need to do. If Jenna knows as much as she does, she's the one you should get your questions answered by, not me."

Of course, Jenna had been accurate about everything. Josh realized if he wanted to know the truth, all he needed to do was talk to her. He'd been avoiding her purposely. Seeing her before the funeral was emotional, a reminder of what he had and lost, or rather pushed away. Until she dumped the news on him, he'd had thoughts of wanting to spend more time with her, wanting her in his life—wanting her back. Josh feared that if he called her now, those feelings would resurface. He'd even wondered before the funeral if possibly a long-distance relationship would work. She could stay in Quebec City until she completed the contract, and see him every other weekend—it could work. Many people had long-distance relationships and were happy. Besides, that job assignment was only temporary. She'd been away eight months. Her term was for six to twelve, she had said, so it must be close to the end, if not already.

After all the internal banter, he shook his head. What the hell was he thinking? It was clear he was thinking he still loved her, but hadn't been able to admit that. He should never have let her go. He wanted her back—fiercely. When he finally admitted that, the knowledge freed him.

Once Josh and his uncle parted ways, he decided he wasn't waiting any longer; he needed Jenna in more ways than one, and hastily booked a flight to Quebec City. Realizing she might not even be there anymore, he called her office to be sure. When the receptionist answered, Josh introduced himself as a family friend looking to surprise her in Quebec City and asked for her address. The voice on the other end said that Jenna no longer worked for *Brandy Thyme Magazine*; Josh flinched and gripped the phone tighter.

"Are you sure? The magazine transferred her at the beginning of the year. Please double-check."

"Yes sir, but that has changed."

"How long ago did it change?"

"It's been three months, sir. But the last address we have on file from her termination record is still Quebec City."

Josh hung up and called Cassie; it went to voicemail. He didn't bother leaving a message and instead headed home to pack—his flight was early in the morning at seven. He was going to make things right, and support her with whatever resulted in her not working for the magazine—he was getting his girl back.

CHAPTER 34

Ready to Learn the Truth

IN WHAT FELT like merely overnight, Jenna's stomach bulged. For the first few months, she was as flat as a surfboard, but when she hit four months, the changes became noticeable. She could no longer hide her bump, and her tight jeans no longer fit. She became frustrated, and tired constantly. Then at five months she gave up trying to button her pants and went maternity clothes shopping.

The last few months had been no easy feat, especially since she was also in the middle of a court battle over a wrongful dismissal case with the magazine.

Seul jumped up onto the couch and laid on her growing bump; she liked the comforting feeling of the baby moving beneath her fur, and purred louder in rhythm with the kicks. Jenna was still trying to get used to the unfamiliar sensation of the fluttery movement, called quickening. It caught her by surprise most days, and when that happened, it brought her back to the realization that she was going to be a mother.

She laid her hand over Seul and gave the court case consideration. The worst thing about it was that she needed a lawyer, and she knew a good one. Junior still, but effective and productive, but she couldn't call him, so she had hired another, bilingual, Toronto lawyer instead.

She still lived in the same apartment. The magazine had paid the lease for the year, and as part of her dismissal package, they agreed to allow her to stay until it was over. She'd been there for eight months already.

The medication she was on for morning sickness finally helped, now that she was over the first trimester, and she had kept busy these last months doing freelance jobs for the local paper. She made more money as a freelancer and could set her hours, but the real bonus was not having to deal with Rachel.

Life hadn't thrown her too many lemons lately, except she missed Liam. She hadn't seen or spoken to him since he called and left that voicemail message while she was in Toronto for the funeral—three months ago. She wanted to call him back, but never did because she was distracted by how things had ended with Josh. After she'd gotten back home from that trip, she'd kept thinking he'd call again, but then a week passed, two, three, and after a month Liam hadn't called again, so she concluded he'd given up on her. She could have called still, but the situation with Josh devastated her and by the time she got over that enough to think of other things, she worried it would upset Liam that she hadn't told him about the baby sooner. She couldn't imagine how to tell him when she was five months pregnant and had kept it a secret for so long. The longer she waited to tell him, the harder it became.

That caused her to stay up, tossing and turning in bed most nights. She wanted to tell Liam about the baby, but the fear prevented her from following through. She constantly thought about Josh, too, and the secret that was kept from him all his life; she didn't want that for her child. She'd witnessed the devastation and pain when Josh discovered Billy wasn't his father, so one afternoon, after not being able to concentrate on work, she texted Liam—it was safer than calling.

Jenna: Hey, it's Jenna here (in case you deleted my contact, and I wouldn't blame you if you did) I know I'm the last person you expected to hear from, but I have a favour to ask you. Can you meet me this afternoon for tea? It's important or I wouldn't ask. And I'm sorry I've been absent for the last while.

His reply came back almost immediately.

Liam: Hey you! So nice to hear from you. I have not deleted you (yet) ☺

Jenna: I'm glad to hear that. Although, I'm not sure I deserve your kindness after not calling you back.

Liam: Your silence told me that you didn't want to hear from me anymore, so I stopped pestering you. When I didn't hear from you after that long voicemail where I confessed my love, I figured I was in way over my head and that you were not interested.

Jenna: I was rude and a coward. I wanted to call you; I did. But things got complicated real fast.

Liam: I would love to see you. Name the time and place.

Guilt. That's what she felt. Of course, he'd made it easy for her. That was the sort of person he was—selfless and kind—and Jenna knew she didn't deserve him.

She assumed he thought she wanted to meet to discuss his past and to tell him about his biological family. That he agreed to meet her must mean he was ready to learn the truth about himself.

Jenna: Great. How about three this afternoon? Our usual spot?

She wanted to get it over with because next week was the hearing in Toronto and she had many meetings between now and then.

Liam: See you then!

Jenna checked the time, eleven in the morning, so she had four hours to fill and regretted not suggesting noon instead.

❦

To her surprise, Josh had been trying to reach her for the last two days. His last text had said he had questions about his biological family and was ready to know more. He said he had needed time to process it all but was ready to talk. After several texts and missed calls from Josh, she called him back but got voicemail and she left a message that she would explain everything. She only wished they could have the dreaded conversation in person rather than over the phone. He didn't call back right away, and Jenna suspected he was busy at work and most likely in court. So, instead, she put Josh out of her mind, getting ready to have Liam see her growing belly.

CHAPTER 35

Long-Awaited Apology

WHEN JENNA ARRIVED, Liam was already sitting with a peppermint tea in hand. He looked up, and his eyes brightened when she smiled softly, then she watched his eyes shift downwards toward her midsection and remained locked there for a moment as Jenna stood frozen at the front door. She centred herself with reminders to breathe and hesitantly made her way to him; her hand placed over her belly protectively. Liam stood, pushing the chair behind him with much force, and approached her, arms flailing.

"How long?" He pointed to her stomach.

She took a deep breath. "I'm five months."

"So... it is..." he shook his head. "Is it mine?" he asked.

"Yes."

"Are you sure?"

"You're the only one I've been with since Josh."

"Five months?" he repeated and shook his head again.

"Yes. I'm sorry…"

He ran his hands through his hair, then gestured for her to sit at the table he was saving and asked what she wanted to drink. He ordered at the counter as Jenna waited at the table for him to return. When he returned with a green tea for her, she continued with her long-awaited apology.

"Liam, I'm sorry I didn't tell you sooner."

"Why didn't you?"

"I… I don't know."

"I have been right here. I called and left you a long voicemail. I told you I loved you. You did not call me back. At first, I convinced myself you did not get it."

"I did and I've listened to it several times."

"Then why did you not return my calls? Why keep me from this? After a while, I stopped calling because I figured you did not want to be around me."

"When I first found out, I was in shock. I wasn't sure what to do."

"About us?"

"That, and other things."

"What else is there?"

"I lost my job at the same time. And there's Josh."

He stiffened. "What about him? I thought that was over?"

"It is. But finding out I was pregnant meant it was also final. We'd never get back together."

Jenna noticed Liam's eye flinch when she said that.

"I didn't realize that was something you wanted still. I had hoped you had gotten over him."

"I was, sort of. Liam, it's complicated. I loved him a lot, and we were engaged. The way things ended between us always felt unfinished."

"Do you still love him?"

Jenna considered his question. "I still care for him deeply. I'm not sure that will ever go away. But I'm not in love with him anymore."

"I think I can work with that."

"I needed to figure out what I wanted, and if I was capable and strong enough to have this baby on my own, or if it was best to have you involved. But the more thought I gave it, the more your situation with Josh came to mind and I realized you have a right to know about the baby. My baby also has a right to know the father. So, that's why I asked you to meet me."

"You did not answer my question about whether you still love him, and I understand you're working on it, but I need to know one thing before we discuss anything else."

"I answered you. I said I'm not in love with him anymore."

"Being in love and loving are two different things. Do you want to get back together with Josh? If you weren't pregnant with my child and he showed up here, would you go to him?" he raised his eyebrows, waiting.

"No. Josh and I have a long history. You've always known that. I've been upfront about my feelings for him and where things stood. He's the reason I could never give myself completely to you... other than that one night. I've never stopped loving him, but it's a different type of love now. We'll never be together again, that I know in my heart. When his dad passed, I went to Toronto, and I told him about you, about the adoption."

"He knows?"

"He does now."

"How did he react?"

"He freaked out. He wanted nothing to do with me. I hadn't heard from him in three months, until the last two days, and I had hoped... I had thought, maybe..." Jenna wiped her nose with the sleeve of her shirt. "I'm so sorry. I'm such a mess."

Liam reached out and took her hand in his. Jenna looked down at their linked hands, surprised by the gesture.

"Jenna," he whispered.

"Yes?" she said in between sobs.

"Do you think he would meet me? I don't know why, but I have an urge to see him, talk to him. Maybe that is crazy, I do not know."

"Perhaps in the future, it might be possible, but right now, Josh is still trying to process that he even has another family, so I'm not sure. Although I got a message from him today that he wants to talk and has questions."

"Hopefully, it means he's ready to talk about his past and not you two," said Liam.

"I can say with certainty that he doesn't want to talk about us. It's over."

"What about my biological grandparents? You said you knew who they were?"

"Yes, I've met them."

"I'm not ready to know about them yet, but will you ask Josh if he'll meet me? Him, I want to meet, even if for the wrong reasons."

"What would the wrong reasons be?"

"Never mind."

Jenna suspected she knew what those reasons were but didn't acknowledge it. "Okay. When the time is right, I will ask. I promise. I just don't know if he ever will be ready, and I don't want you to get your hopes up. But after weeks of no contact, he has reached out, so I will let you know how that goes."

He rubbed his chin. "Jenna?"

"Yes?"

"It will be okay. I have a good feeling everything will all turn out."

"And the baby? You haven't told me how you feel about that? You're going to be a dad. That's not something to take lightly. That's huge, Liam, and if you're not ready to take that on, I understand and promise to be okay with whatever you decide. I can raise this baby on my own."

She looked at him for a reaction; he gazed into her eyes.

"Jenna?"

"Yes?"

"Veux-tu m'émpouser?" *Will you marry me?*

CHAPTER 36

Her Moment

JENNA FLINCHED; HAD she heard him correctly?

"I'm sorry, but what did you say?"

"I asked if you would marry me. We can be a family and raise this baby together. You do not have to do this alone anymore. I will be there for you and the baby."

"You're not thinking this through, Liam."

"I am. In time, your feelings for me will grow. You will learn to love me as you loved him once."

"Liam—"

"He is not here, but I am. It is my child you are carrying, not his. He left you, I did not. He didn't want to be a part of your life, but I do."

He squeezed her hand a little tighter, and Jenna hoped he didn't notice the clamminess accumulating.

"I know I will never be him and will always be your second choice, but I can be a good father and a good husband, too, if you let me."

Jenna's breathing quickened just as the baby kicked. She was so consumed with thoughts about what he'd said. It took a while to notice strangers standing next to them holding up napkins with notes that read: 'Dire oui' *Say yes*. She looked to the other side. More spectators stared, waiting for her answer. One man was down on his knee, hand over his heart. The entire restaurant heard and understood the proposal since he'd asked in French.

"Liam," she said his name softly. "Marriage isn't something we should rush into. We haven't known each other that long."

"I know."

"It's going to get hard."

"I am not afraid of hard work."

"There will be stressful times ahead."

"I am ready."

"Babies are expensive."

"You haven't been to the store lately. You haven't seen how many paintings I have sold this week alone."

"Babies are messy and dirty."

"We will invest in loads of hand sanitizer. I know you are fond of the stuff."

"They're loud, too; really loud."

"Jenna, it does not matter what you throw at me, we will adjust," he said, then added, "together."

Jenna's initial thought was to say she couldn't, but the more she thought through the crazy idea, something inside her awakened. "Can I think about it? I need to make sure this is the right thing, and I don't want to jump into something that we might regret." She tilted her head to the side and studied Liam's face. "Why don't *you* think about it more, too. Give it some thought as well and make sure this is something you want."

"I don't need to give it further thought. Jenna, I love you. I have loved you since before we slept together, and now that I know you are carrying my baby, I want nothing more than to spend my life with you." He cleared his throat before continuing. "But I understand if you want to think this through. I sprang this on you rather suddenly." He lowered his head. "So, take as much time as you need. I am not going anywhere. When you are ready, I will be here, waiting."

"Liam, you are not second choice, and that's precisely why I am not saying yes right away."

❧

She imagined what her life would be like with Liam, married to him. Could they be happy? Could she learn to love him the way a wife should love a husband? She thought she could.

Liam and Jenna stood outside the coffee shop for a few moments before they parted. Liam needed to get back to work; a wealthy couple had commissioned him to paint some pieces for their new home. Jenna had nothing she needed to do, so she lingered a little too long, wondering what had gotten into her.

The weather was cold, breezy, and she hadn't dressed appropriately. She shivered, and Liam wrapped his arm around her. She said she must go before she froze and, before they parted, Liam held her face in his hands.

"I am not letting you run away from me again. Unless you tell me it is what you want." He leaned in and kissed her forehead. "Go, you are cold. Do you own a heavier coat? You're going to need one for Quebec City winters."

She chuckled, assured him she did, kissed him lightly on the lips and left.

Not wanting to go back home, Jenna pulled her thick sweater tight over her belly and stopped at a baby store. After browsing for longer than she expected, she walked out with her first baby item: a little white sleeper with a picture of a baby elephant on the front—she couldn't resist anything with elephants, even if overpriced. Growing up, Jenna's parents had decorated her room like a zoo, with elephants painted on the walls; she fell asleep each night with the elephants looking out for her. Her parents had hired someone to paint it for Jenna on her fifth birthday after she begged and said it was all she wanted that year.

That first baby item purchase was an important first step towards her next complicated chapter. It was time for her to plan for the baby's arrival. Once she left the store, she placed the purchase inside her handbag, reached around for hand sanitizer and walked back to her apartment and checked her phone, remembering the last message from Josh. She still hadn't returned his call, so she hesitated for a moment, then dropped her phone back into her bag; he could wait. This was her moment, not his; she deserved to put herself first and indulge in the bliss that surrounded her for one afternoon.

CHAPTER 37

Love Is Blinding

JOSH WASN'T SURE what he was doing; his mind told him one thing while his heart screamed another—which did he listen to? The true romantics said, 'love conquers all' and 'follow your heart's desire' but the realists said, 'love is blinding' and 'it'll never work'.

He was in Quebec City but didn't know where Jenna lived. He'd pondered the two frames of thought, and, in the end, it was the screaming of his heart that got him there with no plan and a lack of important details, such as her address. He had listened to his heart, pushed away the complicated warnings blasting from his cerebral cortex—now what? Quebec City had over half a million residents, yet he hoped he'd accidentally bump into her—his heart taking over again. Foolish thought.

He'd been shocked to find Jenna no longer worked for the magazine. She had loved that job, and he was curious about what better offer she must have received to have left. He hated that magazine since it caused a great divide between them. Well, that, and coupled with the fact that he wanted to get married right away and have kids and she didn't—the latter, secondary. But the more he thought about it, the more he questioned if it *was* secondary. Should he have been more patient and questioned his desires? Why was he in such a hurry to begin a family? Knowing what he knew about the adoption, he wondered if subconsciously that had something to do with it. Had he always feared deep down that one day he'd lose Billy and be alone with no one to call his own? Is that why he had pushed Jenna? He didn't know. Annoyed with himself for all his past decisions, he regretted having done any of it and wondered if he could have convinced her to stay, had he not told her he was moving out. Would she have given up the promotion if he had come right out and asked her? Did she still love him? Those were questions Josh so desperately wanted answers to.

Josh booked an Air B&B outside downtown Quebec City and sat on the front step of the building trying to get a hold of Cassie to get Jenna's address. Cassie was a hard girl to get a hold of; he'd gotten her voicemail many times and there were three unreturned—but read—text messages. After the last text, he figured she was avoiding him. But had Jenna asked her to? Another question he couldn't answer. He considered calling her parents, or even Kris, her brother, but didn't want to alarm them, so they'd be a last resort if he didn't hear from Cassie soon.

After the way he treated Jenna at the funeral reception, he didn't blame her for not wanting to see him, so because of that fear, he wanted to catch her by surprise. Why couldn't she have moved to a small, quaint town, one where everyone knew each other? It would have made finding her easier. Desperate, he pushed aside his fears and tried Jenna again; it rang a few times before the call went to voicemail. One last idea made him try the magazine again to sweet talk the receptionist into giving him the address, and it must have been the lawyer in him because he succeeded. Voila: he knew how to find her!

With his heart racing, and not wanting to waste another minute, he grabbed his coat to help fight against the cold November breeze and hailed a taxi, struggling to give the driver her address in French. Unlike Jenna, Josh was not fluent in the language.

"You seem excited to get to where you're going," said the taxi driver in French, looking into the rear-view mirror.

Josh leaned forward from the backseat. He'd understood enough of the words to know what he had more or less said. "Oui. Très excite!" *Yes, very excited.*

The drive wasn't long, but Josh's anticipation made it feel as if he'd driven from Toronto. His leg shook, and he placed his hand over his knee to settle the nerves. He didn't know what he'd do or say when she stood before him. Would he apologize for being an asshole? That's where he should start. That, and beg her to take him back. They passed a flower shop and Josh almost asked the driver to make a pit stop, but then decided he didn't have time to lose and wasn't sure how to say it all without getting mixed up in the language. He didn't know how the reunion would go, but he wouldn't make it about himself. He wouldn't ask about the adoption, his dad, or his twin brother. That conversation would be for later; foremost, he needed to get her back, the rest secondary. She needed to know that he'd never stopped loving her, and he'd wait forever if that was what it took.

CHAPTER 38

Some Things Had Changed

*W*HEN THE TAXI arrived, Josh's heartbeat increased. He brought his hand over his chest to slow it. He paid the driver and stepped out in front of Jenna's apartment building. She lived in a pleasant area: quiet, but not too far from downtown, at the opposite end of his Air B&B. He squirmed his way in as someone walked out. He got lucky because he didn't have a code for the building. As he made his way up to the third floor, looking for her apartment number, he didn't know what she'd say when she saw him at her door. He hoped she'd wrap her arms around him and invite him in and not slam the door in his face—a possibility he hadn't emotionally prepared for.

He leaned in close against the door, and her voice emanated speaking French from the other side, so he placed his ear closer to listen. But despite having his ear pressed hard up against the door, he couldn't make out anything other than a few legal words: court date, appeal, settlement. Josh's eyebrows raised in response. When it sounded as if she'd ended the call, he raised his hand to knock when a cat meowed. Odd. Jenna didn't have a cat, but then he remembered there were a lot of things about her he might not know anymore; she'd been out of his life for a long time, enough time that there would be changes.

Aware he looked like a stalker to all who walked by, he still couldn't bring himself to knock. In the time he'd stood outside her door, an older man with a walking stick left and returned. A young mother with two kids carried groceries, making three trips, and Josh even contemplated helping her, but worried he'd miss Jenna leaving. And the janitor had vacuumed the entire building. He'd told each of them he was waiting for her to get ready, but none acknowledged him, carrying on about their business. Fear had him in a tight ball, questioning if he was doing the right thing. He was about to knock when the door opened, and Jenna stood five feet away; his smile widened as he took her in. The familiar eyes, the soft, warm glow from her cheeks, but when his eyes travelled to her midsection, his smile faded.

"Josh, you're here!" she shook her head. "What *are* you doing here? Is everything okay?"

He didn't speak; he just stared at her... at her bump.

"Josh," she repeated.

But Josh didn't answer. He was too busy calculating in his head: How long had she been in Quebec City and how pregnant was she compared to how long she'd been there.

Jenna's eyes followed Josh's, and she frowned. "Josh, will you say something, please?"

Josh shook his head, looked away and then back at her, hoping he'd see a little clearer, but his vision had not betrayed him; because Jenna still had the same bump in her midsection.

"Josh," she whispered. "I didn't want you to find out like this."

He cleared his throat. "I guess... congratulations are in order."

She lifted her arms over her stomach in a protective gesture.

"How far along are you?"

"Five months."

"Hmmm," he said. "Five months?" he repeated, to be sure.

"Yes."

"So, it's not mine. That's all I needed to know," he said and turned around to walk away.

"Josh, wait. Don't leave."

He was already halfway down the stairs when the sound of her slamming the door echoed throughout the hallways.

"Josh," she continued to call out his name as she ran behind him, trying to catch up to him.

"I see you've moved on rather nicely. You wasted no time. That crap about your career being important, you not wanting a family right away, was bullshit. I was your problem all along. You never loved me."

"That's not true. Please don't leave like this. We should talk."

"I have nothing left to say."

"Josh, I never planned—"

He was out the front door and hailed the first taxi he saw, got in and didn't look back; her voice calling out for him was the only thing he heard as he slammed the door of the taxi and told the man to drive.

"Où ça?" *Where to?*

"Just drive," he responded in English, then gestured with his hands as the driver raised his eyebrows, clearly not understanding.

Some things had changed, all right! He was in no frame of mind to think about anything other than: How could she do this to him? How could she have forgotten him so easily? Five months pregnant—three months after she left. It wasn't an overnight betrayal, but still a betrayal, considering she didn't want kids with *him*. That's what he was most upset about. He had expected that she'd have seen other people by this point, but he hadn't expected that. Well, it was what it was; she had done it and there was nothing left for him to fight for.

"Still unsure about where you want to go?" asked the taxi driver, again in French.

"Just keep driving." He made the same hand-rolling gestures. Josh understood a lot more than he could speak.

"We're headed east, so I'll let you know when we've hit the Atlantic." The driver joked in French.

"Parfait." *perfect.*

CHAPTER 39

Life Happens

TIMING WAS EVERYTHING; as a reporter, Jenna knew that, and the timing of Josh showing up on her doorstep couldn't have been worse. She had zero ideas about why he was there, but she knew why seeing her pregnant had sent him into a rage—she didn't blame him. She never meant to hurt him.

After she stood at the front door watching Josh leave in the taxi, she decided she needed a walk to clear her head. Her phone rang and, hopeful it was Josh, she reached into her pocket to answer, but it was Cassie.

"Hey girl, what are you up to?"

"Just walking around here being peachy."

"Well, this might make you even more peachy. I wanted to let you know Josh has been calling for the past two days. Two days, I tell you! I don't know why. I haven't answered because I'm not sure what you want me to tell him about what's been happening. So, you and I must get our stories straight before he calls again, which I'm sure he will, judging by the call history alone."

"And you're telling me now?"

"Sorry, girl, swamped at work."

Jenna didn't want to do this, and she tried to hold back tears, but failed and sobbed into the phone.

"Girl, are you crying?"

"Oh Cas, things are a mess."

"What's happened? Is it the baby?"

"The baby is fine. But Josh was here."

"In Quebec City?"

"Yes, at my apartment. He caught me off guard, and I couldn't cover up my stomach to break the news to him properly. I opened my door to check the mail, wearing a tight T-shirt, and he was just there! He realized right away. I think he was about to knock when I opened the door. And I think he was more shocked to find out than I was."

"Oh boy! So he knows."

"Yes, he knows. He took off in a hurry after asking me how far along I am."

"I wish I was there with you. Do you need me to get on a plane? You know I will."

"No. I know you can't. You've been telling me about that enormous project at work."

"That's not as important as you. Say the word and I'm there, okay?"

"It must have devastated him. He only ever wanted me to give him children, and now..."

"Listen, things happen. Life happens. You broke up and had been apart for months before you got together with Liam. It's none of his business."

"But that's not the point."

"It is precisely the point, Jenna. Just look at it from a unique perspective. Will you?"

"I'll try."

"He left *you*. Don't forget that. You never told him you wouldn't give him children, you just told him it was not the right time, and it wasn't. That wasn't good enough for him. He moved out. You took a position there, and things changed. Your plans changed: the rest is history. I know you still care deeply for him and are worried about hurting him, but he needs to take responsibility for how your relationship ended. You can't control how he will react to the situation, so you're going to have to let him be angry, if that's how he handles it. Are you still there?"

"I'm listening."

"You turned down a dream job for him. How much more convincing did he need that you were in it for life if you could do that? If that wasn't good enough, then I don't know what is."

Jenna considered Cassie's last words for a moment. "But Cas, he didn't know I turned the job down for him."

"What do you mean, 'he didn't know'?"

"I never had the chance to tell him, because that's the day at the hospital when he told me he was leaving, the day he announced out of the blue he was moving in with Billy."

"Wait. At what point did you tell him you took the job?"

"Right after he announced he was moving out. My next words were not to bother moving out, because I'd taken a job offer and was the one moving out."

"Girl, you didn't?"

"What else was I supposed to do? I couldn't let him think he was the one in control."

"This is too bad."

"I know that already. I don't need you to confirm it. I need you to make me feel better."

"I meant that it's too bad that he didn't know about you turning down the promotion. You should have told him you had turned down the job and only took it after he announced he was leaving you. Because to him, it might appear like you had already decided. If he knew the truth, it might have convinced him to not move out."

"He had already said he was moving out. The last thing I wanted was to beg someone to stay who didn't want to be with me. The promotion came at the most convenient time."

"Right, so there you go."

"Cas, I have something else to tell you."

"There's more? I'm not sure how much more drama I can handle, girl. Is this additional information a tequila kind of news? Because if so, I have to go grab the bottle so I'm ready."

"It might qualify as a tequila moment, yes, so go get it. Tell me when you're ready."

"Hold on." There's silence on the other end, other than the stomping sound of Cassie's feet, and it sounded like she was running. Then the clinking of glasses. "Okay, shoot, I poured my shot."

"Liam asked me to marry him."

"Double-shot moment... hold on," she said, then yelled. "WHAT! You make me go on and on about Josh and you say nothing about Liam proposing?"

"It just happened yesterday."

"YESTERDAY!" Cassie screamed into the phone. "I'm still your best friend, aren't I?"

"Of course you are. What kind of question is that?"

"Just checking that you're not calling your new BFF to give her the news first."

"You're the only BFF in my life, Cas."

"That's my girl. Now tell me. Am I going to be a maid of honour? Wait, first tell me how he proposed and then tell me what you said."

Jenna was about to speak, and Cassie interrupted her. "Just tell me the answer first. The suspense is killing me. Am I planning a baby shower and a wedding shower in one?"

Jenna continued walking down the street and arrived at a park. She sat on a frozen swing and twirled with the phone glued to her ear. "I told him I needed time to think about it. He also knows about the baby."

"I figured that's why he proposed. I can't keep up with your life these days, girl. I've got some vacation time left. I'm wrapping up the project soon and I can finish what I need from there. Do you want me to go? I can be there in two days and I can stay for three, but then I have to get back for the project rollout. Take it or leave it."

"I'll take it."

"Done. Will you be okay until I get there?"

"I'll manage just fine; I've got Seul to keep me company."

"Okay. See you in two days. I'll text the details of the flight. Promise me you won't elope before I arrive?"

Jenna let out a screech; Cassie was the only one who could make Jenna laugh during a crisis. "I promise."

CHAPTER 40

Like A Bell Being Played by a Child

DESPERATE TO GET both men off her mind, Jenna immersed herself in the current article for the local paper. Since Josh's unexpected arrival, she had put everything into her work, even more than at the magazine. The trial was coming up, and she'd have to face Rachel again, but she wasn't ready.

She hadn't seen Liam since he proposed, but he called often, not to pressure her, but to check in. She was glad he didn't ask if she'd decided yet and welcomed his phone calls because of it. He was such a sweetheart, and so patient.

When Cassie arrived, Jenna picked her up and their reunion was the same as if they hadn't been apart at all. That was the beauty of a best friend. It didn't matter how much distance was between them, or how long since they'd last seen each other; it always felt safe and familiar.

"Wow, wow, wow. Look at you, girl," Cassie said, and offered Jenna gum from a newly opened pack.

Jenna shook her head at the offer of gum. "I know, crazy isn't it. My obstetrician says I need to watch my weight. I've gained plenty and still have four months to go."

Cassie reached out to touch Jenna's belly and rubbed it, and the baby kicked at the exact moment, startling her. "What the hell was that?" Cassie whipped her hand away.

Jenna chuckled. "That was the baby, kicking."

"Really? They do that in there?"

Jenna's chuckle erupted into a full-out laugh. "Yes, they do, that and a lot more."

As they drove through the city, Cassie commented on the Christmas vibe. "Wow, look at all the lights, decorations, and the music! It's so magical here."

"They sure transform the city at Christmas, you'll see more as we move along," said Jenna.

<hr />

The weather was cold, especially once night fell. But even with the cooler nights, the decorations and Christmas vibe brought crowds out shopping and roaming the streets while sipping hot chocolate. Jenna hadn't put up a tree yet. She was still in limbo; waiting to find out about a new lease on an apartment she applied for, and waiting to decide about her and Liam. At the thought of Liam, her mind lingered on his proposal. The more thought she gave it, the bigger it manifested, and she wasn't sure if she was ready for that next step, so she pushed it aside—again. She knew she couldn't string him along forever, but she needed to be sure for her and her baby. Part of her worried about marrying Liam for the wrong reasons: convenience and security. Although she had grown to love Liam, it wasn't quite the same type of love she had when she'd said yes to Josh. The emotions she had for Liam were different, still—the beginning-relationship type, and not the deep-rooted feelings that came later.

French Christmas music blared outside storefronts as Jenna parked and walked across the street to her apartment. She hummed along, the music playing in the background amidst the loud Christmas air like a bell being played by a child. Jenna thought about how much Josh loved Christmas, and how he always wanted to put the Christmas tree up way too early; she wondered if he had it up, then she swapped that thought for one of Liam instead.

❦

Later that night, Jenna and Cassie lounged around in Jenna's living room with pyjama bottoms rolled up to their knees; Cassie applied a bright pink polish to Jenna's toenails while telling Jenna all about her dating life. Jenna let her go on, and when there was a break in her story, Jenna jumped in.

"Cas, I have more news. I didn't want to tell you over the phone. I wanted to see your face in person."

Cassie lifted the nail polish applicator from Jenna's toes. "You're smiling, so this is good news, I take it?"

"It is. Wait here." Jenna went into her bedroom and returned with a bag from one of the downtown children's stores. "Here." She handed Cassie the bag.

"Watch the toes."

"Oops, so sorry," said Jenna, looking at her smudged big toe.

Cassie looked at Jenna hesitantly, took the bag and peeked inside slowly, as if she were afraid something would jump out. She squealed with delight. "Oh, a new T-shirt. Wait. What does it say?" she asked as she pulled out the stretchy, yoga-appropriate T-shirt, reading: Je suis la tante sexy d'une petite fille! *I'm the sexy aunt of a baby girl!*

Cassie squealed with delight. "When did you find out?"

"Last month," Jenna admitted, ashamed at having kept that secret from her for so long. Cassie would never have been able to keep something that big from her.

"You little sneak! You said you wouldn't find out about the sex. You lied."

"But I had a good reason. I wanted to surprise you with that T-shirt. I thought you'd like that. You can wear it to yoga class. It's fitted enough to make you look good, and I know how important that is." Jenna winked, and Cassie slapped her lightly on the shoulder, giggling.

"I love it, thank you, girl. I also have a surprise for you. I've been trying to figure out how to make it a surprise, but that's going to be impossible. So… SURPRISE, I'm throwing you a baby shower."

"You mean right now?"

"No, silly, next week. You must come to Toronto on the weekend. It's all arranged. The girls from your old office, including Aleshia, will be there, your old neighbours, your parents' neighbours, your family, my family, you know; the usual gang."

"You didn't have to do that. I expected nothing since I'm so far away."

"I'd love to take full credit, but actually, it was your mother's idea. She's bugged me about a baby shower for weeks. We weren't sure how to get you there, and for a while we all considered condensing it to a smaller party and coming to you instead, but that would be more complicated, so I told your mother to leave it to me. I promised I'd get you there on Saturday."

She tilted her head to the side and gave Jenna the eyes she always gave her when she was trying to get something from her.

Jenna placed her hands on her hips. "I see. I'm surprised my mother is going all-out. She took the news better than I thought. I was so worried about telling her, but she was happy she's going to be a grandmother."

"It's like I told you before. You're older now. What can they say? So, anyway, is that cool?"

"That you want me to pretend to be surprised at my baby shower?"

They sat side by side, and Cassie bent forward to embrace Jenna. "Yep. And that is why you're my best friend. So, this weekend works? It has to work."

"The timing is perfect. I'll be in Toronto for the court hearing on Thursday, so I'll extend my stay until Sunday."

"That's why I planned it that way." Cassie scrunched up her nose, then reached out her hand. "Give me your toe so I can fix it."

"You're so bossy."

"Yeah, that's me, Bossy Cassie. Toe, please?" she said with her hand held out.

CHAPTER 41

He Understood Why

LIAM WAS HOPEFUL. Jenna had called and texted more lately, and although he didn't want to push her, he hoped that she'd decide marriage to him was what she wanted. The last time they met up for lunch, Liam was sure she'd say yes then. She was all smiles and seemed generally happier, but then they'd parted with no commitment from her. He understood why she needed to think about it, and he was patient because of it.

He'd taken her to meet his parents when she wrote the feature on him. Jenna had wanted to see where he came from and who had raised him. She'd told Liam it would help make the article more authentic. But Liam still hadn't told his mom and dad that they were seeing each other, let alone about the proposal and that she was pregnant with his child. And he still had mentioned nothing about his living biological grandparents and twin. That was killing him, as he had an open and honest relationship with his mom and dad, so that afternoon, he had gone to see them to break the news about the baby and the marriage proposal. Baby steps, he'd decided. He'd tell them a little that day, and the rest another day.

CHAPTER 42

Time To Refocus
Time To Move On

JOSH'S MOOD CLOUDED his thoughts; they were almost tainted, and he couldn't make sense of anything since he had seen Jenna's swollen belly. Most emotions flowed in and out of his consciousness as fast as a speeding sports car on its way to winning a race, but one thought remained persistent: pregnant, and with another man's child. That one stuck like crazy glue. The biggest betrayal he'd ever faced. And it had been by her. As he sat fuming days later, his phone rang; Cassie was calling him back, finally. Josh had called her so many times, and she chose now to reach out. He contemplated playing her game and not answering, but curiosity got him, so he picked up.

"Hey Josh, I hope I'm not catching you at a bad time. I'm sorry I haven't returned your calls earlier. Things got a bit out of control, but I'm calling to get your aunt's number."

"How out of control have things been, Cassie?"

"I'm sorry?"

"'Out of control', as in: Jenna-is-having-a-baby? Is that why you were avoiding me?"

"Josh, I'm sorry. But this is between you two and I'm not discussing this with you, but all I'm going to say is this: you were a jerk. What did you expect her to do after you announced out of the blue that you're moving out? Obviously, she'd take the job offer. You pushed her to it. The baby..." Cassie hesitated then continued, "They didn't plan it. It just happened, and you two had been apart for months, so really, that's none of your business."

"Stop. Just stop."

"Afraid to hear the truth?"

"No, I'm not."

"Then, what?" she asked.

"She had already sealed the job offer before I ever said anything about leaving. She was leaving me first. I just said it before her."

"You've got that so wrong."

"I don't. She chose her career over me. I always had a feeling it would come to that, and I was right."

"That's not true, and if you think that of her, then you didn't deserve her, or know her at all."

"Whatever!" said Josh.

"Stop acting like a child."

"I'm acting like a child?"

"Yes! You are," said Cassie.

"Why have you always disliked me, Cassie? I was always good to Jenna."

"Yes, you were, I'll admit. And it's not that I didn't like you. I just never thought you were good enough for her. She was much more independent before she met you. You took that from her."

"No I didn't, and besides, would that be a bad thing?"

"For someone like Jenna, yes. So, can I have your aunt's number or not? Now that you know about the baby, I'd like to invite her to the shower since she and Jenna were close."

"Baby shower?"

"You know, the party people throw for new moms."

"I know what a baby shower is, Cassie."

"Then why did you ask?"

"I wasn't asking... never mind. When is the baby shower?"

"This Saturday."

"I doubt Aunt Becky will go to Quebec City on such short notice."

"It's being held in Toronto; she's arriving in two days for the hearing."

"What hearing?" Josh gave Cassie his full attention. He reflected on the craziness of his life: Jenna was pregnant, she had a hearing he didn't even know what for, and she had a cat. How could he know someone so well, but not know anything at all? He stopped himself mid-thought and shifted his thinking. It was not happening in his life—Jenna wasn't in it anymore, that's why he was in the dark.

There was silence on the other end, and Josh wondered if Cassie let the information about the hearing slip. That wasn't his business, but he couldn't help wondering why Jenna had a hearing and why she hadn't called him. Also, knowing that Jenna would be back in Toronto left him confused; he wasn't sure if he was happy about it. Things between them might be over, but he still wanted to talk about his past. Having her there would give him a chance, but it would pain him to see her again, pregnant with another man's child.

After a long silence, Cassie spoke. "She's suing the magazine for wrongful dismissal." Cassie waited for a response, but Josh was busy trying to find order in his shuffling thoughts.

"Josh, you still there?"

"I'm here."

Josh gave her his aunt's number, and before they ended the call, asked one more question. "Cassie, who's the baby's father?"

"You need to ask Jenna."

"Please, just a name. That's all I want, and then I won't involve you anymore. A name means nothing since I don't know her new friends. It's just a meaningless name."

"Then why do you want to know?"

"I'm not sure, I just do. Please?"

There was a pause before she answered. "His name is Liam." She ended the call.

Josh repeated the name over and over. Liam. He reflected on the conversation at his dad's funeral reception. Could it be the same Liam—no. Coincidence, surely? But why did it have to be that name? Any other name, but that one. That name was not meaningless.

∞

Josh couldn't eat or concentrate on work. What Cassie had admitted about Jenna only taking the job because he said he was moving out had also twisted Josh's stomach into a tight knot. Was that possible? Josh shook his head, uncertain. No. Cassie was protecting her to make him the bad guy.

Frustrated over it all, he googled the name 'Liam', attempting to discover how many men named Liam there were in Quebec City. He knew how crazy he was being. It wasn't even a possibility that she was in a relationship with his twin brother. Was it? The nagging feeling that had his stomach twisted intensified the more he thought about it. Time to refocus, time to move on; but instead of moving on, that night he laid in bed thinking of his mother.

CHAPTER 43

Coincidences Are an Unusual Thing

ONE OF JOSH'S earliest childhood memories was of his mother's birthday. He didn't recall how old she was turning, but remembered her smooth, wrinkle-free skin, shiny, long brown hair, and her contagious energy. His dad ran around for days planning a big surprise party. Josh guessed it must have been a milestone birthday. So she was most likely turning thirty. That age made sense, considering he was three. His dad was excited, and constantly reminded little Josh that it was a big secret and he had to be a big boy to keep a big secret from Mommy. Only big boys could do that. It made little Josh feel important, special. So what had he done? What any three-year-old would have. He, of course, told his mother about the surprise, but he also told her it was a big secret and to not tell anyone—like father, like son. That had made little Josh feel even more special, because he had not one but *two* secrets, and that truly left him feeling like a big boy, just as his dad told him he was. He remembered the day of the party. Not well, but enough to recall his mother's expression when she walked into the room full of their friends and family all yelling in unison: Happy Birthday! He watched as her eyes searched the crowd for little Josh, and when she found him, she winked and he winked back, acknowledging the big secret they'd shared. He was pleased that he had a special secret between him and his dad, and his mom, too. Josh didn't think his dad ever knew that he had spilled the beans. Maybe his mom had told his dad, but if she had, his dad never confronted him.

Josh didn't have many memories of his mom dying, but he knew she died when he was almost four, so that birthday memory must have been the same year. Likely just before her cancer diagnosis. Coincidences were an unusual thing. Both his parents died of cancer, and if it wasn't enough to lose one mother, what were the chances of discovering he also had another, but she, too, had died? He'd had two mothers in his lifetime, but grew up with none—what bad luck. It wasn't his fate to have a mother. While it would have been nice to have a mom growing up, he never missed having one—his dad had made sure, filling both roles and giving him everything, and making his entire world come alive for as long as his dad was.

Time had not yet healed his open wounds. Wasn't time supposed to make it easier? If that was the case, surely Josh's pain wouldn't still be as sharp as it had been the first day he'd had to face the world without his father by his side. But the pain was still there, a constant reminder of what he'd lost.

CHAPTER 44

A Warm Safe Space in the Frosty Night

JENNA WAS ON the phone with her lawyer, pacing back and forth, trying to understand the legal jargon. She allowed herself to let her mind go where it naturally strayed: she wished Josh was there to explain things. She hung up, but was unconvinced she understood what the lawyer had said. Still pacing with her cellphone in hand, she called Cassie to tell her the news.

"What do you mean they postponed the hearing?" asked Cassie on the other end of the phone in a panicked voice.

"I don't fully understand all the details yet."

"Did they explain? They must have given you a reason."

"They said something about a requested postponement. That's all I know, Cas."

"Okay, but you're still coming? It's all planned, and I even spoke to Josh's aunt, and she said she wouldn't miss it. Your mother will kill me if we need to change plans this close to the date. She'll somehow think it's my fault."

"Don't worry, Cas, I'll be there, just not as early. I'm arriving on Friday morning. You'll pick me up at the airport?"

"Of course, girl. I'll be there with bells on. You were breathing heavily when you first called. I don't know if you're pleased about the postponement."

"I wanted to get it over with, and now it just means worrying about it longer. So I'm not too pleased about it. My lawyer is fine, but this would have been much easier if Josh were representing me. Instead, I feel like I'm alone."

"You're missing the point. You aren't alone. You have a lawyer, Jenna, and that's what they're there for. They help you through this and explain things in a manner that you'll understand. If you have questions, ask."

"I know I should, but it's complicated. Dealing with him only makes me think of Josh more."

"Well, unfortunately, girl, for the sake of this hearing, you're going to have to learn to separate the two."

"I know, but..."

"Stop. Enough is enough. It's time. You *need* to move on, and it means you *need* to put in that effort."

Cassie's last comment took Jenna by surprise because Cassie wasn't usually so abrupt, but she allowed the words to linger in the early afternoon as she sat at her kitchen table working. She was still doing freelance work for the local paper, and enjoying it. Perhaps it was the freedom of choosing her hours, or the lack of Rachel in her life that she appreciated about the job, but either way, she was working and making a living.

She hadn't heard from Rachel since they'd let her go; she wasn't expecting to, but had prepared to see her in court. Jenna still didn't understand what Rachel had against her. Cassie had always said that she was jealous because the executives knew Jenna was a better reporter and writer, and that between the two, it was Jenna who should have had her job. But of course Jenna's husband wasn't CFO of one of the magazine's major advertisers; Rachel's was.

Jenna had been working since early morning, so she stopped for lunch. There'd been no grocery shopping done yet this week, so when she opened the fridge, it was empty. She got dressed, because she'd been working in pyjamas, and headed out into the city in search of food. It was much colder than yesterday, even though she wore a thick winter coat, pink scarf, and matching winter hat with a pompom high on the top. Her face was pretty concealed, so when she stood at the sandwich truck only a few feet from Liam, he didn't notice her right away, although she noticed him and the sudden increase in her heartbeat shocked her.

"Jenna, I did not even see you all covered up. It is cold, but not that cold. If you are dressing like this now, what will you do in January?"

"I'm planning on not leaving the house in January," she teased. "I wondered how long it would take you to notice me."

"I thought you'd be busy working?"

"I am. Well, I was all morning, but took a late lunch break. There's no food in the apartment. So, here I am."

He held out his arm for her to take. "I have not eaten either. I was hoping a quick sandwich would hold me over, so why not let me buy you a proper sit-down lunch? It will be good for us."

Jenna's thoughts shifted to Cassie's words from earlier. Then, as her stomach growled, she swung her arm and looped it around his as the first snowfall of the year blanketed the earth, leaving white powdered dust on all it touched.

They walked arm in arm down lower Quebec City, the Christmas vibe present in the air. Shops decorated with wreaths and French Christmas music played from the outdoor speakers, creating a backdrop for the many tourists as they chatted about what to buy their loved ones. Sale signs were being hung. People rushed in and out of stores trying to find that perfect gift for that special someone. To the world, she and Liam looked like a happy young couple in love expecting their first baby; Jenna considered that the world would be almost right. But little did those strangers know that there was more history between Liam and Jenna in the time they'd known each other than most couples had after years together.

"What are you in the mood for?" Liam asked, as they passed many restaurants and read the French menus on the windows.

"I could go for some poutine. I have this huge craving, but that would be a bad idea, so how about a burger instead?"

"Is there a problem with eating poutine while you're pregnant? Is cheese bad for the baby?"

"It's not the baby. I have a sensitivity to dairy; although sometimes I'll take the lactose-intolerance pills and indulge anyway, even though my body tells me I shouldn't. It's a weakness, so please never take me to an ice cream shop."

"I did not know that about you."

"We haven't even known each other a year. There's a lot you don't know about me."

"And I would like to change that," he said, looking into her eyes that peeked from between the hat and scarf.

There was that increase in her heartbeat again. Jenna lowered her gaze. After reading a few more menus, they decided, and Liam opened the door to allow Jenna to enter first and requested a table for two. When the hostess showed them to their seats, he pulled out Jenna's chair and offered for her to sit first.

After they sat, Jenna's heart raced even more; she needed to get what was most likely on both their minds out in the open. She crossed her hands on the table to keep herself from fidgeting.

"Liam, I know I've been quiet since..."

"You do not have to explain. I told you to take your time, and I meant it. I am not in a hurry. The last thing I want is for you to rush into something that you are not sure of." He reached for her hands, and the electricity that jolted through her body at his touch made her already racing heart almost jump out of her chest.

"Jenna, I want to be with you, but I also want you to want to be with me, too. I need to know that when you come to me, it is with your heart and not wishing I were someone else—someone I remind you of."

Jenna jerked in her seat. His words brought the reality of the situation to the forefront.

"I've been giving it some thought, a lot of thought, actually," she said.

He raised his eyebrows. "And?" then added, "not that I am pushing, but since you mentioned it..."

"And I have decided on a few things."

"Please do not keep me in suspense."

Jenna reached out to take his other hand in hers and held them both. "Liam, we could be great together. I know that—I see and feel the connection. If it weren't for Josh, I think you and I would already be a lot more than we are. But Josh was my past, and that part of my life is over, and I can't keep making excuses or allowing it to prevent me from living." Jenna shifted in her seat, then continued. "I want us to get to know each other more, the real us. I want to give *us* a chance."

"I think this sounds great, but I'm afraid to ask what it really means?"

"It means we should date, like an actual couple. Let's pick up where we left off after that night we spent together and see where it leads."

"So, you're turning down my marriage proposal," he said matter of fact, head hung.

"No," she said. "I'm not. Not at all."

He lifted his eyebrow. Jenna continued. "I don't want to force anything or rush into marriage. So, what *I* propose is that we date first, see where it goes. Who knows, if things go well, then maybe in the future, we can get a place together and perhaps one day, there might be a wedding, but I don't want to think about that now, it's too soon."

Liam pulled his hands away from hers and ran them through his hair, the way Josh often did, and after making the comparison, Jenna stopped the image of Josh from entering her mind and pushed it out. Cassie was right; it was time she moved on.

Liam looked at her expanding belly when she shifted to adjust her position and smiled. "It is going to get difficult to take you out on dates in a few weeks. Once that little one arrives, she will keep us pretty busy."

He'd said, 'keep us busy', and Jenna thought that was sweet. "You said 'she', is that a wish or a premonition?"

"I am not sure, more like an educated guess."

"I didn't know you were so well educated about childbirth."

"I have been reading a lot, and I have been comparing your pregnancy, what I know of it anyway, to what the books say."

Now that piqued her interest. "And what do the books say?" she asked.

"From the way you are carrying, it would suggest it is a girl."

Jenna smiled, and her heart melted again. That was probably one of the sweetest things that anyone had ever done for her. At that moment, the baby kicked or flipped over and caused much discomfort as she winced in her seat. Liam jumped off of his and was at her side in less than a second.

"What is wrong? Should I call an ambulance?" he had his phone ready to dial.

"No, it's nothing. The baby just kicked me. Oh, here's another one. Do you want to feel it?"

He held out his hand, so Jenna grabbed it. "You're shaking like a leaf, Liam. Don't be nervous, they don't bite, at least not at this point."

She placed his hand over the spot that felt like it was getting bruised, and together they waited for the next kick; when it came, it caused Liam to pull his hand away in a hurry.

"What the hell was that?"

Jenna smiled and looked into his eyes, and for the first time she saw Liam, and not Josh, staring back. "That was your daughter."

He jerked his head back. "Daughter? For sure?"

"Yes, it's a girl."

"Wow, a girl! I was right. The research is paying off already."

Jenna laughed. "I suppose it is."

"But that kick was intense, and yet I have felt nothing more amazing in my life," he said.

"Yeah, who would have thought that being kicked in the gut would be such a magnificent and beautiful experience."

"Does it hurt a lot?"

"It does sometimes, but other times it's more of a discomfort. But every once in a while, she lets one land hard, and those are the ones that take my breath away momentarily."

Jenna looked into Liam's eyes again to make sure that it was still him and not Josh she saw, and a feeling of relief washed over her when she realized it was. He wasn't looking into her eyes though; the rise and fall of her stomach mesmerized him. When the baby pushed up against her ribs, it changed the shape of her belly and the contour of the skin, creating ridges in Jenna's midsection that were visible beneath her shirt.

"Liam," she said again, "to answer your earlier question, if we can't survive dating through the birth of our child, how do we expect to make a marriage work?"

He raised his eyebrows, "That is a good point."

"This will be a test to see how well we are together under stress. If we can survive this," she said, pointing to her stomach, "then we can survive anything."

Liam took her hand in his and brought it up to his lips. "I like that you're referring to us as being together."

His lips brushed up against hers. Jenna closed her eyes and in her mind, it was Liam's touch and Liam's face she saw.

Before they parted, Liam placed his hand on Jenna's chin to lift her face to his, then patted her stomach and said, "Daddy's little princess."

Jenna didn't even ruminate on the fact that it was what Josh had always said he'd call his little girl if he were to have one. That was then and she was moving on.

After lunch, Liam called the store to find out if it was busy, and his part-time worker assured him she had everything covered until the evening rush, so he went with Jenna and they did some shopping together. They spent the rest of the afternoon, at Liam's insistence, picking out cute little things for the baby.

"I don't want to buy too much just yet because Cassie is throwing me a baby shower. I'm leaving at the end of the week. I'll most likely get all this stuff then."

"I didn't realize you were leaving. How long will you be away?"

"I'm sorry. I should have mentioned it sooner. I'm flying out Friday, the shower is on Sunday. The hearing got postponed, or I'd leave earlier. I'll be back by Monday. Do you want to come with me?"

"Shit. I want to, but I can't this weekend. I have the big holiday sale we have been advertising. The store will be busy, and I already gave two of my part-timers the weekend off. I do not have anyone else to cover. If I had known, I would not have planned to take part in the sale."

"Liam, it's okay. I'm perfectly fine on my own. Cassie is picking me up from the airport, and I'm staying with her. She'll make sure I get on the flight safely Monday morning."

"I want to see Cassie again; you talk about her a lot. She seems important."

"She's extremely important; she's the sister I never had. And you will see her again soon." Jenna had a thought that she hadn't considered until then. She was used to doing things on her own, but being in a relationship meant leaning on the other person, so she asked him for help. "I'm returning to Toronto for the hearing in a few weeks, and I wondered if maybe you'd be able to take some time and drive a rented van so that you can help me bring back the gifts. I'm sure there will be too many to manage on a plane by myself. Is that something you're interested in?"

"Interested? Are you kidding me? Give me the date, and I will make sure I get someone to run the store."

"I don't have a date yet, but as soon as my lawyer gives me one, you'll be the first to know this time."

"What will you do with the shower gifts until then?"

"My parents offered to keep them."

"Will you be driving with me or flying when we go to the hearing?"

"I wish I could drive to keep you company, but ten hours in a rental van will be too much; it's difficult to get comfortable. I was hoping I'd fly and you could drive. Would that work?"

"Is it safe for you to fly?"

"My doctor says it's fine. I've had a healthy pregnancy so far, so as long as it's before my thirty-sixth week, I'm good."

"As long as it is safe, it is not a problem for me to drive myself. I'm more than happy to get you and our baby permanently moved here." Liam stopped, opened his mouth to speak, but then stopped again. "Just let me know after the shower how much stuff you receive and whatever else you need to bring so I know what size van to rent." He raised his eyebrows questioningly.

"You're referring to furniture at the old apartment, aren't you?"

"You mentioned you never got around to splitting anything up, so if there is anything you want to bring, that would be the time. I don't mind taking care of that for you. I'm sure I can get it from your old place."

"I won't be bringing any furniture. I'll only have the shower gifts."

"Really?"

"Yep."

"But you said you left all your other stuff behind."

"I did, but there's nothing from that life I want anymore."

"You sure?"

Jenna kissed him softly on the lips, and the kiss lasted for a few seconds. "I've never been surer."

Liam caressed her face, running his finger down her nose, down her cheeks, and then brought his lips to hers once again; as they shared a moment, the snow fell around them and the sound of Christmas music was in the air again, creating a warm, safe space in the cold frosty night.

"I want to take you home to meet Mom and Dad, officially as my girlfriend this time and not just a reporter friend."

"I would love that," said Jenna.

He took her by the hand, and together they made their way to Liam's childhood home.

CHAPTER 45

Breathtaking Indeed

JENNA STOOD IN Cassie's bedroom, looking at the outfit Cassie had picked out for her to wear, insisting she matched the room's décor. Cassie chose a white and soft pink baby doll dress with baby elephants on the front. Jenna laughed and asked where she'd found such an item, but agreed to wear it and go along with pretending to be surprised.

Jenna had already seen her parents; she'd gone to their house to get it over with when she first arrived. As she had often discovered, while she dreaded going, once she was there, the visit wasn't as bad as she'd expected. They were trying, and she reminded herself to try, too. A relationship needed to work both ways, and Jenna knew she needed to do her part. When her mother had asked why she was in town, she'd blurted the lie she'd rehearsed about meeting with a lawyer. Her mother seemed to have bought it and didn't question her further or mention the surprise shower.

"Ready?" asked Cassie, holding out a hand for Jenna to take. Jenna knew that, because of the weather, Cassie was afraid of Jenna slipping on ice.

"I'm ready. Let's go to my 'surprise' baby shower."

They walked outside into the cold, Cassie protectively clenching Jenna's arm.

∞

They had decorated the room with a soft pink colour palette, streamers on the walls, and helium-filled balloons as centrepieces. There were two oversized stuffed elephants at the entrance separated by streamers for guests to walk through. Jenna looked down at her clothes and laughed. When she walked through the elephant-made archway, the guests stood and yelled in unison, "Surprise!" Jenna's mouth forcefully hung open as she raised her hand over it, acting out the rehearsed scene.

The guests played baby games, ate, and Jenna opened presents, and by the time the last guest left, she was ready for bed. Wanting to get back to Cassie's sooner than later, she picked up some light gift bags and was helping to carry them out to Cassie's car when Josh's BMW pulled into the parking lot. She looked twice and recognized the license plate. She took a deep breath, wondering what he was doing there. He noticed her and drove to where she stood frozen, the trunk still open. It was the first time they'd seen each other since he came to her apartment and found her pregnant.

He pulled into the parking spot beside her and stepped out.

"Hey Jenna, can I give you a hand carrying stuff?"

"I'm not carrying anything else."

He peeked into the trunk. "Where are all the other gifts?"

"Inside, but my father is on his way with a truck to pick up my mom, and he's taking the rest back to their place."

He took a step closer to her. "Are you moving back to Toronto?"

"Why would I move back?" she asked.

"I just thought since... never mind. How will you get it all to Quebec City?"

"I'm coming back in a couple of weeks for a hearing. Work stuff. My... someone is driving a truck and meeting me here so we can bring everything home."

"Someone?" Josh asked, as his eyes landed on her midsection.

"My... boyfriend."

Ignoring that, he said, "I heard about that."

"About my boyfriend coming here?"

"No, about the hearing. Why didn't you call me? Jenna, you needed a lawyer, and you didn't call? I'd have expected you to."

"I know, and I also know you would have come to my rescue, but I figured it was easier to find someone on the outside."

"Why was that easier?"

She tilted her head to the side, wondering how he could ask about that. "So we didn't have to see each other." Jenna shivered and her teeth clenched. She brought the zipper of her coat up as high as it would go.

"You're freezing," he said. "Why don't we go inside and talk?"

"Josh, what are you doing here? You show up out of the blue at my baby shower and offer to help. Why? How did you even know I'd be here?"

He kicked at a stone by his foot. "Aunt Becky told me. I wanted to see you." He stopped and looked at her. "For professional reasons, of course."

"Of course."

"I want to know about the adoption, my mother, and even my twin brother; Liam. I wasn't ready before, but I'm ready now."

Jenna noticed that he'd emphasized Liam's name. She became light-headed and grabbed the side of the car to steady herself; the events of the day were catching up to her. She was flying out early in the morning and needed to get back to Cassie's, have a bath, and get to bed.

"Josh, I appreciate you want answers, but unfortunately, tonight isn't a great time. It's been a hectic day, and I'm exhausted."

"Oh, that's understandable. I didn't mean to overwhelm you. How about tomorrow? Can I take you to lunch? We can chat then, my treat."

"I'm flying out first thing in the morning."

"Breakfast then?"

"That won't work either. My flight is too early. It's at seven."

"I see."

Jenna noticed the disappointment in his eyes. "But I'm coming back in a couple of weeks and staying a few days. Can we schedule something then? I promise I'll tell you everything. This isn't about me wanting to keep things from you. I'm just tired today. This pregnancy is taking a toll."

They'd walked back to the building, and he opened the door for her, allowing her to walk through first. "I can wait a couple of weeks; I've waited this long to discuss the truth with you."

"Thanks for understanding. I'll send you a text with the date of my arrival, and we can schedule something then, okay?"

"Sounds good." He looked at her with curiosity.

"What?" she asked.

"Is it Liam?"

"Josh, this isn't the time or place."

"I just need to know if it's him?"

Jenna looked down at her hands and forced them to stop shaking, then let out a slow, "Yes."

"I see." He stayed calm, his breathing even and steady, then peeked into the room. Only a few women remained, either helping clean or waiting for their ride. "Do you mind if I say hello to your mom?"

That caught her off guard. "Sure. Why would I have a problem with that?"

"I didn't think you would. I'm just being polite. It was nice to see you, Jenna, and I'll talk to you again in a couple of weeks." After he'd walked away, he looked back over his shoulder, "Take care."

"Until then," said Jenna, as she watched him walk across the room toward her mother, who wore a perplexed look and glanced at Jenna and raised an eyebrow. Jenna shrugged, showing she knew how awkward it was to have Josh there.

When Josh was far enough away, Jenna let out the breath she was holding in one big swoosh. Cassie was at her heels, startling her out of her trance.

"What's he doing here, and what did he say? Did you know he was coming?"

"Where on Earth did you come from? Were you hiding behind the stack of chairs, listening?"

"I did no such thing. Now tell me everything!"

"There's not much to tell. He wanted to talk about the adoption, wanted to know what information I have, that's all, nothing more."

"And?"

"And what?"

"How did he take it?"

"We didn't get into it. I told him tonight wasn't good. We made plans to get together when I return."

"Hmmm. He better not try anything."

"I don't think he will. He seems different today. At peace with it all."

"Yeah, well, don't let your guard down so soon. Now let's get you home. You look like you need a good night's sleep."

⁂

That night, laying in bed because Cassie insisted Jenna take her room, Jenna stayed up half the night, despite being so tired. She missed Seul and couldn't wait to get back to see her crazy little cat. She'd asked her neighbour to feed Seul every day. She also couldn't get Liam off her mind. Seeing Josh wasn't as difficult as she had expected. She was happy about that; because if Josh and Liam ever met, which seemed inevitable considering they were interested in knowing each other, she would likely see a lot of him. She couldn't imagine what it would be like to be in Josh's presence once the baby arrived—that would be an awkward moment.

Jenna glanced at the time on her phone. It was after midnight when she fell into a deep sleep and her alarm woke her four hours later. When she awakened, she checked her phone for messages and smiled at the message from Liam telling her he missed her and that he'd be at the airport waiting with open arms, followed by a heart emoji. He had sent the message last night at half past midnight. Feeling tired from not having slept enough, Jenna was slow, but Cassie got her to the airport on time. She slept on the short flight, and when she stepped off the plane and walked through to the arrival area, Liam was there waiting, as promised, holding a bouquet of fresh-cut flowers and a box of dark chocolate. She suspected Cassie must have told him she preferred dark over milk chocolate.

"This is a pleasant surprise," said Jenna, greeting him with a long kiss.

He pulled her into him and wrapped his arms around her. "This is not all. There is one more surprise back at your apartment."

Curious about what it was, Jenna raised her eyebrows. Liam took her bag and her hand, and together they made their way through the crowded airport.

During the drive, they talked casually and listened to the news on the radio as Jenna reached into her bag for hand sanitizer. When they arrived at her apartment, Liam walked to her side to help her out. Getting in and out of cars was challenging. Once they were upstairs and standing outside her door, he told her to close her eyes and to keep them shut until he said otherwise.

"Isn't that a little dangerous? Telling a pregnant woman to shut her eyes while she walks could end in disaster," she teased.

He gazed at her. "I will not let you fall," he said and wrapped his arm around her waist and led her into the apartment. "Are your eyes still closed?"

"Yes," she said, waving her hand out in front to make sure she didn't walk into anything.

"Keep them closed, no peeking!"

"I'm not peeking!"

Of course she peeked and noticed they were entering a bright room.

"Okay, open them."

Jenna slowly opened her eyes, allowing the light to accumulate to clear away the fogginess. She gasped, then blinked a few times to be sure she was seeing clearly.

"It's beautiful. Liam, did you do all this?"

"I planned it, and did most of it, but I had help in order to finish before the weekend."

Jenna stood inside the baby's nursery. It was the smaller bedroom and the one Jenna used as a home office, but he'd transformed it. He painted the walls a soft pink, the same shade from the baby shower. There was a massive, human-sized mural of a family of elephants: a mother, father, and a baby. Jenna wondered if the mural represented her, Liam, and their baby. He'd furnished the room with a white crib, a matching changing table and dresser, and the best part was a white rocking chair with another mural of the same family of elephants on the back. It was a different pose and different scenery than the one on the wall, but the same family, the same eyes on all three animals. On the dresser were little elephant figurines, and in the middle of the floor, a rug in an off-white, pink pastel tone that was soft under Jenna's feet, tempting her to lay down on it. The changing table was full of diapers, creams, lotions, and as Jenna opened drawers, she saw he'd filled them, too, with more baby stuff.

"This is the most beautiful baby's room I've seen in my life." Jenna put her arms around him and squeezed tight. "But where did all this stuff come from?"

"I bought some and my family and employees and friends helped with the rest. I went shopping with my mother; she was a great help throughout all this."

"Oh, Liam, I don't know what to say."

"My family wanted to do something for you, since it was awkward for them to go to Toronto, considering... the history. We were going to throw you a second baby shower here, but then I had the idea of just putting the room together instead. I thought maybe two baby show-ers might be too much. I wasn't sure, but Cassie agreed, so everyone dropped off their gifts, and my parents, and brother and sister were here all weekend with me, helping put this all together. Dad assembled the furniture while I painted. I hope you like the painting. If not, we can repaint or cover it with wallpaper."

Liam stood back, allowing Jenna an unobstructed view of the room to take it all in.

"I love it. This is truly unbelievable and so amazing." She turned to him. "You're amazing."

"My parents gifted the crib and dresser. My aunt, the changing table. I bought the rocking chair, that is a special gift from me."

"How did you know I've always wanted one?"

"Who do you think spills your deepest, darkest secrets?"

She smiled, knowing all too well who. "Of course she did."

"It's funny because I didn't get any of these things from the baby shower, so I don't have duplicates," she said.

"We planned it that way. Cassie prepared a list and registered you to ensure there'd be no duplicates. Your parents had to return the crib when Cassie told them my parents had already purchased one. So that's why they gifted the high-tech, most comfortable stroller available."

"Wow! You even know what gifts I received! Cas sure tells you everything. Wait. How did you even get Cassie's contact info?"

"I looked her up on social media and messaged her and then she gave me her number."

"Sneaky!"

"Did she do a good job conveying your vision? I wanted to bring it to life for you."

"Yes. You both did an amazing job. I wish she was here to see it."

"Don't worry, she has already made me send her multiple photos, and we talked over Zoom this morning so she could see it."

"This morning?" Jenna lifted her eyebrows.

"She called the minute you boarded the plane."

"Of course she did."

Jenna took a minute to stretch out her kinked neck from sleeping on the plane. "Liam, thank you so much. I don't even know what to say. I love this." She hesitated for a moment, remembering the last few months and all he'd done for her: their night together, dinners, walks, talks, then added, "And I love you." She hadn't been sure until then, until that moment.

His eyes lit up. "Do you have any idea how long I have waited to hear those words?"

"I know. And I'm sorry I couldn't say it before."

He brought his finger up to her lip. "No, do not apologize. I wanted you to take your time and know for sure that when you gave yourself to me, it was because you truly wanted me and not out of convenience at having my baby or out of rebound. I am glad it took this long for you to tell me you love me; it means it is real."

"It is as real as you and I standing here." She stood with her head against his shoulder when a thought came to her. "Liam, why don't you move in with me?"

He pulled her back slightly. "Did you just ask me to move in with you?"

"Yes, I think it's time. Will you consider it? I'll renew the lease."

"Jenna, there is nothing to consider. I am already packed. I have only been waiting for you to ask."

She smiled. "We're doing this?"

He reached for her hands. "We are, and there isn't anyone else I want to do this with."

Outside the nursery window, the thick snow fell heavily, and they stood side by side as Jenna's eyes wandered to the snow-covered streets.

"I'm not a winter person, but a fresh snowfall in Quebec City at Christmas sure is breathtaking. Don't you think?" she asked.

Liam's eyes focused on her as she focused out the window at the snow.

"Breathtaking indeed," he said, his eyes not leaving her.

CHAPTER 46

Drinks Over a Zoom Call

CASSIE AND JENNA had drinks over a zoom call later that evening; Cassie indulged in white wine and Jenna in a glass of unsweetened almond milk. Not exactly her drink of choice, but her time would come soon. Liam went to his apartment to get an overnight bag and promised to return within the hour. Jenna told Cassie during their call that he was moving in.

"So, you've been talking to Liam a lot. Tell me, what do you think?"

Jenna heard her take a sip. "Real cute. He's such a sweetheart, too. So concerned with making you happy. You have my approval."

"How long have the two of you been discussing me, by the way?"

"Since before you knew about the baby shower. He loves you, a lot." She stopped long enough to have another sip. "How are you going to handle him seeing Josh when you come for the hearing?"

Jenna cleared her throat before answering. "We don't know for sure that's going to happen."

"What do you mean? I thought they said they were interested in meeting?"

"Sort of. They've asked about learning more about one another, but they haven't made plans."

"Well, for your sake, girl, I'm praying it happens after you've had the baby."

"Why after?"

"Because then you can have a few drinks beforehand," she said, and took another sip.

"Are you sipping your wine loudly to make me jealous?"

"Jenna, girl, of course not. That would be silliness," she said, followed by another sip, and Jenna laughed.

⧢

The following afternoon, Liam came home for lunch. He hadn't officially moved in, but he'd only been back in his apartment to get personal things. After lunch, Liam went back to the store, and Jenna had a virtual meeting with her lawyer where she learned Rachel had made inaccurate statements about her that would hurt the case.

When her lawyer divulged that information, Jenna's blood boiled. "This is bullshit, Peter," she said to her lawyer, looking through the project list that Rachel submitted as evidence of unfinished projects towards a right of dismissal case. "None of these stories were mine. She's lying."

"The Information Technology team has already scoured your email for any records about these projects and they found nothing, so that proves that you weren't working on them."

"Well, that's good?"

"We still have to prove that they did not assign you the projects."

"But if there's no email trail, isn't that proof enough?"

"Not exactly. Rachel presented a list of projects assigned verbally."

"It's as if she covered her tracks. Why didn't I plan for this?" asked Jenna.

"I'm not sure you could. But, that's why you have me."

"What are the chances of us winning?"

"Considering everything, we have an excellent case."

After Jenna finished the call with her lawyer, she felt a little more relaxed. She wasn't suing the magazine to get her job back or get Rachel fired, although that would be nice. She was just trying to get what was rightfully hers. They let her go without notice or pay in lieu of notice, and she had worked there for several years, so it was a nice sum of money she could use, especially with the baby coming. Besides, she wanted to prove a point and save her pride.

Jenna was meeting Liam for supper later that night after he finished at the store. With Christmas around the corner, he'd extended his hours to accommodate late-night shoppers. They planned to meet downtown by the store and as Jenna walked, hidden behind her big coat, hat, scarf, and mitts, her phone rang, and she pulled it out of her coat pocket, staring at the display, she saw it was Brenda Mills; Holly's mother. Jenna pulled off her mitt in a hurry to not miss the call and answered with a heavy breath.

"Jenna dear, did I catch you at a bad time? You sound as if you're out of breath. This is Brenda Mills; we met a few months back."

"Yes, of course, I remember. You pointed out that I was pregnant even before I knew."

"Ahh yes, I remember. How is the pregnancy? I assume the child you're carrying is my great-grandchild?"

"I'm swollen like a whale, tired all the time, and hungry, but other than that, it's wonderful."

"Splendid, so a spring baby?"

"First week of April, if she can wait that long."

"So, it's a girl. How lovely. Listen, you're probably wondering why I'm calling, so let's cut to the chase, shall we? We want to meet Liam."

Brenda's comment threw her off balance and Jenna reached out to grab a nearby lamppost covered in Christmas lights. "Just Liam? What about Josh?"

"I apologize. That didn't come out right. Of course we're interested in meeting both, but from what I understood, only Liam knows about the adoption?"

"That's changed."

"I see. My husband and I thought it might be easier to start with Liam since he knew the truth. I didn't know where things stood with the other boy, and we certainly didn't want to upset his life."

Jenna didn't realize how close to Liam's store she was until she saw him outside talking to a young couple who had purchased one of his paintings. When he saw Jenna, he smiled and waved.

"Brenda, let me call you back soon. I'm meeting Liam today, and I'll bring this up. Also, I have information on Josh, but this is not the time to go into that. Can I call you tomorrow, after I've talked to Liam?"

"Certainly, my dear. We will await your call."

"Thank you, and I promise to tell you everything then."

"Looking forward to chatting with you. Take care and stay warm."

After receiving that unexpected call, Jenna slowly made her way to Liam, observing her footing because of the ice. He greeted her cold lips with a warm kiss.

"You look startled. Everything okay, darling?"

"Yes, everything is fine, but, Liam, we need to talk."

◎∿

At the restaurant, after they ordered, Jenna told Liam about Brenda's call. He stared at her with a blank look. She had a hard time determining if the meeting was something he wanted or not.

"Liam? What are you thinking? Do you want to meet them?"

He sighed. "A part of me does, but I do not want to upset my parents. I do not want them thinking I went behind their back." He let out a loud breath. "Let me talk to Mom and Dad. Make sure this won't threaten them. If they are okay with it, I would like to meet my biological grandparents. But if it is going to cause Mom and Dad any misery, I do not want to know anymore. Fair?"

"Of course. We could eat fast and see them tonight if you wanted?"

Moments later, the server arrived with their food.

"Perfect timing," said Liam.

When they finished their meals, they drove to Liam's parents' house to have the painful conversation that Liam had told Jenna he was dreading but was necessary. Jenna was happy to see them again so soon.

"Are you nervous?" she asked.

"I am more concerned with how they will take it than how it affects me, to be honest."

"You're always so concerned with others, Liam. You have a good heart."

"That is because of who raised me. Those two people in there," he pointed to the house as they sat in the driveway, "made me who I am. I do not want to hurt them by having them think they were not enough."

Jenna reached out to touch his shoulder. "Something tells me they won't think that."

As the two sat in the car waiting for Liam to get enough courage, the front door of the house opened. An attractive-looking woman peeked through the opening.

"I never told you before, but your mom is beautiful."

"Inside and out." He let out a breath. "Ready?"

⚮

Liam's parents were not as fluent in English as Liam, so they spoke mainly in French. "Darling, what a surprise. Come in you two," said Liam's mother, already dressed in her robe.

"Mom, we did not mean to disturb you. You look like you are ready for bed; we can come back."

"Nonsense, come in, please. You know I like to be comfortable at home." She wrapped her robe around her waist. "Your father and I were just about to have tea. Would you two like a cup?"

"That would be lovely, thank you," said Jenna, in French as well. "Can I help in the kitchen?"

"Nonsense, in your state, I'm surprised you're even up at this hour." She patted Jenna's stomach. "Sit, I'll get the tea."

"Mrs. Garnier, I wanted to thank you again for your help with the baby's room. It's lovely."

"Jenna, you're a part of the family, so please call me Pat. I'm happy you like it. Please sit."

"Where's Dad?" asked Liam.

"He was taking out the trash but should be along momentarily."

Liam and Jenna took seats at the kitchen table and Jenna noticed Liam's hands shook, so she placed hers over his to help calm him, but she continued to feel them shake under hers. Liam's dad took a seat next to him, and when the tea was ready his mother joined them, placing four steaming cups on the table. There was some general conversation: Christmas, Jenna's pregnancy, the baby's room, and when their teacups were almost empty, the actual discussion began.

"So, what brings you two here on this cold winter night?" asked Pat. Jenna squeezed Liam's hand and gestured for him to go ahead.

"Mom, Dad, there's something I must tell you." He stopped for a moment to check their faces, then continued. "Have you ever heard of Brenda and Bob Mills?"

Pat and her husband looked at one another and both raised their eyebrows. "The names don't ring any bells. Why? Who are they, darling?" asked his mother.

"They are my biological family," said Liam softly, not meeting their eyes.

Liam's mom stood as casually as if she'd just asked them for another cup of tea. "Oh, mon Dieu." *Oh, dear God,* she said, then continued. "Je vais préparer du thé." *I'll prepare tea.*

"Good idea. Sounds like this is going to require a few soothing cups," said his dad.

❧

An hour later, Liam had brought his parents up to speed on how that all came about: Jenna's involvement, Josh, and the discussion ended with him telling his parents that Brenda and Bob Mills wanted to meet him. His parents were supportive and said that they had known eventually some long-lost family member would appear and want to make contact, and they had spent years discussing how they'd react. They told Liam they encouraged him to meet Brenda and Bob and learn about his past. They felt it was important for Liam to know about his origins. Liam told them that his first concern was their feelings. He admitted he worried they would feel replaced and if meeting his biological grandparents did that to them, he'd abandon the idea once and for all and never look back. But his parents told him not to be silly, and that they were pleased that he would get to meet at least some people who were responsible for him being in the world. Jenna listened intently to the exchange and continued to squeeze Liam's hand.

"I don't know why I was so worried about telling you. You took it better than I thought."

"Darling, your father and I only want what is best for you. How could keeping you from them help if that's what you want? If you're happy, then so are we."

"You sure about that, Mom?"

His mother looked to his father for encouragement.

His father nodded. "Son, you have our full support," he said, then added, "and I think I speak for your mother also when I say that we want to meet them too."

Jenna reached out to Liam to wipe a tear that had fallen; he squeezed her hand in return.

"Thanks, Dad, that means a lot."

When Liam and Jenna prepared to leave, his mother wrapped her arms around him tight and squeezed for a long time.

"I might not have given birth to you, but you are, and always will be, my son. You have as much of my soul in you as your brother and sister do. I never want you to forget that, my darling."

"I know, I love you, Mom. Thanks for everything you've done for me and everything you continue to do."

While Liam hugged his father, his mother embraced Jenna. "Now, you take care of yourself and my granddaughter, you hear? Get yourself home and into bed and stay off the streets. The roads are getting icy this time of year."

"I'll be careful," Jenna assured her, and then Liam took her hand and together they walked out the door, more satisfied than they thought possible.

"That went well, I think. Better than I imagined it would," said Liam, speaking English again as he held Jenna's arm to keep her from slipping.

"You underestimate your parents sometimes. They're much stronger than you think."

"You are right, they are."

"You know what this means?"

"I can meet my biological grandparents." Liam let out a sigh, then turned toward Jenna. "I'm ready."

"Do you want to call them and introduce yourself or do you want me to do it?"

"I don't know, what do you think?"

"I think you should do whatever is easiest. But, I'm happy to call and arrange the introduction for you."

Liam was driving on slick roads, and Jenna figured he was trying to concentrate on both the road and what to do because he remained silent.

"Liam? You okay?" asked Jenna.

"You do it. You call and arrange the meeting. It will be easier."

Jenna nodded in agreement. "I'll call Brenda first thing in the morning."

"I could not do this without you," he said, smiled, and squeezed her hand.

CHAPTER 47

Hiding Behind Excuses

ALMOST A WEEK had passed since Jenna and Liam had seen his parents. He'd made Jenna reschedule the meeting with the Millses twice, making excuses, she was sure. Once he'd said he had a headache, which Jenna knew not to be true because he was listening to loud music while painting the same afternoon he was to have met them. Jenna had stopped by the store to check on him, and the loud music blasted from the back room. The second time he'd said he needed to work late, but when Jenna stopped by again to make sure he was okay, his part-time employee worked the storefront while he stood idly behind the counter on his phone. Jenna realized then that Liam was hiding behind excuses.

She brought up the subject, and he admitted he was being a coward; she soothed his concerns and calmed his fears. After she called Brenda Mills again, she promised next time Liam would be ready. They set another date later in the week.

∽

It was the afternoon of the visit, and Jenna watched as Liam paced back and forth for an hour. He changed his shirt three times, his pants twice, and he drank double the amount of peppermint tea that he normally drank, so he was constantly using the washroom. After his last trip, he headed into the kitchen to make yet another cup.

"Liam, sweetheart, relax! It'll be okay. I promise." Jenna took him by the hand and led him to the couch. He sat beside her, but was fidgety; his leg bounced up and down.

"What time is it?" he asked, even though he wore a wristwatch.

"They should be here any moment," said Jenna, and then she turned as there was a knock on the door. "That's them. This is it, you ready?"

He let out a groan. "I think so."

"Stay here. I'll answer it." Jenna kissed Liam's forehead before answering the door. She heard his deep, loud breath and took one herself. She watched him close his eyes as she disappeared around the corner. When she returned, his eyes were open, and he stared at the man and woman he had never met. Jenna stood back and looked at the three of them with a sense of familiarity—the resemblance, astonishing. Brenda stood rigidly, clenching her handbag while Bob paced. Jenna was about to break the silence, but Bob beat her, introducing himself to Liam.

He took several steps towards Liam and spoke in French. "It's an honour to be here and meet you. I imagine you have many questions, and believe us when I say we'll answer them honestly. Not a day has passed that I haven't thought of you and the other boy."

"I have many questions, but I do not know where to begin," said Liam, also in French.

"Take your time. Now that we've found you, we aren't going anywhere."

Brenda remained next to Jenna, watching as Liam embraced his grandfather for the first time. Jenna glanced toward Brenda's hands; they were steady, but she held her purse close to her chest. Then she looked at Jenna and approached her husband and her grandson and joined the embrace. Jenna watched as a tear trickled to her chin.

"Je vais mettre du thé." *I'll put on some tea*, said Jenna.

She left them in the living room and went to the kitchen to boil water, but because the apartment was small, she had an excellent view of them still locked in their overdue, but tender hug.

They spent the afternoon together, talking, crying, and Jenna even pulled out some baby photos which, Pat, Liam's mother, had given her to share with them. Liam hadn't known about the photos, and Jenna observed Liam as he watched his grandparents look at each one, carefully, as if they were committing the photos to memory. The afternoon turned into evening, and they ordered in takeout for supper. Questions poured from both sides; answers created more questions, and before long, it was nightfall.

◠◡

"Here," said Jenna after Brenda and Bob left, handing Liam a steaming cup of peppermint tea. "How do you feel?"

"Relieved. I'm glad I went through with it. They seem like good people."

"They are. Brenda and I have spoken many times. She might have made a mistake twenty-eight years ago, but she is trying to make up for that."

"I'm looking forward to getting to know them better." Liam turned to Jenna. "Thank you."

"I'm glad it worked out," she said.

"You know something? I think this was fate."

"What was?"

"You finding me," he said.

"I think you're right. And we have Rachel to thank for that."

"I guess we do."

"Ha! Imagine that!" said Jenna. "Perhaps that's the reason she was in my life all along."

Liam scratched his head and then stood with his hands in his pockets.

"What's wrong, Liam?"

"I cannot believe I never asked this before, but does Josh know about us?"

"Yes. He showed up at the baby shower to talk, and I told him."

"Why did you not tell me he was invited to the baby shower?"

"He wasn't, he just showed up at the end to talk."

"What did he want to talk about?"

"His past. The truth. You. But we didn't have time to get into any of it. We agreed to meet when I go back for the hearing."

"I suppose I better get accustomed to having him around."

"You have nothing to worry about. Okay?"

"I know. It's just odd knowing that you two were once engaged." He reached for her hand, kissed it, and then took her into his arms.

CHAPTER 48

Nothing Changed

"I'M SORRY, LAINEY, but I've got court all day, so I won't be in the office. Listen, I gotta run. I'll call you later," said Josh into the phone after picking up because he saw Lainey's number appear multiple times.

"Why do I feel you're avoiding me?"

What Josh *wanted* to say was, 'because I am', but what he said was; "Don't be silly, why would I avoid you?"

"Everything between us has changed!" she yelled into the phone.

"How could it have changed if there was never anything between us? I thought you understood where I was at?"

He waited for a reply, but she remained quiet.

Josh ran his fingers through his hair. "Lainey, I have to go. I've got to get into the courtroom," he said and hung up as he walked through the courthouse building doors.

As he rushed through the entranceway, he noticed a familiar woman standing at the end of the hallway and as he turned his head, he whipped it back around. It was Jenna. He blinked a few times to clear his foggy vision, but her image remained. He knew she was back that week for the hearing, but he never expected to see her first thing that morning.

Josh waited for her to notice him, but it took a while. She was busy admiring the Christmas decorations and the large Christmas tree in the main entranceway. But as her eyes scanned the room, they eventually landed on Josh; he smiled at her. She waddled across the room to him, holding her stomach.

"Hey, you," said Josh, reaching out to kiss her cheek. "I wasn't expecting to see you." Josh looked at his wristwatch—he'd be late if he didn't move now. He winced because he wanted to spend more time with her.

"It's nice to see you, Josh. Are we still on for our meeting tomorrow?"

"Absolutely. I've cleared my afternoon. I'll pick you up from Cassie's as planned." He glanced at his watch again. "Shit," he said, letting it slip.

"Go. I know how much you hate being late. We'll talk tomorrow."

Josh waved, already halfway down the hall, rushing toward the elevator.

☙❧

When court ended, Josh rushed back to where he'd seen Jenna, but she wasn't there, so he went to get a tea. As he slowly dipped the tea bag into the hot water, he wondered if Liam was here, too. Josh had a sinking feeling the situation would get ridiculously awkward if he ran into them both. Josh wasn't ready to meet him yet. He'd been curious and wanted to know the whole story, maybe even see a photo or two, but to meet would make it real, and he wasn't sure he was ready to take that tremendous leap because when he did, there'd be no jumping back. What would he even say to the guy? 'Hey bro, how's it going?' or 'I hope you and my ex will be happy together with your new baby?' or maybe, 'Couldn't find your own family, had to take mine?'

He shook his head. All ridiculous—best to avoid the guy. He and Jenna had civilized conversations the last two times they'd seen each other. Josh was happy about that and needed to remain calm and collected so he didn't push her away. Attacking Liam would upset her, and he didn't want to do that.

He still cared for her—loved her—and wanted her to be happy, even if not with him. He'd screwed it up with her; he knew, since Cassie explained why Jenna took the job. He'd not been able to forgive himself since he'd found out. He thought it was her doing, but *he* forced that wedge between them, not her. He did it alone; it had cost him greatly. And he had to let her go because she'd found someone else. Josh found himself once again back in the same spot he and Jenna were at earlier, by the large Christmas tree. He wasn't sure how or why he kept returning. He'd been wandering with his tea when he should have been getting ready for the next court session. He glanced at his watch, three minutes before he was due to meet with his client. He took one sip of the hot tea, burnt his tongue and then tossed it in the nearest trash can, forcing his mind to move forward toward anything that didn't involve Jenna, Liam, the baby, or his past life. Easier to move forward than to lament the past.

CHAPTER 49

No Words Spoken

JENNA'S HEARING WAS in ten minutes, and Liam still hadn't arrived. He'd left Quebec City yesterday evening and planned to drive straight through the night to avoid heavy traffic. He'd told Jenna he'd stop mid-way to get a couple of hours of sleep on the side of the road or at a rest stop. He should have arrived early that morning, but never made it to Cassie's apartment before Jenna left. He wasn't answering her calls or texts either, and she'd had to go to the hearing and face Rachel without him by her side. Where was he? Her mind went through many possibilities: he had cold feet about being a dad, changed his mind about her, forgot his cell phone. At the end of all the mind-banter, she concluded he must have fallen asleep on the side of the road with his phone on silent. That explanation seemed like the most plausible one.

Cassie, of course, was there, but was busy chatting up some lawyer she met earlier. The two seemed to have hit it off, so Jenna left her alone and didn't bother her about her upset stomach—surely because of nerves and not the pregnancy. As she took a deep breath, her lawyer, Peter, approached and asked if she was ready.

"I think so. Let's do this and get it over with."

Before walking into the courtroom, Jenna took one more look down the hallway, hoping to see Liam, but saw Josh standing with a cup of tea in his hands and then tossing it into the trash can. When he looked up, she saw the pain in his eyes, but he didn't notice her as she was quick to turn and made her way inside, following her lawyer.

❦

Inside the courtroom, the air was thick and cold. Jenna hadn't seen Rachel yet, so her eyes quickly scanned the room. When she saw Rachel sitting all smug and collected, Jenna temporarily forgot about Liam's absence. Rachel's arms were crossed over the table, and she held a smile that made Jenna wonder if it was real. The confident look she portrayed reminded Jenna of how she'd treated her. Rachel stared straight ahead and hadn't seen Jenna yet, so Jenna took a seat next to her lawyer. Before the session commenced, Jenna looked back to see if Liam had made it in before they closed the doors. But scanning the crowd only depressed her more. Her mind was full of questions: Where was he? Why hadn't he called?

❦

When they were dismissed for a fifteen-minute recess, Jenna rushed out, eager to call Liam. The phone rang four times before going to voicemail; she didn't leave a message, but hung up and tried again, hoping the ringing would wake him. She killed ten of the fifteen minutes she had and realized she still needed to use the ladies' room, so on the last call, she left a voicemail.

"Liam, please call me back. You're worrying me to death. I'm on recess but due back inside in five minutes, so my phone will be off. Please call me and leave a message so I know you're okay." Reluctantly, she put her phone in her bag and used the restroom before going back inside.

❧

"Well, there you have it. Rachel and the magazine got what they deserved. I hope you're pleased as that went rather well," said Jenna's lawyer with a smirk on his face as he packed up his briefcase.

"Yes, I'm happy. Please excuse me Peter, but I need to make a call." Jenna rushed out, holding her breath as she checked her phone—nothing. She called Liam again—voicemail. Damn it. She called Cassie next, who'd left to go back to the office for an emergency just before the hearing began.

"Hey, is it done? What was the verdict?"

"We won. But listen, Cas, that's not why I'm calling. I'm worried."

"Why are you worried? Did you not get what you wanted?"

"That's not it. I'm worried about Liam."

"What happened?"

"I don't know. That's the problem. He never made it; he's not answering his phone. I don't know what to do. I've got this bad feeling in the pit of my stomach. I can't breathe, Cas. Oh, gosh."

"Okay, girl, relax. I'm sure he just got tired and fell asleep. When was the last time you tried to call?"

"Right before I called you and it went to voicemail. I've called a million times already," she cried into the phone.

"Okay, listen, call him again, and then find a bench and sit tight. I'm on my way to get you. Be there in ten."

Jenna's finger constantly pressed the call button and after it went to voicemail, she hung up and tried again and again. Her breathing was quick and short, and her legs shook. There was a bench at the end of the hall; she took Cassie's advice and sat and laid her head back, letting it rest against the icy wall.

There was silence, then doors opened, and a gush of voices filled the air, but through the chatter, she still picked up on the voice she knew well. Josh was giving someone advice on what to do; a client, she assumed. Jenna brought her head to a forward position to see him, and when the crowd dissipated and he noticed her, he excused himself.

He took a seat next to her. "Jenna, what's wrong? You look pale. I take it the hearing didn't go well?" He placed his hand on her shaky knee.

"No, it's not that. We won. I got a nice severance out of it. The magazine got what it deserved for trying to protect Rachel."

His hand was still on her knee, but when she looked down at it, he removed it quickly. "Then why do you look upset? And don't tell me you're not. I can see it in your eyes, something's bothering you."

Involving Josh was not a good idea and would only make things more difficult—more complicated. She didn't need to complicate her life further, but blurted it out anyway. "It's Liam."

Josh squared his shoulders. "What about him?"

"He's missing." She let out a sob and leaned her head on Josh's shoulder. "I don't know what to do or how to find him."

"Missing?" Jenna suspected he'd asked for clarification, then he prompted her for more information. "How long?"

After Jenna filled him in, he said the same thing Cassie had said. "I'm sure he probably pulled over to have a nap and fell asleep with his phone on silent."

"That's what everyone keeps saying, but this nagging feeling is burning through me. Something is wrong. I just know it. I can't explain how, but I just do."

He looked around. "Is Cassie here?"

"She's on her way back."

"All right, let me make some calls, but I need to know his last name and what type of truck he was driving. Do you know where he rented it from?"

Jenna gave him Liam's last name and the name of the rental company, but that was all the information she had; Josh wrote it down on a notepad that he pulled out of his briefcase, and told her to sit tight for a few minutes, making her promise not to leave that spot.

When Jenna was alone, she laid her head back against the wall, having a hard time holding it up. It felt too heavy. With her head back and her eyes closed, she didn't notice Rachel approaching until her voice was sharp and edgy, close to her ear.

"You think you've won. But you haven't. I'm going to make the rest of your career as a journalist a living hell. No other magazine or paper will ever hire you by the time I'm through with you."

Jenna didn't respond and remained with her eyes closed and head hung back, listening to Rachel's empty threats. Rachel huffed and stormed off, stomping her feet. At least Rachel allowed her a few moments of distraction, not thinking—worrying about Liam, but when Rachel's stomping faded, the worry flooded back full force. Where was Cassie? She was taking a long time to get there. Surely it had been longer than ten minutes.

Finally, she heard the clicking of familiar footsteps down the hall, different from the stomping of Rachel's feet. There was no mistaking Cassie's walk. For a small girl, she sure let a room know she'd arrived.

Cassie took a seat next to Jenna and placed her arms around her. "Oh girl, I'm so sorry I took so long, but I was talking to Josh out front. He said you told him everything. That was smart because he can help. He's making calls trying to find out what happened."

"Cas, something is not right. I can feel it. Does that even make any sense?"

The look Cassie gave her was of pity, unlike Cassie's usual cheerful demeanour.

"What?" Jenna asked, "Did Josh find him? Does he know something?"

"Let's just wait for Josh, and then we..."

"Jenna," said Josh suddenly from behind the other side of the bench, interrupting Cassie. He bent down and placed his hands on her shoulders, bringing her into his arms. "You need to come with me."

There were no words spoken between Josh and Cassie, but Jenna noticed Josh pointed toward Cassie and gestured for her to get up. She got up and took Jenna's arm, lifting her off the bench while Josh did the same from her other side. Jenna swung her head from one to the other.

"What's going on?" she asked.

"Trust me," said Josh.

"Did you find Liam? Are you taking me to him?"

Cassie and Josh each held onto one arm and led her into an empty conference room. There was a board table in the middle of the room, and a coffee station and water dispenser against the back wall. An enormous window allowed the afternoon sunshine to seep in after last night's snowfall. Josh closed the door behind him while Cassie sat Jenna down, then got her a glass of water and forced her to drink.

"Will someone please tell me what the hell is going on?"

Josh was the first to speak. "Jenna, if you've ever had to be strong, believed that things happened for a reason, this is the time."

Jenna looked toward Cassie, but she turned away from her. Josh called Cassie's name, and she turned around and sat next to Jenna, grabbing both her hands in hers. Jenna noticed her nod toward Josh.

"Just tell me. Please. What did you find?"

He cleared his throat before he continued. "Liam got into a head-on collision during the night." He cleared his throat again. "He's in critical condition and might not make it." He leaned in close to Jenna and placed both arms around her shoulder. "I'm so sorry Jenna. So sorry you have to go through this."

CHAPTER 50

Meaningless Words

THE WORDS DIDN'T register—at all. They were meaningless words left in the stale air, floating with no intent or purpose. Jenna convinced herself Josh spoke the words simply to torment her, make her sick, and have her think her stomach was exploding. There was a sharp stab of pain in her midsection—strong, like a knife cutting into her. She cried out while squeezing Cassie's hand so hard that Cassie winced.

The pain was making it difficult for Jenna to breathe. She continued to scream in agony, clenching her stomach. The room spun; she wasn't sure where she was; she'd lost track of where she'd been moments ago. Jenna closed her eyes to focus on breathing as she lay flat on her back. How had she gotten like that? Two people dressed in uniform mouthed words she didn't understand and carried her somewhere. Cassie's hands remained wrapped tight against Jenna's and as the strangers carried her through the hallways, Cassie's hand slipped out of her reach and she found herself alone, surrounded by blackness.

CHAPTER 51

My Strongest Link

JOSH WATCHED AS Cassie pleaded with the paramedic.

"Please, let me be with her."

"Are you family?"

"I'm her best friend, please?"

"Get in."

Cassie stepped into the ambulance and yelled out to Josh. "I'll call you once we get to the hospital and let you know where we are. Can you call her parents and her brother?"

Josh nodded as he'd already scanned his contacts for her parent's landline, ready to call. Her mother answered on the first ring. Josh heard something drop and bang on the floor after he'd told her. She gasped into the phone and cried out for her husband before she hung up. He didn't want to be the bearer of bad news, but it seemed the responsibility fell onto him. There wasn't anyone else, so he stepped up and did it.

Josh texted Cassie to let her know Jenna's parents were on their way, and then he called his office and told his assistant to clear his afternoon.

Jenna would need his support, whether she knew it, or liked it. He'd be there for her when she was rational and calm. He'd be there to pick up the pieces of her broken heart if Liam didn't make it.

On his way to the hospital, a text from Cassie came through his BMW's Bluetooth speaker. Josh pressed the button on the voice command to hear it.

Cassie: Jenna is okay. She's sleeping. They gave her something to calm her nerves. She's not in labour, thank goodness, as it's too soon. It was a panic attack. Liam is in surgery. That's all they will tell me.

As he drove, Josh used the voice activation feature to reply to her text.

Josh: I'm almost there. Don't leave her side, okay?

Cassie: Thank you for coming. I'm going crazy here not knowing what to do!

Josh: I wouldn't be anyplace else

❧

As the elevator doors opened on the maternity ward floor, Cassie was there, waiting to get in.

"Hey, where are you going?" asked Josh, wondering why she'd left Jenna's side.

"Jenna's parents are here, so I was going to find out more about Liam. Someone must call his parents. I don't know if the hospital contacted them." She had tears and could barely get the words out. "Oh Josh, this is horrible. What are we going to do? How is Jenna going to get through this alone if he doesn't make it? I don't even know if Liam's parents speak English, but I have to call them."

"She's not alone. She's got...you." He'd almost said 'us'.

"I know she's got *us* and her parents, but I mean 'alone' differently. Without the father of her baby by her side. Oh gosh, I think I'm going to be sick." She ran off into the nearest washroom, leaving Josh wondering the same thing.

Josh waited outside the washroom. He knew Jenna's parents were with her, so he wasn't too anxious about not being there. His priority was to ensure Cassie understood she needed to pull herself together. She needed to be strong for her best friend, needed to be Jenna's anchor, not the victim. When she came out of the washroom, her face was pale, and she wiped her mouth as her eyes met his. He tilted his head to the side.

"Better now?" he asked.

"Look, don't start with me, please. I know I'm being weak."

"I just asked if you were better."

"But that's not what you really wanted to say." She reached into her purse and, without even looking inside, rummaged through its contents, and pulled out a package of gum, took a piece, offered one to Josh and dropped it back inside the bag. "I'm going to make some calls, get something to eat. Where will you be?" she asked.

"Right here. I'm not going anywhere."

"I'll be back in less than half an hour. Wish me luck with Liam's parents. I'm going to need a Google translator if they can't speak English. Arggg! Could this day get any worse?"

She stepped into the elevator, and Josh went to the Intensive Care Unit to check on Liam first before going to see Jenna. He wanted to be prepared with news, good or bad.

"Are you family?" asked the nurse when Josh approached the Intensive Care Unit desk.

"He's..."

"He's what?" the nurse probed.

"He's my brother."

"I'll send someone around to give you an update in a moment, sir. Please have a seat and be patient."

Josh did as he was told with his head hung. He sat, waiting. He stood and sat again. Still waiting. A pretty female doctor with an unreadable face tapped him on the shoulder.

"You're Liam's brother, I understand?"

Josh nodded in response.

"You look alike; you could be twins."

Little did she know.

"Your brother is in critical condition. He's in surgery, still. He lost a lot of blood. We are doing everything we can. There's not much more I can tell you, other than it is critical." She patted his arm. "I'm sorry." She gestured to the Intensive Care Unit nurse. "Make sure you leave your number with the nurse so we can contact you once he's out of surgery. Your parents should be here momentarily."

"My parents?"

"Yes, we called them when Liam was first brought in. I'm told they jumped on the first flight. I'm surprised they haven't arrived yet."

The nurse walked away.

"Wait, before you go. Can you tell me, please: will he make it?"

"That I can't answer. Only God knows. There's a chapel down the hall if you wish to have a visit. It might help to say a few prayers."

His emotions were all over the place. He was angry, hurt, and sad all at once. He wished his dad were with him to guide him better; he'd have known what to say to calm Josh. He missed him dearly. He braced himself to see Jenna and her parents next, passing the chapel on his way. He stopped, opened the door, and peeked inside, then closed it and carried on, saying a prayer as he walked instead. A couple frantically ran down the hallway with their arms flailing, asking for their son in broken English. Josh's eyes followed them as they broke down in front of the Intensive Care Unit and asked about Liam. Josh watched them as the elevator doors closed.

∞

"Oh Josh, thank goodness you're here," said Kate, Jenna's mother. "Can you stay with Jenna for a bit? We need to get back to the house and get it ready for her to come home tomorrow."

Kate picked up her bag and blew Jenna a kiss as she laid lifeless, hands crossed over her tummy.

Josh looked from her mom to her dad before his eyes landed on Jenna. "I thought she was staying with Cassie? Was there a change of plans?" He directed the question to Kate, but Jenna's father, Brian, answered.

"We're bringing her home. There's no room at that apartment for two grown women for an extended period. She's moving in with us until we know more."

Jenna had been asleep because of the sedative the paramedic had given her, but hearing Josh's voice woke her.

"Liam!" she yelled. "Where is he? Is he okay?"

Josh approached and took her hand in his. "He's still in surgery."

She ripped the blankets off and tried to stand, but fumbled. Josh caught her.

"I need to go to him. NOW. Take me there."

"You can't. He's in surgery," repeated Josh.

She looked at her parents, "Mom; Dad."

"We are here darling, but we're heading out to get your stuff from Cassie's and bring it home."

"Jenna, is that what you want?" asked Josh.

Jenna didn't answer, and stared at her belly.

Kate and Brian said they'd see her in a couple of hours and left.

"Jenna, I'll be right back." Josh walked her parents out.

"Hold on a second," he said as her parents sped ahead. They stopped and turned to face him.

"Josh, don't get in between us. This is for the best. She's pregnant and might not have Liam, so she can't possibly go back to Quebec City. She's got no one there to support her." Kate had raised her voice and people passing by stopped to stare, so she lowered it a notch. "We know what's best for our daughter."

Josh put his palms up, facing out. "Kate, you're speaking as if Liam's already gone. Look, I don't want her going back alone either, but we don't know what will happen yet. Liam is still in surgery. I just want to make sure Jenna had a say and isn't being forced into something she doesn't want. She's not in the right frame of mind to be deciding things."

"Exactly," said Kate, and took a few steps away from him, then stopped. "Josh, I'm happy you're here for her. No matter what happened between you two earlier this year, she's going to need us all, including you."

Josh took a few deep breaths, the way Jenna used to tell him they taught her in yoga. Deep breath in from the mouth and out from the nose, or maybe it was in from the nose and out from the mouth? He couldn't remember the order. What he remembered, though, was her saying to visualize the colour of his breath, and somehow that concept helped to allow the breath to pass more smoothly and intently, so he tried it and visualized his breath as a deep dark blue. After one more breath and still not sure if he was doing it right, he walked back into the room. The air was stale, and he wished he could open a window. Jenna hadn't moved, still in the same protective hold over her belly. He pulled up a chair closer to the bed, refilled her water glass and then took a seat next to her, letting her know with his silence that he was there. She reciprocated, letting him know she understood by allowing the tears to well in the corners of her eyes. He reached out and held her hand and together they remained, hands locked over her unborn, but hopefully not a fatherless child.

Eventually, she fell asleep, and Cassie had already been there and left again to meet Kate and Brian. Everyone had a list, things to take care of, but not Josh; he remained there waiting for her to be ready to talk—she was his only task.

⁂

A couple of hours later, Josh left to go check on Liam. A kind nurse directed him to the family waiting room in the ICU, where he found the same frantic couple from earlier—Liam's parents, sitting and staring at the wall.

Liam's mother looked into Josh's eyes and gasped. "Oh, my!" she said in English, placing her hand over her mouth. "It can't be you? You can't be?"

"I'm Josh, Liam's biological brother, fraternal twin brother."

Liam's father stood beside his wife, a protective arm around her shoulder.

"What are you doing here?" asked Liam's mom, stumbling over her words.

Before Josh could answer, the door opened, and in walked an older man wearing scrubs. His hair was messy, and he was panting as if he'd just run a marathon.

He spoke French. "Liam's family, I presume?"

The couple nodded. Josh remained quiet and listened intently, trying to remember his French.

Continuing in French, the doctor said, "He's alive and out of surgery. He's not in the clear, though. He's lost a great deal of blood and took a tremendous blow to the head. He's still unconscious, and the next forty-eight hours will be critical. If he doesn't wake up in that time frame, I'm afraid he might never wake up."

Liam's mother cried out and fell to her knees; her husband caught her.

"Can I see him?" asked Liam's mom.

"You can each take turns visiting, but only one at a time and only for a few minutes. Talk to him. It might help."

His mom went first, leaving Josh alone with Liam's dad. Josh tried to tell him about Jenna, about the panic attack, but he couldn't communicate that well and didn't know if the man understood what he'd said.

When Liam's mother returned, his dad went next. When it was Josh's turn, he didn't know what to do or say. Did he want to see his brother? He thought he did, so he said his goodbyes to Liam's parents and prepared to walk in through the door to see his brother for the first time.

❧

Josh's eyes were closed when he first opened the door, afraid of what he'd see. He found the courage to open them and approached the bed, hesitantly, not sure what to expect. He gasped when he saw Liam. It was almost as if he were looking into a mirror, but not quite. There were some distinct differences amongst the similarities. How odd this was for him. He thought of his dad and the big secret he'd kept all these years, then sat next to the bed, reached for his brother's hand and held it tight. Just when he thought he'd lost all his family, first his mom, then his dad, he'd found a brother.

CHAPTER 52

Don't Let It Be the End

IN THE MATERNITY ward, Jenna waited impatiently to hear news about Liam. How could it be like this? How could this be their fate? It couldn't; they'd just found each other. "Please, God, don't let it be the end," she prayed aloud.

Her stomach growled, but she ignored it. As if on cue, her dinner arrived at the same time as Josh.

"Liam?" she asked.

Josh nodded. "He's alive. I can take you to see him if you want, but your doctor said you have to go by wheelchair."

Jenna let out a deep breath and then a loud sob. Alive! He's alive. That was the only word she'd registered.

Josh wheeled her to the ICU and waited outside the door while Jenna braced herself to see Liam tied up to machines. Once she sat on the edge of the bed, she grabbed his hand, and placed it over her stomach as the baby moved. There was a knock at the door, then it opened.

"Oh, Jenna, dear, thank goodness you are here," said Pat. "What a tragedy."

CHAPTER 53

Black Ice Is the Devil

ONCE HE WAS back in Jenna's room, Josh opened the food containers and brought the tray closer to her, prompting her to eat. She shook her head.

"Jenna, you need to eat something, if not for you, for the baby. Do you want to spend more time here? That's what will happen if you don't eat. You need to be strong for when Liam wakes up."

She seemed to consider that, then reached for the orange juice and took a small sip.

"Good. Here, take this." Josh handed her the fork, and she took it reluctantly, but ate a little.

When she finished the orange juice and roast beef with mashed potatoes and gravy, which smelled good to Josh because he was hungry, she finally talked.

"Thank you for being here. But I understand if you need to go. I'll be okay on my own until the others get back. Liam's parents will be up shortly to see me." She spoke the words, but without life in them.

Josh pulled the food trolly away from the bed so that he could get closer to her. Sitting on the edge of the bed, he took her hands in his. "Jenna, I'm not going anywhere, at least not until he's awake and you don't need me."

Tears filled her eyes again and that time, came with deep sobs and laboured breathing; it appeared to Josh as if she'd just remembered— realized that Liam was helpless—fighting for his life.

"Oh my God, I can't... I can't breathe, Josh." She was hyperventilating. He reminded her to do what her yoga instructor taught her, and after a few minutes, her breathing calmed, allowing her to relax.

"I want to know what happened, Josh. I need to know everything. How, why?"

"It's too soon to talk about it."

"I need to know. I can't sit here in the dark any longer."

"Are you sure you're ready to hear the details? Maybe tomorrow might be best, after you've had some time to process this and rest."

She interrupted him. "I want to know now. Please. Be straight with me. I can handle it."

"The report I received from the station confirmed Liam slid from his lane and into oncoming traffic. Unfortunately, it was a transport truck, and it hit the van head-on." Josh searched her face for clues that she wanted him to stop, but she wore an expressionless look. So he continued, "They think black ice caused him to lose control as he was going around a bend. There's severe head damage."

Jenna took a deep swallow. "What about the other driver?"

Josh considered how to answer that. It was going to hurt, no matter how he said it. "He was fine, just a few scratches."

She lifted her hands to her face and cried into them. Josh walked to the window to give her space.

After a few minutes, she said, "Do you know anything about the other driver?"

"Male, late sixties, divorced with two grown kids. That's all I know."

"It's not fair. I'm glad that he's fine; it's just not fair. Liam has his entire life to live. This man got to see his kids grown, but Liam might never hold his baby."

"No, it's not fair, but you sound as if you've given up. There's still hope. You know what?"

She removed her hands from her face long enough for him to see how red and swollen her eyes were. "What?" she asked.

"No matter what happens, you will always have Liam, and not just in your memories and heart." Josh pointed to her stomach. "You'll have a piece of him."

"It's my fault, Josh," she said in between sobs.

"No, this isn't your fault at all."

She shook her head. "You don't understand, but it is. I asked him to come and pick up the shower gifts. If I hadn't, if he'd just flown with me, he wouldn't be fighting for his life. He didn't have to drive. We could've hired a moving company. But no. I asked him, and he said yes, and so I caused this."

"Jenna, do you think for a minute that he'd not have helped you, anyway? I don't know him, but you do, so think about it. Is Liam the man that would let you figure it out on your own? Or would he have come up with that plan, eventually?"

She considered Josh's question and wiped away a tear that rested on the tip of her nose. "He is that kind of man, generous, kind, and he'd have done anything for me and the baby. I know that. But I still should have talked him out of driving by himself at night. I should have insisted he get a good night's sleep and drive during the day. Why hadn't I thought of the dangers he was putting himself in?"

"There was black ice on the road, Jenna. Even after a restful night, black ice is the devil. You need to stop blaming yourself for the accident. Jenna, are you listening to me?" He brought her chin up so her eyes met his. "This is not your fault." He looked around the room, desperate to find a distraction for her. "How about we watch TV?"

There was a small television in the room, so Josh turned it on and flipped through the few available stations. He stopped on a scene with puppies at the local humane society, thinking that would be a pleasant distraction, but that story wrapped up quickly and the next one was coverage of the accident. Josh hadn't expected that. He reached for the control to turn the TV off. But Jenna's breathing was once again short, shallow, and quick.

"I can't imagine how his parents felt finding out the way they did. Oh, God. How horrible to find out from a stranger? I need to talk to them again. They are my strongest link to Liam." She looked at her belly. "Until, of course, the baby arrives."

"They said they would be up in a few minutes."

There was a knock and then Liam's mom peeked her head inside. "Is this a good time?" she asked in French.

Josh offered to leave to give them privacy. "All right, well, I'll go to the cafeteria to get a bite. I'll be back in about half an hour."

Josh bent to plant a kiss on her forehead before he stepped out.

CHAPTER 54

Fighting For His Life

FTER JOSH LEFT, Jenna held Pat's hand close to her heart.
"Oh, Jenna, thank goodness you and the baby are okay.
We were getting worried about you and have been trying to
locate your parents. How are you holding up, darling?"

Their son was the one fighting for his life, yet they showed concern
for her. They truly were the most selfless people she'd ever met; Jenna
pulled herself together, needing to reciprocate and support them.

"I'm so deeply sorry for all this. I feel responsible. This is the hardest
thing I've ever gone through; I can't imagine how you must be feeling."

"Oh, darling, life sometimes isn't fair. I've been crying all morning.
Every time I think I can't possibly shed another tear, I think of him
being alive still and then I feel happy again, and the pain begins all over.
I still can't believe this happened. Liam will make it, though. He must."

Pat sobbed into Jenna's chest, and Jenna, not able to control her
emotions, joined her. They spent the next several minutes reminiscing
about good times; Pat told Jenna about when Liam was a young boy

and all the silly things he did, and Jenna shared the laughter and joy he brought into her life in the year she'd known him. Jenna listened intently to another childhood memory and noticed Josh had returned. Jenna wondered how long he'd been listening to her go on about what a great man Liam was. Jenna held up a finger, showing she'd be another minute, and then she and Pat said goodbye.

"I've been back a while but waited outside the door to give you some privacy," said Josh.

Jenna turned toward the window. It was dark outside, and snow covered the rooftops. "When did the snow start?"

"Listen, Jenna, Cassie called me. She's not able to make it back. It's been snowing for the last few hours, but it's coming down harder now. There's a storm watch; twenty-five to thirty centimetres expected this evening. Cassie is stuck in her driveway. The plow blocked her in. She was going to call an Uber, but even they couldn't get there quick enough. I told her not to worry about you because I'd be here."

"Why didn't she call me?" Jenna checked her phone to see if she'd missed a call while talking to Pat.

"She wanted to make sure I was still here so you wouldn't be alone."

Jenna wasn't sure how she felt about her best friend calling her ex to take care of her.

"It's sweet of her to worry, but you don't have to be here. You've already been here long enough. I'm sure you have many things to do." Jenna paused for a moment then continued, "You should go home. It's late."

"Jenna, don't start with that nonsense. I'm not leaving. Have you heard from your parents?"

"No, but I should call and tell them not to come back. I don't want them driving in this weather, there's no need."

"We finally agree on something."

After talking to her brother in Bali, Jenna talked to her parents and then passed her phone to Josh. They wanted confirmation he was still with her, not believing her. They said they'd been getting her room ready: changing sheets, washing the carpet, and they even picked up a litter box for Seul, who was at Cassie's. Because Jenna had planned on staying for a week, she'd brought Seul with her.

"I've got so much to do before this baby comes, and it's almost Christmas. How am I ever going to do any of this now?"

"You need to take one day at a time. Remember what the doctor said? The next forty-eight hours are crucial for him. Is there anything important that you need from your apartment that you can't replace?"

"Just the baby stuff. Other than that, I have what I need, or at least enough to manage for a while. I'm not planning on staying too long. If Liam gets transferred to a hospital in Quebec City, I'm leaving right away."

"Of course," agreed Josh. He opened his mouth to say more, then stopped.

"What?" Jenna asked.

"It's just... have you thought about what you'll do if Liam doesn't make it? Will you stay?"

Unable to answer, Jenna turned away. A tear formed and then another, and before Jenna knew it, Josh was handing her the package of Kleenex and she was going through it like water.

"I'm sorry."

"Don't apologize for crying over someone you love. It's natural. I'm the one who should be sorry. I shouldn't have asked that."

Josh and Jenna hadn't talked about her feelings, so she wasn't sure if he assumed she loved Liam or had overheard her telling Pat how she felt. But it was true. She loved Liam with all her heart, and she was glad she'd told him. She had imagined them together in her future, as a family, taking their daughter to the park, going for walks. It would be their first Christmas together, and a memory she prayed would materialize. She longed for more memories of her and Liam, more good times to experience and remember.

Josh pulled the chair up and sat next to her, but said nothing. His silence meant so much, and filled her heart. She needed him as a friend more than ever.

Jenna eventually fell asleep while Josh sat at her side. She remembered saying goodnight, thinking he'd get up to leave shortly, but they must have plowed him in; because when the nurse did the routine check through the night, he was still there. Instead of the chair, he laid on a larger, padded recliner with a blanket over his legs. Jenna watched him sleep while the nurse checked her blood pressure; he didn't stir and slept through the check-up. When the nurse left, Jenna fell back asleep and dreamt of Liam.

When she awakened early the next morning, she stretched and peeked out the window. It was a new day; the city covered in snow. Jenna didn't like the cold, but she found beauty in a fresh snowfall, especially first thing in the morning, too early for anyone to have yet created footprints, destroying the beauty. Jenna got up and walked to the window. The snow hadn't stopped, although it was only a light dusting, and from her window, up high on the eighth floor, the city looked like a snow globe. Jenna was admiring the beauty of the snow-covered city when the events of the day before flooded her memory—Liam, the accident. That realization first thing in the morning punched her in the stomach. She slowly turned to go back and bury her head under the pillow when she saw Josh sleeping in the same position he was in last night. He stirred, then opened his eyes.

"Hey, I can't believe I slept longer than you. How long have you been up?"

"I just got up, maybe two minutes if that."

"Did you sleep well?"

"Considering everything, I slept pretty well. Exhaustion will do that. I'm surprised to see you and so sorry you got stuck here through the night because of the storm. I didn't mean to be such a pain."

Josh stretched his back, squaring his shoulders, and it reminded her of Liam that time, instead of the other way around.

"The storm didn't keep me here," he said, lowering his eyes.

"I need to see Liam. I need to know if there's any change."

"Of course. I'll take you down right away."

❦

After seeing that Liam was still unconscious and there'd been no change, Josh took her back upstairs. Breakfast arrived seconds later, so Josh went to the cafeteria for coffee and left Jenna alone with her thoughts and, considering where she was at emotionally and physically, this was not a good idea. By the time Josh returned, she'd already had another panic attack, alerting the nurses to run to her aid to calm her. Josh arrived right at the tail-end of the commotion, and the next call he made was to his office, where Jenna heard him asking his assistant to clear his schedule, again.

❦

The doctor came to see her, and discharged her, but only because Josh insisted she wouldn't be alone.

She spent the morning making calls: a few to clients, another to Liam's siblings who were boarding flights to Toronto. When she spoke to his parents that morning after her breakfast, his mother seemed even sadder than she was yesterday. Yesterday she had cried a lot, but was talkative. Today she appeared sombre, quiet. The hours were ticking by. These forty-eight hours were crucial. Jenna heard the strain in Pat's voice that was not there yesterday.

While waiting for the discharge paperwork, she sat at Liam's bedside.

She held his hand and pleaded with him to wake up. She cried, then dried her eyes and laughed, remembering his silly jokes. She cried some more. Liam never stirred. She watched the rise and fall of his chest and placed her head on it, and then curled up on the bed next to him and slept.

CHAPTER 55

She Was No Longer His

JOSH OPENED THE door to Liam's ICU room to check in on Jenna. He saw the two of them together. Jenna curled up like a ball, her head rested on Liam's chest. That was when he finally realized that she was no longer his. He'd lost her, even if Liam died. It should have filled his heart with worry that he'd lost her forever, but he was glad she'd found Liam. He was glad that Liam made her happy.

Careful not to disturb her, he tiptoed to the closet and pulled out another blanket, selecting an extra thick one, rolled it out and covered them both. As he walked out the door, he looked back and smiled, hoping that Liam would wake up soon to enjoy his family. He was the better man; he was the better twin. He deserved her. Josh realized that he and Jenna were over forever. And closed the door behind him.

CHAPTER 56

That Little Crazy Cat

JENNA DIDN'T LEAVE the hospital that day. She stayed with Liam, and the doctors didn't kick her out. Liam was approaching the end of his life—the end of the critical forty-eight hours—and he was still not awake. Jenna only left his side long enough to allow his parents and brother and sister a chance to visit. She was in the family waiting room when she realized she hadn't heard from Josh since yesterday morning. She checked her phone. There was a text from him.

Josh: Thinking of you during this tough time. Stay strong. Please call me if you need anything.

She texted back a quick thank-you while she waited for her turn to sit with Liam again.

Cassie arrived moments later and placed her hand over Jenna's and squeezed when Jenna was quiet for too long; Cassie knew when she struggled; she knew her well. The smell from Cassie's watermelon-flavoured gum caused Jenna's stomach to growl. She had eaten little the last two days, and it was then that she remembered Seul needed to be fed. Cassie promised she'd arranged for her neighbour to check on Seul. Thinking about Seul brought some comfort. She missed that little crazy cat, climbing her curtains, jumping up onto her counters when she wasn't in the room. Despite her current situation, thinking of Seul made her smile, and she never thought it would have been possible. It's astounding how calming animals are to one's soul, especially during times of sorrow.

∾

Jenna tried to sleep in the family waiting room but couldn't. The noise was too much, the not knowing, too overwhelming. So, instead, she took out her phone and swiped through photos of her and Liam together. She stopped on one. They were downtown while the snow fell over them. She zoomed in on the photo, admiring his face. He looked happy.

Jenna had brought the copies of the letters that Holly wrote while pregnant with her to the courthouse, so they were in her bag. She'd brought them along in case Josh had wanted to see them when they met. She also intended to share them one day with her daughter, since Holly would have been her baby's grandmother.

She re-read them all again, and it was the last letter she decided was the most heartfelt.

∾

Dear baby,

There are going to be things in life that will throw you for a loop: things will creep up on you when you least expect it. These unforeseen situations might strangle you, cause you to become derailed or demotivate you, but it's how you'll deal with these mishaps that will shape the person you become and set you up for a fulfilling life. Often, we use these moments as excuses to give up on goals and accomplishments, but if you channel that same energy to do the opposite, you will be unstoppable.

Let no one prevent you from doing the things that you want to do. Let no one tell you that any dream of yours is too big, unachievable; because you can do whatever you want—be whoever you choose to be. I think you'll be great. There is no dream larger than my love, hope, and encouragement for you, so when the time comes, and you're in deep despair, do something with it—turn it into something positive and realize your great potential. Always stand up for yourself and for the things you believe in; always believe in yourself and your life will be complete.

Love, Mom

Needing a change of scenery, she folded the letters, safely tucked them back into her bag, and made her way out into the hallway where she bumped into Pat, who wore a slight smile for the first time since she'd arrived.

"Jenna, dear," she spoke in French. "It's your turn to see him."

"Okay, I was just on my way, thanks."

As Jenna turned the corner toward Liam's room, she thought she saw a twinkle in Pat's eyes. She hesitated at the door, and then she opened it and gasped. He was still hooked up to machines, but his eyes were open, and the blue in them grew wider when they landed on her.

"Liam!" she yelled as she ran to him and into his arms. At that moment, she forgot everything. Liam was awake. There would be life-long memories of them together after all, she just knew it.

It had taken a while, but after Liam was discharged, they had temporarily moved in with her parents after he'd left the hospital. Jenna had been afraid he wasn't strong enough to travel back to Quebec City right away, so she found him a therapist in Toronto to help him with his long recovery.

During that time, Jenna had also made copies of all the adoption paperwork and research she'd gathered and mailed a package to Josh along with a note to say thank you for all he'd done for her while Liam was in the hospital. She told Josh to reach out if she could help answer any questions. She'd given him all the information, so the rest was up to him.

∽

They were still in Toronto during the holidays, and Christmas arrived with much joy that year. On Christmas Eve, her parents had held a gathering at their home and most of their relatives had come for a Christmas drink. Liam, not yet fully recovered, was there by her side. Even his parents and siblings had come for Christmas. Jenna had much to be grateful for.

It was a white Christmas when she woke up on Christmas morning. She made herself a decaffeinated coffee and took it with her to the spare bedroom that her parents had converted into the baby's room for their future visits.

Her mother was suddenly at the door, nursing a coffee. "Merry Christmas, darling."

"Merry Christmas, Mom."

"Hey, there you two are. I was looking for you. Everything okay?" asked Kris. "Dad wants a family photo. He told me to find you two."

"Everything is fine," said Jenna and her mother in unison.

"All right, come on then." He left, and together Jenna and her mom stood in the baby's room, arm in arm when Jenna's phone chimed.

Josh: Merry Christmas Jenna and thanks for the package you sent. I've connected with Brenda and Bob already.

She smiled but wondered when he'd want to connect with his brother, then she put her phone away and went to look for Liam.

Her father set the automatic camera with a five-second delay and ran to join the others.

"Smile everyone," said her father.

Jenna's arms wrapped tight around Liam's who stood behind her; his arms folded over her stomach.

CHAPTER 57

Laughter Is Contagious and Therapeutic

IT HAPPENED THE beginning of March. Jenna and Liam were back in Quebec City and living together when one cool, crisp morning, she had crouched over in pain. It was time. Liam had taken her to the hospital while she held her belly, waiting for the next blow. She was four weeks early, but her obstetrician had assured her it was fine, that the baby was fully developed. Her parents were in Quebec City visiting that week, and so her mom had accompanied her and Liam to the hospital. They gave Jenna a wheelchair and took her to the maternity ward and found out she was fully dilated. Her mother had already called Cassie on their way to the hospital, so she could jump on the next flight. A nurse then wheeled Jenna to a labour delivery room.

Six hours later and, thanks to the support of her mother and Liam by her side during the labour, Jenna held her baby girl in her arms. She had the same almond-shaped eyes as both Liam and Josh, but she didn't have Liam's fiery red hair, instead she had Josh's lighter brown. When she finally opened her eyes, both men's blue gaze stared back at Jenna.

Jenna's mother patted her forehead with a wet cloth, and Cassie arrived a few minutes later, announcing that she'd just seen Jenna's father and he looked happy.

As Jenna held her daughter, she thought about when she and Josh argued over having a family and how adamant she was that she wasn't ready. How strange that she had ever thought it was such a crazy idea; because holding her little angel, she couldn't imagine not being a mother. It was just never meant to be with Josh. It was never right, and that was why she'd felt that way. Liam was right.

"Sweetheart, a delivery came for you," said Liam, placing a bouquet next to Jenna's bed.

"They're beautiful."

Jenna picked up the card and read.

Dear Jenna

Josh called to give us the news. We've been in communications and are enjoying getting to know him thanks to you Congratulations to you and Liam We can't wait to meet our great-granddaughter

With Love,

Brenda and Bob Mills.

"Have you thought of a name, darling?" asked Jenna's mom as she wiped away the sweat from her brows. Jenna looked at Liam and he nodded, urging her to tell her mother the baby's name.

"I have. Mom, meet Holly."

"Holly, that's an interesting choice. Is it short for something? I've never heard you mention that as a possibility."

"No, just Holly." Jenna hadn't taken her eyes off her baby. "Holly was her grandmother's name."

"Whose grandmother? The baby? Liam's mom's name is Pat, not Holly."

"Mom, there's so much I need to tell you."

Of course, her mother knew a part of the story, mainly that Pat and her husband adopted Liam, and that he was Josh's biological brother, but she didn't know everything that had transpired the last year about the Millses and Holly. Her mother sat on the edge of the bed. Jenna shifted to the side to give her more room.

"I'm here darling. You can tell me anything."

The conversation about Liam's and Josh's past was the first genuine conversation they'd had in a long time, and the start of many more.

Josh hadn't come to the hospital, and Jenna hadn't expected him to. He was in Toronto and too far away for a quick visit. Besides, she knew seeing her with the baby would hurt, and if Jenna was honest, she'd hoped he wouldn't come. She hadn't wanted to put Liam through more than what he'd already been through with the accident and therapy either, so one afternoon, when Holly was almost a month old, and to avoid having Josh just show up unannounced, she snapped a photo of herself and Holly and texted it to him:

Jenna: Meet Holly, your niece!

That was all she said. No pleasantries, no fluff.

His reply came fast.

Josh: Congratulations. Cassie has sent several photos and has kept me updated. She's beautiful.

The news about Cassie being in contact with Josh came as a surprise. She didn't know they had remained connected. Curious, and while the baby slept peacefully in her arms, she called Cassie.

When asked directly about Josh's comment, Cassie said, "He's often reached out to find out how you, Liam, and the baby were. This is nothing new."

"Really? I didn't know."

"Yeah, he did. Do you think he would have just disappeared?"

"How long has he been asking about us?"

"Since the day of the accident. When Liam was going through his recovery, a day hasn't passed that he hadn't checked in. He actually impressed me. Maybe I've been too hard on him over the years."

"I'm surprised you never mentioned this."

"I didn't think you wanted to know. You didn't ask about him, so I thought you wanted to move on from that life. Besides, he asked me not to. He didn't want to interfere. He's truly happy for you and Liam, and didn't want to come between you two. But if you'd mentioned him even once, I would've told you. You know that?"

"I do."

"Since you never brought him up, I figured it was best not to. I thought you wanted to forget the past."

"You're right. I do. I have my little family and that's all I need."

⁂

In the summer, when Holly was almost five months old, Jenna and Liam took her on a trip to Toronto. Jenna's parents were watching Holly while she and Cassie were on their way to an early morning outdoor yoga class by the lake. Jenna had complained it was too hot to do yoga outside, but then admitted that the heat wasn't so bad early in the morning, so she went along to spend time with Cassie. During a downward dog and while chewing gum, Cassie never got over that habit, she told Jenna about her newest love interest for the week, and Jenna gave her a hard time about still finding fault with all the men she dated.

After yoga, the girls went out for lunch and while sitting in the shade at an outdoor café, already melting because of the rising afternoon heat, Jenna's phone rang. She checked the display; it was Liam.

"Jenna, I think it is time. I want to meet Josh while we are here."

"Liam, are you sure?"

"Yes, I am sure. Can you arrange it before we leave?"

"It would be my honour."

⁂

Not wasting a moment, she dialed Josh's number. She hadn't talked to him in months. He answered right away. "Jenna?"

"Hey, Josh, I hope I didn't catch you at a bad time."

"Not at all. It's just a surprise, but nice to hear from you. Is everything all right?"

"Josh, I have a huge favour to ask of you."

Josh was reluctant at first. He said he wasn't sure if he was ready. Wasn't sure how he'd react, how he'd be able to face him, carry on a conversation, but after some time agreed to meet Liam. Jenna was speechless and tried to hide her emotions from him. She hadn't known how he'd react, and she'd prepared for the worst, but in the end, he'd surprised her.

❧

Jenna, Liam and Holly sat in a café in The Danforth area of Toronto waiting for Josh. How odd that she'd met both men at cafés and that they would meet each other at one, too. This would be the first time that Jenna'd seen Josh since the morning after the accident, and she wasn't at all nervous. It almost felt natural, having the two men meet after all they'd been through. She looked at Liam and searched his face for clues that he was sure he was doing the right thing. His big smile confirmed to her, he was sure.

Holly was wide awake from her afternoon nap, fed and happy as she sat in the stroller while Jenna rolled her back and forth; her belly laughter emanated through the room and caused strangers to stop and stare. Jenna was so enthralled by the way her daughter's laughter pulled people to her like magnets that she hadn't noticed Josh standing over the stroller until he spoke.

"Wow, look at that face, it looks so eerily familiar."

Jenna looked up to find him looking into the stroller. "Josh, I didn't see you come in." Jenna got up and gave him a friendly hug; he planted a kiss on her cheek.

"So, this is Holly."

Jenna let out the breath she didn't realize she was holding. "This is Holly. Your niece." She cleared her throat. "And this here," she pointed to Liam, "is your brother."

The two men nodded slightly, acknowledging each other, but neither spoke. Jenna held her breath again, watching the two of them watch each other.

Josh broke the silence. "May I?" he asked, directing the question to Liam, reaching his hand out to touch Holly.

"Of course," said Liam.

Hesitantly, he held her little hand, and it disappeared in his; Jenna held her breath again, anticipating something—she just didn't know what. It was surprisingly almost natural being there with Holly, Liam, and Josh, considering all that had happened and why they were even at this point in their lives. Liam didn't say anything more, but stared at his brother, examining him.

Jenna leaned into him and whispered in his ear. "Are you all right, darling?"

Liam nodded, then stood and took a step toward Josh. Josh did the same. Liam reached out his hand, but Josh leaned into him and pulled him into an embrace instead.

"I'm glad to see you alive. You gave everyone a scare," said Josh.

"Thank you for taking care of Jenna after the accident. I know that must have been difficult, considering everything. I wanted you to know, sincerely, how grateful I am."

Josh wrapped his arms tighter around his brother. Jenna let out a long sigh.

A moment later, after the embrace, Josh picked up Holly's little hand again, and she smiled back and let out another belly laugh, causing Josh to laugh along with her, and then Jenna and Liam joined in the laughter and before long, the entire café was laughing so loudly that others walking by joined as well. Laughter is contagious—and therapeutic.

Forever Home

Three Years Later - 2020

*I*T TOOK THREE years for Liam and Jenna to get there, but they made it—together.

After that meeting, when the brothers met and it had ended in laughter, they saw each other often, at first just occasionally, but eventually the relationship developed into a closer one, and Josh and Liam found what each had never dreamt they would—friendship with one another.

Holly had grown to love Uncle Josh and was happy when he visited them in Quebec City.

❦

"Holly, come here and stop pulling the flower out of your hair or you can't be Mommy's flower girl." Jenna's daughter looked at her, and then in the full-length mirror, and pulled the flower out and threw it on the ground.

"Want Daddy," she cried.

Jenna embraced her. "I know you want Daddy, but Daddy is with the boys getting ready for our big day."

"Uncle Kris," Holly said, not as a question, but Jenna knew that's what she meant. Kris and Xavier had been so wonderful with Holly lately, and she really enjoyed having them around. They made her laugh uncontrollably.

"Uncle Kris is with Daddy, Uncle Xavier, and Uncle Josh. They are all getting ready, just like us girls are. You'll see them soon. I promise."

Little Holly crossed her arms in front of her chest. "Hmmm," she said in a huff, still refusing to keep the flower in her hair.

"Come on little one, help me with Mommy's dress," said Cassie, already dressed herself, her long flowing locks pulled back into a loose chignon pinned at the top of her head with a decorative pin to match her maid-of-honour dress. Jenna had told Cassie she could wear whatever she wanted as long as it matched the colour scheme of silver and blue, and Cassie had outdone herself with a simple but classy off the shoulder knee length dress, with silver trim along the sleeves and bottom. A modest slit revealed her shapely thigh. Jenna wore a traditional white satin gown that covered her feet and with a train so long that her seamstress had to sew in extra buttons for her to hook the train on to; it would prevent her arms from getting tired carrying it around. Her dress was a halter-style top with sequins around the breasts, pinched at the waist with a flare at the bottom. Detailed sequins ran along the bottom half, making her look like a princess. Her hair matched Cassie's, in a loose chignon under her crown headpiece.

Cassie was trying to figure out how to get the train buttoned up and was having a hard time.

"Why don't you call my mom? She's in the other room. I'm sure she can figure it out."

"Nonsense, I got this. Besides, your mom is in charge of the food. I'm in charge of getting you dressed, since I'm your maid of honour. Oh, there we go. I did it!" She threw an air punch, and they laughed at her over exaggeration.

"So, who's the guy, anyway?" Jenna asked, referring to the man Cassie had added to the guest list last minute as her plus one.

Cassie smiled. And that was how Jenna knew that one was a keeper. "Kevin, and please be nice to him; because he's shy."

"Wow, look at us."

"Look at you, girl. You've come a long way. You and Liam truly are a fairy tale ending. You two have been doing a fantastic job with Holly. You should be so proud."

"It took us a while to get here, didn't it?"

"You didn't want to rush it. I get that."

Cassie turned to Jenna; they were facing each other. "It's good you two waited. It allowed your feelings for Josh to get worked out."

"True," agreed Jenna.

"It also enabled them to figure out where they stood with one another before getting more complicated with your marriage to Liam."

"Since when did you get so smart?" asked Jenna, teasingly.

Cassie winked. "I've always been smart. You just rarely listen."

Jenna and Cassie chuckled, and then Jenna wiped the tear that fell down her cheek. "Happy tears. I promise," said Jenna.

Cassie squeezed Jenna's hand as Holly came up behind and yanked on the wedding dress so hard that she caused the train to become unbuttoned.

"Oh, damn it," said Cassie.

"Cassie, words!"

"So sorry, I meant darn it."

Holly covered her mouth and giggled.

"How are you girls doing in here?" asked Jenna's mother. "We only have a few minutes before we have to leave for church. We don't want to be too early, but we don't want you missing your wedding either, do we!"

"We're ready," Cassie and Jenna said at the same time.

"Okay, let's go."

⚬∾

The church was full when Jenna peeked through the back window; every seat occupied. The wedding co-ordinator told them to take their places, and before Jenna knew it, her best friend was walking down the aisle, followed by Holly carrying flowers, but the one in her hair was missing.

Jenna was next. When the music grew louder, the guests stood, and Jenna linked her arm through her father's as the two walked down the aisle. On their way to the altar, they passed all their friends and family, including Josh. She smiled at Josh, and he smiled back and then gave her a thumbs-up. Josh was sitting next to Brenda and Bob. Josh had met them shortly after Jenna sent him all the information on his adoption, and over the last three years, they formed a relationship. It filled her heart to see Josh with them. She missed Billy and wished he could have been there but was glad Josh at least had found other family to sit next to. When her eyes locked with Brenda's, tears formed, and Jenna had to force them away and tell herself it was too early to cry. She had to at least get through the vows.

Her eyes continued to wander and landed at the front of the altar where Liam stood waiting for her. He wore a big smile to match his enormous heart. Jenna's father hugged Liam and whispered something in his ear, but Jenna couldn't make out what. Liam's hands squeezed her father's shoulders in response to what he'd said. The two men nodded, and then her father placed her hand in Liam's hand and together they stood before the minister as they, finally, after three years, exchanged vows.

Jenna whispered to Liam, "What did my father say?"

"That I'm finally a part of the family, officially."

"Yes, finally." Jenna said and then answered the question asked by the minister, "I do," and Liam mouthed the words 'I love you' at the same time. They turned toward the crowd. Sitting in the front-row seat was Holly, kicking her legs, pulling flowers out of her bouquet. Jenna watched as Liam's eyes locked with Holly's—the same eyes.

"That's my daddy," said Holly, pointing to Liam. Liam's smile widened.

When Jenna looked into Liam's eyes, she knew she'd found her forever home.

ACKNOWLEDGEMENTS

I first started this story when I was a teenager, but scrapped it, thinking the twins plot had already been told too many times. Then, as I got older, I had the idea of Jenna being the centre of the twins' saga and revisited it with a new enthusiasm. I'm glad I did; because I'm really proud of this one. While my past two stories will always hold a special place in my heart, *The Angolan Girl*, being the story of my grandmother's life, and *From Far And Wide* being inspired by a special trip, *Twenty-Eight Years* allowed me to grow as a writer as I challenged the boundaries I had set with the last two.

Sara Graham, you have always been a faithful beta reader, supporter and sounding board for me as I struggled with the first word in *The Angolan Girl*, to the last in *Twenty-Eight Years*. It was you who first inspired me to revisit the twins tale. We were working out together in my home gym when you told me about a book you'd just finished about twins separated at birth. As you told me about the book, I got to thinking of this book, not yet written then, and realized it was different from any twin story I had ever read. Thus, thank you for your years of encouragement and support throughout my writing journey.

Elsa Miranda Daniella, without your honesty, and suggestions about the French culture, *Twenty-Eight Years* would not be the same. You've always gone above and beyond providing detailed thoughts on what worked and what didn't. Thank you for taking the time to translate all the English phrases.

Melanie Hunter, while we're an ocean apart, and have never met, your opinion is one I've come to lean on and trust. Your insights, thoughts, questions, and suggestions about the relationships in the book, and especially around the adoption, were vital. Thank you for being so willing to help me every time I questioned something and for being such a strong supporter of my books.

Lindsey-Anne Pontes, although you were super busy, you took the time to read through my book, and provided such insightful comments. You made me realize something I had forgotten about Jenna, in that she is a strong, independent woman, because of that, came the new ending, which I absolutely love.

Tiffany Guerra, even though you were off on your sailing adventure, you still took the time to go through my book. Your love for Liam made me develop his character more and give him his happy ending. Thank you for always believing in me, dear sister!

Catherine Muss, your dedication and passion with what you do shines through in every correspondence we have. Thank you, again, for polishing my book. It's so imperative to have another set of eyes, and I'm so happy that I have found you to look over my work before publication.

Tara Mondou and Pam Urie, thank you for being another set of eyes as my proof-readers.

Terry Rocha, thank you for the beautiful cover design and promotional material once again. I can always count on you to capture the essence of the story and bring it to life in your beautiful covers.

To all my readers, writing a book is a very personal journey. As a writer I live with the characters in my head for the duration of the writing process. They become almost like friends. Then to share them with the world is like putting my most vulnerable self out there for others to judge and criticize. It's a hard thing to do, but my love of writing keeps me doing it. So, if you liked this book, please consider leaving a review on Amazon, Goodreads, or any other reviewing platform. Reviews help authors to get the word out. Even a simple, "I liked it" helps. Thank you!

ABOUT THE AUTHOR

*T*ELMA ROCHA is an avid reader and reviewer. She documents and shares her reading and writing journey on Instagram and on her blog: www.turnthepageofbooks.com and is an active member of various groups dedicated to promoting local talent.

Telma lives in southern Ontario with her husband and two sons. When she is not reading or writing, you can find her enjoying the outdoors with her family or sharing meals and laughter with good friends.

Born in Angola, Telma immigrated to Canada as a baby in 1976, avoiding the turbulent civil war that erupted there in 1974. She documented these events in her first novel, *The Angolan Girl*: the story about her grandmother's life from childhood through the early stages of the war.

Telma is currently working on her fourth novel.

Social Media Links:

Website: www.Telmarocha.com
Instagram: https://www.instagram.com/turn_the_page_of_books
Goodreads: https://www.goodreads.com/turn_the_page_of_books
Twitter: http://twitter.com/turnpageofbooks
Blog: www.turnthepageofbooks

Printed in the USA
CPSIA information can be obtained
at www.ICGtesting.com
LVHW092005090424
776877LV00004B/448

9 781999 066727